THE QUEEN'S QUIET END

SHADOWS OF CAMELOT BOOK 2

BREE MOORE

INNATE INK PUBLISHING

This is a work of fiction. Names, characters, places, events and incidents are used in a fictitious manner. Any resemblance to actual persons, living or dead, or actual events is purely coincidental.

Cover Design by Moonpress | www.moonpress.co

Previously published as "Bound" by Phase Publishing, LLC

First Ebook & Print Editions

August 2017

Library of Congress Control Number 2017947436

Cataloging-in-Publication Data on file.

Ebook ISBN: 978-1-956668-05-6

Paperback ISBN: 978-1-956668-07-0

Hardcover ISBN: 978-1-956668-15-5

PRAISE FOR "THE LADY'S LAST SONG"

"Bree Moore achieves a radical new vision of King Arthur and his court in this imaginative and creative tale...This absorbing tale creates unconventional binds between certain characters that are so strong, they will either dispel the most terrible of curses or destroy an entire kingdom."

-J.B. Richards, *author of Miriam the Magdala*

"...A story woven with poetry, riddles, chivalry, tragedy, and revenge. It is truly a tale 'where one thread is tugged, the entire web vibrates'."

-Wendy L. Anderson, *author of the Kingdom of Jior series*

"The way [Moore] weaves these familiar tales together is delightful...definitely full of twists, in many ways turning the tales upside down...and because we're already in a world of magic, nearly anything is possible."

-C.A. Gray, *author of the Piercing the Veil trilogy*

PROLOGUE

THE DUINE WITCH HAD BEEN HUNTING, and she had found her quarry in a king.

Elizabeth's blood rushed through her chest, pumping through her heart at a rapid pace. Her king. She would not allow any witch to have him. She breathed in and out at a great pace, almost matching the breakneck rhythm of her horse's pounding hooves.

A second set of hooves sounded in discord behind her.

"We shouldn't be doing this. You shouldn't be here, not in your condition," a voice called out, breathless.

Elizabeth gritted her teeth. "Would you let yours be taken?"

Elizabeth panted heavily. Her large, pregnant belly prevented her from leaning further over the horse. Her face grimaced in pain, not from the words she spoke, but from the pain of her contractions. They had come gently that morning, but her focus on the impending labor fled once she heard the Duine witch stole her husband.

A king-killer. Once she seduced them, they never returned.

"I understand, my queen, but this is a job for the knights."

"And let them get seduced, too? A man cannot be trusted with the Duine," Elizabeth snapped, then gasped and released her horse's reins, doubling over. Well-trained, the beast slowed to a trot, then a halt. Lirael passed Elizabeth, then slowed and trotted her steed back to meet her.

"My waters," Elizabeth moaned. Her time had come; this babe had chosen to be born.

Lirael slid from her saddle and took the halter of the queen's black mare, the animal's feet stamping, its eyes rolling with fear.

Elizabeth bent over in the saddle, panting and moaning, then releasing a short grunt. Her pale skirts glistened with dark stains in the moonlight.

Lirael took her arm. The forest swam through Elizabeth's vision, and the moon seemed to blur. Another pain took her, and she pressed her forehead to the neck of the horse, carried away by the force of the contraction.

"Your majesty."

The queen didn't respond.

"Elizabeth," Lirael said, more firmly.

The queen looked up, exhausted beyond bearing. She could have hours of labor yet.

"Come down from there. Come on, I have you."

The black mare's eyes rolled at the smell of the blood that dripped down her flank; she stamped nervously at the ground but stayed steady as Elizabeth fell into Lirael's arms, screaming when another labor pain took her.

Lirael held her until the contraction ended, then half-carried, half-dragged her a short way across the forest floor and lowered her against the rough trunk of a wide tree. Cradled in its roots, Elizabeth writhed and yelled again.

"Something...isn't right!" she said through clenched teeth, then gasped, eyes going wide, hands scrabbling for something to hold. One hand reached toward Lirael, who responded by taking the cold, trembling hand in her own.

"It will be alright," Lirael insisted. "I am here. Your babe is coming, it will be alright. It's almost over." She babbled, but her words seemed to help the queen focus. She pulled the queen's ruined dress back over her knees and looked between the laboring woman's legs.

Her face blanched at the blood. The glistening top of the baby's head barely visible through a coin-sized opening as it stretched, growing wider as the queen bore down.

Elizabeth's grunt ended in a scream, and her nails dug into Lirael's hand as she pushed again.

"That's it, good work."

Elizabeth panted, leaning back. "I can't, Lirael. I'm not...I'm tired. I can't."

"Shh, enough of that." Lirael stroked the sweat-dampened hair from the queen's face. "You will give birth to this child, hear me?" Lirael tried to keep the desperation from her voice.

She reached out her other hand and Elizabeth took it, eyes wild with pain and fear.

"Now, hold to me. Take a deep breath."

The queen locked eyes with Lirael and breathed, tears coming down her sweating face, glistening in the moonlight. A moment later her muscles tensed, and she began a guttural moan.

Lirael bent her head, watching the opening with ever-widening eyes. Instinctively, she let go of Elizabeth and reached her hands below the opening as it stretched over the large, round head, and the baby slid out. Lirael's hands held it off the dirty ground below, and she heard a gurgling sound as the baby struggled to take its first breath.

"Push again, Elizabeth! Your baby needs to come out," Lirael cried.

Elizabeth gave a primal yell, stretching her neck and body out,

arms pressing into the earth below as first a shoulder, then an entire body slid from into Lirael's waiting hands. A gush of blood followed the babe, bathing both his skin and Lirael's a dark crimson, slick and shining.

Lirael brought the babe up to her chest and rubbed his back. "Come on, little one, breathe for me."

The baby gagged and coughed, then let out a lusty cry. Lirael laughed with relief and smiled at the queen.

"What is it?" Elizabeth croaked, eyes half-open as she slumped against the tree.

Lirael looked past the waving limbs. "A boy. Oh, Elizabeth! It's a boy!"

The queen managed a smile and reached out her arms. "Give him to me."

Being careful with the cord, Lirael passed the naked, squalling babe over, guiding Elizabeth's trembling arms until she held the babe securely against her chest. Lirael removed her shawl and spread it across the babe and his mother. Warm now, he settled, staring into his mother's eyes, his own wide and unblinking.

"Ah, me, what a sweet little lad," Elizabeth whispered. She tilted her head back, looking at the sky. "He's as good as gone, isn't he Lirael?"

"Hush now, your babe is fine."

"Not the babe." The queen swallowed. "My husband. That witch—"

"Shh," Lirael replied. "His men were not far behind us, my queen. They will retrieve him."

Lirael tugged the queen's skirts down. She could do nothing for the bleeding. Either it would stop—God willing—or it wouldn't. She clasped her bloody hands in her lap, trying not to look at them.

The queen drifted, her head starting to nod. She shivered, and her eyes seemed unable to focus.

"It's so cold, Lirael."

"I know, my queen." Lirael adjusted the shawl, tucking it around Elizabeth and the baby. Lirael had seen that same distance in her own grandmother's eyes when she passed from this life.

The queen was dying.

"Alas!" Elizabeth cried out, squeezing her eyes shut, then looking at the calm babe in her arms. "Alas, my babe, you have killed your mother. Oh, it's not your fault," she added, "but it is what it is. You'll be a knight, no doubt, and mete revenge on life for taking your mother from you, by removing sons from their mothers in many great battles. You must grow, then, and be a man among men."

She paused, taking a long, shuddering breath, her voice a whisper. "Whatever you are, whatever you turn out to be, be good." Elizabeth leaned down and kissed her babe's forehead, then looked imploringly at Lirael.

Lirael understood and reached for the baby, wrapping him more tightly in the shawl.

"His name is Tristan. Do not let anyone tell you different," the queen whispered. She sighed then, and her body relaxed. The breath of life left her.

Lirael looked on as Tristan, snuggled in his tight, warm swaddle, slept unawares. It was not his to know as a simple babe, but tragedy and suffering would follow him all his life, each step marked by this one moment when his mother died having borne him earth-side.

His very name would serve as a reminder of what he had unintentionally done, for Tristan meant sorrowful.

CHAPTER ONE

Love, that is flesh upon the spirit of man
And spirit within the flesh whence breath began;
Love, that keeps all the choir of lives in chime;
Love, that is blood within the veins of time;
That wrought the whole world without stroke of hand,
Shaping the breadth of sea, the length of land,
And with the pulse and motion of his breath
Through the great heart of the earth strikes life and death...
"Prelude: Tristram and Iseult," from "Tristram of Lyonesse"
by Algernon Charles Swinburne

Thirty-six years later.

The hawk's rust-colored feathers stood out against the vivid blue sky as it wheeled around. Tristan followed it with his eyes. It felt good to be back in Cornwall, no longer on the road eating dried food between inns, and, worst of all, getting rained on and riding a horse for days on end. His backside ached at the thought. He jogged forward through a copse of trees to bring the hawk back in sight.

His winged companion, Astor, hadn't much liked the trip from France, either. Tristan kept him hooded most of the time to calm him. The numerous horses, rough and loud conversation, and the sheer number of men that thought they could reach out and pet the raptor at any given moment without warning drove both Astor and Tristan mad. Astor skinned more than a few fingers, despite Tristan's warnings. By the end of the journey, they trailed far beyond the main group, rather eager to be done with the whole thing.

Cornwall hadn't happened soon enough. Now Astor stretched his wings, exploring the geography of his new home. Tristan gazed upward, shading his eyes from the brilliant sun as he peered through the autumn foliage to glimpse his red-tailed hawk, a tiny speck in the sky.

For a moment, Tristan worried this might be where Astor left him. He had been through several hawks while in France; most hunting hawks left after a season. Astor had stayed with him for two seasons so far and showed no indication of leaving, but after the harrowing journey Tristan put him through to get here, Tristan wouldn't blame the bird for leaving him. All he could do was convince Astor life was

better with him providing good hunting and a safe place to roost.

The speck in the sky jerked and dove faster than Tristan could follow. He broke into a jog, breaking through the trees in time to see Astor make the kill, a fat rabbit making its death scream. Astor tugged at the still-warm body with its impressive beak, tossing tufts of white and brown fur into the air.

"Now, then, leave some for me," Tristan said, chuckling. The bird of prey cocked its feathered head, as if listening, then went back to the rabbit. Tristan let it work this one. Two pheasants and a large rabbit weighed down his bag already. A good day's hunting. The quarry was plentiful and well-fed this time of year.

Astor moved on to the rabbit's stomach, and Tristan took a short walk. He had grown used to the gore involved with hawking, of course, but he hadn't eaten his first meal of the day yet, and the sight of the large raptor shredding the innards of its prey churned his empty stomach.

He walked to the top of a low hill nearby, still able to see Astor from a distance, and looked out at the scenery around him. He could see Tintagel Castle with its towers looking out over the sea.

From that direction, Tristan spotted a rider, white messenger's coat flapping in the wind. Horse and rider disappeared for several long minutes, then Tristan caught a glimpse as the rider turned his way. He would be upon Tristan in a short time.

His uncle, no doubt, deigning to see Tristan. Resigned, he headed down the hill and came upon Astor, whose bloody beak trailed intestines and bits of fur.

Tristan whistled, calling the bird to perch on the heavy leather glove covering his right arm. The strong talons gripped Tristan's arm, and he rubbed a piece of fresh meat against Astor's beak, keeping his fingers clear as the raptor snapped it up.

He talked soothingly to the bird and scooped the rabbit's remains into his catch bag and out of sight. Astor was well-trained and, fortunately, distracted by the meat in his beak. The scar across Tristan's left eye, the result of a foolish lad crossing a stubborn, newly-trained goshawk, served as a reminder of the trouble caused by taking a hawk's prey.

He heard hoofbeats before he saw the rider come up through the copse of trees.

The horse galloped right up to Tristan, who tried not to flinch or step away from the massive snorting animal.

The young man sitting astride the saddle cleared his throat and recited his message. “His Majesty, King Mark of Cornwall, formally summons Tristan de Liones to court...”

Tristan whistled. “A formal summons, eh? He didn’t need to go to that sort of trouble for me. He might have just sent archers with instructions to shoot on sight.”

The messenger arched an eyebrow.

Tristan sighed. An older messenger would have cracked a smile, at least.

“Carry on.” He motioned to the messenger, who started again. Astor repositioned, his claws gripping Tristan’s arm through the glove. Tristan stroked his feathers.

“...to engage in a battle to the death against...”

“Wait, what?” Tristan asked, turning his attention back to the messenger.

The messenger sighed, his mouse-brown hair flopping over his eyes. He tossed his head and opened his mouth to repeat. “His Majesty, King Mark...”

“No need for that, messenger. I’ll go ask him myself,” Tristan growled, stomping away toward Tintagel.

A moment later, the messenger brought his horse trotting up beside him.

“I have been asked to take you on my horse. The king does not wish to wait.”

“I’ll not ride on that monstrous beast. No, I will walk. You can tell King Mark to take a bath or imprison someone unjustly, whatever kings are doing for enjoyment these days."

The messenger followed Tristan for a stretch filled with awkward, expectant silence on his end, while Tristan carried on a conversation with King Mark in his head.

A fight to the death? Only if it's against you. You think you own me, well it's time I put that thought from your mind once and for all. I will not be your puppet. I will not be the one you run to when you're frightened. Fight your own battles for once. I...

"Tristan?"

Tristan glanced up. Somehow, he had gotten from the field to the mews. Astor left his arm to perch on a beam high above.

He'd lost the messenger along the way, too.

The mews master ran his fingers through his stiff, grey hair, standing it even more on end. His gap-toothed smile made Tristan smile back, even though he didn't feel much joy.

"I'll make sure he gets settled in fine, Master Tristan. My birds all get treated right. More'n right. They're made out to be kings and queens o'the sky, I assure you."

Tristan dug into his pocket and handed him a few coins, accompanied by lint.

The mews master pocketed them, licking his lips. He pointed at Tristan's hands.

"Ye might want to wash those afore ye see the king."

Tristan stuffed his bloodied fingers out of sight. "How did you know he summoned me?"

"Ye were gabbling about it as you came in jus' now. Ye spend too much time alone, ye ken?"

"I know," Tristan replied, nodding to the mews master. "Thank you for seeing after Astor. I'll be in to fly him tomorrow."

I hope.

Tristan stood in front of the throne room door, staring at the carvings. He had stared at them since age seven. He'd gone to France at fourteen and visited every year, pawned off on his uncle so his stepmother wouldn't kill him.

Never mind that he had saved her life once; she was furious her own children wouldn't inherit the Scillian Isles when her husband, Tristan's father, passed.

They could have it, the whiny little bastards.

Tristan rubbed his hands together. In this lighting, it almost looked like they still had blood on them.

What would he do with an entire kingdom? Go mad like his uncle, he supposed, locked up in a stone box all day, arguing with peasants about taxes and bargaining with neighboring kings, jostling for the highest spot on the hill before he died and ended up lower than them all anyway.

Tristan sighed. Tillman, a friend he'd left back in France, always said Tristan needed to lighten up or he would die a dull flame.

Tristan forced a smile and pushed open the doors. He stepped into an empty room, footsteps echoing.

"Hello?" he called.

Light spilled out from a small annex room. Tristan walked towards it. A man sat inside, head in hand, arm propped up on the arm of his chair. He mouthed words as he stared at a paper clenched in his trembling fist.

"I can read that for you if you are having trouble, Your Majesty." Tristan emphasized the last word.

King Mark looked up, dazed for a moment, then a grin split his round face. He rubbed his free hand over his shiny head, making the last few hairs on it stand straight up.

"Tristan, my lad! It is good to see you."

"I wish I could say the same. I thought you might have put a price on my head by now."

King Mark chuckled, setting the paper down on the tiny table beside him, next to a full goblet.

"I only think about it once or twice a year."

Tristan cocked his head and counted on his fingers. "Oh, so, just about every time I visit."

His uncle stared at him, grinning like a fool. "It's good to have you back, Tristan, I miss your humor."

"I didn't quite get that impression, judging by the way I was received by your men the last time I visited..."

Mark's face went the shade of a beet. "Your dalliance with Earl Segwarides's lady ruined a crucial political alignment and nearly cost me my life!"

"You're only angry because it interrupted your own dalliance with Earl Segwarides's wife," Tristan shot back.

The two men glared at each other.

Mark's mouth twitched, and his red face grew to an even deeper shade. Tristan kept his face impassive, waiting. Mark snorted, straightening his face, until he burst out with a roar of laughter, slapping his knee, tears streaming from the corners of his eyes.

"The image of you, naked as a newborn babe, leaping from her bed and grabbing your sword...my men and Segwarides' chasing you across the moors...I can never... unsee it..."

Tristan joined with the man's infectious laughter, shaking his head. He crossed his arms as their laughter died down.

"You have put me in many a tight spot," Tristan said.

"I always get you out, too," Mark pointed out. "Segwarides wanted you hung, if I remember, and I sweet talked him into settling for a flogging."

Tristan rolled his eyes. "When I then conveniently failed to show up, you sent your men hunting for me."

"You know I had to."

Tristan stared at Mark. His familiar ruddy complexion and red, bushed-out mustache were counterpoints to the sparkle of mischief dancing in his blue eyes. After a moment, he cleared his throat.

"Yes, all right, you've gotten me out of a fair number of binds. But I haven't neglected you, either."

Mark's mustache drooped. "Aye, lad, that you haven't."

"A fight to the death, though? What have you done this time, Mark?"

Mark cleared his throat and looked away. He straightened the curling roll of paper on the table at his side. "It's King Angeus."

"The Irish king? What does he want?" Tristan stepped over to the table and skimmed the missive. "Seven years of tribute! Mark, you haven't paid him?"

"Money's been tight for many seasons, you know that. I don't want to increase the taxes on our people. Angeus is seeking war unless the tribute is paid, or..."

"Or I fight his champion." Tristan leaned on the table, looking at his uncle, who nodded. Tristan breathed out in a huff, then stood upright. "Where and when?"

"The Isle of Mann, a week's time."

"It will take that long to get there! When will I train? I'm not exactly in top dueling form."

"Tristan, I'm not one to beg, but I've asked all my men, and none have responded. Have I been so poor a king that none of my men will defend their kingdom?"

"Who has King Angeus chosen?"

"The queen's brother, Sir Marhaus," King Mark said, face miserable.

"There's your problem. Sir Marhaus is a knight of King Arthur's court. No one here could match him."

"Humility does not become you." Mark smirked, tapping his fingers on his chin. "You know you could defeat him."

"I don't *like* fighting."

"Despite an unnatural amount of inborn talent for combat, you prefer your harp and hawk," King Mark said. His face darkened. "Is there a wife and children you have stashed somewhere? Did my brother die at last and leave you the isles? Should I be bowing, King Tristan?"

Tristan shook his head. "Nothing like that, Mark." He sighed and rubbed the back of his neck beneath his shoulder-length hair. "Are you certain there's nothing else you could do? King Angeus has a daughter of age, doesn't he?"

King Mark raised an eyebrow. "You want me to marry?"

"All good men do."

"Do I get to set you up, then?" King Mark quipped. His emerald ring flashed as he waved his hand in the air, then shifted, reseating himself in the velvet chair. "I would consider it if we had more time, but there's barely time to get you to the isle. I can't risk war. Besides that, I have little to offer Angeus through marriage, except to ensure his daughter would be comfortable and her sons would inherit my holding here."

"It's an impressive holding, my liege." Tristan drawled out the last word. "Some might say the pairing is advantageous."

Mark shook his head and brought the goblet to his mouth, taking a sip of wine. He swirled the ruby liquid, glancing from the cup to Tristan.

"I can draft a contract, stating my intentions towards King Angeus' daughter. But you will have to deliver it for me, to Sir Marhaus on the Isle of Mann. If he accepts the terms on behalf of his king, you will go with him to retrieve the daughter."

Tristan laughed, hands on his hips. "There is one problem with your plan."

"Oh?" Mark said with a grin on his face. "And what might that be?"

"I cannot fight Sir Marhaus."

"But you said—"

"I am not a knight, King Mark," Tristan insisted.

Mark clunked the goblet down on the table, and a few droplets of wine spilled onto the missive from Ireland.

"Tristan, you had me worried it was serious. Knighting you will be simple. I can do it tonight."

It was the last thing Tristan wanted. But for Mark, for Cornwall, he would do it. He would fight Marhaus and win, or he would retrieve a bride for his uncle and bring her to Tintagel.

"Tonight, then. I must ready myself."

"And I must warn the cooks." Mark chuckled, pushing himself to stand.

"You know my father will hate you for this."

"He would have done it himself, years ago, if you'd let him," Mark said. "I think it may be you he will hate."

Tristan let out an amused grunt, but his throat constricted when he thought of his father. He let his legs lead him to the door of the throne room antechamber.

“I will pen a letter. I'll only blame you a little,” Tristan said, turning back to face Mark while walking backward.

“Wait, Tristan,” Mark said.

Tristan halted, halfway through the doorway. Mark's face looked earnest. “What is her name, the Irish princess?”

“Er, Isolde, I think.” He tossed a grin off at his uncle. “You had me thinking it might be serious, Mark.”

He laughed as he walked away, the king's mutters of “King Mark and Queen Isolde,” making him chuckle all the way down the corridor on his way to the armory.

CHAPTER TWO

Love, that sounds loud or light in all men's ears,
Whence all men's eyes take fire from sparks of tears,
That binds on all men's feet or chains or wings;
Love, that is root and fruit of terrene things;
"Prelude: Tristram and Iseult," from "Tristram of Lyonesse"
by Algernon Charles Swinburne

Breath entered Morgan. Her chest pinched and her breathing hitched with each inhale. Her eyes blinked open, sight blurry at first, and then her world sharpened.

White stone walls. A narrow window, looking out toward pale, grey clouds.

The wind whistled across the window, but a heavy pile of blankets and a fire crackling at her back made Morgan warm. Almost too warm.

She pushed herself to sitting, leaning back against the pillows on the large bed. She was breathless from even this, the slightest of movements.

Knotted, discolored scars twisted their way up her fingers, snaking over her palms and the backs of her hands, and crawling up her arms.

Morgan lifted the loose shift she wore, revealing tiny purple marks covering her stomach. Her hands rested on the covers, then in one swift motion peeled them off her legs. Mottled purple scars covered both legs.

She closed her eyes and replaced the blanket, breath catching in her throat and emotion tightening her chest. She clenched and unclenched her hands on the covers. She felt no physical pain, hardly anything at all.

She wished she could say the same for her heart.

A figure appeared in the open doorway, and Morgan jerked her head up. The person smiled.

"Glitonea?" Morgan asked. It couldn't be. That would mean. "You've brought me back to Avalon."

Glitonea inclined her head, bright red hair glistening. Her blind eyes stared sightlessly in Morgan's direction. "Thiton said you would be awake."

Thiton. The island's physician.

Morgan remembered her as a mousy-haired woman, small-bodied and with grey at her temples. Deft hands, though, and she'd taught Morgan much of what she knew about healing with herbs and salves.

Healing with magic was reserved for healing emotional pain, a craft Glitonea had mastered.

The tall, blind woman walked into the room, sitting in the chair beside Morgan's bed without hesitation.

Morgan's mouth felt like cotton. She swallowed hard and ran her tongue around her mouth, but there was nothing there to offer moisture.

Glitonea handed her the metal cup from the nightstand a moment before Morgan reached for it.

"Here. Drink."

Morgan gulped. Clear water flowed over her tongue and down her throat. She emptied the cup and held it out for Glitonea to refill. The woman used the small metal pitcher on the nightstand to fill the cup, and again Morgan emptied it.

Wiping her lips, she gave the cup back, and Glitonea replaced it on the nightstand. Working with Glitonea was like a seamless dance. The blind woman had an enormous capability to sense what one wanted or needed, or what one didn't want.

It made Morgan extremely uncomfortable. The last time she'd been here, she hadn't been prepared for Glitonea's way of sifting through her emotions swiftly and automatically, without any regard for what Morgan might want her to know. She said it was a sense, like smell or hearing, not something she could control.

"Thank you," Morgan said. She realized her hands clenched the blankets again, and she released them. Glitonea couldn't see her physical nervous cues, but she sensed far more than that through her empathic powers.

Glitonea cocked her head. "There is no need to fear me, Morgan. I mean only to help you."

Morgan sighed. "I am not afraid of you, so much as what your presence means."

Glitonea's brow creased. "It means you are safe, rescued and cared for by friends."

"I am not sure about that," Morgan said. "Last time we met, I was...defecting, with a woman who turned out to have evil intentions towards the Order."

"Niviane. Yes. We wish you had chosen a different path, but what is done is done."

"I caused the downfall of Camelot, surely forgiveness isn't so quickly given." Morgan looked down at her hands, following the raised rivers in her skin. Burn marks. A permanent reminder of everything that had happened. What did her face look like? Had the flames reached that high? She couldn't remember. She resisted the urge to touch her face and find out.

"Argante is furious. Many of the others, had they been lesser women, would have let you die as well. I appealed to their better natures, as I know your heart," Glitonea said.

"How did I get here?" Morgan asked, glancing up and watching the priestess's face.

"We retrieved you from the tower, brought you here, healed you. It was a simple task, inspired by the Goddess. She still has a purpose for you, Morgan." Glitonea's soft voice struck at Morgan's heart like a spear.

Morgan looked away, swallowing. She had abandoned the Goddess. What purpose could there possibly be for her?

"I am here to open your heart," Glitonea said after a moment. Her long fingers glided across the bedcover and found Morgan's own, grasping them in her thin, cool grip.

The room spun.

"What? Why? I am no longer an initiate of the Goddess."

"Until you complete the Rites or die trying, you will always be an initiate. You knew this when you first came to Avalon."

"I am not ready," Morgan insisted. "I never completed the Rite of the Mind."

"They are not always done in order. My sisters agree this must be done without delay. You are broken, Morgan. The fragments of your heart call to me; they ask to be made one."

“But…what will happen?” Morgan whispered. She knew of Glitonea’s methods. It was one reason she’d left Avalon with Niviane so many years before. After completing the Rite of the Mind, all initiates went through the Rite of the Heart. Some didn’t survive.

“No one can know, except the Goddess. Will you deny her will again?”

“I don’t want this!”

“Your choice was made many years ago.” Glitonea’s voice twisted

into a deeper version of itself, rough and grating. She stood, towering over Morgan. Heavy silver cords appeared in her hands, and before Morgan could react, Glitonea bound her wrists to the oak bedposts. Morgan struggled and pulled, the ropes biting into her skin. She kicked the covers from the bed in her panic. A whimper escaped her lips.

Glitonea’s clouded eyes lit up, lightning blue, and peered into Morgan’s soul. Her hands reached into Morgan’s chest, and Morgan screamed, agony lancing through her body. Glitonea moved through skin and sinew and bone, gripping Morgan’s heart. Morgan clung to the bedpost, trying to pull away, her chest anchored by Glitonea’s grip. Glitonea squeezed.

Morgan’s soul wrenched from her body. With a single, swift motion, Glitonea’s hands broke open Morgan’s astral heart. Morgan’s back arched and blackness erupted from her mouth, chest, and womb, shooting upward in a writhing column of darkness.

It stopped abruptly, and Morgan’s body collapsed, limp, on the bed. She could not move, could not feel anything. A thousand black worms wriggled on her skin, but her hands would not move to swat them. Bile rose, burning her throat.

Glitonea, eyes clouded once more, tipped Morgan to the side and held a silver bowl for her as her body vomited again and again, first a tarry, black substance, then thin, yellow bile tinged with blood.

Morgan's vision wavered. She saw a giant, plumed bird of silver light hovering over Glitonea's shoulder. The bird sang a song of such crystal purity that Morgan gasped, and her vision went white, filling her eyes until she could see nothing but the bird, its beak open in pure song.

I am dying, Morgan thought. And the thought brought relief to her soul. She could let go, leave this world and move on to the soul's realm. "Morgan." Glitonea's voice called her, anchoring her soul back to

the mortal realm. Tears broke forth from Morgan and sadness drowned her, enveloping her like a wave in the ocean, crashing down and sending her spinning through its depths.

Arthur appeared, standing beside the silver bird, his bearded face solemn, his eyes kind. His kindness undid her, again and again, each time she looked on him. Her eyes would not obey her; they would not close. She found her hands unbound now, but even when she covered her eyes, she saw Arthur and the silver bird in the air beside him.

Sadness poured from her, its sour taste pervading her mouth. Tears washed over her face and hands. Her eyes became puffed and

inflamed until she could not see. She tried stuffing her fists into her mouth to stem the flow, biting down until she bled, the metallic tang mixing with vomit on her tongue, but nothing could stop it. She would be weeping for eternity, like the banshee women of the tales, forever crying for lost love and doomed to punish others the way she had been punished.

Her gut wrenched inside her. She felt cramping in her womb. It started off irregular, painful but bearable. The next cramp bent Morgan in half, arms pressing down on her middle as if she could stop it from happening. Another cramp, then another, her body consuming her in waves of contractions.

Wetness drenched her thighs, and bright red blood flowed from her, staining white sheets. She gasped and heaved, grasping the sheets and screaming. Her eyes went wide, and Glitonea came into focus, passively looking on, hands clasped within her wide white robe sleeves.

"Glitonea, please, stop this!" "I cannot."

"I am dying!" Morgan's body clenched in pain and her voice erupted from her throat.

"What the Goddess wills will be done," Glitonea intoned, her unseeing gaze looking through Morgan.

More blood came out in a rush, bringing with it a lump, glistening and dark. Morgan gasped and looked away, body shuddering. She felt bile, hot and stinging in the back of her throat, but there wasn't enough left to expel.

A little boy with curly, dark hair appeared in the air beside Arthur, and Morgan cried out, reaching for the child. Her body shook, trembling with the fierceness of the mother-love that flowed through her, something she had never let herself feel.

Her son. Did he belong to Arthur? Or one of her half-brothers? It didn't matter which one had impregnated her. The child would never be born.

Rage replaced the love pouring from her. Her fists clenched, and she sat up, screaming her rage to the sky. Blackness forced its way from her throat in a thick column that choked her, made her gag and retch, but she couldn't move, couldn't stop it as it poured from her.

When it stopped, she slumped forward, breath rattling. She struggled to focus on breathing as the last bits of rage leaked from her.

"Please," she rasped. "Please, end this," "It will end when it is done."

"No," Morgan moaned.

She would not survive any more. She could feel more darkness stirring within her, as more memories churned to the surface. Fierce anger at Avalon, the priestesses, at Niviane, for lying to her.

The Goddess didn't exist, or if she did, she didn't care about Morgan. Anger at Mordred, for betraying her, for lying to her.

It coursed through her, white-hot, filling her with energy, energy to seek out those who had wronged her and make them suffer.

The image of Arthur stepped forward, mouthing words.

I am sorry.

Sorry? For not believing her? Letting her get burned at the stake?

Not loving her?

"You should know that Arthur is dead," Glitonea said, gazing straight at Morgan, connecting with her eyes as if she could see.

"Dead?" Morgan whispered. Her arms wrapped around her shoulder.

Anger washed out of her with a wave of sorrow. Her vision tinged blue-grey, muting everything. Glitonea's vivid red hair became purple, her robes grey. Everything became dark and Morgan fell into despair. He was dead. She could never make him answer for what he did,

or hear him say that despite it all, he loved her. Keening filled the room; her own voice, rising and falling like the call of a mourning dove. It grew in volume, then faded away to nothing.

A third figure appeared beside the little boy. She smiled at the little boy beside her, then up at Morgan.

Morgan's heart stopped beating.

"Elaina, no, you're alive. You have to be, you saved me." It had been smoky, and Morgan in agony, but she had seen the face behind the helm, a face she recognized better than any other besides her own. Elaina had saved her. So how had her form come to be here, standing beside two others Morgan knew to be dead?

"I am alive, Morgan. For now." For now? What did that mean?

"All must die, Morgan. But it is not your time; not yet. Live." "Why?" Morgan couldn't manage more than that. Weight on her

shoulders crushed her. Each breath in took massive effort and grew more difficult by the moment. It would take no effort to let go of this life.

Elaina smiled sadly but said nothing. Beside her, a mirror appeared. Morgan turned her head away, gripped with fear of what she

would see.

Glitonea's broke through the crippling fear. "You are not seeing something that is, Morgan, but something that could be, depending on your choices. Your sister lives, and she seeks you."

"Why does she waste her life seeking me?" Morgan cried out. "She understands more than you do."

Morgan curled her legs to her chest. "I should be dead to her. I should be dead to everyone. I do not deserve to live."

"Look into the mirror, Morgan." "What will I see?" Her voice trembled. "Your true enemy."

It wasn't Morgan who rolled her body over on the bed, facing the figures and the mirror. It wasn't Morgan who opened her eyes, forcing her to look at what reflected. It wasn't Morgan; and yet, who else could it be? She stared at the reflection in the mirror, not comprehending, and then, with great effort, she sat up.

Her own image gazed back at her. Covered with blood from the waist down, burn marks on her hands, arms, and legs up to her hips, and scattered across her torso, one on her face, a streak like a tear streaming down from the corner of one eye almost to her jaw. Her dark green eyes, staring straight forward.

Her chest burned, and her reflection in the mirror glowed with a faded silver light. Morgan rubbed at it, looking down, but saw nothing. The burning intensified, grew to an unbearable point, stinging across her skin like a thousand burning needles.

Her reflection dimmed, and the burning sensation stopped. In the mirror, Morgan saw the gleaming, silver figure of a large, plumed bird, as if painted into her skin, its wings brushing her collarbone, its clawed feet coming down between her breasts.

Morgan touched it with awe, then looked at her finger, almost expecting it to rub off, like freshly applied ink.

The mirror vanished. Elaina, Arthur, and the little boy blinked from existence. The room whirled about, spinning inward on Morgan, moving faster and faster. Her stomach clenched painfully, too weak to vomit. She shut her eyes tightly, wondering if she would survive whatever else happened in the Rite of the Heart or whether she had already failed and would die now.

She hated that the thought came as a relief.

Morgan slumped, as if her muscles melted and left her body as a sack of bones. Glitonea took her by the shoulders and leaned her back

against the bedpost with no resistance from Morgan. Glitonea's blind eyes seemed fixed on Morgan's chest, face impassive.

Morgan's eyes closed, and she drifted, the silver bird chasing the edges of her restless dreams.

Low murmurs woke her mind first. Morgan tried to focus on the indiscernible words, but the raw wound of her heart presented itself, drawing all of her attention. In her mind's eye, her heart lay in shreds, torn open, laying bare in her chest with everything exposed. It seemed tender, inflamed by what it had gone through, though she could sense some parts beginning to heal, parts she had supposed would always hurt.

"It isn't possible," Glitonea's voice insisted, floating in the darkness beyond where Morgan lay. She tried to open her eyes, but barely managed a flicker. She relaxed, breathing deeply. Better to hear them discuss her while they assumed she slept.

"The Rite of the Heart is as mysterious as the others. It is not exempt from exceptions," Thiton said.

"And yet, sister, in seven hundred years there has not been such an exception recorded. The Rite of the Heart cures or it kills, it does not leave half-healed sisters walking the earth!"

"Perhaps it is associated with the symbol chosen for her," Thiton replied, ever the logical, practical one. Morgan's finger twitched, itching to touch the painted wings now emblazoned on her chest, but she didn't dare. What was the bird called? She knew she had seen it depicted in a book somewhere. But her sluggish mind moved more slowly than her body. "The phoenix symbolizes rebirth. Perhaps Morgan has not chosen life again, yet. This is why I argued we should wait for the Rite of the Heart until after we had offered her the choice." "You could not have predicted this would happen. Moronoe, did you see this?"

"I saw the bird, but not the woman it belonged to." Moronoe's flat tone sounded strange to Morgan. Morgan wasn't certain she had ever heard the woman speak, and she struggled to recall the sister's face. Dark hair, a straight nose...she wished her eyes would open.

"Did you see whether the phoenix turned?" Glitonea asked, almost eager.

"It is silver in all my visions," Moronoe replied. Glitonea cursed. "I have never failed to purify a heart."

"Beware of pride, sister. It is not yours to purify, but the Goddess's."

"She awakes," Moronoe said, a moment before Morgan's eyelids fluttered open.

The three sisters gazed at her, each one so different, and yet similar. Sisters of the Oaths, not of blood. Moronoe's pale skin like death and a long, straight nose were hidden by the sweep of black hair falling forward into her face.

Morgan's eyes went to Thiton, the warmest of the six leaders of the Order of Avalon. She did not make eye contact with Morgan, but sat between her taller sisters, head bent downward, lips muttering unintelligible words.

Morgan didn't want to meet Glitonea's unseeing, yet disapproving gaze. Her fiery red hair was twisted in an elegant bun that pulled away from her face. Lips pursed, arms folded, her clouded eyes bored right through Morgan.

"There is a wrong belief your heart manages to cling to," Glitonea said to Morgan. "I could not see it before, as you slept, but understanding has opened itself to me now. I have never seen this in my time. I have seen many a heart turn to wrong beliefs, even after taking the Oaths, but I have not seen one fail the Rite of the Heart the way yours has."

"I failed?" Morgan said, sitting up, rubbing the crisp, clean sheets. Had she imagined the blood and vomit? Her body felt new, fresh, resilient, though easily exhausted. Her arms trembled when she pushed against the mattress and her lungs expanded hesitantly, straining against exhaustion in her body. "How is that possible? I thought failure meant death."

"I think what my sister means here is not that you have failed, but that the Rite has failed to complete its work," Thiton said in a rush, glancing to her sisters for support. Glitonea only snorted, and Moronoe stared ahead blankly. Did she see the past or the future? Thiton cleared her throat. "Moronoe, perhaps you could add to the conversation?"

"No," her alto voice intoned, and she continued staring, straight past Morgan and into the wall behind her. “I see only darkness surrounding this woman.”

“And I see only those silver wings,” Glitonea said, sounding like

a sulking child.

Morgan touched the mark on her chest; the mark of a large, plumed bird, spread across her skin as if painted by a master artist. “What is wrong with them...with it?”

“It is supposed to be gold,” Glitonea snapped. She jerked down the neckline of her white robe, showing a large golden eye above her own heart. “Every sister of Avalon has one after the Rite of the Heart. Every single one. The mark is unique to each sister, but speaks to certain strengths, usually indicating the path she will follow. When the Rite is completed, the mark turns gold. Yours has not, which means something I do not understand.”

“It is not ours to question the will of the Goddess, nor the path she would have you walk, Morgan. For some reason, she would not have you complete the Rite of the Heart now. Perhaps someday we will understand why,” Thiton replied.

“Her heart is unprotected; she will not be prepared for what comes,” Glitonea said, gesturing wildly. Morgan had never seen her so agitated.

Thiton held up a hand; a seemingly useless gesture against her blind sister.

“It all depends on her choice,” the lilting, cool voice said from across the room.

Morgan bowed her head. Argante. Head Priestess of Avalon, rumored to be a queen from another realm and over a thousand years old. She flowed more than walked across the floor. Her almond-shaped eyes rested on Morgan.

"We have a deal for you, Morgan le Fay."

The use of her full, true name from Argante's lips made her shudder. She would not be able to refuse this woman anything she proposed, she could only hope the priestess would be fair and offer a true choice.

"I do not deserve any deals," Morgan said. "I am responsible for the downfall of one of the greatest kingdoms, one of the greatest men, the world has ever known." She bowed her head, hands clutching the sheets. "What I deserve is death."

"There is our answer," Glitonea hissed. "She wishes for her own death. How could the Rite of the Heart be completed in the face of such selfishness? It could not kill her, not without exonerating her. Nor could it heal her."

"Glitonea." Argante's voice was not sharp, but it cut Glitonea off all the same. She looked at Morgan. "My sister is correct in theory, if not in manner. You dishonor the Goddess in your desire to throw away your own life, Morgan."

Morgan kept her head bowed. "I do not wish to dishonor, priestess. It is only that I cannot see another way to absolve my wrongdoings."

"The Goddess has shown us two possible paths for you, daughter Morgan. A choice lies before you, not to be made lightly."

Morgan looked up, meeting Argante's gaze.

"The choice is yours, and we will not try to persuade you. All may be made right, though nothing is certain."

Morgan waited.

Argante gestured to Thiton, who nodded and spoke. "You could choose to travel to an obscure abbey, far north of Camelot. There you would take vows as a nun of a strict Christian order, where you would make a daily penance for your crimes. You would not need to make any confession, but take a vow of silence. You would neither speak nor view the outside world until you passed from this life. You should know that your use of magic makes it possible for your physical form to outlast that of most mortals, perhaps adding twenty or thirty years to your time there."

Morgan nodded. Inside, her mind reeled. If she made this her choice, she would die. Far sooner than Thiton predicted. If not at her own hand, then from despair at living a truth she didn't believe. Guinevere had believed in the God of the Christians.

Morgan had always aligned with the religion of the Goddess. Why would the priestesses send her there, to live out her life in a lie? To take Christian vows she could not commit her heart to? Did they mean her to condemn herself through blasphemy of two kinds; unable to fulfill the Rites of the order of Avalon and only going through the motions in the oaths she took as a nun?

Thiton interrupted her racing thoughts. "There is another option. It involves the use of time magic. We do not take its use lightly, so you are warned. You have used the spell before, we believe, in your pursuit of your arrangement with the sorceress Niviane."

Morgan took a sharp breath in. The thought of going through it a second time made her lungs stall before she forced the air out again. Her hands shook. She clasped them together.

"Yes, we would send you back in time. There is another path we have arranged for you."

"Where would that path take me?"

Thiton shook her head. “Far from Camelot. We believe that if you do not meet with Niviane as Guinevere, her plans will be disrupted and the fate of both Camelot and King Arthur would be changed.”

“But I did very little. My mind was too broken to complete her plans successfully. She used Mordred, in his form as Lancelot, to complete her tasks. All I did was…”

“Distract King Arthur. Yes, you played a more significant role than you think, Morgan.”

“So, you would have me avoid him completely?”

Argante nodded. “Never meet him, never go to Camelot. Live out the rest of your life essentially banished. You could go anywhere or stay in Carmelide. You could marry, or not. Your task would be to avoid Niviane, Arthur, and Mordred at all costs.”

“Without me, Arthur still might fail,” Morgan insisted. “I could go, knowing what I know now, and warn him. I could prevent the fall of Camelot, kill Niviane and Mordred before they know that I have changed. I could —”

“You could ruin it all again by being allowed to return,” Glitonea seethed. She stood, towering over Morgan. “Do you not see? Time spells are unstable. The healing you have experienced with the Rite of the Heart may be enough to keep your mind from dividing this time, but it isn’t for certain. We could send you back only to repeat history exactly as it happened before, since the Rite of the Heart wasn’t completed.”

Glitonea turned to Argante. “I do not think we should even give her this choice, priestess. It was contingent on the Rite of the Heart, which has failed.”

“The Goddess intended for us to give her this choice, Glitonea, and she knew what would happen during the Rite. The choice is yours, Morgan. You can accept the risks and requirements that come with being sent back, and also enjoy a long life of relative freedom, or end your days in silence and seclusion. You have three days to decide, Morgan.”

Morgan looked up. “Only three days? Why so few?”

“The sky is in alignment for the spell to be used. If we are to lower the risk of your mind dividing, we must perform the spell when all is right,” Argante said.

Morgan hesitated, then nodded. “Could I have clothes?”

Thiton gestured. “A robe and undergarments are at the end of your bed. You are free to walk the grounds, participate in meals, and

speak to anyone you like. You are not a prisoner. You may also access the library, should you wish to study, though I urge you to avoid recreational texts and personal accounts. You may study and practice spells, however.”

“Thank you,” Morgan replied.

As they stood to go, Glitonea lingered. Morgan feared what the tall woman would say, but her face held a surprisingly compassionate expression. “You may wish to seek out Merlin. He is here in Avalon, as our guest.”

“Merlin?” Morgan looked at her with shock. The last she had known of Merlin, he was trapped in Elaina’s tower in an enchanted wooden chest at Niviane’s hand.

“When we came for you in the tower of Shalott, we also freed the sorcerer Merlin. He is largely responsible for offering you the choices we have.”

Morgan stared at Glitonea. Merlin was on a long list of people she never wanted to speak with again. She had made a fool of herself in front of him, refusing to accept his help when she most needed it. Besides that, he had her to blame for killing the man who was like a son to him. He wouldn't want to see her, either.

Glitonea followed her sisters out without another word, leaving Morgan alone, surrounded by cold, impassive marble walls and a choice.

CHAPTER THREE

Love, that the whole world's waters shall not drown,
The whole world's fiery forces not burn down;
Love, that what time his own hands guard his head
The whole world's wrath and strength shall not strike dead;
"Prelude: Tristram and Iseult," from "Tristram of Lyonesse"
by Algernon Charles Swinburne

Tristan's stomach heaved with the ship, but fortunately, he kept his last meal down. Bile rose and burned the back of his throat. He swallowed hard and took a stiff breath of sea air. The Irish seas were choppy, and he wished for nothing more than to be back on land, preferably by himself, flushing out game for Astor.

The poor bird would be confused when Tristan didn't show up to take him out. Of course, the mews master would make sure he got flown, but Tristan had to prepare himself for the likelihood that Astor would leave without someone he trusted there to call him back.

It hit Tristan harder than it ought to, harder than leaving his companions in France. His stomach lurched again. They sailed for a few hours, their tiny ship navigating the choppy sea with difficulty, at least in Tristan's eyes.

The captain of the Spanish six-man crew seemed in a good mood, for all the drizzling rain and unexpected gales. Happy to have a job, perhaps. He said the windy season made the waters dangerous to sail, and many ships remained moored until early spring. The captain claimed he didn't mind, having a great amount of experience sailing in inclement weather. He would wait at the Isle of Mann for Tristan, trading his merchant goods to the inhabitants there.

Alive or dead, Tristan supposed he would return to Cornwall on the ship. He would rather be buried in Cornwall than the Scillian Isles,

where his family resided. Hopefully, his uncle would follow through on his wishes. Tristan had penned them out before departure and had asked for the will to be delivered to Mark's chambers that morning, two days after leaving. He didn't want to debate the will, or face Mark's unerring confidence that Tristan would be victorious.

Tristan leaned on the railing, watching the low waves as they carried the ship along toward the Isle of Mann. No hole in the ground for him. His body would be burned, some ashes put in a capsule on a hawk's leg, to be scattered by the hawk's flight over Cornwall. Yes, that would be a fitting end, if Mark honored his wishes.

If Tristan's father heard, he would be furious that Tristan chose burial outside the family burial lands. Perhaps Mark would find a way to placate him. Either way, Tristan would be gone and wouldn't have to worry about the politics and emotions that would arise from his death.

Crossing the wet deck, he double-checked his armor, making sure the oiled, sealskin bags kept it protected from the elements. He turned next to a much longer package containing a new sword, gifted by his uncle, next to his old sword. He didn't dare open this package; the wooden scabbards could be ruined if they got too wet, despite their beeswax coating.

He hunched down beside his belongings, staying out of the way of the crew. The merchant ship had no covered place for a passenger. Fortunately, they would only be traveling about a day longer. They should hit shore before nightfall, the day before King Angeus had decreed the challenge would take place.

At least Tristan would get to sleep on land that night. Hopefully, the Pict villagers would accommodate him with an actual bed.

Sucking on the dried, salted meat that served as his evening meal until it softened enough to chew kept Tristan awake until nightfall. His destination was visible in the distance, a dark mass on a red horizon. The shore was hours away. He wrapped an oilskin cloak around himself and leaned his head on one of the packs. Within moments, the rocking of the ship sent him to sleep.

Tristan woke after a fitful night's sleep to the cry of gulls and a tremendously stiff neck. The grey birds wheeled in the air as he rolled his head around, trying to stretch the muscles. Around him, men performed their various duties in relative silence.

They worked flawlessly as a crew, each knowing their duties and working the ship without the need to communicate. Tristan didn't pretend to understand much of what they did; he was no sailor. At the moment, four of the crew's six men pulled at the oars, slicing them through the water, directing the ship toward shore in the absence of a strong wind.

The gales from the night before had died down and changed direction, leaving the ship to rely on her own manpower for getting to shore.

An ever-brightening pink dawn sliced through the grey sky. Ahead, color washed over the isle in patches of green and brown grass, cut through by rifts of grey rock.

Tristan squinted at the tiny white dots scattered about this face of the isle; sheep. If the tales he heard held any truth, sheep living on the Isle of Mann had four horns, instead of two. He looked forward to seeing them himself.

"We aren't landing on the isle itself, Sir Tristan," the captain shouted from the ship's head, his beard buffeted by the wind. "King Mark said the fight will take place on an island off the coast of Mann, to avoid disturbing the locals."

As he spoke, Tristan realized the ship turned away from the main isle, headed toward a colorless, wave-beaten bed of rock.

Trust Mark not to mention that little detail. They would be staying the night in pitched tents on the rocky ground of an abandoned island, with their enemies sleeping on the other side. There would be little to explore, no native hospitality, and fresh meat only for fortunate hunters.

Tristan hoped that there would be a small valley, or flat area better suited to fighting than the rocky ground he saw. In a short while, he would be able to see for himself.

The wind picked up again as they came ashore, biting through Tristan's clothes where his cloak didn't cover.

The pale, cold sun peeked infrequently from the clouds as Tristan helped the crew pitch two tents, pounding the stakes into the rocky ground. They positioned their tents on the leeward side of several large, jutting rocks, then set about in pairs to hunt for game.

Tristan followed two of the men, then split off on his own; he had no bow and would be of little use to the hunting parties. He spotted what appeared to be a stone chapel a short distance away. He felt inclined to visit whomever might reside there, so he stretched his legs walking through the wet, waving grass to the only structure on the island. Perhaps they would house a knight the eve before a duel.

Knocking on the wooden door sent echoes through the hall on the other side. A face appeared in the peephole near the top of the door, and muffled voices spoke briefly on the other side.

Tristan put on a friendly face, despite his exhaustion and the hunger twisting his belly.

After a moment, the door cracked open, revealing a squat, round-faced monk with a full head of brown hair. He spoke a Pictish garble that slightly resembled what Tristan had learned during his time studying Northumberland.

Tristan replied, trying to make sense of what he heard.

He learned from the monk that Sir Marhaus had arrived two days prior and secured the chapel as shelter for himself and his people. The monks would not admit Tristan and his crew, despite expressing their willingness and their pity, and Tristan suspected Sir Marhaus paid them well, an advantage Tristan did not have.

Tristan made his way back to the crew and their camp, a sour taste in his mouth.

He joined the men huddled near the fires, warming his chapped hands and face and putting his back to the bitter wind.

Several pheasants and fish roasted on spits, their juices sizzling as they dripped into the flames.

The captain welcomed Tristan back, expressing disappointment when he heard about the chapel. He clapped Tristan on the back and led him to a spot at the fire, telling him about the special seasonings he had sprinkled over the birds and fish.

It did smell good, Tristan had to admit.

He sat on the rock, listening to the friendly conversation between crewmen, drinking a spiced wine that warmed him while the meal cooked. The men brought him into the conversation, but Tristan didn't feel much like talking.

Shortly after the sun set, a messenger appeared at the edge of their camp; a soldier bearing the crest of King Angeus.

Tristan walked out to meet him.

"The terms of battle, from his majesty, King Angeus," the soldier said in his native tongue.

Tristan knew this one, being proficient in several languages and dialects. He thanked the messenger, who waited while he scanned the letter.

The terms were straightforward; a fight to the death, fairly fought between two men. Angeus' champion Sir Marhaus, and Mark's champion, Tristan. No help from outside parties, each allowed armor, a shield and a sword. The battle could be delayed, if agreed on by both parties, for inclement weather. Judging by the clear sky, that wouldn't be necessary. The fight would take place at mid-morning, on a sloped field near the chapel.

Tristan nodded at the messenger and agreed to the terms, marking the missive with his signature. Sir. The messenger hesitated.

“Sir Marhaus wishes to know who he fights on the morrow. What name shall I give him?”

The growing darkness seemed to close in around Tristan. He swallowed. “Sir Tristan de Liones, of Cornwall,” he replied. The messenger bowed slightly and took his leave.

At his side, the crewman ran a finger through his hair. “I have heard of this Sir Marhaus. He is a famous Knight of the Round Table, no?”

“He is,” Tristan replied, settling in his place at the fire.

The captain handed him a piping hot pheasant leg. Tristan let the evening air cool it. A couple of the men weren't so patient, and the others laughed at those who took hasty bites, then had to pant, mouths open, to cool off. The captain pressed servings onto Tristan until he complained of being overfull. He shrugged as Tristan refused the last bit of pheasant, taking it in his own mouth.

“I only want to be sure you are prepared, Sir Tristan.”

“I'll need it more in the morning, Captain,” Tristan replied.

“I will be sure you eat breakfast, Sir Knight. I have been saving something special.”

Another of the men spoke up, a small, mustached man with great agility in the rigging on the ship. “Do you know how you will defeat the knight?”

“A moment at a time, Cardon. Sir Marhaus is a strongly-built man with renowned skill in hand-to-hand combat. I trained in France and was considered to have great skill with the blade, but I'm relatively untested against Camelot's knights. I've also not studied Sir Marhaus's fighting style, but we both hold that disadvantage, as I'm unknown to him." Tristan shrugged, licking the drippings from his fingers before wiping his hands.

"You do not seem troubled at all," Cardon said, looking around to his fellow crew members. "I know I would be quaking in my boots!"

"And that is why you sail, my friend," Tristan replied good-naturedly.

He didn't need to tell this man that he was afraid; an intelligent man was always afraid the night before. During the fight, he knew his instincts and training would take over and grant him a calmness he looked forward to each time he experienced it. This time would be no different.

Tristan slapped his knees and stood. "I must retire early."

A chorus of voices bid him good rest as he retreated.

He made his way to one of the tents, where he found his belongings laid out beside three bedrolls. His appeared to be padded with an extra roll, courtesy of the captain, no doubt. If Tristan lived, he would ask Mark to commend the man, perhaps offer extra payment for his service to the crown.

Tristan took a moment to unwrap his swords and hold them on his lap. He couldn't see much by the shadowy light from the distant fires that shone through the tent flap, but he could feel the difference in the sheaths; the worn, familiar design on his own, the crisp, sharp lines on the new one.

Which should he use in the morning? He wasn't certain he could use an untested blade in one-on-one combat. His sword was old and worn, but tried and true. He laid them on opposite sides of his fur bedroll, then laid down between them.

He stared up at the tent ceiling, gripping the carved wooden cross that hung beneath his clothes. He didn't believe in big displays of spirituality, but he did know someone had to be up there, watching and caring.

He preferred to believe in a loving Father on high than the condemning God often portrayed, and this was who he muttered his prayers to this night; prayers for good rest and fair weather in the morning, prayers that he might do his best and give his all, for the good of Cornwall. Prayers for his opponent to be as well-rested as he and that a fair fight would be fought.

In the midst of his prayer, he decided which sword he would use; he would take into battle whichever one he woke up facing in the morning.

CHAPTER FOUR

Love, that if once his own hands make his grave
The whole world's pity and sorrow shall not save;
Love, that for very life shall not be sold,
Nor bought nor bound with iron nor with gold;
"Prelude: Tristram and Iseult," from "Tristram of Lyonesse"
by Algernon Charles Swinburne

Hard stone pressed against Morgan's knees as she knelt on the floor of the temple, its coldness seeping through the thin fabric of her robes. Morgan resisted the temptation to ignite a fire in the air beside her.

Thiton had warned that trying to use her own magic so soon after the Rite of the Heart would result in her losing consciousness. It would be a long time, she said, before Morgan regained her full ability with magic.

Morgan pressed her palms together in front of her chest, and the robe slid down, revealing the twisted burn scars on her arms. She looked up at the stained glass rendering of the Goddess of Avalon, the greens and purples and blues of the dress of nature that she wore casting their light from the sun outside and speckling the floor around Morgan, marking the white cloth of her robe in a dazzling array of color.

This was her favorite of the five likenesses that occupied the five small temples on the mystical isle of Avalon. Among them, two stained glass windows, including this one; two carved statues, one wooden and one stone; and one painting.

She loved this window for its color and the look of compassion on the Goddess's face. Her second favorite was the wooden statue and its life-like image. She preferred that temple, actually, but found it too far for her to walk in her condition on this brisk, autumn day.

Morgan took a deep breath, clearing her mind. She saw an impression of the Goddess behind the darkness of her eyelids, helping her focus. She drew in her breath, and imagined, like she often did, that she spoke directly to the Goddess, and that the Goddess, in her mercy, replied.

It wasn't too unlike how it felt to have herself divided, the other voices speaking to her and in her place. Perhaps she had always been mad, in a way.

Mother?

Yes, daughter?

Mother, I am lost. Please help me find my way. I always have. Except when I have been foolish and have drifted. I see now that Niviane does not heed your will and led me astray to destroy Camelot.

Did she?

The question made Morgan pause. The tenets of the Goddess always taught that everything happened for a reason, and that the reason always led back to the Goddess. But how could something so horrible be the will of the Goddess?

Morgan breathed in again, holding her palms together, swaying on her knees so the hard marble beneath her knees wouldn't hurt so much.

I have been given a choice, but I do not know which to choose. Would you have me return, to live out my life avoiding Camelot, avoiding Arthur, and finding a new path through my old life as Guinevere?

She waited, trying to feel whether she received an answer. The cool air swirled around her. Leaves tumbled outside. She felt nothing.

Or perhaps it is your will that I become a nun of the Christian God? As punishment for my crimes against your will and your name?

Nothing but silence and frigid air wrapping its fingers around her, leaking through the fabric of her robes.

Show me the way, Goddess, please! You know the way.

Morgan clenched her fists, anger rising hot and fast inside her chest. Why did the Goddess not answer her? Didn't she care? Silence, in the building and in her mind.

Morgan stood and pivoted, walking hastily from the building. She felt a lump catch in her throat, blocking tears from falling, choking her with the force of her feeling.

She stopped along the leaf-strewn pathway, breathing in, and out, trying to clear the lump from her throat as it spread to her chest, paralyzing her with fear. She did not know the way.

In fact, as she looked around her, she realized she felt disoriented, despite having walked all the way here without an issue. Mist closed in around her and obscured the path at her feet. She walked forward, then stopped, confused.

The heavy mist left drops of dew glistening on the dark strands of her hair. She shivered, wrapping her arms around her. Ahead, she caught a glimpse of a figure.

"Hello?" She called out, swallowing again. "Please, I need help!"

The figure turned, blonde hair swept up in a hasty bun, face creased with concern. "Morgan, where are you?"

Morgan halted. Elaina. Morgan stared at the woman before her, her body mostly obscured by mist.

"Elaina?" She asked. Her sister turned, looking straight through Morgan. She couldn't see her.

A pathway existed between the real world and Avalon, but not many could find it on their own, and if they did, a guardian stood protecting the inhabitants of the Isle of Apples, often to the death.

Morgan lowered her hand. She hadn't realized she held it up. She watched as Elaina seemed to move through the fog, searching for her. A prickling of her neck hairs made her turn around. Merlin stood behind her and to her left. Morgan blinked at his sudden appearance.

"She cares for you greatly," Merlin said, tucking his hand into his wide sleeves. Did he feel the cold?

Morgan turned back to face Elaina. "I do not understand why. She should hate me after what I've done."

"It isn't easy to understand love."

"Will she find me?" Morgan asked. "Can she reach through the mists of Avalon?"

"Who knows? She has the same blood as you, which technically qualifies her to enter. I do not know if she wants to enter, however. She may be waiting for you to come out. Or she may not know you are here at all."

Morgan shut her eyes tight. If she entered the convent, Elaina may never find her. Would she spend her whole life searching?

"I should send her a message, tell her not to keep looking, to settle down."

"She is unlikely to listen. You are her last remaining family."

Morgan turned on Merlin. "Is that supposed to help? Or make me feel guiltier?"

His blue eyes blinked at her anger. "Do you feel guilty, Morgan?"

She folded her arms and turned back to Elaina, whose form grew more distant in the fog. "Yes, if you must know. I betrayed Camelot. Even if I didn't consciously know what I was doing, part of me knew. And I didn't do anything about it; I let it all happen."

"Perhaps you were meant to let it happen."

"The priestesses say I should go back in time and change it. That's not light magic. They wouldn't be offering it unless it were crucial that Camelot remain."

"Do not presume to know every answer at once. There are meanings hidden within meanings, and it is only by making a choice that we can live to see the answers made clear." He waited for Morgan to respond, but she only hunched herself over against the cold wind. "Have you made your choice, Morgan le Fay?"

"No," she replied.

Merlin paused. "It was noble of you to offer yourself for execution earlier."

Morgan shut her eyes tight, her breath visible in front of her as she breathed out.

"I didn't...I didn't offer myself. It was a trick, meant to, first, see if they planned to kill me, and second, convince them not to. I know my sister priestesses well, Merlin. If I asked to die, they would not kill me. They have a strong preservation instinct, and often preserve life to a fault. I knew my suggestion that I needed to die to right the wrong would infuriate Glitonea. She sees life so much as a gift that it blinds her."

Merlin's eyes gleamed. "Very clever."

Morgan scoffed, shuffling her feet on the ground. "More to feel guilty about. Even as they're deciding my fate, I manipulate them into letting me live. They make it sound like I'll be a hero if I choose to go back and save Camelot. I'm no hero, Merlin. I just don't want to die."

"So, go to the convent. Punish yourself with guilt for the rest of your life." His tone made it clear he wasn't serious, but Morgan stared

at him all the same. At last, she shook her head.

"No. It would be more reward than punishment, in a way. A life of ease, silent and simple. I do not think I will accept it."

"And yet you feel too guilty to accept a second chance?"

She froze. How could he read her so well? Elaina's form faded into the distance. If Morgan went back in time, could she free her sister? Morgan chose not to respond to Merlin, instead turning in a circle. The fog lifted gradually around her in Elaina's absence.

"Do you know the way back? I'm starting to feel tired."

"Have they told you yet that you will not succeed?" Merlin said to her back.

Morgan closed her eyes, then turned around and opened them, gazing at his wizened face.

"There will be a price, and I do not think you are prepared to pay it."

"What is the price?"

His face was solemn as he stepped toward her, head towering

above her. "Everything you are, everything you have become, must be sacrificed if you are to succeed. And success may not look as you expect it to."

"That isn't an answer."

"No, it is not. I imagine, if you ask the same question of Argante, she may give you a different answer." Merlin smiled then, a sudden, bright thing that shone into Morgan's soul.

She cringed.

Merlin gestured straight behind her. "Head up that path, my dear. You will find what you are looking for."

She muttered her thanks, then went the way he indicated, the path clearing as she walked, revealing the Mother House up on the hill. By the time she arrived, she was completely chilled, and Thiton gave her a lecture on wearing proper clothing out in the elements.

Morgan let herself be ushered into her room and held the offered mug of herbal tea in her trembling hand.

Thiton pulled back the covers and waved Morgan toward the bed.

Morgan took a step forward, then stopped.

"What are you waiting for, child? Goddess knows you need rest, and I'll be certain you get it."

"Why didn't you heal me?" Morgan said, looking up at the older priestess.

Thiton's mouth dropped open. "I did heal you, child. What makes you..."

"You've healed my body, but not my mind. I remember everything. Why didn't you take it away?"

"It is not the Goddess's will that we remove your memory."

"I do not care about the Goddess's will, Thiton! I want to be able to close my eyes without seeing their faces!"

Morgan clenched the mug in her hands, breathed deeply. Her throat ached with choked emotion, but the tears seemed stuck somewhere below her breastbone.

"Oh, my dear." Thiton took the tea from her hands and set it on the table, then grasped both of her arms, stroking them with her thumbs.

Morgan didn't look up. Her breathing became ragged, the space in her chest near her heart throbbed and ached, like a wound reopened.

"You will understand in time why all of this has happened," Thiton said, her voice gentle. "We all have hurts inside of us. Yours will be close to the surface for a long time, after what Glitonea did. It is part of the healing process. You cannot heal those heart-hurts without acknowledging they exist."

She led Morgan to the bed and sat her down, bringing her legs up onto the bed for her and pulling the covers up to her chin.

Morgan let herself be treated like a child. She didn't want to face those feelings she had when she thought about Arthur. Love. Hate. Sorrow. Hurt.

She rolled onto her side, away from Thiton, who sat on her bed and stroked her hair for a time. She sang a quiet lullaby in her lilting Irish accent, and Morgan found her breath slowing, her body sinking further into the down mattress, her mind clearing. Thiton's weight left the bed as sleep claimed her.

Morgan woke on the final day with a pounding in her heart and her head. Her mind swam with strange bits of fading dreams. The last impressions of her dream ran through her head.

If you go back, you will never see Arthur again. If you stay and become a nun, you will see him every day for the rest of your life. And if you return, you may be able to free Elaina.

It left her with only a single question.

Thiton bustled into her room, giving Morgan a curious glance as she set a tray of food on her lap. "Are you feeling well enough today? Has the exhaustion left you? Any fever or aches I should know about?" She didn't wait for Morgan's reply, but put a hand to her forehead.

"I am well enough, Thiton. But I do have a question."

Thiton hesitated. "If it's about what we discussed yesterday, I won't—"

"No, not that."

"Very well." The woman brushed her greying hair behind her ear and straightened the blanket, then clasped her hands in front of her white robe.

Morgan stared down at her food. "What would you choose, Thiton? If you were me?"

Thiton made a surprised sound. "You are asking me? We are different people, Morgan."

"I am not asking you to decide for me."

Thiton smiled, shaking her head. "I will not be put in that position, Morgan. It is a decision for you. I do not know what I would choose, for I am not you."

She reached her soft, cool hand up to Morgan's cheek and patted it.

Morgan turned her face away.

Thiton sighed. "What would Guinevere do?" she asked, then left Morgan alone in the room.

What would Guinevere do? What kind of fool question is that? Guinevere was never real. And yet, despite how many times she told herself this, Morgan knew it was a lie. She had become Guinevere for a while, gone mad with talking to herself, blacking out, waking up hours later without knowing what happened.

The core of herself never left, but her good, innocent sides— Guinevere, Morgause—and her bitter, angry sides —Morgaine, Morgan—came out intermittently and at their own will, each distinct from the other, until they integrated, and their will and purpose became one. Arthur had been part of that healing. His love for her changed her, and his betrayal nearly destroyed her.

What would Guinevere do? Guinevere would become a nun. She loved that patriarchal God her father believed in. She would find healing in a life devoted to the church.

In an instant, Morgan knew that life would torture her. She wouldn't spend her days seeking healing from God, she would spend them agonizing over the memory of Arthur and all she did wrong.

No, she could not go to the nunnery.

She'd go back, then. Back in time and avoid Arthur all together. She clenched her fists and bowed her head, choking on the feeling of emotion welling up without any tears falling.

When I was Guinevere, I cried all the time. Now I can't shed a tear! What is wrong with me?

Was it a side-effect of not completing the Rite of the Heart?

"You will find emotions...difficult, until the Rite of the Heart has finished, and your phoenix mark turns golden," Argante's high, thin voice said from the doorway.

Morgan's head shot up, and she had to catch the tray on her lap as it slid.

"Argante. I'm sorry, I wasn't prepared for your visit. I'd hoped to be dressed."

Argante walked into the room. “It is all right, sister. No one expected it. It is rather early. Just after dawn, actually. I am pleased to find you awake.”

“Do you want my answer?”

Argante blinked, then pulled up a chair and sat, smoothing the soft fabric of her robes. “If you have it, we could use all the time you give us to prepare. But I promised three full days, and today has only begun. I intended to ask you how your spiritual practice was and how your personal relationship with the Goddess has developed. You showed much promise as an initiate when you first came, and I have hope that I might make you an apprentice someday.”

Morgan stared at the priestess in shock. “I…well, it’s been difficult. Do you know what happened to me when Niviane cast her spell?”

Argante tilted her head to one side. “I have heard some things, but sifting through rumors is difficult and unreliable. I would rather hear it from you.”

“I will tell you all of it, some day. For now, you only need to know that when the spell was activated, my mind split, dividing the abused parts of me from my core self, protecting me as a child again from remembering those terrible things, almost like I was reborn. Guinevere…I…was terrified. And the split parts of my mind were strong and unbalanced. I’m afraid the past twenty years have been a waste, as far as my spiritual and magical training.”

Argante hummed with interest.

Morgan bowed her head, examining the cold tea and poached eggs on her tray.

“I would not say wasted. You are here before me a very different person. You are less rash and softer around the edges. More teachable, perhaps. I wager the Goddess will be able to speak to you more clearly from here on. Be sure you are listening," Argante said.

"Yes, priestess," Morgan said. And then, "Can you tell me anything more about the decisions before me? Where will I go, what will I do if I choose to go back?"

Argante stood. "The path will appear as you step forward."

"Could I come here, you know, after time is turned back?"

Argante hesitated. "You know how the magic works, Morgan.

Avalon's paths close for a time to the person on whom the enchantment is worked. It is to prevent the magic being traced back through you by someone who wishes ill intent upon the inhabitants of Avalon. You will find your way back when the Goddess wills it, and not a moment sooner."

Morgan looked down at her hands. "One more question?"

She looked up to see Argante incline her head, gesturing for her to ask what she would.

"Merlin said there would be a price. I know now the price for Niviane's magic. What will be the price of yours?"

Argante froze, her expression closed. "I cannot lie to you. Not when you were so ill-used by Niviane. Should you choose to go back, you will risk fracturing your mind again, although that outcome is less certain than others. You also already know that as an initiate, rather than a full priestess, your magic will grow weaker the longer you are away from Avalon." She hesitated, then, and her eyes grew distant, as if she was seeing far off. “You will see someone die, someone you love deeply.”

Morgan sucked a breath in and closed her eyes. If she went back, she had a chance to try to rescue Elaina from the tower; no one said anything about staying away from her.

But if what Argante said held any truth, she would have to stay far away from anyone she loved to avoid seeing them die.

She opened her eyes, and Argante was gone.

CHAPTER FIVE

Fate, that is fire to burn and sea to drown,
Strength to build up and thunder to cast down;
Fate, shield and screen for each man's lifelong head,
And sword at last or dart that strikes it dead;
Fate, higher than heaven and deeper than the grave,
That saves and spares not, spares and doth not save.
"The Sailing of the Swan" by Algernon Charles Swinburne

Tristan woke in a cocoon of warmth, eyes on his trusted old sword. He grinned.

An extra layer of furs lay across him, thrown on him in the night; no doubt the generous captain again. The warmth only made it harder for him to push them off and sit up, rubbing the crusted sleep from his eyes. By the look of the dawn outside, he had several hours until mid-morning. Beside him, his tent partners slept, buried in their own furs like bears in their dens.

He stood, taking the well-worn sheath with him, its weight comfortable in his hands. He also grabbed the large, unwieldy package that held his armor and shield, the second, newer sword, and tucked a fourth package under his arm.

Tristan staggered out of the tent, dropping his shield as it slipped under his arm. He retrieved it, placing it on top of the precarious pile in his arms.

A stunning, pink-shot sunrise greeted him, streaking through the sky with gold and orange hues.

Tristan took a deep breath of the crisp air. The morning's dawn invigorated him in a way no grey skies could have, and he sent his thanks to God above for the gift. It was one man's last sunrise, this day. He hoped Marhaus enjoyed his view from the abbey.

The captain tended the fire. His grey mustache twitched as he sniffed the cold morning air. "Ah, I figured you one for the early rise," he said, adding another log to the fire as it ate its way through a spark of kindling, hungry for more.

"Thank you for accommodating me most comfortably, Captain. Were you up the entire night?" He set his packages down with a clatter and drew his old sword, inspecting it in the growing sunlight.

The captain grinned toothily at him. "No, Manuell took first watch. I relieved him. It is one of my greatest pleasures, staying out in the isolation of night, feeling as if I am the only man alive in the world, communicating with the stars and God. A man needs this, now and again."

Tristan smiled, nodding his agreement as he put the sword down, balancing it on the rock in front of him, the back of his legs becoming warm against the crackling fire.

The captain watched Tristan unwrap the armor, moving each piece, making sure it wasn't stiff or rusted in any area. "Why do you not have a squire, Sir Tristan?"

"I was knighted only a day before I met you, Captain," Tristan explained, pulling on a gauntlet and flexing the metal fingers. "I saw no sense in choosing a squire who might only serve me for a few days."

One thing he did appreciate was well-fitting armor. He had gone to great pains to get his fitted by France's best, and, strange though it seemed, he would miss it when he passed from this world. Armor this light, this well-fitted, this durable, was hard to come by.

Instructions to King Mark had included finding a new home for it. He set the armor aside, wrapped loosely in its package, and picked up the new sword next. He held it out to the captain, who hesitated, then took it, admiring the pattern on the sheath and hilt. He drew the blade halfway out.

"It is a masterful blade," the captain admitted.

"I want you to have it," Tristan said.

The captain stared at him, then shook his head. "No, you mustn't. What will you fight with?"

Tristan gestured to his old sword. "I cannot fight such a crucial battle with an untested sword. I will not fight in top form if I am uncertain of my weapon."

"It is bad luck to take such a gift while you yet live, *mi compadre*," the captain said, holding out the sword.

Tristan reluctantly took it back. "You must agree to take it if I die today, then."

"I prefer to believe I will never get that chance," the captain said.

Tristan smiled and set the sword on the ground, then sat on the smooth rock and picked up the fourth package, unwrapping it with great care. He stroked it as he would a lover, feeling the polished wood beneath his fingers, the delicate strings singing slightly as he brushed them.

Across the fire, the captain perked up. “You play?”

Tristan adjusted the tuning pegs, then plucked a few individual strings. “Aye, I do. There wasn’t much opportunity to bring her out earlier.”

“The harp is a beautiful instrument. It surprises me that a fighting man such as yourself plays. Do you play well?”

“Some say so.” Tristan shrugged. “I have devoted many hours to learning.”

The captain’s eyes gleamed. “One can tell that you love the instrument.”

“That I do,” Tristan said, settling the bottom of the small harp between his thighs. “This is Peu d'Amour, Little Love. I have a much larger harp at home, a cherry wood that fills you with sound at each stroke until tears leak out your eyes and you beg me to never stop playing.”

“Let us hear, then. It is a fine way for the men to wake, hearing your music. And while you play, I will warm breakfast.”

Tristan let his hands wander tunelessly along the strings, trying to determine what mood the harp had this morning. Nothing seemed to fit with the glorious sunrise and impending fight to the death.

He stopped the thrum of the strings by laying his hand flat against them, then sighed and closed his eyes, hanging his head.

After a time, his fingers wandered along the strings, volume growing as he gained confidence. His fingers trailed along the harp strings, weaving the notes together in a composition of his own, burbling like a river, trilling like a bird, a piece he had written to put the forest into song.

He drew in his brow, fingers falling hard and plodding on the low notes, letting each one play until it disappeared, transitioning into a solemn tune he had heard at an inn once.

Tristan had a good ear; once he heard a tune, he could play it almost immediately.

He played anything that came to his hands and heart. A short, happy folk tune from a little French village. A Welsh ballad. A love song. His fingers flexed to pluck each note with perfect agility.

One by one, the rest of the ship crew woke, the remaining five men coming to sit around the fire, even at Tristan's feet. As if a spell wove itself around their eyes, forcing them to watch those white hands play, weaving around their ears and on to their hearts. None leaned in to whisper, none glanced around at the seabirds calling.

In the lone chapel on the hill, the monks' morning chants wove around the echoing sound of the knight's harp as it made its way to Sir Marhaus's room, by now a Scottish war song, declaring the player's ferocity and strength, singing of his mighty deeds through the power of a stream of notes.

Sir Marhaus glanced up from binding leather greaves on his arms to listen as the faint notes played. It could almost be said that something like fear took him in the heart then, but like a mosquito buzzing about his head, he ignored it and went about his morning, muttering a prayer of protection.

Oblivious to all who heard him, Tristan played. He lost himself in the music, as he would lose himself in the fight. No one could make him lose focus. Nothing would take him away from his purpose.

He heard a poorly-disguised sniffle from among the men and opened his eyes. Every eye glistened. Tears streamed down his own face, dripping onto the wood of his harp, and his fingers moved to play the last notes of a widely-known lullaby..

He let the notes linger in the air, then laid down the harp in its waterproof wrapping. No one stirred. A last tear dripped from his nose and fell onto the harp before he closed it.

In his will, he had asked King Mark to burn the harp with him. A beautiful instrument such as this deserved to be played, but he couldn't bring himself to leave it to anyone.

He faced the men, slapping his knees and grinning. "Well, then, what's for breakfast?"

And like that, the harp's spell broke. Some men laughed, others chattered.

The captain brought Tristan a bowl of warm gruel, cooked in a pot with the bones and juices from the game caught the night before.

It was warm and filling, and with the addition of salt and herbs the captain had brought with him, it was rather savory, too. Tristan was given the last scraping from the pot as seconds, after which he licked the bowl and profusely thanked the captain. A fine meal to be his last, be it according to God's will.

The sun climbed, lending its warmth at last as its rays forced their way through the partly-clouded sky.

Tristan took to his feet, walking through his stretches, touching his toes, reaching for the sky. He twisted his torso one way, then the other, then went to pick up his armor. It wasn't there. He frowned and straightened.

Before him stood small, dark-skinned Manuell. He looked at Tristan solemnly, his straight black mustache quivering on his lip. He held Tristan's armor outstretched in his arms.

"I have some experience in this area, señor. Would you allow me the honor of assisting you?"

Tristan's heart swelled and his throat closed. He coughed to clear it, wiping at the moisture in his eyes.

"My squire for a day? I would appreciate that, Manuell. Thank you." Tristan inclined his head to the man, then stretched out his arms.

Manuell began with the padded gambeson, a long, thick vest that went on over Tristan's clothes, with matching arm pieces. Next came the chainmail shirt, rattling as it poured over Tristan's head and body.

Tristan allowed Manuell to do what he would, only pointing out minor adjustments as he preferred. The last item was his helm, which he accepted from Manuell and tucked under his arm. He did not have his scabbard attached; he wouldn't take it into a duel. Instead, Manuell would hold it for him.

Followed by the captain and crew of six, Tristan walked towards the chapel. Wet grass flattened beneath his feet. If he breathed deeply, fear didn't have time to invade him.

Focus on breathing, he told himself.

The chapel came into view. A knight in gleaming silver armor stood outside the doors in the company of ten other men. They spoke to the monks, then started down the hill.

Beside him, Tristan heard one of the crew mutter in Spanish. He smiled grimly. French and Spanish were similar enough he understood the basic meaning; *God above, he is big*, was roughly what the man said. A true statement.

Tristan himself wasn't small, but as they got closer it became apparent that this man, Sir Marhaus, was enormous. Built like a bear with massive hands and feet, towering a foot and a half over the shortest man on Tristan's line, and several inches over Tristan himself.

Height didn't make Tristan nervous, skill did. And he had heard rumors, legends, even, of Sir Marhaus's skill with the blade, particularly in hand to hand.

Visor up, Sir Marhaus approached. Beaked nose and bearded jaw, but otherwise pleasant-faced.

The two men faced each other, each one with a foot higher and a foot lower so they were on an even plane, despite the hill. The one on the upper side of the hill would hold a slight height advantage, though he would also be facing into the sun.

"Sir Tristan." Sir Marhaus inclined his head, the crest of his helm gleaming.

The crest on his helmet was unusually exaggerated, a thick, heavy piece of metal meant to discourage opponents from bringing their swords down on the wearer's head.

Tristan's own helm held no such advantage. Simple, straightforward, functional, the way he liked most things.

The rest of Sir Marhaus's armor matched his helm in every respect, both elegant and functional, etched in the Irish way. A Celtic symbol displayed prominently on the breastplate and shield.

Tristan returned the knight's nod. "Sir Marhaus. I hope you slept well."

The knight's mouth split into an amiable grin. "I did indeed."

Tristan gestured to Sir Marhaus's shield. "What does your coat of arms mean?"

"It symbolizes my loyalty for Ireland, for my king and people, as does yours, I assume."

Tristan glanced down. A borrowed shield from Cornwall. Fitting, for that is who he represented here. His heart swelled as he thought of the land of his childhood. His uncle sought freedom and honor of his own making. Tristan would be proud to stand and fight for that right to be free from King Angeus' tribute.

"My liege has a request, to avoid all bloodshed, if possible," Tristan said, reaching his hand to the side, where Manuell stood with the missive King Mark had sealed with wax, proposing a marriage union.

Sir Marhaus hesitated, then reached out for the missive, grasping it in armored fingers and reading swiftly. He held it back to Manuell, who hesitated, waiting for Tristan's nod before receiving the rolled parchment.

"The king suspected King Mark might try to delay the fighting and escape being held accountable for his crimes. On behalf of King Angeus of Ireland, I reject King Mark's proposal. This will be settled here between us or in blood on a larger battlefield. And our steward will take record of the results of our duel, to be sure all is recorded with accuracy."

Tristan nodded. "Very well." He placed his helm. It settled on his head, narrowing his field of vision. Manuell retreated to a safe location where the rest of the crew stood watching. Tristan held his shield and sword at ready, relaxed.

Sir Marhaus put his visor down and tapped his sword on his shield. “Are you quite ready, Sir Tristan?”

“Aye, I am. Why the rush?”

Sir Marhaus shrugged. “I appreciate efficiency. The terms are agreed upon, we are met at the assigned place, I see no reason to hesitate.”

“Very well. On your man’s mark.” Tristan said.

Sir Marhaus nodded to one of his soldiers, who stepped forward on the incline. He extended his arm between them. Sir Marhaus raised his sword, readying.

Tristan settled into his beginning stance. The music from this morning had calmed and focused him.

The soldier’s arm went up and he barked a word, and Tristan’s blade darted close enough to touch the tip of Sir Marhaus’s weapon. The knight batted Tristan’s weapon aside easily, then made its own attack. Easily parried. A test.

Tristan rushed forward, his slashing met with a parry from Sir Marhaus.

Immediately, Sir Marhaus pressed Tristan back until they turned, and Sir Marhaus held the upper hand on the hill. Each of his blows landed heavier on Tristan’s sword until Tristan batted his opponent’s sword away and moved from lower to upper ground.

The sun made him squint, but the power increased with each swipe of his sword, and he forced Sir Marhaus to the ground.

His sword whirled around and swiped at Sir Marhaus’s leg, slicing him above the knee. The other knight rebounded with a jab into Tristan’s left arm above his elbow where the plate parted. The first blood drawn.

They stepped away for a moment, a non-verbal understanding between them that lasted a split second before they pressed into another exchange, sword on sword.

Tristan got in close enough he couldn't maneuver his weapon, so he punched Sir Marhaus's helm with a gauntleted fist. The weak blow didn't do much damage, but it gave Tristan time to reposition his sword for an attack.

Sir Marhaus stepped away, missing the parry, and Tristan's sword crashed into his armored chest, denting the metal.

Tristan's breath came heavy, loud in his helm as he stumbled back from the blow. The field was eerily silent. This wasn't a tournament match, with jewels or a lady waiting on the outcome. Kingdoms were at stake. Lives. Freedom. A war in miniature. Two men, one would survive. Men did not cheer a war.

Sir Marhaus renewed his pursuit, pounding Tristan's sword with his own.

Tristan stumbled, blocking one blow with his shield that made his bones ring with the force of it. He didn't stop to nurse it, as it didn't feel broken, but pressed back onto his opponent.

They changed places, one on the uphill, the other on the downhill, each with different advantages. Both breathing heavily, both faces slick with sweat.

The clouds drifting by covered the sun, removing the glare from Tristan's eyes as Sir Marhaus came in close and fast, slipping in the mud and ramming into Tristan, bringing him to the ground with a dagger in his hand.

It pierced Tristan's armpit on his left side, making him yell. With a surge of anger, Tristan bashed his shield into

Sir Marhaus's head, knocking him to the side.

Tristan pushed to his feet, tossing aside the split shield and gritting his teeth against the pain in his side and arm. He brought his sword down with two hands on Sir Marhaus, who struggled to get his arm from his shield stuck deep in the mud beneath him.

He saw Tristan coming and rolled, removing his head from the striking line. Tristan's sword cleaved into his arm, and Sir Marhaus screamed as the bone in his shield arm shattered.

Sweat stung Tristan's eyes. He blinked and Sir Marhaus swung towards his leg. He stumbled backwards down the hill, his own sword a moment too slow to stop the attack. His opponent's sword struck the side of his calf, punching through the armor and slicing his leg.

Tristan went down howling, but instinct brought his sword up to block the follow-up blow that came for his head. Metal clashed. Tristan blocked another two-handed attempt on his life, then thrust his sword upward.

It screeched as it skidded up Sir Marhaus's arm, point landing in his armpit and skewering his sword-arm shoulder. Sir Marhaus bellowed, pulling away, blood drops landing on Tristan as his sword came loose. He limped up the hill, barely able to use his leg, getting above Sir Marhaus.

Tristan chopped his sword downward to the space between Sir Marhaus's helm and breastplate. The man saw it coming and stepped out of the way, slipping on the wet grass and falling to one knee, head down. Tristan's sword sparked as it cut through the enormous crest on the helm and lodged itself there. Sir Marhaus collapsed.

Tristan went down with him, pulled by his lodged blade, tumbling a short way down the hill. The sword came free from Sir Marhaus's helm. Tristan landed on his back, winded. He scrambled up. Sir Marhaus didn't move. Tristan held his sword out, inching toward the fallen knight, breathing heavy, waiting.

Sir Marhaus lay still.

Tristan glanced at his sword, looking for blood. What he saw stopped his heart cold. The tip of his sword was jagged, several inches of its length and point missing. He looked around the ground for it.

A pool of blood formed around Sir Marhaus's helm, and in the top of it, stuck in a crevice between the crest and pan of his helm, rested the remainder of Tristan's sword.

Several of Sir Marhaus's men rushed forward, and Tristan stood, breath heaving, broken sword dangling downward. The soldiers knelt at their man's side, rolling him over. His eyes were wide and sightless, blood leaking from his helm and staining the ground.

Tristan pulled off his helmet. His leg trembled. How much blood had he lost?

Manuell rushed forward, shouting celebratory things in Spanish and leaping about like a mad rabbit. He calmed down enough to hand Tristan a rag to wipe the sweat from his face.

Tristan took a knee, gesturing to Manuell. "Get...it off," he rasped. The underside of Tristan's left arm throbbed.

Manuell rushed to unfasten the armor, starting with the breastplate, then working on the arms and legs.

The chainmail came off, a huge weight lifting with it, and Tristan took a deep breath in, testing his lungs. He breathed well, but a red stain spread down his left side, the cloth of his underpadding glistening as it collected his blood. His leg also bled, and judging by the depth, it needed special care.

He looked toward the chapel, then gestured to Manuell. "I need to get up there."

Manuell shouted to his fellow crewmen, and four of them rushed to Tristan's side, pulling him horizontally into their arms. They took off at a jog.

Tristan glimpsed the men surrounding Sir Marhaus through darkening vision. They seemed to be discussing how to move him. He closed his eyes.

The bouncing of the uphill journey made every wound burst anew with agony. He tried to open his mouth to tell the men to slow down, but either nothing came out, or no one responded.

Manuell spoke to one of the monks at the chapel door. Tristan couldn't make it out.

The monk addressed Tristan, and he replied with a low moan.

The door widened, and the men carried Tristan through, his eyes catching a blurred glimpse of whitewashed stone walls and a dark wooden cross over his head.

CHAPTER SIX

I will put by my violent days, and the ill deeds that I have wrought,
All wayward sins of a wild heart, all empty joys I sought,
I will forswear the fruitless year and the deedless day,
And the long gold tresses and false caresses of Morgan le Fay.
"Morgan le Fay" by Cicely Fox Smith

Morgan didn't get another chance to speak with one of the priestesses until the midday meal. Stomach rumbling, pinching painfully after not touching her breakfast, she ate seconds, even thirds of the savory vegetable soup being served. She ate as fast as the scalding liquid would allow, her body melting into the warmth and flavor of the soup.

Satisfied, she spotted Glitonea sitting among a group of sisters. Morgan cleared her dishes, then walked over to the red-haired priestess. She stood beside her for a moment, then placed her hand on Glitonea's arm.

Glitonea glanced behind. She excused herself and took Morgan's arm, leading her from the main hall where everyone ate.

"What do you need, Morgan?"

"I wish to go back. I will return through time and correct my wrongs." Morgan spoke in a rush, her entire body trembling.

Glitonea's face went rigid for a moment before she recovered from her shock. "I will pass your message on to Argante. We will prepare for tonight. There is nothing you need to concern yourself with." Glitonea turned to leave.

"How far are you sending me?" Morgan blurted.

Glitonea moved her head back toward Morgan. "You know it's impossible to predict exactly how far back you will go. It's imprecise and unstable dark magic to alter the time stream. If we didn't think we had a chance of preventing the fall of Camelot, we wouldn't dare try it."

"What if there's nothing I can do, and Camelot falls anyway? What if my mind breaks again?" Morgan's voice choked on her last words.

Glitonea sighed and faced her. She put her hand to her heart. "I promise you will be safe, Morgan. I have seen your heart, remember? It was already healing when I touched it. Even exposed as it is with the unfinished Rite, it is more whole than it has been since you left Avalon all those years ago. Now, if we can keep your mind and body together, then we will have a true success."

"What?" Morgan asked. "That can happen? The mind and body can separate?"

"We will have all twelve conducting the spell, all focused on making sure it goes as planned. You will be safe. Remember, you have done something like it before."

"Niviane de-aged me, she didn't send me back in time."

"It is a similar magic." She put her hand on Morgan's shoulder and gave it a squeeze, a reassuring smile on her face. "I will see you tonight. Come to the Grove of the Maiden at the tenth hour. Thiton will be waiting to prepare you."

Morgan nodded and made her way into the corridor. She thought she heard Glitonea call to her and turned back, but she saw no one. Perhaps she only wished the priestess had more words for her. Morgan's throat closed up. Despite all the risks, she had to try, didn't she? For Arthur's sake. For Camelot. Everything would be better if she wasn't there to mess it up.

She could go to Northumberland. Maybe Ireland; she had read of the beauty of that land. What trouble could she get into on the small, isolated land of rolling hills? She could take up weaving. She didn't have the patience for it, but when trying to avoid fate, doing something boring was likely a safe bet.

A doubt niggled in the back of her mind like an itch she couldn't scratch. She ruminated on it as she walked across Avalon to the Hall of Records, but nothing specific came up. She spent the day studying bits of everything.

Avalon was a wonder for its records alone. How the priestesses obtained them, Morgan didn't quite know. Books would appear on the shelves for a time, then disappear again, as if taken back to their true place in the universe.

The Keepers in the Hall of Records tried to document new titles, so the information could be used by the priestesses. One of the Goddess's gifts to them, a secret resource hidden from outsiders even in the face of death.

Morgan found a few basic spellbooks and memorized some enchantments; perhaps she would find a use for them. She thumbed through a thin volume of poetry, tossing it aside after the first few pages, then went browsing for a more specific genre: folktales.

She found a volume with an intriguing emerald cover and settled into a plush armchair with it, sitting sideways, her legs dangling over the arm. The heavy volume laid open on her lap, drawings of various Irish Fae practically coming to life in full color on the page.

Her fingertips brushed the page; men and women, their half-beast forms contorting beautifully. On the opposite page, the royal Fae, elegantly dressed in silk as fine as spiderweb, their ethereal faces gazing back at her. She turned the page again, pushing her back deeper into the cushion behind her.

It had been too long since she'd read for pleasure. Her eyes soaked in the words on the page, letting them sink deep into her soul.

Outside, the world darkened. She reluctantly replaced the tome on its proper shelf, stretched the kinks from her back, and made her way back to the main hall to eat supper. She enjoyed a lovely savory pie and a bowl of fruit with cream.

Morgan tried not to think about what would happen with the spell, or what she would do upon her return.

She shoved aside the swirl of confusion, guilt, and, oddly enough, excitement, and took a walk in the cool autumn, letting the peace of Avalon pervade her. She found a labyrinth pathway, the kind without walls, simply a path in the ground, meant to lead you to your center as you walked.

Morgan took it, winding around. As she did, her mind cleared, and she felt a deep peace settle inside of her, an anchor she could cling to amidst the exposed emotions.

Breathing deeply, she moved out of the labyrinth and made her way to the Grove of the Maiden.

Thiton waited for her outside a short hut, golden light illuminating it from within. She inclined her head, smiling at Morgan and opening the door to her.

The door closed behind her with a click of finality.

"This is the path you have chosen, Morgan le Fay?"

Morgan swallowed. Some of the peace inside her seemed to shift, and she felt her nerves begin to tighten the muscles in her neck and shoulders as she gazed around the tiny hut. It held a small bed, a cabinet, a table, and a single chair. Did someone live here?

"Morgan? I need you to answer. You have chosen this path?"

"Yes."

"And you have chosen it of your own will, without being persuaded, bribed, or otherwise coerced?"

"I have chosen it of my own will," Morgan replied.

"Let it be according to the will of the Goddess," Thiton said, touching her first two fingers of her right hand to her forehead between her eyes. She stepped forward, indicating Morgan needed to undress.

Morgan obliged, grabbing the hem of her long robe and bringing it upward to pull it over her head.

Thiton's strong hands helped her, and the woman spoke, her voice muffled through the layers of fabric.

"We want as little interference with the spell as possible," Thiton explained, helping Morgan change from her robes down to her knee-length linen shift. "No jewelry of any kind?"

Morgan shook her head.

Thiton rubbed her down, double checking, even running her fingers through her hair. "When did you last eat?"

"At suppertime, with everyone else," Morgan replied.

"You may feel a bit sick as the spell is activated." Thiton turned to a tall cabinet and opened the cupboard doors, eyeing the bottles lined on the shelves. "Where were you before now?"

"The Hall of Records."

"Reading?" Thiton asked sharply. "What have you read?"

Morgan shrugged. "A few spells. Some books of tales. Nothing serious."

Thiton jerked the cupboards shut, slamming bottles of infused oil down on the table at their side.

Morgan jumped. "Reading is one of the worst things you can do before a spell like this. The words seep into your mind and heart and can affect the outcome of the spell. Even something as simple as reading about a location can alter where you turn up."

"We could do the spell tomorrow..." Morgan replied, trailing off at the sigh that Thiton released.

"The time is ripe for the spell. The heavens are aligned. Waiting a day could do worse damage than your reading might."

She looked at the array of bottles and selected one, then grasped Morgan's wrist and turned it upright, dripping some oil on it. Thiton set the bottle down and rubbed up the inside of Morgan's forearm, briskly massaging the oil into her skin.

It smelled of roses, a rare and expensive oil. Morgan couldn't get enough of the scent. It filled her nostrils and entered her head. She breathed in again and again, taking in as much as she could.

Thiton poured more onto her other wrist, rubbing until the air became thick with the heady scent of roses. She dripped some onto Morgan's head, then turned Morgan around and ran her hand up her shift, wiping the oil from the crown of her head to the base of her spine.

Thiton turned Morgan around to face her again, holding her hands. She sighed, shoulders relaxing, and smiled at Morgan. "It is all in the Goddess's hands now."

She kissed Morgan's forehead, then took her arm, leading her to the door of the hut.

"You are ready. Do not speak as we enter the grove. Keep your mind and heart free, clear of any distracting thoughts or feelings. You must feel at peace, not nervous or afraid, so practice your meditative breathing."

Morgan followed Thiton as she opened the door. Golden light spilled out onto the stone pathway outside, then darkened as the door shut behind her.

The two women moved in silence on the walk to the grove. Morgan shivered, bumps rising on her skin as the autumn cold kissed her bare skin.

The Grove of the Maiden stood as a clearing surrounded by a ring of twelve tall trees. Twelve white-robed and hooded figures stood, one in front of each ancient tree, each holding an offering for the spell in her left hand.

Some held precious stones, imbued with magical energy. Others held bottles of oil, or little pots of herbs. One held a fistful of smooth, tiny bones. Yet another held a long, thin reed, likely picked that morning.

Morgan shivered. Each item had been chosen by the priestess that carried it, an object she would use to channel her own powers.

Morgan glimpsed Argante, her short frame standing out amongst the others. She did not look at Morgan but stared at the ruby in her hand. It glowed dimly, the light brightening as Morgan watched.

Thiton led Morgan to a stone table at the center of the grove. She helped Morgan onto it, laying her down on the hard surface until her face gazed up at the night sky dotted with stars.

Morgan swallowed, breathing deeply, trying to find her center, like she had in the labyrinth.

A warm glow filled the grove, lighting the tree trunks that reached for the sky. A low murmur of female voices began a chorus of chanting, words in a strange tongue that sounded simultaneously foreign and familiar to Morgan.

The hard stone pressed against her back, and the scent of rose wafted into her nose. Above her, the sky spun in time with the priestesses' chants, pulling her towards the stars. She found nothing to hold on to, nothing she could do but spin and let the stars take her.

CHAPTER SEVEN

Love that is fire within thee and light above,
And lives by grace of nothing but of love;
Through many and lovely thoughts and much desire
Led these twain to the life of tears and fire;
Through many and lovely days and much delight
Led these twain to the lifeless life of night.
"Prelude: Tristram and Iseult," from "Tristram of Lyonesse"
by Algernon Charles Swinburne

Queen Eithne gripped the edges of her wooden throne tightly, forcing her knuckles to go white.

"My brother is...dead?" she choked out.

Her frame trembled, making the beads threaded through her matted, rust-colored locks click together in the silent room. Her gaze rested on the litter on the ground, which held the empty, damaged body of her only brother.

His eyes, glazed over with death, stared blankly upward through the open visor on his helm, his body already beginning to swell and stink with age. The queen jerked her head up, then thrust herself to her feet.

"Tell me who did this!" she barked out, her voice hoarse, straining to hide her emotion. She adjusted the fur on her shoulders, but she hardly felt the chill in the room through the chill in her heart. “Tell me!”

She slammed her staff on the floor, the crack of wood on stone the only sound in the room.

One man stepped forward, hair and clothes damp from the rain. He reeked of fish and filth.

The queen sniffed. “Who are you?” the queen asked. “Conan, my Queen.”

“And the man who killed my brother?”

“I heard his name, it was Sir Tristan, sure, Majesty.”

“Does he yet live?”

“Aye.” Conan nodded his head firmly up and down. “King Mark is his father’s brother, to be sure, and he lived when we left the isle, though he was hurtin’ something terrible.”

She glanced again at the body of Marhaus. “Why hasn’t his helm been removed? I wish to look on my brother’s face.” She didn’t, really. Even she had a stomach.

“Sir Tristan delivered his killing blow there, and he left a piece of his sword...Well, see for yourself, My Queen. We feared we might spill his brains if we tugged on it at all.”

Queen Eithne hid her grimace as she stepped down from her chair, walking stiffly past Conan and kneeling beside her brother. She would show her strength to them, and she would see her brother one last time.

No one in the room dared question her. They watched with bated breath to see what the mad queen would do. Queen Eithne touched the helm where the broken sword tip was embedded, and pulled. It took several tugs before the helm ripped free from her brother’s bloated face. She swallowed the bile that rose in her throat and gestured for her handmaiden to take the bloodied helm, sword shard stabbed through the crown of it.

"Clean it," she growled, wiping her hands on a cloth the maiden handed her. "Put it in my collection."

She approached Conan, who had a look on his face that crossed somewhere between disgust and admiration. "You have a new position, Sir Conan."

The man straightened at the addition of the title before his name, eyes gleaming.

"You will choose a surveillance team. Scout the borders along the coast that faces Cornwall. Ask if any have seen this Sir Tristan. You know his face, you can identify him should he choose to wander into our land."

"Aye, Your Majesty. How long would you have me do this?"

"As long as it takes," Queen Eithne hissed. She stepped back to her chair and sat down, twirling a matted strand between her fingers.

"And what would you have me do, my queen, if we discover him?"

"Bring him to me," she said, gazing past the man, into a distant view only she could see.

She would find the man who did this, this Sir Tristan. And if he never deigned to show his face in her land, she would go to his and hunt him until the end of his days.

Fire burned its way through Tristan's blood. His body shivered. He rolled his head from side to side, moaning through the pain. Above him, monks talked in hushed tones, applying poultices, offering tinctures, and most of all, praying for his soul.

Tristan was dying.

The fire in his side and leg spread tendril-like through his veins.

When it reached his heart, he would die.

His head spun. Above him, the ceiling opened up into stars and the roof peeled back to reveal thousands of glittering lights dotting the blackness above. Tristan gazed upward. The heavens were opening to welcome him home.

A woman in a simple white dress appeared in the stars, flying over him with her black hair flowing behind her. Her green eyes shone brilliantly against her fair skin. She smiled down at Tristan, who stared in wonder back at her.

"You are dying," she said. Her voice seemed to echo. Tristan tried to answer, but only a moan escaped from his lips. "I can see the poison in your blood. You must receive the antidote."

Poison? Sir Marhaus's blade. Tristan moaned again, body contorting, twisting in the sheets. The stars swirled above, and the woman swirled with them.

"Go to the source of your wound!" the woman called out. "Wherever the weapon comes from, there you will find healing!"

The stars, and the woman, disappeared in a blink. Tristan bolted awake, startling Manuell, who muttered prayers at his bedside. Manuell's hands went to his chest.

"Sir Knight, you startled me! I have been afraid you would die. Are you well, now?"

Tristan shook his head, then motioned for the water, gasping through his dry throat.

Manuell provided the cup, holding it for Tristan.

Water spilled down his throat and out the sides of his mouth, soaking his undershirt and the bedding, but still he gulped. It seemed to quench the fire somewhat, but he could feel it simmering in his blood.

"I had a dream," he rasped, pulling the bedsheets aside.

Manuell tried to put them back over him, insisting that he should stay in bed, but Tristan pushed his helpful hands away and tried to stand. He collapsed back onto the bed, agonizing pain shooting through his leg.

"The sword was poisoned. I must go to the source of my wound, where the weapon is from. I must go to Ireland to be healed."

Manuell stared at him. "Are you mad? Go to the land of your enemies? They will destroy you for killing their champion."

Tristan grimaced. Manuell could be right. He might not be received well for killing the queen's brother. His mind slogged, but he forced it to work, to figure it out.

"We must have a different story." He looked straight at Manuell. "King Angeus rules over Mumhan." He reached up a hand, grabbing the front of Manuell's shirt. "You must take me there, please. I will make sure the captain is paid."

"I-I will see what we can do." The man hesitated, then pressed firmly on Tristan's chest. "You must rest while I consult with the captain."

"We must go now," Tristan croaked, laying his head down on the pillow, his eyes closing, his body already exhausted. "Do not...wait."

Strong ropes pulled on Tristan's wounds as he woke. He cried out and started thrashing.

Manuell's concerned face appeared above him. "All is well, compadre. It is your friends. We are going to

Ireland."

Tristan stopped moving. Each drop of rain that fell on him felt like a knife slicing through his skin.

The men tied him to the deck of the ship like their merchant goods, crisscrossing ropes over his body. One man walked around, testing the tightness of each tether. Tristan felt bulges strapped down on either side of him; gear and supplies, no doubt.

Manuell patted Tristan's shoulder. "I have been assigned to keep you safe, but I may not always be here if I am needed to row or tend the ship. It is less than a day to reach the shore of Ireland. Did your dream say where you must go?"

"The source," Tristan muttered.

Manuell grimaced. "Depending on where we strike shore, it may be several more days on foot, unless we can get some horses."

Moments later, the ship cast off. It jerked as the waves caught it. The gale howled, wind lashing sideways through the air, and the waves towered above them.

Tristan's heart sank in his chest. He might not survive the trip. All of them could die. What had he done?

He blacked out after the first wave sent the ship plummeting towards the sea. Hours later, he awoke to Manuell shaking his shoulder frantically.

"Tristan! Tristan, we made it." His face lit up with excitement. Tristan blinked his eyes open against the sun shining in his face. Manuell was untying him. "I hope you are still alive, my friend, because we made it!"

Manuell poured water into Tristan's mouth, practically choking him. He removed the damp blanket, its usefulness gone. Tristan's clothes were less easily replaced. He had to bear the muddy, rumpled clothing.

The men carried him from the ship and transferred him to a brilliant carrying device. Apparently, the whole thing had been thought up by Manuell.

He had strung a blanket between two heavy sticks, tying it off until the knots held firm when weight was added. Five men would go with Tristan and one would stay with the boat, Manuell explained. It was far beyond what King Mark paid them to do, but the captain insisted on seeing Tristan safe before they left for their regular routes.

The crew laid Tristan in the center of the litter, then four of them grasped each end of the two sticks and hoisted Tristan into the air. Hanging mid-air made Tristan's mind swim. They started walking, making the whole contraption sway.

"How far to King Angeus?" Tristan asked, wiggling his arms to find a comfortable position. Manuell squinted in the sunlight, looking south.

"Oh, perhaps two days on foot, I am told. We asked a local, mostly played a game of gesture and guess, if you know what I mean. Did you know they only speak Ga-leg here?"

"Gaelic, you mean? Aye. I speak it with some decency," Tristan said, resting his head back and closing his eyes against the sun. His entire body hurt, and his head burned with fever. His lucidity was a good sign, but he wasn't sure how long it would last.

Manuell snorted, glancing down at Tristan, his voice straining with the effort of carrying the wounded man. "How many languages do you know, Sir Knight?"

"I speak five well and understand several others. I could probably figure out most any language. Take your Spanish, for example; it's awfully close to French, and I recognize about half of the words you and the others use." He shaded his eyes and watched Manuell's grow wide with amazement.

"Where did you learn all of that?" Manuell asked.

Tristan told him about being sent to France after his step-mother tried to kill him multiple times. Since he insisted on her being allowed to live, and since his father didn't truly want to sentence her, Tristan agreed to go to France. He finally experienced true freedom; freedom to learn anything he wanted, to be anyone he wanted without his father breathing down his neck, blaming him for his mother's death at his birth.

After several hours, the captain rotated in, taking a turn carrying a corner of Tristan's litter, and continued Manuell's questions. It took some time before Tristan realized they kept him awake on purpose; they couldn't be certain he would wake up should he fall back to sleep. "We need to find people," Tristan said, his voice rasping. "Do we have things we could trade for a horse, perhaps a wagon? It makes no

sense to continue walking."

"Those things may be quite expensive here," the captain said, his wispy white hair waving in the breeze on the air. "A horse and wagon are a person's livelihood, ofttimes. They will not be trading for a broken sword."

He turned and spoke in Spanish to one of the men not helping with Tristan, who nodded, then set off at a jog back toward the boat.

The captain glanced down at Tristan. "Do you have a plan, boy? I don't aim to walk my men into more danger than is necessary."

"I have been thinking; when I've been conscious, that is." He grinned.

The captain shook his head, not appreciating the joke.

"They never knew the name of my uncle's challenger, but their men will make it back before we do and tell them who killed their man. We can give them a false name, one they won't connect back to me, and tell them I was in a duel and poisoned, and that a wise woman told me to come here."

"It is a weak story, too close to the truth, but it will have to do," the captain said.

"The truth is easier to tell convincingly. You don't have to lie as much," Tristan replied. The captain fell silent, and Tristan drifted off to sleep.

When he woke again, he felt groggy and irritable. His wounds were on fire. The cramped space in the litter, the sun beating down on them, and the constant swaying on an empty stomach wore at his normally congenial attitude.

Fortunately, they had stopped in a large village. People milled about, staring at the newcomers in their midst.

"Ah! He is awake. Come, speak with our translator." Manuell ushered a craggy old gentleman over. He had a permanent squint and a curve to his back that made him even shorter than Manuell. Tristan smiled up at the man from his litter.

"Nach tu," he said, trying out the foreign words on his tongue. Long years had passed since he last practiced them. Is it not yourself? Such a strange way to greet another.

"Ta," the man said, face lighting up. He repeated the greeting, and Tristan answered, then he gibbered rapidly, and Tristan tried to keep up, despite his pounding head.

"I think he said the weather has been grand, and is complaining of an ache in his back." Tristan explained to the captain, who stood at his side watching the exchange.

"Well, tell him of your own aches, and ask about a horse and wagon," the captain snapped. He seemed much in the same state as Tristan. "And inquire about food. We are famished."

Tristan relayed the message. The man's eyes grew wide as Tristan explained his injuries and the crew's hunger.

"Do we have gold or something to trade?" "Gold," the captain replied.

"Then this man's son has a wagon, and his cousin has a horse. He says one of them will take us where we need to go if we pay in advance."

"Half now, half when we get there," the captain bartered.

The old Irishman squinted at the captain, then at Tristan as he explained, then nodded, smiling.

"He says his wife and daughters will feed us to the pigs. No, that's not right. Feed us one of their pigs, I think."

"I should hope so," the captain said, eyes gleaming. Tristan laughed. It simultaneously hurt and felt like medicine to laugh.

The men lifted the litter and followed the Irishman through winding village pathways until they reached his home, a beautiful stone house set amongst crags on a hill. Short stone fences kept herds of sheep in their fields. Tristan thought his eyes would burst looking at all the green.

In an instant, children swarmed them, all belonging Ardan, the old Irishman. They were grandchildren, he explained. He had seventeen, borne from his eight daughters and three sons.

They propped Tristan up on a pile of blankets and pillows in the main room outside the kitchen. Everyone walked past him and constantly asked after his well-being. Ardan's wife, a plump and sprightly woman, brought him a mug of herbal tea, sweetened generously with honey. He had strength to drink on his own, but barely. The mug shook in his hand.

The pandemonium caused by the children's antics made him smile. Despite it all, pain and brain fog overtook him, and he found himself drifting to sleep.

That night was a blur. He woke at some point, crying out for water with a dry, burning throat, his body throbbing.

Manuell presented him with water and broth, giving Tristan much-needed sustenance. His body shook uncontrollably, and none of the blankets Manuell piled on him made him warmer. A cold cloth went on his head. He tossed it off, thrashing about with the pain and discomfort. Somehow, he fell asleep.

He woke briefly to movement. He was being carried. Tristan felt himself laid down. His eyes flickered open and glimpsed the sky. Moments later, the crew piled into the wagon beside him, several holding packages Tristan recognized as his belongings.

Through his fever, his hands ached to hold his harp and play, but he couldn't even stay awake for more than a few moments at a time. The wagon bumped and jolted beneath him, seeming to hit every rock and divot the road offered. He closed his eyes and drifted.

Sometimes he dreamed; strange dreams with no sense or meaning. Once, he saw the woman in the stars again.

He reached for her, longing to escape his abused body, but she disappeared, and he remained, spiraling into the darkness.

It rained later that day. Manuell held a blanket over Tristan's head, keeping the rain off his face.

When they stopped again, rain continued to fall. Tristan felt the drops on his face as they lifted him down from the wagon. He screamed when they accidentally pulled his arm, the wound in his side stretching, ripping open wider.

Manuell looked down at Tristan, concern deep on his face as he walked beside the litter.

"Tristan, are you awake? We have reached the castle of King Angeus. We do not speak the language, and we need you awake." He reached into his pocket and pulled out a small metal flask. "This might help."

He pressed the cold metal against Tristan's lip. Alcohol trickled in, its taste crisp and acrid. Tristan swallowed, feeling the burn as it hit the back of his throat, but he didn't choke.

Almost immediately, he felt more aware. He opened his eyes, blinking up at the clouded grey sky.

"Why have we stopped?" he croaked. He cleared his throat. "The guards. I think they want to know why we are here." "Gesture to one of them to come over; I can't speak loud enough

from here."

A guard in chainmail came over, his face visible beneath a helmet that only covered the top of his head. He peered at Tristan, face impassive.

Tristan took a deep breath, and the story spilled out. He spun a tale of his own making, giving himself the name Tramtrist, a knight from France who had won a duel, but was losing his life.

Though poor at lying, Tristan seemed to convince the guard of his plight. He waved the entire group forward, accompanying them to the seat of royalty within the castle. There, the guard obliged Tristan by relaying his story for the king. From the litter, Tristan could see very little, being unable to sit up.

"Call for Isolde," the king said, his deep voice thrumming through the hall.

Isolde? His daughter? Why call her? *I don't want to get married, I need a healer!*

Moments passed. Doors opened and closed several times.

A soft, feminine voice spoke to the men holding Tristan, speaking his language with a lilting Irish accent.

"Can you put him down?"

The litter lowered, and an angel's face appeared over him, an angel with gently curling blonde hair and green eyes. She smiled at Tristan. "I d'be checking your wounds, Sir Tramtrist."

Her hands were cool and gentle as she observed his fever, feeling his neck.

"Do you have any dizziness? Numbness? Tingling? Shortness of breath?"

Tristan tried to take in a deep breath and ended up coughing. He gasped for a moment, wheezing, then smiled wanly. "Yes, to all of it. And a rotten headache."

Manuell pointed out the wounds in Tristan's side and leg. She removed the old bandages, then sat back and turned to the king. Her father.

"I can help him, if it is agreeable with you to do so?"

“It pleases me to aid these foreigners,” King Angeus’s rich voice spoke again. “You may put Sir Tramtrist in the infirmary. His men are welcome in the soldiers’ quarters.”

“Thank you, athair.”

She asked the men to hoist Tristan up again. Tristan craned his neck to look up at her as they walked. Her smooth hand picked his up from the litter and held it.

“My name is Isolde,” she said in lilting English.

I know. Tristan wanted to say, but his mouth wouldn’t work, and a moment later he passed out again.

CHAPTER EIGHT

Chance cast him westward on the low sweet strand
Where songs are sung of the old green Irish land,
And the sky loves it, and the sea loves best,
And as a bird is taken to man's breast
The sweet-souled land where sorrow sweetest sings
Is wrapt round with them as with hands and wings
And taken to the sea's heart as a flower.
"The Sailing of the Swallow," from "Tristram of Lyonesse"
by Algernon Charles Swinburne

Swirling stars and ghostly faces filled Morgan's memory. Her trip through time was nothing but a blur now. Morgan opened her eyes and glanced around. This wasn't the room she remembered from her father's keep in Carmelide.

She pushed the heavy fur covers off her body and stood, gasping as her toes hit the cold stone floor. As she stood, movement—the reflection in a large mirror beside a table at the foot of the bed—caught her attention. Her heart pounded in her chest as she approached the mirror. Had she seen what she thought she saw? She stepped directly in front of the mirror's rippling glassy surface, and her eyes went wide.

Morgan brought trembling hands up to touch smooth, pale cheeks. Fingers touched the soft, blonde hair that curled past narrow shoulders. She stared in the mirror with disbelief. She took in the longer, daintier nose, the delicate, swan-like neck, the green eyes, and that pale, golden hair, hair she had dreamed about as Guinevere, always hating her long, straight, dark hair. She couldn't find a single burn mark marring the flawless skin.

This wasn't her body.

Morgan felt for the chair beside the table and fell into it, unable to take her eyes from the image in the mirror; her own reflection, yet not her own. Who was she, and where was she, and how had the spell gone so wrong?

Argante would know. There had to be a way for Morgan to communicate with her. She eyed the metal bowl filled with water for washing up that sat within arm's reach. She pulled it towards her, careful to not spill, then watched until the surface of the water stilled. A crystal or laurel wand made hydromancy, the art of scrying in water, much easier, but Morgan had neither. And the bowl had carving around the lip, which would interfere with the connection.

Morgan gazed at the water sideways, looking at the smooth surface from the corner of her eye. She focused her intention, calling upon Argante to answer her scrying. The water rippled.

Argante was practiced in sensing when someone contacted her; she would choose whether or not to answer Morgan's scry.

Morgan breathed in deeply, keeping her panic and fear at bay. The slightest emotional disturbance would break the connection. She couldn't afford that; she needed answers. She breathed out through her nose, slow and focused.

An image appeared in the water's surface, growing in clarity and sharpness as Morgan watched. She waited until Argante's face came into full view, then turned her gaze straight on the scrying, no longer looking from the corner of her eye.

Argante wouldn't be able to hear her until Morgan sent the first message. She breathed, keeping her emotions as calm as the water's surface.

"Argante, priestess, it is I, Morgan le Fay. I have need of your wisdom." The high-pitched voice that came from her lips was not her own, either.

"You do not look like the Morgan le Fay I know," Argante replied in her familiar, cool voice. Her face stayed impassive. Morgan could not see beyond the priestess's small, narrow face. Scrying only allowed one to see whomever they scried, not the room or people beyond. Morgan swallowed.

"Something has gone wrong. The time spell you performed...it did not send me back to my own body." Her voice quivered.

Argante's gaze became sharp. "I performed no such spell. Of what do you speak?"

Morgan's heart froze. She licked her lips. How could she not remember? The surface of the water quivered as Morgan's emotional state became more unstable. She breathed in, then out, and then the answer struck her. She had been sent back in time. If the spell had worked correctly, which it hadn't, she should be back in Cairhaise, living Guinevere's life, about a year and a half back in time.

Argante's form faded as she pulled away from the connection.

"Wait, Argante, please!" Morgan said. Argante's face became clear again. "I cannot explain it all. A time spell was performed by yourself and eleven sisters to send me back so I might fix...certain mistakes. But it has gone wrong, and I'm not where I am supposed to be, or who I am supposed to be."

"Did you read, sing, or play any music in the day before the time spell was cast?" Argante asked, raising an eyebrow.

The books. Ireland. Did that mean...Morgan resisted the urge to run to the window and look outside. She swallowed past the lump in her throat and grasped her fingers to keep them from fidgeting.

"Yes."

"Then you are in a location near wherever the book or song originated from. As for your physical form, this is why time spells are rarely attempted, and only when the need is dire; when you jump time, you create a rip. Mother Nature in all her wisdom mends that rip by whatever means necessary. Her way of doing that likely resulted in a body-switch or a mind-share. Do you hear any other voices in your mind?"

Morgan barely contained her panic as she listened. She heard no voices. What if she had trapped the true owner of this body? Or worse, erased her?

"I do not hear anything."

"A body-swap, then. It is a known side-effect of that particular type of magic."

"What should I do? Whomever I switched with will be in great danger, she must be prepared for it, or the spell will have been for naught," Morgan cried. Her emotion made the water ripple; she almost lost the connection.

"You must do what you were told to do when the spell was performed. If you must warn her, use hydromancy as you are now. She may not know how to answer. If that is the case, perhaps you might use a more conventional method, such as a letter or messenger."

Morgan nodded. Emotion clenched in her chest, stuck beneath the surface. She didn't cry, though she wished her body would allow her.

Argante's face vanished in an instant.

Morgan's hand reached out and splashed in the bowl of water. She could try scrying Argante again, but to what purpose? She had her answers, at least some of them. The Argante of this time did not know her location, or the identity she held. Morgan would have to discover these answers for herself.

A knock at the door caused her to jump, the bowl of water splashing as she jostled it. She breathed in, calming herself. She had to let them in or they would think something was wrong and barge in anyway.

Morgan cleared her throat. "Enter."

The word flowed off her tongue in Gaelic, a language Morgan herself did not know or understand beyond the few spells she had memorized in the tongue. Before she could analyze the discovery further, the door opened.

A woman curtseyed. She was not the least bit distinctive in dress or appearance. A dirty, white kerchief kept her hair wrapped up on her head and she wore a brown dress overlaid with a filthy apron. She gazed wide-eyed at Morgan, making Morgan feel self-conscious. She had to find out who she was supposed to be, but she had to be subtle about it; servants talked.

The servant pulled herself together. "Princess Isolde, you are not well again?"

Isolde. My name is Isolde. And I'm a princess...princess of where? She kicked herself for not being a better study of nobility.

"I am well," Morgan said, then bit her tongue. "Well, actually, no, I am not feeling myself this morning."

The servant clucked her tongue. "That is a shame, it is. Shall I tell your patients not to expect you until later?"

Morgan turned away from the maid, hiding her face and mouthing to herself. Patients? Was this Isolde a healer? She had a little natural healing ability, and some knowledge from her time in Avalon. If Isolde kept decent records and journals, as well as a library of healing books, Morgan could get along all right.

"Milady?"

"You should," she blurted, turning back around. "Yes, tell them. Am I expected elsewhere this morning?"

"I suppose you'll be taking breakfast in here, now? Instead of in the main hall? Your mother will want to have a look at you." The maid stared at Morgan, as if expecting her to do or say something.

Morgan stared back for a moment, stretching the silence out.

"I will be expecting her, then, miss...?"

"Aideen, Banphrionsa." She looked at Morgan as if she had two heads. "Will you be wanting help with your dressing now? Or perhaps I should return later?"

"Later," Morgan agreed. The woman turned to leave. "Aideen?"

The woman hesitated before the door closed.

"What year is it? And the season?"

The maid's eyes grew even wider. "I will send for another healer right away. Rest yourself, now."

"No, Aideen, I simply forgot, I am not ill. I..."

Morgan sighed as the door clicked shut. She did not know a way to determine what time she now lived in. Perhaps her location would be easier to determine. She stood and walked to the window, peering out through the narrow slit between stones.

What little she could see was an ocean of green. The hills rose and fell, dotted with sheep like the foaming crests of waves. Ireland. She couldn't be certain which part. Hopefully, that would become clearer when she met Isolde's father.

Isolde!

Morgan turned and rushed back to the little table and chair. The bowl held plenty of water for scrying. She didn't have a moment to waste; Isolde would be more bewildered than she was, waking up in a strange body and a strange land. Morgan would call to her, and hopefully the woman would be aware enough to pick up on the vibration and answer Morgan's hydromancy.

She settled in the chair, trying to ignore her distorted reflection in the mirror. It disturbed her every time she glanced and saw herself as, well, not herself.

Her breath flowed in, then out, then in, and she turned her head, looking at the surface of the water from the corner of her eyes. The surface stilled. The reflection of the room vanished, and a muddy form appeared.

Her own face cleared, then blurred, then cleared again. She looked at her own dark hair, heart-shaped face, and straight nose. But someone not-her stared back through those eyes.

"Who are you?" the woman-not-her asked. "Or should I be asking, who am I?"

"I am sorry," Morgan started, "there is too much to explain. Can you tell me where you are?"

"I woke up i-in a castle," the woman stammered, glancing all around her. Morgan wished she could see the woman's surroundings. Which castle? Was it King Leodegrance's holding in Carmelide, or Camelot? "There was a feast, and hundreds of knights, and a king..."

Morgan blinked. "King Arthur?" "I-I think so."

"Was there a large man with red hair who called you daughter?"

The woman nodded. "He became very concerned that I was ill; I feel so bewildered. Can you tell me what is going on? Where am I?" The woman's voice was rising in pitch with her panic.

"You are Isolde."

The woman looked straight at her and straightened. "Yes, how did you know that? Who are you?"

"I am an initiate of the priestesses of Avalon. I am afraid it is my fault we are in this situation."

"Why are you in my body? Am I in yours?"

"You are." Morgan nodded. Sharp, this one. Morgan could appreciate that. At least it wasn't some fool-headed girl using her body. "Tell me, who has spoken to you?"

"I can't remember their names. A maidservant, Mary? Both kings. Is one of them your father? And a knight, with black hair. He seemed to know me. Who are you?" The last part was said in a demanding tone that befitted the Irish princess. "Not your name; I need to know why I am here, and what is going to happen to me."

"You are in England, near Camelot, in the role of Guinevere, daughter of King Leodegrance. You are in grave danger. You must leave, now. Do not speak to anyone. If someone named Niviane appears, you must escape. Do nothing she asks you to do. Stay away from King Arthur, from Lancelot. Do you understand? You must not go to Came—"

"There is someone here," Isolde said, looking away from Morgan, showing the back of her head.

"Isolde, you must listen to me. An old woman may appear to you tonight. Do not speak to her. Pretend to sleep, find your maidservant or father, keep away from Niviane."

"What will she do to me?" Isolde's voice was trembling.

"She is a dark sorceress. Do not speak to her, Isolde—"

The connection broke off. Morgan lashed out, striking the bowl with the back of her hand and sending it clattering to the floor. She put her head in her hand, leaning against the table. Her hand rubbed down her face, moving across her chin, as she stared at the now-empty silver bowl.

The spell had sent her back too far.

In her life as Guinevere, living in Carmelide, she was meeting Arthur for the first time. The priestesses sent Morgan back in time to prevent that meeting and the subsequent union; would having Isolde there in her place ruin everything the priestesses had intended?

The door opened with a bang, crashing into the far wall as it swung too wide too fast. A woman stood there, taller than Morgan, chest heaving, her red hair twisted into ropes that hung beside her narrow face. Her green eyes blazed with anger, her fists clenched. She moved into the room with the unspoken might of a force of nature; like a terrible storm had come into the room.

Morgan stared at her in shock from where she sat. The woman adjusted her fur cloak, advancing on Morgan, a snarl on her lips.

"What makes you think I believe your little charades? You have been laid out for more than a week, Isolde, with no symptoms other than 'fatigue' and 'headaches.' Enough pretending."

"I-I-"

"Do not speak!" The woman snapped. "I may be your mother, but I am also your queen, and you will not interrupt me!"

Morgan shut her lips tight as the woman advanced on her, using every bit of willpower she had to not shrink back away from the irate Irish queen.

"You cannot fool me," the queen continued, the beads in her hair clattering together as they swung next to her face. The queen's hand reached out and jerked Morgan from her seat by her wrist. "I can see that you are well. And while you sit here and whine, there is a man in the main hall bleeding to death, having been poisoned. You must help him, Isolde. Do not shirk your duties."

"I will not," Morgan managed, pulling her wrist from the woman's grip. She cast her eyes down, attempting to appear contrite. Might as well play the part, for now. "Should I go down in my nightgown?"

It slipped out before she could stop it, a quip she might have said to Mary. Not something she should have said to the queen, even if the queen was her—Isolde's—mother.

The queen's eyes grew so large, it seemed they might fall out of her head. She wheeled around, stormed to the wardrobe, yanked the doors open and pulled out a dress, tossing it onto the bed.

"Get yourself into that. It will be acceptable. No servant will help you dress today. I expect you downstairs in less time than it would take a soldier to work into his armor."

Morgan nodded, but the queen had already turned and stormed out the door, slamming it shut behind her. Morgan breathed out, her breath almost visible in the cold air of the room, then ran to the bed, stripping her nightgown off.

She didn't bother with a new shift; she had no time to search for where they were kept. Had Morgan done something to invoke the queen's ornery mood?

As she picked up the dress, she found it different than anything she had worn in England, soft, linen fabric made into a simple smock-like design that seemed baggy and unflattering.

The pale blue color was pretty, but the shape left something to be desired. It fell to her ankles, and as she looked in the mirror she noticed the circular neckline dipped low enough to reveal the silver phoenix, gleaming as if painted on her chest. She gasped, hands flying up to touch it. How could that mark be there?

Morgan rushed to the wardrobe and shuffled through the items hanging there, grasping the heavy wool fabric of a purple cloak and pulling it out. A broach attached to one shoulder, which she fastened with some difficulty, her fingers fumbling on the gemmed object, threading the sharp pin through the thick wool.

Before she turned from the wardrobe, she noticed a pile of belts at the bottom, beautifully wrought in metal, thread, and leather. She selected an intricately woven belt, then went to stand before the mirror, tying it around her waist. As she did so, the dress took on form, and suddenly made sense to her.

With the embroidery at the end of the long sleeves and on the bottom hem, it made for a rather pretty garment, though less ornate than the gowns she wore as queen in Camelot. The cloak covered her chest neatly; it seemed the right season for wearing it, given her frigid room.

She moved towards the door and caught sight of her hair. Knotted from sleep, the golden tresses poofed out from one side of her head and lay flat on the other, reaching down to her backside. Normally, a servant might help her with it, but the queen had denied her such help this morning.

Morgan reached for a comb and a leather tie and moved towards the door, pulling it through her hair until the mats on the back of her head smoothed over. Then she began twisting it into a single long braid, which she secured with the leather tie in her hand.

Tossing the braid over her shoulder, Morgan looked around and realized she did not know how to get to the main hall. The corridor branched a number of ways as she walked. How could she know where to go? Her pace quickened; she didn't want to anger the queen further.

Coming out of a doorway ahead, Morgan caught a glimpse of the servant from earlier.

"Aideen!" she called out, her own voice high-pitched and foreign to her ears. The servant tried to act as if she hadn't heard, but Morgan saw her straighten at the sound of her name. "Aideen, I require your aid," she said.

"I will give it, Princess Isolde," Aideen said, hesitating a moment before falling into a curtsey.

"The main hall...remind me which direction I go?" The servant's eyes widened again.

"The queen is waiting on me, Aideen. Please?"

She jerked at the mention of the queen, fear taking over her stunned gaze. She motioned for Morgan to follow and began walking down the hallway, taking on a brisk enough pace that Morgan, with her rather short legs, ran several steps to keep up.

Her heart pounded, and her breath came loud in her ears. She focused on the servant's uneven gait in front of her to calm her nerves. How had the woman gotten such a limp?

They walked down a long corridor, down a flight of winding stairs, and before Morgan could collect herself, she stood before a set of double doors, one of the attendants opening the door before her. Aideen had disappeared, leaving Morgan alone.

One glance from that fiery-haired queen and Morgan forced herself forward. The man sitting beside the queen, presumably the king, smiled at her, genuine affection and pride in his eyes.

She turned her gaze to the group of haggard-looking men in the center of the room, standing protectively around a man who lay in a makeshift litter they carried. Right. The reason for her summons. She took a deep breath and squared her shoulders, walking across the floor to the men. She gave them a welcoming smile.

"Can you put him down now?" she asked. They obliged, moving slowly so as not to jostle their companion. Morgan knelt on the floor.

The man looked familiar, and she thought she remembered him from Camelot. Was he a knight? She remembered so few of them by name.

She licked her lips and addressed one of the men. "What is his name?"

"Sir Tramtrist, my lady," the man said, the way he rolled his r's making his accent unfamiliar to her.

She wished she had paid better attention in Thiton's healing lessons, now. But she must have learned more than she thought, for as she glanced over the wounded man, she noticed his waxy, pale complexion, likely due to blood loss and pain, and his eyes followed her as she observed him.

Always a good sign, despite the pinch of pain she could see at the corners of his eyes. He seemed familiar, and Morgan wondered if she had met him before, but she couldn't dwell on it now. She needed to determine the extent of his wounds.

"I d'be checking your wounds, Sir Tramtrist." She put her palm on his brow. Heat radiated from his head. She tried to keep her face neutral, despite her concern. "Do you have any dizziness? Numbness? Tingling? Shortness of breath?"

The knight tried to take in a deep breath and ended up coughing. He gasped for a moment, wheezing, then smiled wanly. "Yes, to all of it. And a rotten headache."

The short man leaned down and pointed out the wounds in his leg and beneath his left arm. Morgan lifted the bandages there and sucked air in through her teeth; it was a deep, furious-looking wound, pus oozing from the puckered red skin where a sharp weapon—a sword? —had gone through. It must have been shorter than a sword, however, as his lung wasn't pierced.

The queen had said something about poison. She would need to find any journals Isolde might have kept, and pray they were organized so an outsider could find important information.

Morgan sat back on her heels and looked up at the king and queen. "I can help him, if it is agreeable with you to do so?"

"It pleases me to aid these foreigners," the king said. "You may put Sir Tramtrist in the infirmary. His men are welcome in the soldiers' quarters."

"Thank you, athair," Morgan replied, inclining her head.

She felt the wounded man's eyes on her, and her face flushed. Why did he stare at her? Her hand reached up and subtly checked the position of her cloak; it still covered the silver mark. Relieved, she instructed the men to lift Sir Tramtrist. On a whim, she reached her hand down over the side of the litter to grasp his.

"My name is Isolde," she told him, forcing the words out in English. It felt right that he should have a name to call her by. She glanced down at him with a smile, only to see that he had passed out.

She found Aideen lurking outside the doors of the main hall. Morgan snagged her again, requesting that she escort the men to the infirmary. The maid gave her a suspicious, narrow-eyed look.

I will have to speak with her alone again; she may be someone useful to have on my side. Morgan walked beside the litter, continuing to hold the wounded man's hand. Fever radiated from him and sweat beaded his brow. He didn't have long.

Morgan glanced at him, unable to shake the feeling that she knew him. She racked her brain, wondering if the after effects of the Rite of the Heart could have impacted her memory, when it suddenly came to her.

Sir Tristan. One of Arthur's inner circle of knights.

She remembered him. She could not doubt it now; his long brown hair, the way it curled down to his shoulders. She remembered him standing with the others, laughing. She knew him as lighthearted, respectful, skilled with a sword and rumored to be a talented musician, although she had never heard him play.

In the past timeline, she knew him as a Knight of the Round Table.

What would become of him now that she had taken Isolde's place?

CHAPTER NINE

Yet was not love between them, for their fate
Lay wrapt in its appointed hour at wait,
And had no flower to show yet, and no sting.
But once being vexed with some past wound the king
Bade give him comfort of sweet baths, and then
Should Iseult watch him as his handmaiden,
For his more honour in men's sight, and ease
The hurts he had with holy remedies
Made by her mother's magic in strange hours
Out of live roots and life-compelling flowers.
"The Sailing of the Swallow," from "Tristram of Lyonesse"
by Algernon Charles Swinburne

It was a miracle from God. Tristan took a deep breath in, filling his lungs near to bursting before breathing out in a rush. Pain twinged in his side, and he had a dull ache in his leg. He could feel the pressure of the bandages holding him together.

A familiar face appeared beside him, grinning from ear to ear beneath a black mustache. "You have slept like the dead for two days, my friend, and here you are, alive again. Is there nothing you cannot do?"

"Dance or cook," Tristan said, his voice grating from his throat. With Manuell's hand supporting his arm, Tristan sat up and accepted the cup of water he was handed. "Where are the others from the crew?" he asked, sipping the cool water.

Manuell waved his hand in the air. "They are about. Dueling with King Angeus's men, wooing local women; it is a time to relax for them. The captain wants us to go back to the ship and bring it down the coastline. Waiting to see your fate was a priority, however. The captain will be pleased you are awake."

""I am much indebted to him," Tristan said. He shifted under the covers, feeling his side tug painfully. "Did she sew me up?"

"Who, the princess? I do not know. I wasn't here. You might ask her. She went foraging early this morning. Ought to be back soon."

Tristan stared around the room. Two empty beds, one, besides his, filled. An old woman, staring off into empty space with glassy eyes. She didn't stir as the men talked. Tristan noticed her eyes drooped.

He turned his attention back to Manuell. "I need pen and paper. King Mark should know of our victory."

"You cannot send a message to King Mark from here, of all places," Manuell hissed. He glanced around them. The room was empty except for the old woman, who now slept. "If you do, they will know you lied to them and we'll be caught."

"Fortunately for you, I made sure a message was sent." The captain approached Tristan's bed, clasping his hand, other hand patting Tristan's shoulder.

"How?" Tristan asked.

"On the isle, the monks receive a visitor every couple of days. This visitor brings supplies and news, as well as relaying messages. They took one detailing the account of your victory back to the main Isle of Man, where it will have gone out with the next ship to England. It may take a few weeks to get there, but it will get there."

Tristan felt tears prick the corners of his eyes. He sniffed, as if the action could bring those tears back inside his head. He looked up at the captain. "Thank you, Captain. For everything. I would not be alive now if you hadn't been willing to do more than your hire."

"I trust you will make sure it was worth my while," the captain said, voice gruff. Tristan thought he caught a glimmer of moisture in the captain's eyes too, and he smiled. "Listen, I am going to take the other men back to the ship. We intend to sail down the coastline, to be closer to the castle should we need to depart with haste. I will leave Manuell here with you to be safe. It is a trip of four, maybe five days. Will you be all right until we return?"

"Aye, I will be all right. I have a feeling I am in good hands."

"So long as nobody discovers who you are," Manuell muttered, then jumped as a voice spoke from behind him.

"Ah, the invalid awakes. How are you this morning?" Princess Isolde's voice, with its lilting Irish accent, drifted through the room and into Tristan's ears like a song. She greeted the captain as he walked from the room, and Tristan looked to her, expecting that his fever may have exaggerated her appearance as he remembered it from earlier.

It hadn't.

She wore a long tunic, the color of a pale pink rose, tightened around her waist with a belt of ornate silver. A silver circlet pressed her hair down on the top of her head. A smile graced her face, and her blonde hair cascaded over her shoulders. She walked to the table beside Tristan, unloading the basket from her arm and sorting the roots and leaves into distinct piles, tying stems with strings to hang the bunches of herbs.

"I am well enough, it seems, thanks to your ministrations," Tristan said in a graveled voice.

He cleared his throat, taking another sip of water, trying to keep his eyes anywhere but on her. The way her tunic flowed over her hips as she moved to tie up the herbs kept drawing his gaze. Tristan glanced at Manuell and at the sight of the man's besotted face, spit his water back into the cup, trying to cover up his burst of laughter by coughing.

Princess Isolde turned around, eyes wide. "Are you quite all right?"

Tristan caught his breath. "Yes, I am. Perhaps you could tell me some about my healing. How is it progressing? Will I lose my leg?"

Isolde folded her arms and pursed her lips. "You are actually paralyzed, I am afraid."

Manuell gasped. "You don't say! Sir Tramtrist, try to move your legs."

Tristan made a great show of trying, then failing, and did his best to put a crestfallen expression on his face. Princess Isolde covered her mouth, failing to hide the snort of laughter that escaped her.

Manuell looked from Princess Isolde, to Tristan, then back again, his face growing beet red. "Oh no, you two pull my leg..."

The princess and Tristan both dissolved into helpless laughter, and even though the stitches in his side pulled something fierce, Tristan couldn't stop. He laughed until he cried, and his laughing kept the others doubled over.

"We haven't been introduced. I am the Princess Isolde of Mumhan. My father, King Angeus, says that you have traveled from England to come here. How did you know to seek healing here?"

Her green eyes pierced him, and he swallowed hard before answering. "It sounds odd, milady, but I had a dream. I believe it was divine guidance, sent that I might live."

"Not odd at all. I believe most dreams have meaning, if we have the wherewithal to interpret them correctly. You were wise to heed your dream."

"You did not truly answer my question from earlier; how am I mending?"

She shrugged. "You are doing well enough, considering. I identified the poison as Monkshood. Beautiful flowers, deadly poison. It appears the knight you were fighting had attached this to his dagger, filled with the poison." Morgan used a pair of small metal tongs to hold up a thin, needle-like casing.

Tristan frowned. Poison was a low, dirty trick for a knight. Why would Sir Marhaus do such a thing? Or had someone else gotten to the knight's weapon?

"I was able to use a little-known remedy for Monkshood. It is likely that if you had gone anywhere else, they would not have known of the remedy and you would be dead. You might also have been dead faster, but for the needle being clogged by some substance, preventing most of the poison from leaking out. You are very fortunate."

"I keep telling him this; he has the most incredible luck," Manuell stated.

The princess kept her eyes on Tristan, who found that he could not bring himself to look away. Did she suspect his tale was false?

"Do you mind fetching Sir Tramtrist some food from the kitchens, Manuell? A simple broth, to start. The servants ought to have something they can warm for our knight."

Manuell agreed and within a moment, Tristan and Isolde were alone, except for the elderly woman, who snored softly in the other bed.

Isolde uncrossed her arms and closed the gap between them, coming right to the edge of the bed. "I do not think you are who you say you are," she said quietly.

Tristan could see the faded sprinkling of freckles on her nose that weren't visible from farther away. He swallowed, throat dry again.

"What would make you say that, princess?"

"I...I have a source that recognizes you. They say your name is Tristan. I wondered why you would hide your true name, and then I heard it spoken in court as the name of he who killed Sir Marhaus. My uncle," she added the last words almost as an afterthought.

Sweat pricked at Tristan's brow. She didn't seem angry, more curious. Could he trust her? He realized he had to. She hadn't told the king or queen yet, or Tristan would be dead.

"Why would you help the enemy of your kingdom?" he asked, in way of answer. She looked up towards one of the windows, sunlight streaming past her face.

"I was taught to save life where possible, not take it away."

"You ought to hate me," he said, wondering what manner of woman this was, who forgave so easily.

"Hate is a waste of this precious life," the princess said. She reached up and tucked a loose strand of hair away behind her ear. "I have seen it destroy a person."

"As have I," Tristan replied.

Silence stretched between them. Isolde returned to the table after a moment, straightening books and tools on its surface. Her fingers tapped the wooden surface, the only sound in the still room.

"You know that I..." Isolde began, as Tristan blurted, "Do you know where..."

"Sorry," Tristan said. "You go ahead."

Isolde smiled, and it lit up Tristan's heart, lifting him up to a place he had never been before.

"I wanted to tell you that you do not have to worry about me revealing who you are. I am not on good terms with my mother," she practically spat out the word, "and my father will not inquire. He admires knights for their nobility and honor, blind to all their faults."

Tristan raised an eyebrow. "Do we have so many faults?"

"Do not take it personally, all men suffer from them."

"And women do not?" He pressed.

Isolde turned and gave him a long, steady stare, pursing her lips. She returned back to the table, a small bottle filled with oil from the shelf in her hand. She carefully crumbled dried herbs into it, stopped it with a cork, then held it up at eye level as she swirled it around.

"I simply meant to convey that you are safe here."

"Thank you," Tristan replied.

"What were you going to say?" Isolde asked.

“Oh, it sounds foolish now. I was going to ask whether you knew where my things were being kept? There is something I would like to have while I am on the mend.”

“Ah, yes. You shouldn’t walk on your leg for at least a week. Your side will take longer to mend. It might feel great now, but that’s because I’ve given you herbs to dull the pain. When they wear off, well, you’ll wish they hadn’t.”

“How soon can I travel? I would like to return home.”

Isolde came to the bedside again, bending down and dragging several bundles out.

“Everything is here that your men brought with them.” She stood up, putting her hands on her hips, her face rosy with the flush of exertion. “You might travel in two weeks’ time. Perhaps a little sooner, if needed.”

Tristan frowned. “I would rather be off sooner. The queen may catch on to my identity in that length of time. I only planned on holding the ruse for a few days. Would your...sources...be inclined to bribery, should the queen approach them?”

Isolde shook her head. “No, they are not the kind of sources that can be bought.”

Tristan cocked his head. Most people could be bought or threatened. What made her sources so different? Loyalty to their princess, perhaps. Not a far stretch from what he had seen of her.

The princess continued. “My mother is cunning and bears grudges eternally. She has vowed vengeance against you, and her men are scouring the coast, hoping you will show your face.”

Tristan’s heart leapt into his throat. “I should have warned the captain. Do you know if any of these men were with Sir Marhaus when I fought him?”

Isolde shook her head, the strand of hair falling loose again. "I am afraid not. I assume there might be one such among them, but I have no way to be certain."

Tristan raised his left arm to run his fingers through his hair but gasped in pain as the motion pulled on his wound. Isolde looked at him with sympathy.

"I can bandage that arm to your side if necessary, so you do not forget and try to use it."

"No, that won't be necessary," Tristan said. He combed through his hair with his right hand, distracted by the fact that his hair felt rather too clean for what he had endured.

"You gave me a bath!" he exclaimed.

Isolde blushed. "Someone had to, you were filthy. I performed the task with the utmost discretion, I assure you. Some areas I avoided. And Manuell assisted me when you needed to...well, relieve yourself."

Tristan's face burned hot as a summer day. He laughed nervously, raising his left hand out of habit, dropping it when pain split his wounded side.

She, a princess, had seen him naked. He wasn't sure how he felt about that. Had she liked how he looked? He snorted at the thought, making Isolde turn around and stare at him.

Tristan smiled. She didn't look on him as anything other than a drooling invalid. She likely thought of him as nothing more than a patient, and a crippled one at that.

"Hand me that triangular package, if you will, milady?" Tristan asked.

Isolde hesitated, then hefted the harp onto the bed in its waterproof packing. Tristan removed the wrapping and ran his fingers across it. One snapped string and a single dent in the wood below where he placed his hands while playing. Another miracle. He took his time restringing and tuning it, Isolde watching as she bustled around the room, straightening various items, shuffling through her books.

"Are you any good?" Isolde asked.

"They say when I play the birds take vows of silence," Tristan replied, keeping a straight face.

"Truly?" Isolde asked, clearly skeptical.

Tristan launched into telling her about one of his favorite memories. He had played for a court in France once during a three-day feast, and every time he stopped, the people had almost rioted until he started again. They wouldn't even eat at times during his playing, often holding each other and weeping or laughing or cursing.

He embellished the story by playing bits of the songs he had played for the court, plucking out jolly and sorrowful tunes alike, and he could tell Isolde enjoyed it all. The story ended with some members of the court claiming they had seen the heavens open and deposit a chorus of angels to accompany Tristan's playing.

In the end, his pay far exceeded the original agreement and several nobles offered their daughters' hands in marriage.

Isolde laughed when he finished, eyeing him a little warily. "You are quite the storyteller, Sir Tramtrist," she said, his false name sounding odd coming from her lips. "I am not sure what is truth and what is fable."

"Perhaps that is because it is all truth," Tristan replied.

And then, he launched into a lusty tavern ballad, a jaunty, hilarious tune about a miller's wife tricking her foolish husband into thinking she didn't have a lover. His voice was merely fair, in his opinion, but he found that the sound of his harp more than made up for it.

Both Isolde and the woman in the other bed clapped along, laughing at the fate of the poor, idiotic miller.

Tristan played for Isolde every day after that. She sometimes suggested songs, but most times listened to whatever he felt like playing. If she had any other duties, she abandoned them to hear him play, sitting with him throughout the morning and early afternoon. Sometimes others came to ask for remedies, and once she set a bone for an older gentleman.

Every afternoon, she drifted off to sleep, either crawling into one of the beds, sometimes falling asleep at her table, surrounded by open books and herbs. Otherwise, she only left Tristan's side to care for the elderly woman in the next bed. She fell asleep at odd times and rarely went out. He wondered at it, but did not pry, and she didn't give any reasoning for it.

Every day, he grew fonder of Isolde's company, and every day had to remind himself that this season would pass, and he should not become too reliant on Isolde's company, for soon he would return to Cornwall.

CHAPTER TEN

But, what hinders that the two,
In the spring of their young life,
Love each other as they do?
Thus the tempting thoughts begin -
Little recked they of the sin;
Nature joined them hand in hand,
Is not that a truer band
Than the formal name of wife?
"Tristan and Isolde; The Love Sin"
by Jane Fraqncesca Wilde

Morgan fell asleep in the afternoon after lunch, as she had every day since arriving. Her head pounded with a monstrous headache, and her body seemed excessively fatigued. She wondered, as she drifted off, if perhaps Isolde's body had a wasting sickness. Her eyes flickered shut, and her mind wandered.

Tristan's gaze followed Morgan into her dreams. She woke in the darkness with no memory of what she had dreamt. How long had she slept?

Her nightgown twisted around her, the bedcovers strewn on the floor. A dark form stood over her. She opened her mouth to shriek but a hand clapped over her mouth.

"Hush, my dear. You were dreaming poorly." The softness of Aideen's voice made Morgan shiver. The maid slowly removed her hand from Morgan's face and bent down, retrieving the covers.

Morgan pushed herself to sitting. "Aideen, what are you doing in here? It's the middle of the night."

"I am never far, Banphrionsa. I heard you cry out. I came." Aideen held up the covers, her face cloaked in darkness. The waning moon didn't provide much light.

Morgan remained sitting upright. She stared at the woman, her mind not grasping what Aideen said.

"Where do you sleep, Aideen?" Morgan wasn't sure what made her ask.

The maid paused in her straightening of the covers. "Beside your door on most nights. When I am able."

Morgan gaped. "Why?"

Aideen hesitated, then sat at the edge of the bed, making it dip slightly from her weight. Her hands clasped in her lap, and she gazed downward at them. Morgan wished she could see the expression on the older woman's face.

"As a babe, you were often sickly. Do you know that the queen could not give you suck? She was lost to her mind in those days. Your father grew concerned and called for nursemaids. I was chosen. I slept on the floor beside your cradle. Your mother was distant, would not hold you, would not touch you, and if left alone...she would attempt to kill you, along with herself. I prevented her with my presence."

Morgan's back had stiffened, and her shoulders were tight. She forced herself to relax them, exhaling slowly.

"My mother? She is well now, though, isn't she?"

"I am not certain she ever recovered. The queen has always been...forceful. Manipulative. Quick to anger. She has grown...unpredictable in recent years."

Morgan could see Aideen's face now, as the sky outside had begun to lighten. She saw the lines of worry creasing out from her eyes, the downturn of her mouth as she looked on Morgan. The servant turned away, rubbing one hand over the opposite, wringing them together.

"I am sorry for what she has done to you, Banphrionsa," Aideen muttered.

"Aideen?" Morgan asked.

Aideen's head jerked up, and her eyes widened. "I spoke aloud?"

Morgan nodded.

"She must not know. She must not know you know."

"Know what?"

Aideen leaned in, face closing in on Morgan's until their noses touched. "I cannot stop what is coming. Do not eat her food." The maid fled from the chamber.

Morgan stared at the closed door for a long moment, trying to decide if she should follow the woman and pry more information from her, but decided against it. Dawn was close. Soon, other servants would be stirring and might hear if Aideen became upset. She didn't return to sleep, however.

What did Aideen mean about the food? Why would the queen want to poison her own daughter? Morgan frowned to herself. Her left hand drifted up to rub her chest, where, to her eyes, a silver phoenix stretched across her skin, its wings grazing her collarbone.

Morgan's nightdress was low cut, revealing the bulk of the mark she had received from the Rite of the Heart. Aideen couldn't see the mark; or if she could, she made no comment on it.

She had spent her days getting Sir Tristan settled in the infirmary and familiarizing herself with Isolde's books. The woman had kept meticulous medical journals so organized that anyone could have followed along with the Irish princess's notes, fortunately for Morgan, who understood rudimentary herbs and medicine but nothing beyond the basics.

It also seemed that Isolde was a solitary person, avoiding everyone but her patients. It seemed an easy enough personality for Morgan to portray, but the fear of discovery kept her alert, afraid that she would say or do the wrong thing at the wrong time and be suspect.

This threat from the queen complicated matters. Morgan thought about how tired she had felt after her noon meal. Was the poison slow-acting? One that would kill her eventually? Or did a more abrupt plot against her have Aideen worried?

Morgan laid her head back down, unable to fall back to sleep. From where she lay, the bowl she had scried with the first morning she arrived stood in view. She sat up and pushed the covers from her legs, swinging them around and touching down on the cold stone floor.

She stared into the water. She needed to talk to Isolde again. She could ask her what she knew and get a clearer message to her about Niviane and Camelot. Morgan flexed her fingers and took a breath, letting go of any thoughts that might disturb the connection.

Isolde? Morgan's own face appeared in the water, wavering. The astronomical alignment could be off, or perhaps the poison in her system interfered with her magic.

Morgan...that you? I cannot...you. Isolde's voice came inside Morgan's head, her image rippling in the water's surface.

Why couldn't either of them speak aloud? Hydromancy usually allowed one to both see and speak. Could Isolde see her?

*Niviane...can't...she...*Isolde tried again.

I cannot hear you well, Isolde. The connection is poor. Morgan thought toward the other woman in a rush. *Do you know what kind of poison your mother is using against you? How can I counteract it?*

No*...antidote...possibly...live long.*

Live long? *Won't live long*? Morgan cursed to herself. *What has Niviane said?*

We are...hiding. She...plans...involving Camelot...go to court...What...debt...?

The connection wavered more as Morgan failed to suppress her frustration. She tried breathing again to calm herself and thought about the words she could discern from Isolde. A debt. The debt she owed to Niviane, in exchange for keeping Elaina safe.

Morgan cursed out loud and the scene wavered.

Morgan's door opened.

"Banphrionsa?" Aideen asked.

Morgan turned from the now-empty bowl. "It is nothing, Aideen. I struck my foot in the dark."

"I thought you struggled to sleep again. I brought warm milk." Aideen hobbled into the room with a mug and set it beside Morgan on the table. "Sweetened with honey, the way you like. And extra cream." The woman smiled. Morgan eyed the mug with trepidation. Could it be poisoned?

"Aideen, why are you helping her?" Morgan asked, glancing boldly up into Aideen's face. The maid's eyes widened, but she did not speak at first.

"I am compelled. I have no choice."

"What is she using? Please, you must tell me."

"I do not see how she prepares it. And if I neglect to give it, I am punished. If you do not eat it, you will be punished. Or perhaps your wards in the infirmary. Your mother knows how you care for them. She has staged accidents before, if you remember."

Morgan didn't, of course. Isolde would, but Morgan couldn't scry her again right now. The tips of her fingernails bit into her palms.

"I understand, Aideen. Thank you for the milk."

Aideen nodded and left the room. Morgan felt a pit open up in her stomach as she grabbed the mug, feeling the heat of the clay seep into her hands. She smelled the sweetness of the honey as it wafted through the air into her nose. Her stomach growled.

She stood and crossed the room to the narrow window, looking out onto the dark, blueish light of dawn. In the distance, lightning flickered, and the wind blew towards Morgan, bringing with it the heavy scent of rain. Lightning interfered with magic, sporadically enhancing or blocking communication and other spells. One took the chance of being killed by their own spells, even benign ones, when they practiced during a storm.

Morgan's breath shuddered as she drew in the fresh air. Her hands felt hot, holding the mug of milk Aideen had brought.

She smelled the honey and rain, a comforting scent that didn't match the thickness in her chest and the weight in her stomach at the new truth she had learned.

Her hand trembled as it reached out the window and tilted the mug. She watched as the milk splashed to the paving stones below, leaving a dark stain that spread as rain poured down from the clouds in a sudden sheet.

Morgan turned from the window and crawled back into bed, pulling the covers over her head, as lightning flashed in synchronicity with the crash of thunder outside.

CHAPTER ELEVEN

Murmured vow and clinging kiss,
Working often bane as bliss;
All the wild, capricious changes
Through which lovers' passion ranges.
Yet would love, in every mood,
Find Heaven's manna for its food;
For love will grow wan and cold,
And die ere ever it is old,
That is never assailed by fears,
Or steeped in repentant tears,
Or passed through the fire like gold.
"Tristan and Isolde; The Love Sin"
by Jane Fraqncesca Wilde

Tristan woke one night to find Isolde with her shoulders shaking and gasping for breath as if she were crying. She leaned over one of the beds across the room, a sheet covering the old woman's form; she had died in the night.

Without a word, Tristan took out his harp and made it sing of death and sadness and comfort, until sometime near dawn he found himself gazing down at the sleeping Isolde, her head on his uninjured leg while the rest of her curled at the foot of his bed, and his heart thumped in his chest as he reached out to touch her hair. It felt so soft beneath his fingers.

He didn't move until she stirred, and then only regretfully. He couldn't deny, then, his feelings for her. He lived for her laughter and his heart yearned whenever she tended him.

Manuell visited on the eighth day. He was getting restless for the ocean, he said, and the captain and the other men were eager to be on their way.

Tristan almost told him to leave him. He would gladly live out his days here, if not for the truth that hung over his head. He had killed the queen's brother, and there would be no chance for recompense if the queen found out.

The days passed, and with each one he grew stronger, getting out of bed and taking short walks around the castle, sometimes with Manuell helping him, but more often with Isolde on one arm, laughing and talking with him.

On the tenth day after he had awoken, the captain himself showed up at Tristan's bedside. He was there when Tristan woke in the morning, rubbing the cap that usually rested on his balding head. He looked up when Tristan pushed himself to sitting.

"How are you, Sir Knight?"

"I am well enough. Thank you, again, captain, for your generosity."

The man nodded, smiling down into his fidgeting hands. "I cannot help but notice your fondness for a certain señorita," he said, expression flattening. "I do not think I need to tell you how dangerous this is for you and for my men."

"It's nothing, captain. She's a lovely woman, but I'm aware I must return to Cornwall."

The captain placed his cap back on his head and stood. "The weather is bad this season, but we have a dry spell now. I will keep watching the skies. We will leave in four days, weather permitting. I am told you will be well enough to return with us."

Tristan nodded, not trusting his voice to speak. He had never felt so torn. His heart oscillated between going home and staying in this foreign land, the land of his enemies, to try and convince this Irish woman to love him in return. He swallowed the emotion, trying to harden himself against it.

Tristan knew what he had to do, for his sake and the crew's. He owed them. Getting them killed by association with him would be poor repayment for their kindness.

He did not allow her to fall asleep on his bed again, but would shake her awake if his playing made her drowsy, making certain she went to a separate bed or across the room before her afternoon fatigue struck.

He also tried to limit their conversations, avoiding personal questions she asked, and biting his tongue before asking what she thought about this or that.

She was amiable, always open to conversation, and he cursed the need for his coldness every time she looked at him confused by his unwillingness to answer or return her teasing. Despite his efforts, he found himself watching her embroider while she sat at her table, asking such harmless questions as he could think to ask. She answered with distraction, focused on the thread and needle and probably put-off by his own apparent inattention.

"Why do you fall asleep so many afternoons?" Tristan asked.

Isolde looked up from her embroidery. He was fairly certain she only did it to keep her hands busy. The design wasn't anything to be applauded, nor was it something he even recognized.

"I am tired after dealing with you all day," she jibed, but her smile didn't reach her eyes.

"Would you like an excuse to stop torturing that cloth?" he asked.

Isolde dropped the embroidery into her lap, mouth open at him.

He smiled at her, and gradually, a smile appeared on her full, lovely lips.

She held up the embroidery. "What, you don't appreciate my depiction of a bird?"

"Is that what that is? I thought it was a mouse. Or maybe a bug?"

She laughed and shook her head, standing up and taking the embroidery over to the table against the side of the room. "I have always been terrible at embroidery, or doing anything beautiful with my hands."

"So, you're basically terrible at being a woman?"

This time she smacked him in the shoulder. "You are walking a dangerous line, Sir Tristan." She whispered his real name, teasing in her eyes. She seemed pleased that he returned her flirtation, and though the guilt rose inside Tristan, seeing her smile after days of rebuffing her made him feel light as air.

"You shouldn't tease, you know. I could be killed if anyone found out." He meant it to sound joking, but her face fell, and she started picking at the blankets. He regretted saying anything.

"I know, that went too far. I'm sorry."

"Apology accepted. What I said was offensive. Forgive me?"

She laughed at his exaggerated, wide-eyed begging face. "Only if you play for me." Her eyes seemed to sparkle, and she reached down with both hands to pick up his harp from where it stood on the floor beside the bed.

Tristan took it from her, positioning it between his outstretched legs. He closed his eyes, resting his cheek against the dark wood of the instrument, hands stroking the smooth wood, brushing over the strings and making them hum their first notes.

"You hold that harp like it's a beautiful woman."

"That's what she reminds me of," Tristan replied.

Isolde smiled and sat on the bed once more. He plucked aimlessly for a moment, thinking, then played an experimental chord, letting it reverberate through the room, and began a lively tune, singing as he played.

"A fair maid sat in her bower door, Wringing her lily hands;

And by it came a sprightly youth, Fast tripping o'er the strands.

"Where gang ye, young John," she says, "So early in the day?

It seems me think, by your fast trip, Your journey's far away."

He turn'd about wi' surly look, And said, "What's that to thee?

I'm ga'en to see a lovely maid, Mair fairer far than ye."

Isolde's laughter filled the room as through the next several stanzas, the besotted maid followed the frustrated John from town to town. He bought her gifts at each town, trying to bribe her to leave him, until at the last he bought a wedding dress and married her, having fallen in love again.

Isolde's cheeks were flushed and her eyes bright.

"That was just the thing I needed," she said. Tristan noted that her shoulders had relaxed, and the pinched fatigue seemed to have disappeared from her eyes. "You weren't lying when you said you played well, that is for certain."

"It is my first love," Tristan said. "I have found in my travels that there are few people who don't appreciate music. I have played my way to many free meals and stays, especially in taverns. Good music brings customers, you see, and prevents brawls."

"I can see that. Your playing is like an enchantment, it creates such a positive feeling in others. Maybe you ought to play for the queen."

Tristan laughed nervously, adjusting one of the pegs and plucking to hear the new sound. Perfect. "I am not certain she is one of those people who appreciates music."

"You may be right, at that," Isolde said.

A knock came at the door, and a servant entered carrying a large tray of food.

"Thank you, Aideen. You may put it over there." Isolde gestured to the table, and the servant complied. She curtseyed to Isolde. "Milady, this serving is meant for you," the servant said, pointing to the dish on the right. It was identical to the other dish of stew from what he could see.

"Thank you. You may leave," Isolde replied.

The servant hesitated, as if wanting to stay, but instead curtseyed and left the room. Isolde walked over to the tray and stared at the two servings, then took the indicated bowl of stew and threw it in the fire. She set the bowl calmly back on the tray, brushing her hands together.

Tristan gaped at her. “Not hungry?” he asked.

“Not hungry, sure. I do not feel like being poisoned today.”

“Who would poison you?”

Isolde nodded. “Who do you think was behind the poisoned dagger tip Sir Marhaus stabbed you with?” She raised an eyebrow. “It is her preferred method. After all, she is the one who first taught me of the healing, and deadly, properties of herbs.”

“Your mother? Why aren’t you dead yet? How long has this been going on?”

“Months, at least. She is slipping it into my food, a little at a time.”

“Yes, but how? She never comes in contact with your food.”

“I told you she had people watching me. Aideen is her little puppet,” she said bitterly, bringing Tristan his bowl.

He stared at it, his mouth starting to water. “You don’t think mine is poisoned too?”

“Unlikely. Why go to the trouble of indicating which serving was meant for me? I will wager yours is safe.” She dropped the spoon into it, splashing a little.

“Share with me,” Tristan said, looking up into her face.

Her eyes went wide with shock. “What?”

Tristan moved over in the bed, trying to hide his wince of pain. He patted the mattress beside him. “There is a second spoon. Have some of mine. Your mother will never know the difference.”

Isolde said nothing, but climbed onto the bed, moving her skirt out of the way and bending her legs to the side. Did she do everything gracefully?

They ate at turns, Tristan holding off his desire to slurp the whole bowl and waiting until Isolde took a spoonful before digging his spoon in again. The soup contained large pieces of meat and root vegetables that made it hearty and filling, but by the time they slurped up the last dregs, Tristan's stomach still felt empty. He let Isolde take the bowl and she returned it to the tray. As he watched her, he felt no regrets.

"You ought to get some rest," Isolde said, pressing on his good shoulder to make him lay down. He didn't resist, and she pulled the covers up to his chin, tucking him in.

"I feel like a small child," he said.

She smiled down at him, a look almost like sadness in her eyes.

"Thank you," she said. "For the meal. You may have saved my life, you know."

"Nothing so dramatic as that," he replied.

She picked up the tray containing the two empty bowls and turned to go.

Tristan sat up on his elbows. "Why don't you leave?"

Isolde stopped and faced him. "I do not know where I would go," she replied.

"You could go anywhere," he said. "You could come to Cornwall with me."

She smiled, then walked from the room without a word. Tristan lay back down and stared at the ceiling, gradually giving in to exhaustion.

When he woke, he felt groggy and disoriented. It took a moment before he realized the voices he heard were real and not part of a dream. Tristan's ears perked up. In the hallway outside the room, he heard two individuals having a discussion. A heated one, at that. One of them was Isolde. He smiled when he heard her voice, even though it was loud and irate.

"Father, how could you do this without asking me?"

King Angeus? Tristan slowed his breathing, listening as hard as he could for the response.

The king spoke in a hush, as if afraid of being heard. "My dear Isolde, you know what your mother has been trying to do. I cannot protect you in any other way than this."

"I am certain there is another way. There has to be."

"There is not. You must leave here, and this is the only way I know of that won't make her suspicious. Even now, she watches me as a hawk watches its prey. I am followed wherever I go."

"You are king here, are you not? If anyone else plotted against me the way she does, would you allow them such leniency?"

"Of course not, daughter. You do not understand; she is powerful, far more powerful than I. Her allies are my allies, so long as I do not cross her."

"You are a coward." Isolde's voice was cold and harsh, unlike Tristan had ever heard her speak. It didn't sound like her.

King Angeus's response came after a long moment. "That may be, but I love you, and I am doing what I can to protect you."

The door creaked open a moment later as Isolde stepped inside. She saw Tristan awake and managed a tight smile, but the anger didn't leave her eyes. She walked straight to his bed and sat on the edge.

"I am sorry to wake you. Did you...did you hear anything?" She looked at him sideways.

"I did not mean to hear," Tristan said. "I am sorry to intrude."

Isolde sighed. "It is all right."

"Would you like to talk about it?"

"I would." She stood up and walked to the door and shut it, then dropped the latch across the frame. "Now no one can barge in on us," she said, returning to the bed and adjusting her seat until she seemed comfortable.

"I finally have you all to myself. Too bad I'm crippled," Tristan joked. "Though I am almost better. I am sure I could manage some scandalous behavior."

He was rewarded with a small smile.

"Always jokes with you," Isolde said, and then she shook her head. "I'm sorry. I feel so overwhelmed." She took a shaky breath and wiped at her eyes.

"My father has informed me that he is putting on a tournament in three days. The knights have already been arriving. Knights from across the land will compete in open melee. He's calling it the Lady of the Lands tournament. Three guesses as to the prize," she said, her voice bitter.

She gazed down at her hands.

Tristan stared at her. "Isn't there anything you can do? Talk to him? Refuse to be married?"

"You heard our conversation. It was rather one-sided. With my mother trying to poison me, he believes the only way to keep me safe is to marry me off. She has hated me since I was a babe; my birth nearly killed her."

Tristan rubbed his chin, feeling stubble. He hadn't shaved in almost a fortnight.

"Your life story sounds an awful lot like my own," Tristan said. "My mother died bearing me, and my father remarried. The woman is awful. She had several of her own children with my father but seemed furious that none of them would inherit my father's land, so she tried to off me. Several times."

Tristan noticed Isolde's hand drop to the covers, within inches of his own. He itched to reach out and take it, but instead swallowed hard and continued.

"During one of her attempts, she accidentally killed one of her own sons. My father saw what was happening and condemned her to die, but as a young lad my heart was soft enough that I entreated him to spare her. He did what any good father would do; he agreed to my request and sent me away to study in France."

The tips of Isolde's fingers brushed his hand. It sent a thrill up his spine, and his body shuddered with the pleasure of even that brief moment of contact.

He left his hand there, their fingertips barely touching, and cleared his throat. "I suppose that is what your father is doing; getting you away from your mother the only way he knows how."

"But why must it be marriage? Why not send me off to apprentice with another healer, maybe in England? Why is that acceptable for a lad, but not a lass?"

"Marriage is safer; then he knows you're being cared for. You won't have to fend for yourself."

Isolde snorted. "Too often marriage is a disguise for church-mandated, socially accepted abuse. Women aren't safe with men. Every time a man gets involved, there's hurt and manipulation and misery." She withdrew her hand from his, folding her arms into her chest and hunching over, as if she could make herself disappear.

Tristan studied her. His mind reeled; what to say? He had never spoken this deeply with a woman before. It had always been light-heartedness and uncommitted wooing. He wasn't sure he wanted to know, but looking at her now, slumped over and silent, he found he couldn't leave the conversation there.

"What happened to you?" Tristan asked softly.

She collapsed further, and her shoulders began shaking with silent sobs. He couldn't begin to understand. As a man, he held far more weight in society than she. He had seen that female servants were treated more poorly than their male counterparts. And the things his fellow knights said about women sometimes turned his stomach. He had seen it with Earl Segwarides' wife.

God help him, he didn't even remember her name, and that fact made him feel ashamed. She had been fought over by himself, his uncle, her own husband, captured by another knight, rescued and returned to her husband; a parcel without say in her destination. Tristan knew she loved him. Given the choice, he might have married her. Her own marriage, loveless though it was, held her captive to a jealous husband.

Tristan regretted ever getting involved.

"I can see why you feel the way you do, in part. I have seen it happen to women before," Tristan said, keeping his voice low. He reached out and touched her arm.

Isolde didn't move, didn't look at him. Her proud head bowed low, her body pulled in on itself, as if she could hide from it all. Suddenly, he knew how he could stop it. She may not appreciate it, but he had nothing else to offer.

"I will fight for you," he said, gazing at her. Her head came up, and she stared at him with red, but dry eyes. "I will enter the tournament, I will win your hand, and I will set you free."

"You cannot. You are wounded."

"I have two days to heal further. I will be well enough to fight."

"You cannot," Isolde insisted, turning her whole body to face him.

Suddenly, her face animated once more. The sight made Tristan grin. "Besides, your ship leaves in two days, before the tournament."

"I will ask them to stay a few more. When I tell them why, they will stay."

She pursed her lips, possibly the only woman Tristan had ever known to look attractive while furious. "I will not allow it. You'll be killed!"

He forced his face to become solemn once more. "That may be. But you have never seen me fight. I have more skill than you know."

Cornwall could wait a few more days. Mark would be chomping at the bit waiting for him to return.

"Even the most skilled knight can die of an addled brain," she retorted.

"Addled in the best way," he said, wishing his eyes could convey the message so that she could understand how he felt by looking into them. He wished he was brave enough to say it out loud. But she looked away, and he couldn't muster the courage.

"You're an idiot," she said, her voice breaking. She slid from the bed and before he could reply, ran from the room.

Tristan watched the door swing on its hinge, coming to a close. Then he pushed the covers off, sucking in his breath at the pain in his side. He took it slow, swinging his legs off the bed, then putting his weight on them, testing how his injured leg felt. It seemed well enough. He twisted at the waist, wincing again when he went right and his left side pulled.

He bent down to touch his feet, and while he was down, he pulled the package out from beneath the bed that contained his armor. The long, thin package on top of it slid to the floor, clattering. Tristan picked it up first, setting it on the bed and unwrapping it.

Inside, two swords lay in their sheaths. The first was the new sword King Mark had gifted him.

Tristan set it aside. He would fight this tournament with it.

The second he held before himself in both hands, then drew the blade. He stared at the jagged end, uneven and pointed where the tip had broken off inside the helm of Sir Marhaus.

Tristan caught movement from the corner of his eye and quickly sheathed the blade, gazing at the door where Isolde's handmaid had stood only a moment before.

CHAPTER TWELVE

Star with star molten, soul with soul imbued,
And all the soul's works, all their multitude,
Made one thought and one vision and one song,
Love—this thing, this, laid hand on her so strong
She could not choose but yearn till she should see.
So went she musing down her thoughts; but he,
Sweet-hearted as a bird that takes the sun
With clear strong eyes and feels the glad god run
Bright through his blood and wide rejoicing wings,
And opens all himself to heaven and sings.
"The Sailing of the Swallow," from "Tristram of Lyonesse"
by Algernon Charles Swinburne

Morgan woke to the dark of predawn with crusted eyes. Rubbing them as she sat up, she noticed the fire had died. The air around her felt cool. The usual achiness had disappeared from her limbs.

Hunger gnawed at her stomach. Her only food was what she could pilfer from the kitchens without arousing suspicion. Since she had stopped eating what Aideen brought her, the achiness and fatigue had diminished, but it would take some time for the poison to leave her system.

She stretched and sat up, disoriented for a moment until she realized she was in Isolde's chambers rather than the infirmary. She had woken up in that room so often the past two weeks she had gotten quite used to it.

Belt fastened around her waist, stockings and slippers keeping her feet warm, Morgan went to the small table and peered sideways at the bowl of clear, still water sitting there.

She opened a wooden box on the table and drew out a rosy pink crystal she had procured from a local market. She set it down and took out a curved yew stick next, placing it on the other side. Together, they enhanced the hydromancy that Morgan performed.

The image wavered, and then filled with color. Golden hair. Blue eyes. Petite nose. Familiar face. Elaina. With the aid of the yew and the crystal, Morgan called forth a wide enough image to see Elaina's form sitting at the loom, her hands moving back and forth through the threads, wielding the shuttle that Morgan's mistake bound her to.

She had scried Elaina twice now, but never spoken. What could she say? The connection was possible through the mirror Niviane used to bind her sister; if Morgan held the connection too long, Niviane could notice.

One thing she would do with her new life would be to free Elaina from that prison. Trapped with no ability to see out. Morgan understood that feeling now. Safe or not, Elaina didn't deserve that trapped fate. Morgan dropped the scrying, letting it ripple from the water as if it had never been.

Her body felt drained. It shouldn't be after a single scrying, but Thiton warned her it might take months to recover her magic ability, and by that time, she would be losing it, having been away from Avalon for so long.

Taking away the potency of your magic was one way the Goddess made certain her priestesses stayed loyal to her. When one returned, the potency grew again and the reserve was made deeper so one could be away longer the next time. Niviane spent decades building her reserves, and she had many powerful artifacts that enhanced the potency of her spells.

Despite her exhaustion, Morgan brought up an image of Isolde, straining to hold her intention until the image wavered to life in the bowl. Morgan's heart stopped. With the power of the crystal and yew wand, she could see the one to whom Isolde spoke. She held it for an instant, straining, until the yew wand snapped, the crystal cracked, and the water in the bowl splashed as if an object had dropped into it.

She spoke to Arthur. King Arthur. The very person Morgan was supposed to be avoiding. She held up the crystal, examining the crack. It shouldn't have done that, unless someone had placed a barrier over Isolde. Someone like Niviane. It would take a vast amount of effort to scry Isolde in the future. How would she know if Isolde married Arthur?

Morgan breathed in and out through her nose, her heart pounding, feeling like she couldn't get enough air in. Her vision closed around her.

It hadn't worked. Isolde had met with Niviane, despite Morgan's warnings. And now they were together in Camelot.

It took several long moments before Morgan could move from the chair, her energy so drained from the two scryings. When her limbs regained their strength, Morgan rose and fled to the infirmary, needing to see Tristan. It would calm her to speak with him about mundane things.

When she got there, she found his bed empty, the covers smooth, almost looking unslept in. She scrambled across the room. His harp stood next to a long, thinly wrapped parcel. His sword. Today, the tournament began, the Lady of the Lands.

He would be out at the field, warming up, getting into his armor. Morgan grabbed the sword, intending to take it to him. He would need it today, of all days.

The wrapping slid off easily, and the hilt caught her attention. Battle-worn, clearly well-used, and if the little she knew about weaponry meant anything, the sword needed to be replaced. Perhaps he would be better off with a sword from King Angeus's armory. Curiosity getting the best of her, Morgan gripped the hilt in one hand and pulled it from the sheath. She gaped at what she saw. The tip was gone, leaving a jagged, broken edge in its place.

And then she remembered how Sir Marhaus had died, with Sir Tristan's sword tip buried in his skull. Bile rose to her throat and she re-sheathed the sword.

"Good morning, Princess Isolde." Aideen's smooth voice made the hairs on Morgan's arms rise, and she dropped the sword with a clatter.

"Aideen! I was just putting Sir Tramtrist's things together for his departure," Morgan said, wrapping the sword back up and thrusting it under the bed.

Aideen walked into the room, tray in hand. “I heard he wasn’t leaving until after the tournament.” The servant smiled, a dark gap showing between her teeth.

“It is so,” Morgan said, coming to stand. Aideen passed her and set the tray on the table, then came up behind Morgan and put her hands on her shoulders.

“Come, now. I have brought your breakfast.”

Morgan licked her dry lips. “I’m not hungry.” Her stomach rumbled in protest at the lie.

Aideen’s smile widened, and her hands guided Morgan to the chair, pushing to make her sit.

“Please, eat.”

Morgan closed her eyes. She picked up the fork and stabbed the steaming turnip hash, tines grabbing a piece of sausage with the white vegetable strings. Her mouth burst with saliva. She hesitated only a moment before forcing the food into her mouth, scalding hot. She chewed as fast as she could and swallowed.

Aideen watched her eat the entire meal, down to drinking the last dregs of fresh milk in her cup. She smiled as Morgan finished, then took up the tray.

“There. Now you will have the strength to watch your knight battle for your hand in the tournament.”

Morgan’s stomach churned. She felt sick, and none of the herbs on the shelf would help her.

“Thank you, Aideen,” she managed, and, feeling more than a bit unsteady, she staggered from the room.

Her head spun, and her heart pounded. She hadn’t had a dose of poison for several days; perhaps it had affected her more rapidly this time. Somehow, she made it outside, the warm autumn sunlight spilling over the frostbitten ground. People walked past her, chatting on their way to the arena. She ought to call for a horse, or at least wait for Aideen to escort her, but Morgan didn't have a care. She had to warn Tristan.

Dozens of brightly colored tents stood around the arena, and here, people milled around, pages and squires running errands for lords and knights. Ladies, dressed in their best, preened for the knights' attention. Men in armor, testing weapons. The weapons flashed in the sunlight, and Morgan jumped each time she caught the gleam of metal from the corner of her eyes, imagining each one burying itself in Sir Tristan's flesh.

He was going to get himself killed.

Morgan pushed her way through the crowd, fighting the nausea building in her stomach. In her frantic state she neglected to acknowledge those who greeted their princess. She moved so fast she ran straight into the barrel chest of a tall, olive-skinned, black-haired man. She muttered her apologies and moved to leave.

A smile split from beneath the man's thin mustache, and his gauntleted hand caught her arm, holding her with him.

"Ah, princess, your beauty has been understated. I know flowers that would wilt in the presence of your loveliness." His voice glided from his lips like oil spilled from a lamp. Morgan tugged on her arm. "Please release me," Morgan said, voice coming out hard between her clenched teeth.

The man let go of her arm and swept into a bow. "Sir Palamides." He reached for her hand and his lips brushed it.

Somewhere behind her she heard the whisper. "A dirty Saracen dog, come to steal our princess away." She stiffened.

Someone pushed their way through the crowd, tall and well-built, dressed in full armor. Even before he spoke, some part of her knew him. Tristan. His appearance made the sickness in her stomach diminish. She took a deep breath and straightened.

He approached the Saracen, visor up on his English-style helm, and extended a hand to him. "The battle to the best man, aye?"

Sir Palamides eyed him up and down, then spat at his feet. "I can defeat any arrogant English churl who approaches me on that field. Do not underestimate my ability because of my origin."

Tristan held up his hands. "No one is doubting your skill, my friend. Some of the best men I know come from your land."

The man cursed in a harsh tongue Morgan didn't recognize, then split the crowd as he walked away.

"Good morning," she said to Tristan, the circle of people scattering back to their tasks. They sounded disappointed there hadn't been more of a fight.

"Good morning, Princess Isolde," Tristan replied, bowing a little.

She watched how he hesitated before straightening, and frowned.

Tristan saw her face and laughed. "Don't start with me. I won't be talked out of this."

"I know," she said. "That doesn't mean I don't think it is possibly the most foolish thing you will ever do." She paused, then pulled a piece of blue cloth off of her arm. She held the silk scarf out to him. It fluttered in the breeze. "I brought a favor for you. You don't have to wear it."

Tristan reached out and took hold of the delicate fabric. It looked out of place against the gleaming metal of his armor. "Indeed, milady. I would be honored." He grinned at her. "Would you tie it for me? On my arm will be fine. Make sure the ends are tucked in."

Morgan approached, wrapping the fabric several times to shorten it. She snorted at his comment. "Wouldn't want a silk scarf flying into your eyes to be your downfall, would you? Hardly a ballad worth harping about."

He let out a belly-shaking laugh at her pun, roaring and slapping his knees until tears came out his eyes and people walking by stared.

Morgan waited for him to finish, a smile finding its way onto her face at his infectious laughter.

"I do hope I will get to hear you play again."

"Aye, me too. And I wager you will, at that. I am more capable than you might think."

A horn sounded in the arena, calling all fighters to the ring. A melee match, to weed out the weakest and start the competition. Some would die; it always happened in melees. The men would fight until twenty men were left standing, and those would duel each other in open-weapon hand-to-hand combat to first blood.

Tristan nodded to her, dropping his visor. She watched him go, noticing the way he limped slightly and the too-stiff swing of his arm on the side he had injured mere weeks before. He could die.

She wanted to speak, but the words caught in her throat. It brought poor luck to say goodbye before a duel. They would keep until the fight finished and he came out alive.

Morgan made her way to the stand where Isolde's father sat. She chose not to speak to him, putting on an offended front as any daughter would when her father elected to marry her off to the strongest set of muscle. The sickness returned, churning and thick in her stomach, and the second symptom of the poison, a raging headache, pulsed behind her eyes.

In his wisdom, or perhaps for lack of words, the king did not break the silence. She stood at the barrier between the royal dais and the arena, watching men gather on the field. She placed a hand on her head and rubbed, distracting herself from the pain.

"So many," she muttered. There had to be over a hundred of them.

"You are well-admired, my dear," King Angeus said, taking her words for permission to talk. She said nothing in response. A servant arrived, bowing to both Morgan and King Angeus before proffering a carved wooden box. Morgan hesitated.

"For me?"

"They hope you will remember their gifts and deny the winner his due." The king spat off to one side. "Others look on it as good fortune, as if they could trick fate into making them the winner."

"From Sir Tramtrist, milady," the servant said, bowing as he left.

Another servant arrived, two such gifts in hand. Morgan gestured to an empty place, and the servants left them, informing her of the names of knights who had bestowed the gifts.

Names spun in Morgan's head as she watched, still holding the wooden box, until two dozen gifts were laid around her. Most of them appeared to be jewelry, though she saw several bolts of cloth. Five of the gifts came from one familiar name, Morgan noticed; the Saracen, Sir Palamides.

"Cocky bastard, that one," her father growled. "Don't think I enjoy this business any more than you, Isolde. The man who wins you better not be a dog."

Morgan lifted the lid of the wooden box she held, the one from Tristan. The carvings were beautiful and intricate, decorating the outside and inside of the box in a way that was both simple and ornate. Emotion welled up inside of her and she snapped the lid shut, then buried the box among the other gifts, throwing a garish bracelet on top for good measure.

She'd noticed that Tristan fancied her, but until now she had fooled herself into believing it was friendship. Her face heated. She acted like a lovesick milkmaid who blushed at every passing flirt from the stable boys.

No, she was an imposter who fell in love with kings.

Arthur's face, with a quick smile and those brilliant blue eyes flashed into her memory. She expected pain but felt a mere echo. Arthur as she knew him, and her chance to be with him, was gone. He would want her to be happy, wouldn't he?

Her heart swelled within her chest, practically bursting with the assurance that, yes, Arthur would wish her every happiness she could find in this life.

Sir Tristan was neither king nor stable boy. He was so different from any of the men she had known; could she dare to hope that this time, this one would be right?

"You have an admirer." The low voice of the queen behind her sent a chill up Morgan's spine. "Many, it would seem."

She passed Morgan and touched one of the necklaces, a beautiful pearl piece. She moved on to a delicate ruby necklace set in silver, touching her own throat as she fingered it. Morgan watched her, swallowed past the knot that rose in her throat, praying she wouldn't insist on seeing every gift for herself.

Queen Eithne picked up the ruby necklace and brought it to Morgan, gesturing for her to turn around. Morgan lifted her blonde hair away from her neck, allowing the queen to clasp the necklace, skin crawling when the queen's fingernails brushed the back of her neck.

Another servant, a young, blonde-haired page, ran up to the dais, huffing. "Princess Isolde, Sir Palamides has gifted you a horse. A stallion from the best stock in the Middle East, milady. It is set up in the stables. He wanted you to know it was from him." Morgan stared at him, stunned.

"Pay the page for his trouble, dear, and send him on his way," Queen Eithne said.

Morgan stammered her thank you and pressed a coin into his hand, then fell into the seat on the king's left-hand side. A horse? He had gifted her a horse? That man was...well, what Isolde's father had said. A cocky bastard.

She looked out over the gathered crowd of armored men, noticing some of them wore nothing more than leather; those would be the lads of poorer lords and chieftains. Others wore chainmail and various bits of well-used and hand-me-down armors.

Only about a dozen full knights had shield and sword and the entire ensemble; Sir Tristan and Sir Palamides were among these. They would likely be among the lead competitors. Morgan sat up and strained her eyes, trying to see who had come and whether any of them were from Camelot.

Yes, she saw Sir Kay and Sir Gawain. Sir Agravaine also stood nearby.

"There are several kings here, did you notice?" Queen Eithne gestured to the field. "The King with a Hundred Knights and the King of Scots are most notable among them." Her eyes seemed to flash, though with anger or jealousy, Morgan could not discern.

She was so caught up in thought, she almost missed the start of the melee. One moment they stood there, more than a hundred men, gripping weapons in sweaty hands and waiting for the horn, and then the king gestured, the horn sounded, and all hell broke loose.

Chaos of the worst kind erupted. Some men, having realized their lack of preparedness, fled the arena within moments, cowards who would not deign to show their faces again for some time.

Others tapped out, raising their weapon high and moving to the side of the field to wait out the melee with guilt-ridden hearts pounding in their chests. Guilt for the gratitude they felt at being alive, and for the cowardice they would be chastised or punished for on their return.

Morgan kept her eyes on the field, watching that streak of blue silk as it moved among the remaining competitors, whittling them down. Tristan avoided the others in armor, knowing they would be among the last and saving his energy for those fights later. Instead, he stayed in one place, fighting any who approached, swinging that huge sword only when he had to, even stopping to rest.

"Why is that knight out there, Isolde? Did you give him leave to fight?" Queen Eithne asked, watching the forty-odd men left.

The field attendants were trying to remove the dozen or so bodies that lay scattered about, but the fighting was too fierce. Sir Palamides had killed many of them himself, reckless and unrestrained with deadly skill.

"I could not stop him," Isolde said, watching as Tristan parried blows from two simultaneous attackers. "He insisted on participating."

"Well, he is holding his own. It seems you have made quite an impression on him," the king said. He sat back against his chair, hand stroking his short beard.

In the end, one man held out against Sir Gawain and Sir Kay for a rather long time, until at last he stumbled and one of the knights drew blood. The horn sounded, and twenty remaining men stepped up to the dais, some stepping over bodies.

The death count came to thirty-six, they told her. Her fingers clenched into fists, her jaw set. Thirty-six needless deaths. Dozens more with injuries. All for her hand—Isolde's hand—in marriage. Men did foolish things for women.

Tristan stood at the end of the line. He had spent hours without food or water in open melee combat. Morgan restrained her urge to rush to his side, but once King Angeus acknowledged the winners and announced the first match in the morning, Morgan fled the dais. She heard her mother requesting several servants to take the gifts to Isolde's room. How many of those men were dead now?

Morgan threw herself into a frenzy. She ordered food for Tristan, then rushed to the infirmary and began pulling things off shelves.

In the midst of it all, Tristan limped in, Manuell supporting him.

"You are incredibly heavy, my friend," Manuell complained.

"At least we took off my armor first," Tristan replied, voice strained.

Morgan waited impatiently while he got settled on the bed, then handed him a plate of toasted bread topped with shredded meat and gravy.

"Eat," she demanded.

He smiled, but she wasn't having any of it. She stood and watched him, eyes glaring, while he ate, offering water when he asked. His eyes watched her, too, from the corners, and it seemed to her he deliberately slowed his eating, to keep her waiting.

Her temper grew to a boiling point, and then, in a swift moment, dissolved. She couldn't keep this up; the charade of being Isolde, eating poisoned food or no food at all, watching Tristan fight for his life in that ring...her frail nerves fell to pieces and she sobbed with no tears, just a horrible, choking pain blocking up her chest. She couldn't stop. She collapsed to her knees on the floor, hiccupping and trying to breathe, fully aware of the fool she made of herself.

The men stared at her, neither one sure what to do.

She caught Tristan's gesture to Manuell, who went around the side of the bed, passing Morgan, and picking up Tristan's harp.

Tristan settled it between his knees and played a tune that wove an enchantment through the air, singing straight to Morgan's heart. He didn't sing, only played, the haunting, beautiful melody vibrating through the air until her breath deepened and her heart stopped pounding.

Morgan calmed enough to pull herself into the chair behind her, rubbing her temples until the music trailed off, leaving the air with a final note.

Tristan said nothing, handing the harp back to Manuell, who returned it to its place beside the bed. Morgan feared to look up. She had made quite a fool of herself over this knight she had only known for a moon.

She slapped the tops of her legs with her hands, rubbing them across the smooth fabric of her dress, then stood and took a jar from the table beside her. She opened it and scooped the goopy substance out with her fingers, then gestured with her head at Tristan, who sighed and stripped off his cloth undershirt, gritting his teeth when his arms went over his head. Bruises covered his body.

Manuell stood to the side, wincing as he watched Morgan apply the salve to his friend's back.

"One would think you were the injured one," Tristan said to the Hispanic sailor.

"No offense, mi compadre, but I would not do that for any woman."

Tristan laughed, and Morgan felt a smile spread on her face. "That feels nice, Isolde. What is it? It is tingling, almost cold."

Manuell's eyes widened. "Oh, man, she's trying to kill you."

Morgan laughed at that. "No, it is wintergreen. It will dull the pain and help the bruises heal."

"It is getting hot, now," Tristan said, rolling his shoulders, face in a grimace. "It is the strangest sensation. Are you certain it is safe?"

"I d'be fixing you up, sir knight. No harm will come to you in my care." It was still strange to her how easily Isolde's Irish accent rolled off her tongue.

She put the pot of salve down and reached for a few more items. The kettle would be hot. She used a thick cloth to pull it from the fire and pour a cup of tea.

"Some for you, Manuell?"

"No offense, milady, but I think we all need something stronger than tea."

"Your friend does not get to drink tonight," Morgan said, adding a spoon of honey to the steaming cup and stirring. "He must be sober and clear-minded for tomorrow."

"I, for one, will enjoy the taverns, then," Manuell declared. He bid them both a good evening, then slipped away.

Morgan brought the cup to Tristan. "Drink this."

"It is scalding," Tristan said, indignant. His grin told her he teased her, as usual. He took a sip and made a face, then set it beside himself on the bed.

"I want to look at your side," Morgan said.

He hesitated, then lifted his left arm. Morgan hissed at the angry red wound. Several stitches had pulled out. She grabbed her materials from the table, bringing them to the bed. She numbed it with the wintergreen salve, then picked up a needle and gut thread.

"Hold still. This will hurt."

"I am a baby when it comes to this sort of thing," Tristan murmured.

She slid the needle through his skin, trying not to think too much about what she did.

Tristan sucked air through his teeth, muscles trembling as she stitched.

Finishing the last stitch, Morgan cut the thread with a knife. "I cannot guarantee that will hold with what you plan to do tomorrow, but at least you won't fall apart on the field."

He gazed at her, eyes shining. "Thank you, Isolde."

Morgan couldn't explain the irritation that rose inside of her at his use of the name. She busied herself about putting things away, moving back and forth between the bed and the herb shelves and table several times before Tristan caught her arm with his hand.

"I mean it. Thank you."

"I didn't save your life so you could lose it in this foolish tournament," she snapped, pulling her arm free.

"I am doing this to repay you for your kindness," Tristan said.

"You do not need to repay me," Morgan said, gesturing wildly. "I have always done this for free." At least, that is what she had gathered in her few weeks as Isolde. The woman must be a saint. Morgan was not.

Tristan reached out and grabbed her hand, bringing her close.

Morgan's heart beat wildly, and her chest burned in a strange way.

"I know you are upset about me fighting, but can you accept that I want to repay you?" he asked, voice low.

Her mind panicked; memories flashed through. Arthur. Mordred. Not ready. Morgan licked her lips, freezing her muscles, afraid to move. Afraid not to move.

"Isolde."

The queen's voice. Morgan spun around as Tristan released her, heart pounding in her ears, face burning in the darkened room lit by the fire in the grate giving off its glowing orange light.

"You did not show up for dinner."

"I was tending to Sir Tr-Tramtrist's injuries."

The queen's eyes narrowed, then she smiled. "Of course, you were. Is he well enough to leave yet?

"He d'be well enough," Morgan said, sparing Tristan a glance.

The queen reached out a hand. "Then come with me, darling. We will get you something to eat, since you missed a meal. You must be starving."

Starving, yes. For a poisoned meal, no. She hadn't fallen asleep today, but with another toxic dose running through her bloodstream she would no doubt find it impossible to stay awake tomorrow. During the tournament.

What if she missed Tristan's duels? What if he died? Morgan swallowed past the dryness in her throat. She looked one last time at Sir Tristan.

"Do you have all you need?"

His hand twitched at his side, and she could see the concern, the warning in his eyes. *Don't go*, they seemed to say.

She shook her head, subtle enough to avoid suspicion.

"Aye, I am well enough to fall asleep. My thanks to you, Princess Isolde."

Though it pained her, Morgan nodded, then turned away, moving towards where the queen stood in the open doorway. The queen was unstable, to say the least.

Morgan's escape plan, she realized now, was incomplete. Once Tristan won, hopefully, and announced that he would not marry her, how would she get away? Have a horse ready and gallop off somewhere? What about Tristan? Would she ever see him again?

The queen's cold hand took hers, leading her away from the infirmary.

A pale glow shone in the darkness of the hall. Her mark, the phoenix, shining as a silver beacon beneath her tunic dress. She put her hand up, blocking the light, though the queen made no indication she had seen it.

Queen Eithne didn't speak until they entered Isolde's quarters. A meal of meat with gravy beside a slice of bread, such as she had served Sir Tristan, sat on the table beside her scrying bowl. The broken yew wand and crystal were gone. Morgan swallowed hard. She forgot to remove them in her rush to get to the bout that morning. A careless, foolish, deadly mistake.

She moved to sit in the chair, but the queen stopped her, fingernails digging into Morgan's shoulder from behind.

"Articles of spell casting were found in your room. Who were you scrying?" The queen asked with a low, dangerous voice.

Morgan licked her lips. "No one. Just practicing. I was unsuccessful."

"Unlikely. The crystal and wand were broken. Why?"

"The connection was tenuous. I got frightened and the power surged." It wasn't entirely a lie.

The queen's grip loosened, and Morgan stumbled forward, her momentum released. She stopped herself on the back of the chair and sat, staring numbly at the meal before her. How could she eat without ingesting the poison? No doubt the queen would stay and watch her.

"Eat, daughter. Satiate your hunger, then rest. Tomorrow your knight will fight for you. You wouldn't want to miss that, would you?"

With a smirk on her narrow face, the queen closed Morgan's chamber door. The latch clicked with finality.

Though her stomach rumbled, Morgan only dared reach for the bread. They most likely powdered the poison, stirring it into the gravy where it would dissolve and go unnoticed. Besides, since eating non-poisoned food again, she found that the poison had a bitter aftertaste. One bite of the bread would tell her what she needed to know.

She bit into the crusty bread, rolling it around on her tongue as she chewed, then swallowed. Nothing but the nutty flavor of the bread. She finished the thick slice, her belly hollow with hunger afterwards.

Morgan unfastened her belt and pulled the tunic off over her head.

A glimmer caught her eye in the mirror. The phoenix. Even in the low torchlight, Morgan could see it had changed. The tips of the wings gleamed gold, instead of silver.

It turns gold when the Rite of the Heart is complete, Morgan remembered. She touched the new gold edges of the bird on her chest. What had she done to make that happen?

Confused, she pulled a clean shift over her head and crawled into bed, her head spinning with ideas until, at last, she drifted into a dream-tossed slumber.

CHAPTER THIRTEEN

When out of vision and desire was wrought
The sudden sin that from the living thought
Leaps a live deed and dies not: then there came
On that blind sin swift eyesight like a flame
Touching the dark to death, and made her mad
With helpless knowledge that too late forbade
What was before the bidding: and she knew
How sore a life dead love should lead her through
To what sure end how fearful; and though yet
Nor with her blood nor tears her way be wet
And she look bravely with set face on fate,
Yet she knows well the serpent hour at wait
Somewhere to sting and spare not;
"The Sailing of the Swallow," from "Tristram of Lyonesse"
by Algernon Charles Swinburne

Tristan slammed the visor of his helm down and stormed onto the field. He had made such a fool of himself with Isolde last night. All that mush-talk, trying to tell her how he felt, had clearly failed. He was an absolute fool to think she felt anything for him after these short weeks.

He adjusted his hands on his sword, the unfamiliarity of the grip putting him off.

This afternoon he faced a short, burly man who wore rusted chainmail. Tristan had watched him fight in the arena yesterday; he defeated his opponent with a fierce fighting style, using a mace to bash his opponent to the ground. What was his name again?

Tristan should've been afraid, but he only managed more anger as his words from last night, and Isolde's reaction to them, swirled around in his mind.

Never go to a fight angry, his mentors taught him. Despite their differences, they all believed that one thing. Clear your mind.

Tristan heard his breath, rapid and loud in his helm. A horn blew, and the man charged.

Tristan dodged, letting the man sail past him, stumbling at his unmet momentum. Tristan whirled in time to parry the counterattack as the man—Sir Gardon, he remembered—rushed him again. The strike rattled his arm.

Tristan gritted his teeth and thrust the mace off his sword, backing up two steps. He swept in with three quick and short thrusts, each one knocked aside by the mace. If that weapon struck Tristan, well, first blood being drawn and losing the tournament would be the least of his worries. Fortunately, he held the advantage with a longer weapon.

Tristan darted in again, making quick footwork in to strike at Sir Gardon's mace-hand, then back. He did it again, coming from the other side. Each time the man moved out of the way enough that Tristan's sword scraped chainmail, rather than cut.

His breath came in gasps. The salve Isolde gave him worked wonders on his sore muscles but did little for his overall state, still healing from the battle with Sir Marhaus.

Tristan gritted his teeth and settled into a defensive stance as the mace-wielder came swinging. His sword struck the dense metal handle, a block he felt to his rattling teeth. He stabbed and struck, but didn't punch through the mail, as his opponent leapt back.

Tristan grabbed his blade in both hands and swung toward the man's mace-arm again. This time, moving backwards did not work out in his favor. Tristan's sword sliced into the outside of the thumb above the man's wrist.

Sir Gardon howled and dropped the mace with a thud to the dirt, gripping his injured hand as blood flowed down and dripped to the ground. The horn sounded. Tristan held up his arm, fist pumped into the air at the victory.

The crowd cheered, and Tristan glanced up at the dais, looking for Isolde. She wasn't there. The smile left his face. Where could she be? Had he offended her so much that she refused to attend the tournament he fought to win for her sake?

He retreated to the tent loaned to him by King Angeus. He shared it with three knights from King Angeus's own court. Two of them had been eliminated the first day. The third man approached as Tristan entered the tent, clapping him on his shoulder with a grin, partially hidden by his mustache.

"Good work, Sir Tramtrist."

Tristan nodded. He didn't feel like socializing. He went to his side of the tent, where Manuell stood waiting for him, practically bouncing with joy on the heels of his feet.

"We will bring that lady home with us yet, eh my friend?" Manuell said, beginning to unclip the armor.

Tristan grunted in reply, and Manuell caught his mood, falling into silence. Tristan had fought twice already that morning, winning both. He didn't have another bout until later that evening. Bouts were being fought faster than anticipated; likely the winners would be decided tonight, an entire day early.

Tristan lifted his arms with care, trying not to stretch his side too much. The new stitches itched terribly, but at least he didn't have to worry about the wound reopening in battle.

Manuell pulled his mail and padding off, setting them aside. Tristan squatted a few times, loosening his muscles. He stretched his arms and legs, rolled his shoulders and neck.

Thank God above he hadn't been struck by that mace; through his armor, it could have cracked several ribs or given him a bruise that would last months, not to mention what could have happened if the spikes had punctured the metal plate, giving Isolde more patching to do. He didn't hate that idea, even if he desperately wanted to avoid the circumstance that would give him more personal time with her.

Cheers erupted outside. Had another bout ended already? "Who was that, Manuell?"

"Sir Palamides and the King with a Hundred Knights." Manuell grimaced. "That one should have lasted longer. This Sir Palamides is a hard one, Sir Tr-Tramtrist." Manuell stumbled over the false name, glancing to the other side of the tent where King Angeus's knight spoke with his squire after suiting up for his bout.

"He has won all three of his bouts this morning, and in less time than it takes a man to suit up or take off his armor. He is swift and dangerous. You had better watch your head."

"I am not worried."

"You are never worried when you ought to be," Manuell tossed back, setting the last piece of Tristan's armor on the pile. "But I can tell that something does worry you. Is it the queen?"

Tristan shook his head and sat down, rubbing his sweaty forehead across his arm.

Manuell nodded, mouth posed thoughtfully. "It is the princess, then. Mi compadre, have you ever been with a woman?"

Tristan's head shot up. "What?"

"It is okay to tell me, I will not make fun. I myself have been with dozens of women, and then I settled with my Rosita. She is a flower. The one that makes you stay, that is the one worth fighting for," Manuell said. Tristan snorted. "You do not believe me? Look at yourself. Wounded, willing to risk yourself for a señorita you have known for a fortnight? It is love."

"I will be honest, Manuell. I do not know what love is." Tristan laid down on the bench, arm across his eyes to block the light out.

He fell asleep like that, listening to the roar and groan of the crowd as they responded to the happening of the next bout. He didn't wake until a cheer sounded outside, and he jolted upright, glancing around the tent. The sun had shifted, and the shadows covered the opposite side of the tent. It disoriented him.

Tristan stood, groaning, and Manuell burst into the tent, urging him to don his armor. The time had come for his next bout. The sailor-turned-squire alternated between putting on bits of armor and forcing pieces of chicken into Tristan's mouth. He hadn't eaten all day.

"Who is it? Who is the opponent?" Tristan asked, voice muffled as Manuell tugged the padded shirt over his head and arms.

"It is Sir Palamides," Manuell said, gritting his teeth as he sped through fastening each catch of Tristan's armor. "He has cheated his way to the top, to be sure. Each of his bouts has been fought dirtier than the last. Keep your head clear, my friend."

Tristan double-checked his armor. It would be a terrible disadvantage to have a catch come undone in this fight. The silk scarf from Isolde came last. He didn't much hold to luck winning a battle, but seeing the favor on his arm stoked a fire in his breast that made him stand taller, despite the ache in his side from the still-healing wound.

Manuell handed him his sword and pushed him from the tent, Tristan chewing rapidly on a final mouthful of chicken and taking a swig from the waterskin that Manuell held for him. The food and drink gave him a much-needed boost of energy, and to loosen up his muscles, he jogged into the arena.

The sunset cast a low, orange glow over the field. Tristan shaded his eyes and looked to the dais. Isolde's vacant seat stood out sorely beside the king. Would she stay angry at him this long? Or had something happened to her?

The queen did not sit in her seat, either, and Tristan's heart beat faster in his chest.

He adjusted his grip on his sword and the horn sounded, loud and clear through the near-silent arena. Sir Palamides, in gleaming armor and a helmet that revealed the lower half of his face, came swinging. He had defeated kings to be here, and Tristan could hear the shorter man growling.

Tristan swung to defend against the fierce attack. Sword struck sword, clanging, then back and striking again and again, relentlessly pressing Tristan back until he thrust him against the barrier between the arena and the dais.

The castle court gasped at the fight taking place immediately before them. Tristan grunted and parried a blow that came close to his face.

His side split with lack of air. He took a deep breath in and thrust his opponent back, then came in swinging with his own attack. He tried to match the Saracen's fighting style, pressing the other man back. His arms felt heavy. He had to end this fast. He wouldn't last more than a few minutes on this field, especially if the Saracen tried anything underhanded.

Thrusting his blade point forward, Tristan drove Sir Palamides into defense, holding him there until the Saracen smashed his sword downward, tipping the point of Tristan's blade into the dirt and making him stumble.

Sir Palamides raised his blade for a final thrust, but Tristan parried. His blade whistled toward the knight again, slicing through the edge of the Saracen's exposed ear.

Tristan blinked at the cheers that erupted around him.

Sir Palamides knelt on the ground, pulling off his helm and yelling to the sky, fists clenched. Whether in pain or in fury at his loss, Tristan wasn't sure.

Panting, the defeated man stared up at Tristan. “You have won the day, Sir Tramtrist. I am at your mercy. My life is yours.”

“The tournament is to first blood. Quarter is not mine to give.”

“I am defeated and ashamed of how I have acted. Please...” The Saracen crawled on his knees towards Tristan, hands raised up, clenched together before him. “Give me what my lack of honor deserves.”

Tristan stared at the man’s desperate, sweaty face. He had no quarrel with him. Men did and said foolish, prideful things when they felt too confident, and the Saracen had more cause than others to be boastful and try to prove himself. But perhaps he had something to learn of humility.

“Very well, then. Sir Palamides, there are two conditions you must hold to. The first is that you will not wear armor or bear a weapon, except in self-defense, for a twelvemonth.” Tristan expected anger, but the Saracen had already begun removing his armor, even as Tristan added the second condition. “And you will not approach the princess Isolde again.”

The anguish on the Saracen’s face told Tristan the knight would hold to that until the day he died, and a strange sense of satisfaction overcame Tristan.

Blood streamed down Sir Palamides’s neck as he stood and stripped his armor, not waving his squires over for help, but struggling on his own. It almost made Tristan feel guilty, seeing that man stripped of his armor as if it were his dignity, but it was what the man had asked for, and Tristan had a feeling that nothing short of death would satisfy the prideful knight more.

Sir Tristan approached the dais, stopping an appropriate distance away, then knelt on the ground, bowing his head before the king of Mumhan.

King Angeus shook off his stupor and stood. “Your victor!” he hollered.

The watching crowd erupted in a wild, earth-shaking cheer, stomping their feet and waving colors flags.

“That was the fastest tournament I have ever seen fought,” the king said to Tristan.

Tristan stood, the weight of exhaustion pulling at him, threatening to drag him down to collapse.

“I, myself, have never seen the likes of it,” Tristan said. He nodded towards the empty chairs. “Where are your wife and daughter? Did the tournament not please them?”

King Angeus’s shoulders drooped. “My wife informs me that Isolde has taken ill. I…I fear for her. After all my planning, I…” The burly man’s voice broke, and he turned his chin to his shoulder, looking away.

Tristan stood and came near, placing a hand on the king’s shoulder. “I know your fear, Your Majesty.”

The king glanced up, tears shining at the corners of his eyes, and smiled, placing his hand on Tristan’s opposite shoulder. “But now, I have less reason to fear, yes? You are the victor, and you may claim her hand and take her away from here. Though her absence will bring me grief, her freedom, bought by you, will bring me joy.”

Tristan took a deep breath. “I have indeed bought her freedom, Majesty, and I return that freedom to her. I will not claim her hand against her will. She is her own, and I ask that she be allowed to go whithersoever she will from this point on.”

King Angeus's eyes widened, and he sputtered. "In all my days, I never knew I could meet a man like you, Sir Tramtrist. Please, rest here and prepare for the departure to your homeland with my full aid at your back."

Tristan bowed at the waist, strength faltering as he straightened.

"You must bathe, Sir Tramtrist. I will have a servant prepare water for you."

"I intended to find your daughter first, Your Majesty, and see that she is well."

"And you will, good knight. But not stinking as you are, if you don't mind me saying."

Tristan managed a smile through his worry. He wouldn't linger getting cleaned up and would ask a servant to inquire after Isolde's health.

God willing, he would find Isolde and have the chance to apologize to her and tell her of her newfound freedom. It would be a new start for the Irish princess. She might even consider coming with him to Cornwall.

The thought brought a smile to Tristan's face. He walked through the crowd to his tent, congratulated the whole way by knights and common folk alike.

Manuell stood grinning from ear to ear as he moved to relieve Tristan of his armor. A page was sent, and Tristan gave the boy a coin and the request for a hot bath and any news on Isolde's health.

An hour later, after fighting his way through the celebrating crowd and turning down the proffered hands of unmarried village girls, Tristan soaked in a deep bathtub filled with steaming water and herbs. Their heady scent wafted through the air, making Tristan's mind drift off with relaxation.

Across the room, Manuell cleaned and polished Tristan's armor and sword, making it fit for the next time Tristan would need it. Which, preferably, would be a long time from now. The Spaniard chattered as he worked, and Tristan leaned his head back against the tub, murmuring the appropriate responses as needed.

The door to the infirmary opened. Tristan glanced up, feeling exposed, hoping it wasn't Isolde.

"Queen Eithne," he stammered, splashing water over the side of the tub.

The woman stalked into the room, eyes burning, face murderous. Manuell scrambled to his feet. The queen's hands came out from behind her, holding an enormous, gleaming sword with a shattered tip. Tristan's heart stopped.

"For my brother!" the queen howled. She rushed toward the tub, sword high in the air, held ready to run Tristan through. Tristan scrambled, slipping in the tub trying to escape, but he couldn't move fast enough. She would—

Brown arms encircled the queen's, pinning them to her side. With a deft twist of her wrist, Manuell disarmed her, broken sword clattering to the ground.

Queen Eithne screamed and writhed, trying to get free. She bucked against Manuell's grip, stomping and kicking and making a racket like feral cats fighting.

Tristan leapt from the tub and grabbed a blanket, wrapping his naked, dripping body in it.

"I have no quarrel with you, Queen Eithne," he said.

"You killed my brother," she spat, "and then you dare seek quarter here? You are a filthy, traitorous liar." She went still in Manuell's arms.

Guards poured in from the hall, weapons held at the ready, pointed at Tristan and Manuell.

"Arrest the knight, Sir Tristan," the queen barked. "Release me," she snarled at Manuell, who immediately let her go and stepped to the side of the room, eyes wide.

The guards held Tristan at spear-point while he quickly dressed in his old, tattered clothes, and marched him from the room.

"Tell Isolde," Tristan said as he passed Manuell, "then leave. Tell the captain to go." He swallowed past his fear as he said it. He could not in good conscience risk their lives by asking them to stay.

"He will not go without you," Manuell called out after him.

The Irish soldiers led him down several floors and through a long corridor, until they came to a wide room where half a dozen men lined the walls, each chained far enough away from the others so they could not touch. They stopped before an empty space near the end, and clapped a set of heavy irons on Tristan's ankles and wrists, and an iron collar on his neck.

He stood, though he felt like collapsing, and stared straight ahead, ignoring the tortured howls of those around him. He had done nothing wrong. The duel he fought with Sir Marhaus demanded his death or his opponent's. Now, to convince the Irish king and queen of that.

Tristan swallowed. For the first time since arriving, fear crept into his heart. Fear that he would be killed before he had a chance to speak to Isolde. Fear that she wouldn't return his feelings, even if he did get the opportunity to tell her. And fear that the queen, in her fury, had killed the princess with her poisons while he fought in the arena.

The thoughts weighed heavier than the chains as he waited in the prison for his fate to be decided.

CHAPTER FOURTEEN

So Tristram looked on Iseult face to face
And knew not, and she knew not. The last time—
The last that should be told in any rhyme
Heard anywhere on mouths of singing men
That ever should sing praise of them again;
The last hour of their hurtless hearts at rest
The last that peace should touch them, breast to breast,
The last that sorrow far from them should sit,
This last was with them, and they knew not it.
"The Sailing of the Swallow," from "Tristram of Lyonesse"
by Algernon Charles Swinburne

Morgan's heart pounded as she flew through the corridors and down two flights of stairs. Tristan had done it. He had won the tournament and freed her from any obligation to marry. He had no idea how much that truly meant to her; to Morgan and to Isolde both.

Now they held him imprisoned, and it was her fault.

How had she slept so long? The Queen and Aideen must have used a new poison, one she didn't recognize. She ate only the bread, but when she woke, the tournament had ended and Tristan was imprisoned.

Queen Eithne had gone Pict-warrior on him in his post-tournament bath, or so the servants whispered as Morgan rushed through the halls, following the directions to the dungeons.

If she hadn't complained about the tournament, he would be a free man by now, sailing on his way to Cornwall. She was a selfish fool.

She rounded the last corner and charged down the corridor to the holding cell. A guard blocked her way with a spear, holding it out across the entrance to the room where, beyond, she could see men lining the walls, all in shackles, filthy, long, ratted hair, dirt and beards obscuring their faces, all except their eyes, some feral, some empty, as if the man inside was dead.

Among them, standing tall and stoic, head forward, jaw set in anger, was Tristan. Morgan looked to the guard, whose face was stern.

"Ye aren't allowed ter see him, milady; queen's orders."

Morgan reached into her pocket and took out the small bag of coins, pressing it into the guard's hand.

"Please, for love's sake," she said. She said it at first to convince him, then realized the truth behind it and her mouth went dry. The hope of his returned affection swelled within her, making her throat constrict.

The guard considered the coin, weighing it in his hand, then pocketed it and nodded to her, moving his spear aside. Morgan walked through the center of the room, keeping her head high amidst the howls from the men. Some strained at their chains, reaching for her, growling and snarling like beasts.

Tristan's face became furious.

"Silence, fiends!" he bellowed, and even with the heavy iron chain around his neck, hands, and ankles, Morgan thought he looked magnificent.

Chains rattled as men shuffled, most crawling to lean back against the dank walls. Morgan approached him, taking his hands in hers.

"I cannot believe you did it," she said, her voice coming out sharp, all of her stress and anger pointing at him. She took a deep breath. "I was poisoned, I couldn't be there, I am sorry."

"Your freedom matters to me," he said gruffly, and she could tell he held back tears. Her emotional knight. He reminded her of Arthur, with his kindness. She had never encountered his ability to feel, and to show those feelings, in any other man.

"I wish that meant more," she said. "My father is losing the argument with my mother that your wish for my freedom should be honored. She claims you have no honor, having killed her brother. He says that is why you have honor, because you fought for your king." She hesitated. "I cannot stay here, Tristan. And yet, I cannot leave while you remain imprisoned."

"You must," he urged, blue eyes gazing into hers. She could see the urgency in them but could not bring herself to feel it. "My imprisonment will hold them distracted. You could leave."

"And go where?"

"Go to the captain. Tell him I said not to wait for me. He will take you wherever you want to go. Go to Camelot."

Morgan gave a hollow laugh at the irony of his suggestion. He did not yet know her true identity, nor why she could not go to Camelot. She shook her head, looking up into his face and trying to memorize every part of it.

"I wish I had a chance to know you better," she said.

"And I wish you would leave, and at least give me relief in death knowing you are safe," he replied.

"You're a fool," she whispered. "This afternoon, my father is having you brought before the court for a trial. You may yet be free."

"What about you? How will you escape?"

"Do not be concerned for me. Focus on getting out of here with your head." The coldness in her voice couldn't be helped. She had to distance herself, to think on how she could escape, and to make sure he made it onto that ship. Morgan turned away, feeling his eyes on her back following her out.

This place held nothing for her now. She could go anywhere— anywhere but Camelot. Anywhere but the one place Morgan wanted to be. Where Isolde dallied with Arthur in Morgan's body. Where Elaina wove her tapestry and waited for someone to free her.

Where could Morgan go? She paced back and forth in the infirmary. It felt more private and more welcoming than Isolde's room, though it seemed tomb-like without Sir Tristan in the bed at the end.

The old woman, Cara, had passed over a week ago. Medics cared for injured men from the tournament in a large tent beside the arena, and so the vacant beds stood sentinel, the only witnesses to Morgan's indecision.

She could go north, to Northumberland. She could go to France. She could go farther, to the lands of the Saracen knight she had met the other day. She would go to Avalon, but for the recency of the spell cast on her. The residue wouldn't fade for months yet, and until it did, she would be prevented from finding the sacred isle.

She could go to Cornwall, with Sir Tristan. She knew he eventually ended up as a knight of the round table, at least in her own time. Would that history remain true if she followed him? Would fate lead her back to Camelot after all? Better to stay far away.

But her heart pulled her towards another chance at love, and perhaps the Goddess meant for her to discover it. True love, after all the heartache her life had held. Fear repelled her from entertaining that thought too long.

"It is time, Princess Isolde." Aideen stood in the doorway. Loyal to her mother, perhaps, but still enough Isolde's servant to inform her when the trial started as she had requested.

Morgan held her head high. She wore a white tunic, blue and gold threading her belt, with a blue cloak to fend off the chill. The golden circlet on her brow made her feel regal. She wanted to look her best; it helped her feel confident that she might persuade Isolde's father to release Tristan.

She wasn't familiar with Irish law, but anywhere else, with a just and fair king, Tristan would never have been imprisoned. Even with the queen controlling most of his political maneuvers, King Angeus maintained his sense of honor. She relied on using it to defeat the queen's prejudices and unstable tendencies.

Morgan saw Tristan first, noticing his hands bound before him. She didn't see Queen Eithne, her chair sat empty.

King Angeus noticed Morgan staring and reached for her hand. Morgan offered it. "Your mother is resting. She has had quite an ordeal," her father whispered, his tone almost...conspiratorial.

Her eyes widened. “Did you…?” she stopped herself before she could say it aloud. It would not do well to speak of drugging the queen in the midst of the court.

She faced those gathered to hear Tristan’s fate, mostly his ship’s captain and crew, including that man who acted as his squire, Manuell, and King Angeus’s soldiers. Everyone else enjoyed a feast set out of doors. She found it a mercy King Angeus did this quietly.

“What have you to say in defense of yourself?” King Angeus’s rich voice boomed out into the room. His face held a stern mask as Tristan took a single step forward.

Tristan raised his head to face the king, expression neither too lofty, nor betraying any fear or uncertainty. “I did battle for the love of my uncle, King Mark, and for love of the country of Cornwall, King Angeus. It gives me no pleasure to have had part in Sir Marhaus’s death. Your own hand signed the agreement over the battle we fought that our countries might remain at peace, and I should not suffer for that, having won a fair fight. Your men and mine can testify to that.” He nodded to the men lining the hall.

King Angeus rubbed his chin with his fingers. “My wife lays ill, spent by her encounter with you. She is devastated, and understandably angry. You lied to us, seeking our aid in a time of mourning the one you killed.”

“My only debt is to your hospitality,” Tristan replied. “You have no right to my life, not when Sir Marhaus gave his life willingly in the name of your country.”

“So help me God, you did as a knight should. It was your part to do, for your quarrel,” King Angeus agreed, and Morgan’s shoulders relaxed. “However, I may not allow you to stay. It would distress my wife and her kin greatly.”

Tristan's face broke out in a grateful smile. "I thank you for your goodness, your Majesty," he turned to Morgan, eyes connecting with hers, "and that of milady, your daughter. You may yet win more by my life than by my death. I pray you honor my right to her hand as champion of this contest."

Morgan's heart beat faster. As much as she hated being bandied about as a prize to be won, it held her best chance at escape. And she trusted Tristan; trusted him enough to believe that if she desired, he would release her as he had promised.

"You would have me banish my only daughter with you? I will never see her again."

"So long as your queen insists on treating me as a criminal, that may well be."

The king considered for a long moment. The few men that stood by shuffled their feet, and one coughed in the silence. King Angeus dragged a hand down his face.

"I am a selfish man, Sir Tristan, and find I cannot do as you ask. My wife's power is far greater than you know, and none could stop her wrath should she learn her daughter married the man who killed her brother. No, I will not allow it, though it pains me to make this decision."

"I understand," Tristan replied.

He nodded to Manuell, who produced the parchment bearing the broken seal of Cornwall. He presented it to King Angeus with a bow.

"I presented this to Sir Marhaus before our bout. King Mark wished to avoid bloodshed, if possible. Sir Marhaus refused on your behalf."

The king opened the missive. It was far enough away that Morgan could not make out the words. She searched Tristan's impassive expression.

The king's eyebrows raised as he read, and he glanced at Morgan, then Tristan. "This missive is asking for my daughter's hand to be given in marriage to King Mark of Cornwall."

Morgan's heart plummeted. A knot formed in her throat, and her hands gripped the arms of her chair. How could he? How could he do exactly what he had fought that tournament to prevent? She wanted to scream and rage at him; instead, she let her fury ruminate inside of her.

"I see you have my kingdom's interests at heart, Sir Tristan. I presume you would accompany my daughter to Cornwall yourself?"

"Yes, Your Majesty," Tristan replied, voice wooden. He deliberately avoided Morgan, his eyes staring straight forward.

"And how would you guarantee her safe arrival there, Sir Tristan?"

"With my life, Your Majesty." He turned his blue eyes to Morgan's, at long last. His entire face trembled with effort to stay composed. "I have proven my loyalty to her in the tournament these days past. I also promise you that I shall, in all places, be my lady's, your daughter's, servant and knight. I shall always protect her, putting her life before my own. I shall never fail her."

Morgan felt her lips begin to quiver. She couldn't do this; she couldn't stay quiet. She opened her mouth to speak, but Tristan glared, stopping her words in her throat.

He is trying to save me, she reminded herself.

An understanding seemed to pass between King Angeus and Tristan. Morgan saw it as she watched them, an almost tangible thing that passed between them through their gaze.

King Angeus nodded, then motioned to an attendant, who brought a quill and inkwell. The king signed the parchment, then stamped it shut with a wax seal.

"Very well, Sir Tristan. Your life for my daughter's safety. It is a strange position you put me in, I am sure you can see. My daughter will be prepared; you must leave with all haste. One final warning, before you go."

The king took a deep breath. "I must hold you to your agreement. Should I receive word that she has not made it safely to the holding of King Mark, and if their marriage is not held forthwith, war will be waged upon Cornwall until no men remain to defend it." He gritted his teeth, and Morgan understood that the law constrained him to make this claim of war.

Her blood ran cold in her veins, her fingers numb from gripping the arms of her chair. If Tristan planned to run away with her, this would prevent it. They could not ignore the impending war that would start if they escaped together.

Tristan bowed, face impassive, then held out his manacled wrists. King Angeus waved and a guard came forward with the keys. Morgan sat still, briefly registering the clank of chains releasing.

"I take my leave to prepare our ship, and my men, at your grace," Tristan said.

"Several of my men will accompany you," King Angeus said, "to aid your preparations. Any rations or repairs you need, they can arrange for you to receive."

The king had wisdom. Cowardice, as well. He sent men less because Tristan and his men needed the help, and more because he needed some assurance that they wouldn't flee without his daughter. But he didn't know Tristan.

Morgan stared at the man, handsome despite his disheveled state, and she knew he would not leave without her. What if Isolde's father had not accepted King Mark's offer? Would Tristan have attempted to fight his way out with her? She wouldn't put it past him.

Tristan broke their gaze, accepting the newly sealed missive, from one of six soldiers that surrounded him and his men. He walked out without looking back. King Angeus dismissed the rest of the court with a wave of his hand, and the room emptied.

"Father?" Morgan said.

King Angeus sighed, rubbing down from his forehead to his chin with one hand. Then he looked at her, and Morgan recognized pain in his gaze.

"You realize I will not be able to attend your wedding? Your mother, she...needs me here."

"We both know that is only partially true," Morgan replied. "She is going to be furious that you've done this."

King Angeus smiled, the corners of his eyes crinkling. "Better I bear the brunt of her anger. You will slip from her grasp and be out of her reach forever."

He reached out and placed a hand tenderly beneath her chin. Morgan stiffened at the touch, but the king didn't notice.

He gazed at her. "My precious Isolde. I hope you remember me fondly, when all of this is over. I have tried to be a good father. There is much I will miss about you being sent away, but it is for the best."

"I..." Morgan swallowed hard. The ruddy face of her own father appeared in her mind. Had he known what her half-brothers, his sons, did to her all those years ago? At least King Angeus tried to help, even if his method was disagreeable. “Thank you, athair. I shall miss our rides together.”

King Angeus’s eyes welled up with tears, and he leaned forward, dragging her into an embrace, patting her back.

Morgan held him, feeling awkward. She had none of Isolde’s feelings for this man she called father. She didn’t even know whether Isolde liked him or despised him. So, she pretended, wishing she wasn’t being forced to live someone else’s life.

Eventually, the king sat back, wiping away the tears. “You are a good lass, Isolde. Not many would tolerate the blubbering of a fool like me.”

“I need to pack my things,” Morgan said.

King Angeus waved her off. Morgan went immediately to Isolde’s rooms. She froze at the sight of maids scurrying about the chamber, folding gowns, filling an enormous trunk with her things. She noticed Isolde’s medical journals were inside the trunk, thoughtfully wrapped in waterproof covering and tied with string.

“All is being made ready for you, Princess Isolde,” Aideen said from behind. The title sounded strange coming from the maid; she always called her Banphrionsa before. “Come, the queen has requested your presence in her chambers.”

Morgan hesitated. She didn’t have to go. In her heart she knew Isolde would say goodbye, even though the woman had tried to kill her. She was, after all, Isolde’s mother.

Morgan turned away and followed Aideen’s uneven gait down the corridor, turning a corner and coming to a stop before the door.

All this time the queen's chambers stood only doors away from Isolde's. Now, she stood before it, palms sweating, heart pounding. Would the queen demand she stay? Would she kill her on the spot? Every fiber of her being told her to run, to meet Tristan at the dock with nothing but the clothes on her back.

But instead, she watched as Aideen swung the door open, stepping inside before her and announcing her presence.Morgan moved into the room like a wraith drifting through a graveyard.

Queen Eithne looked pale as death, her matted red hair splayed out on the pillow around her. She lifted a thin hand up toward Morgan, and a smile, an actual smile, played at the edges of her lips. "My child, come here."

Morgan took a step closer, glancing at Aideen, who stood watching them, a smile of her own creeping across her otherwise dull face.

"Close, child. I will not bite you."

Morgan obliged, suppressing her instincts to run. She swallowed. "How are you feeling, Majesty?" She could not bring herself to call this woman 'mother'. She had a feeling Isolde would be in agreement.

Queen Eithne snorted. "How do you think I am feeling?" she snapped, sounding much more like herself as Morgan knew her. "I discovered my daughter is in love with the man who killed my brother, failed to exact my revenge, and then discovered that same daughter is planning to run off with my brother's killer and abandon me on my deathbed."

A snarl obscured any trace of the smile that grew on the queen's thin lips, and she pressed herself to sitting with trembling arms. "You betray me, daughter."

"I-I…" Morgan stuttered. What could she say?

"Do not speak!" the queen roared, hair quivering around her with her rage. "If I were not laid up so, I would beat some sense into your small mind. Does this King of Cornwall know of your feelings towards his knight? Do you plan to betray him before or after you warm his bed as his wife?" She spat the last word, like snake spitting venom. Morgan straightened her shoulders.

"And you pretend to be better than I?" Morgan said, stepping towards the queen, looming over her. "Did you think I wasn't aware of what you have been doing these past few months? I am leaving, Your Majesty, whatever you say. My life is my own to do with as I will." Morgan rushed through the last part, feeling every bit of the lie. Though she didn't think Isolde would begrudge Morgan escaping on her behalf.

"You have no hold on me, not like father. Someday, your anger will be your death." She turned on her heel, leaving the stunned queen gaping like a fresh-caught fish.

"Wait," the queen called out after her, voice rasping.

She cleared her throat. Morgan turned, hands clasping the cloak at her sides, eyes defiant. The queen motioned to Aideen, who held an amber-tinged wine bottle in her hand. She reached it out towards Morgan, who eyed the item, but didn't receive it.

"Tell me what it is," she said.

"A wedding gift," Queen Eithne croaked. She took a swig of water and continued, her voice smoother. "A love potion of the strongest kind, brewed by my grandmother for my mother, who, in turn, brewed some for me. Now I pass the same chance on to you."

Her eyes glittered as she gazed at Morgan. "Please accept it. Share a drink with your intended and you will be bound together with a love unshaken, unbroken, and unmatched. None will ever take him from you, and none will persuade you away from him into paths of infidelity and unhappiness."

Morgan considered the queen's face; she looked open and sounded sincere. "Did you ever share it with father?" she asked.

Given how the man tolerated his daughter's poisoning at his wife's hand, it seemed obvious now.

The queen's face froze. "I did," she said.

Morgan stared at the bottle again.

"If you truly intend to honor the arrangement that has been determined for you, then this gift of true love will give you happiness until the end of your days, no matter his temperament, no matter his looks or who he is. I will send it with Aideen. She will pack it in your things and be sure it makes it safely to Cornwall with you."

The statement, said so matter-of-factly, made Morgan's blood freeze. "Aideen...she is coming with me?"

The queen's eyes widened in shock. "Why, of course. I wouldn't leave you alone to fend for yourself in a foreign land. Consider it another gift. Aideen, I trust above all of our servants. I send her in my place."

I do not doubt that you do, Morgan thought, her fists tightening on her cloak. *Now you can be sure I will be killed.* She would deal with that situation later; perhaps an accident could be arranged, or...

A knock came at the door. Aideen set the bottle on a nearby table and opened the door. A bearded man, dressed in messenger's livery, stood at attention.

"Princess Isolde, the wagon is packed, and we are ready to depart. Sir Tristan and his men are eager to set out before dark."

Thank the Goddess. She pushed past Aideen into the hallway.

"Fare thee well, daughter," Isolde's mother called after her. Morgan didn't bother playing the role of a daughter distraught to be leaving her mother. She didn't wait for Aideen, either.

Instead, she passed the messenger and rushed down the hall, running from that amber-colored bottle and the Irish queen's sly smile.

The wagon and travel party indeed waited for her, practically at the steps of the castle.

King Angeus sat atop a black stallion, holding the reins of another, smaller mare. "I thought I would ride with you one last time, daughter."

It couldn't hurt. Morgan managed a smile and, gripping a fistful of the mare's brown mane in her fist, jumped and swung herself onto its back. Her skirts rode up to her knee, but her cloak covered her well enough that she didn't care. She would never see any of these people again.

Morgan made a show of waving to those bidding her farewell in the courtyard. Her last glimpse revealed Queen Eithne, standing at the window, watching her go. She waved. Morgan ignored her. She clicked her tongue and nudged the horse forward, following her father as he made his way down the winding stone pathway.

The keeper of the horse pulling the wagon that held her two trunks came after, and a dozen mounted and armed men surrounded them.

Aideen caught up to her on a chestnut mare a hand shorter than the one Morgan rode, cradling a bulging satchel in an almost motherly way. She noticed Morgan eyeing her and smiled. The woman didn't appear quite herself today.

Unsettled, Morgan looked away, gazing at the winding road ahead. In a few brief hours they would reach the shore. They faced days of sailing to the shore of Cornwall, and several more days of travel by foot before they reached Tintagel.

She had until then to find a way to escape Aideen and circumvent her marriage to the King of Cornwall.

CHAPTER FIFTEEN

And with light lips yet full of their swift smile,
And hands that wist not though they dug a grave,
Undid the hasps of gold, and drank, and gave,
And he drank after, a deep glad kingly draught:
And all their life changed in them, for they quaffed
Death; if it be death so to drink, and fare
As men who change and are what these twain were.
And shuddering with eyes full of fear and fire
And heart-stung with a serpentine desire.
"The Sailing of the Swallow," from "Tristram of Lyonesse"
by Algernon Charles Swinburne

"Damnit," Tristan cursed, knots slipping through his numb fingers. He re-tied the ropes holding down their provisions and belongings, cold making his breath puff out into the air.

The ship rocked as a strong wave picked it up and brought it back down. The gales blew strong today, stronger than yesterday. A furrowed brow seemed to have permanently etched itself onto the captain's brow.

He didn't like how the sun had set yesterday, or how the air smelled, or the way the ship tilted, or the lack of seabirds searching for fish among the waves. Some other sense told the experienced seafarer that no ship ought to be out on the sea tonight, and it made him unsettled, which made the crew jittery.

Tristan checked a final rope, then turned and looked for Isolde. It had become a habit. She occasionally asked one of the crew a question, but she avoided him. He could only keep track of her by sitting across the ship and watching. Why wouldn't she speak to him?

Of course, he knew why, but it wasn't right. He had saved her life. Twice. Why did he feel like she deserved an apology?

As if hearing his thoughts, Isolde glanced towards him, her blonde hair damp from ocean spray, her woolen cloak collecting water droplets on its felted surface. She looked away almost immediately, towards the woman, her servant, sitting some distance away, clutching that odd-shaped package like an infant.

Tristan considered them for a moment, then made his way across the ship, passing Isolde and stopping before Aideen.

"May I sit here?" he asked loudly, gesturing beside her. Aideen gave him a gap-toothed smile.

Tristan took up the place, crossing his legs, one hand holding the edge of the ship above him as the ship rode another wave, tilting upward.

"Some weather we're having," he said, keeping his voice raised above the sound of the crashing waves.

The captain shouted orders. Manuell darted past, then shimmied up the mast to disconnect the sail as it flapped out of control in the wind. They would be trusting in God's direction to get them safely home now.

He glanced at the woman again, who huddled away from him, arms tightened around the object she carried.

"Why are you here, Aideen?"

The servant paused, hair whipping into her face and sticking to her damp skin. She stared past Tristan to where Isolde sat at the other end of the ship.

"Her majesty gave me to her daughter, as a gift. Along with this." She hoisted the package. If she felt poorly at being treated like cattle to be traded, she didn't show it on her face.

"What is it?"

Aideen considered him. "Spiced wine," she said, voice low enough he had to lean in to hear. "A special family recipe. It is tradition to give it to the bride and her intended, for their wedding night."

Tristan shifted and glanced down, then away, discomfort squirming in his gut. A bride and her intended. Isolde and Mark.

"You love her," the woman said louder.

Tristan jerked his head and met her knowing green eyes, storm clouds reflecting in their bright surface. Aideen broke the gaze first, looking out into the storm.

"How do you know?"

"I know because I see you, how you look, how you don't look. How you touch, how you don't touch. Everything you do speaks of your feelings for her."

"And her feelings for me?" he couldn't help asking, like a lad asking a fortune finder at a May Day celebration to read his palm and tell him his true love's name.

Lightning flashed, making contact with the sea and lighting it up, tendrils reaching for the boat. Men scrambled.

Tristan looked to Isolde, hunched over, alone. He didn't wait for Aideen's reply, if she was going to make one. He crawled across the slick, wet deck, reaching

Isolde, and without a word, pulled her into his side. She didn't resist.

Damn his uncle. He didn't know it, but he would ruin Tristan's life for good, unless Tristan could convince Isolde not to marry him, and somehow prevent the war that would surely ensue if he didn't keep his word with King Angeus.

Tristan pressed his cheek into Isolde's damp hair and rode out the waves, his thoughts as agitated as the water.

Another storm struck in the middle of the night. Tristan's stomach heaved as the waves grew taller. Lightning flashed, disorienting him and making spots in his vision.

Isolde cried out, and he wrapped her tighter in his arms as the ocean tossed their ship into the air like a giant's plaything. Each crash back down sent waves over the side, dousing them in freezing sea water.

A wave struck sideways, and the ship tilted. Tristan held onto Isolde as long as he could, but the ocean's grip tore them apart. The ship flipped over, tossing everyone into the raging sea. Tristan sputtered and swam, praying the others would survive. A large, flat piece of the ship bumped into him and he clambered on, gripping for his life.

When the storm calmed, Tristan found himself gazing at a flat, empty ocean, yelling until his voice grew hoarse, but none of his comrades, nor Isolde, replied.

Tristan dragged himself onto the shore and collapsed, breathing heavily, blowing sand away from his mouth. Dark shapes dotted the shore. He opened and closed his eyes, waiting until the feeling of being tossed about abated, and he could sit up without his head spinning.

Among large chunks of wreckage lay several bodies. Tristan closed his eyes, breathing. Then he stood and limped across the beach to see who he could find.

The first was Aideen. Tristan's fingers on her neck told him what he had feared most; she was dead.

He eyed the package clutched in her arms. Spiced wine, she told him. It might save their lives. He slipped the bottle free and held it by the neck as he stumbled to the next body. One of the crew.

No captain. No Manuell. Smaller bulges, most likely ruined provisions. Pieces of the ship.

One more body. Feminine. Cloak draped over. Blood matting her hair.

Tristan fell beside Isolde, hand rolling her onto her back. She breathed.

His relief made him cry out. He dropped the amber bottle into the sand and put his hands on Isolde's sand-crusted face.

"Come on, Isolde. Wake."

She sputtered and coughed water, but her eyes remained closed. She needed something to revive her, something warm. The wind on the beach bit at their wet skin and clothes. Isolde's body shivered.

Tristan grasped her shoulders and heaved her into his lap, propping her up. He used his teeth to grip the cork and popped it free from the mouth of the wine bottle, then held it up, sniffing. It smelled of cloves and fruit. Would he be able to discern if it were poisoned? Surely the Queen didn't desire to start a war with Cornwall.

He couldn't smell anything unpleasant. He took a sip. Unremarkable, with an acrid aftertaste, but nothing alarming.

Tristan set the mouth of the bottle against Isolde's lips and tilted it, pouring a small amount in. A bright red drop trailed from her lips and down her chin. He put the bottle down and wiped it off, then waited. Nothing but steady breathing.

Then her mouth and throat moved as she swallowed the liquid, and coughs racked her body. A strange tingling blossomed in his veins as he watched her. It warmed him from his heart outward, reverberating to his fingertips, pulsing through him.

He blinked, and a glimmer of gold shot from his chest to Isolde's, connecting them with a thread of light. He blinked, and it disappeared. Had he truly seen it?

A sensation like a wave came over him, and he fell forward, unable to see, unable to think, unable to feel anything but the liquid fire now running through his veins.

Tristan woke to the call of gulls. His arms held a warm, feminine body. She moved and stretched in his arms and a smile spread on his face. He burrowed his face into her hair, nuzzling her neck, brushing it with his lips. He could hold her for hours, feeling her body pressed to his.

Isolde turned rigid in his arms.

His eyes blinked open. "What is wrong?"

She pulled from his embrace, sitting up, staring at her hands, then moving them up her arms, rubbing her chest, touching her forehead. "I don't feel right. My arms and legs, my chest, they're burning. It is like fire in my veins. What happened?"

Tristan frowned. Fire in her veins? That didn't sound good. He sat up beside her, a hand on her back, his other hand reaching up to touch her brow. Normal. No fever.

"We shipwrecked. The storm caught us up and set us down here."

"Where are the others?" She glanced around at the debris-strewn beach.

Tristan took her chin in his hand, bringing her focus to his face. "The ones I've found, they…" he took a deep breath. "They are dead, Isolde. I found one man from the crew. Not the captain, nor Manuell. I found Aideen."

Her eyes widened. "Aideen is dead?"

Tristan nodded, somber.

Isolde's face lit up, a grin spreading on it. "Thanks be! I was afraid I might have to have her killed."

"Killed? What in God's name, Isolde?"

"You don't remember? She is, was, my mother's lackey, Tristan. I would rather her than me…" she trailed off.

Tristan felt numb, his mind unable to form a cohesive thought, his mouth twitched as he looked for words.

"Tristan, are you feeling well?" Her hand on his wrist brought clarity.

He shook his head, then glanced at the bottle sitting beside them on the ground. It had tilted in the sand, spilling half of the remains into the damp sand below. What had he done?

"Do you happen to know what kind of poison your mother used on you?"

"No, why?"

He picked up the bottle, cork missing from the top. He swallowed past the cotton feeling that coated his tongue.

"The…wine?" She hesitated, then her eyes went wide. "Tristan, tell me you didn't," she pleaded, desperation shining from her eyes. She took the bottle, sniffing at it.

She reeled away, holding the bottle at arm's length. "Quick, the cork."

Tristan fumbled, scattering sand until his fingers gripped the small cork. He handed it to her.

"Did you drink any?"

"Isolde, what is..."

"Did you drink any?" She insisted again, her eyes boring into his.

He swallowed, then nodded.

"And I gave some to you," he said.

She exclaimed indignantly, and Tristan held up his hands. "You were freezing, you needed warmth. I thought it was spiced wine. I was only thinking of you, of making sure you survived."

"That wine was a gift from my mother, Tristan. The queen who tried to poison you with Sir Marhaus' spear head and poisoned me almost unto death. Did it not occur to you that it could kill us?"

All feeling drained out of Tristan. "I-I didn't think. I was concerned about you."

"We won't die," she said, glancing at him. "Our fate may be worse than that."

Worse than dying? Besides physical torture or watching the one you loved die, Tristan wasn't sure he could think of anything he would consider worse.

Isolde gathered her feet beneath her, moving the tattered edges of her skirt out of her way, then stood, brushing off sand. She looked out across the waves, then in the other direction.

"Where are we?" she asked. She looked out across the shoreline, blonde hair blown about by the wind, looking more beautiful to him than ever.

"What did you mean, about our fate?" Tristan asked, unfolding his legs and coming to stand beside her.

Her proximity made his blood sing, making him swell with excitement at the prospect of being near her. It was massively uncomfortable. He adjusted his clothing, angling himself away from Isolde. She didn't notice, her eyes busy scanning the horizon in all directions.

"Since we aren't dead, it is most likely a love potion of some kind. That is what my mother claimed at least. I thought she might be lying, but apparently not." Isolde stepped through the sand, poking around the debris.

Tristan followed her, chuckling. "How is that a fate worse than death? Forced to love someone as beautiful and intelligent as you?"

Isolde stopped and looked at him, her stare making Tristan wish he could swallow his teasing words.

She straightened, brushing sand off her hands, and approached him, closing the gap between them until he could feel the warmth of her body radiating towards his.

His heart rose with the thrill of her closeness, and he leaned in, her lips begging him to kiss them. Her face tilted up, and she leaned in. He reached a hand up to cup the back of her head and in a blink, she batted it away, stumbling away from him, almost running.

Isolde made it several feet away and turned, and even from the distance, Tristan could see her eyes becoming red, but no tears welled up. She crossed her arms over her chest and looked out to sea. His whole being cried out to follow her, but his mind told him to wait, to give her distance.

She drew closer by a few steps, this time leaving a wide space between them. Tristan's muscles released the tension they held, and he trembled, arms aching to hold the woman before him.

"It feels good, doesn't it? The way your blood sings when I am near. The fire...well, everywhere." She actually blushed, and the color in her cheeks made Tristan smile. "I can feel it, too. The trouble is, neither of us have a choice."

Tristan's chest and groin both throbbed painfully, a dull ache he somehow knew would go away if he touched her. His fingers brushed the sleeve of her dress and Isolde ran again, this time putting significant distance between them. Tristan's heart pulled after her. He took a step. He couldn't stop it; his body answered the call...her call. The call to be near her and to never be apart.

Isolde looked small in the distance, and he couldn't make out the expression on her face. She halted, faced him, then took a step backward, away from him. He couldn't bear it. The throbbing intensified, pain stabbing through his chest.

"No," he gasped out, reaching a hand for her. He took several steps forward and the pain eased. Isolde stepped back; the pain returned. Could she not feel the pain?

Tristan broke into an all-out run. Isolde stood, seeming frozen, as he approached. He didn't stop, didn't hesitate when he reached her, but took her in his arms. Relief flooded his body. She trembled.

Gradually, his breathing slowed, his heart stopped pounding. Beneath it all, he could feel a slight, warm sensation flowing through his veins, if he paid attention, feeling for it.

"The potion binds us by distance." Her head rested against his chest. "Other kinds work in other ways.

Often the afflicted couple is so affected, they spend every moment making love until their bodies give out and they die. Or, as it seems to be in this situation, we cannot be apart without suffering physical pain."

Her face turned up to look into his eyes. Tristan could see a war being fought within them. A gust of wind blew past them, and Tristan found himself shivering. He didn't have the benefit of an extra layer, as Isolde did.

"So never leave me," he said.

Isolde's laugh put a chill in his heart. "You still do not see. What happens if you are called to fight a battle in some far-off land? Do I come with you? Even if I am with child? There are thousands of situations that could call for us to be apart, but we do not have that option, it has been stolen from us. We are bound, for better or for worse. It is a curse, and there may be no cure."

"I do not want a cure," Tristan said. "This is what I hoped for; a reason to be near you always, an excuse to make you mine."

She smiled, a small, sad, lovely thing that made Tristan's heart twinge with the desire to take away her sadness.

"You say that, but how can I know it is your true feeling, and not the potion?" She shook her head. "What of my father, expecting to hear of my wedding to your uncle? If I marry you, he will start a war. Isn't a war what you were trying to avoid by fighting that duel? We can't cause one because we want to be together."

Tristan frowned. He considered what she said; rolled it around in his mind until the edges of his thoughts became dull and he didn't want to think about it anymore. The silence stretched between them. He swallowed, stepping back, but keeping her hands in his.

“All I can think about is you, and how, if you marry King Mark, my whole reason to be alive will vanish.”

“I know,” she said, visibly wilting before him. “Besides that, how could we remain bonded while I am married to him? My duties as his queen, and yours as his knight, would often require us to be more than a hundred feet from each other. We would never survive.” she shuddered, looking out toward the grey ocean. “I have felt madness before. I wasn't exaggerating when I said it was a fate worse than death could bring.”

Tristan considered, following her gaze out to the churning waves.

He felt as if he was still out there, being tossed about in a storm. “Then our first recourse is to find a cure,” he said.

“As I already said, there isn't one,” Isolde replied.

“There must be. An enchantment against this...curse. A potion to burn this substance from our veins.”

And if we find it, then you will know this is not the potion making me feel this way, do these things, say what I say, he thought. The words sat on his tongue, lingering like the taste of salted meat. He wanted to say them out loud; he meant to say them. Above them, lightning flickered.

Isolde looked up at the darkening clouds and the moment dissipated.

“Our first recourse should be finding shelter, unless we want to be caught in this storm.” She took a few steps, then bent down and heaved a long, broken plank up, letting it thump to the side in the sand. She picked up a large, wrapped waterproof package.

Tristan's heart leapt to his throat, and he reached out his hands for the object.

"My harp," he said.

"It doesn't seem broken," she said, releasing the package into his grip. "Perhaps it needs to be aired out, maybe restrung, but she should still play."

"Thank you," Tristan managed.

He tucked the package under his arm and turned around, almost tripping on a long object that stuck halfway out of the sand. Another package; this one half-unwrapped, contents gleaming in the muted daylight. His sword, the new one his uncle had given him. He groaned at the sight, pulling it from the ground. The wooden scabbard was soaked, cracked, ruined. He unsheathed the blade, inspecting it.

Tristan frowned to himself. Normally he would be feeling the urge to sit down, right there, and clean and polish the blade back to perfection. But he felt nothing other than that unsettling desire to be near Isolde.

"You're right, we need shelter," he said, eyes scanning the horizon, trying to distract himself.

Based on the direction the winds blew during the storm, they were near Land's End, the edge of Cornwall. In the worst case, they had two days' walk to get to Tintagel castle. He squinted. He thought could make out what looked like houses, perhaps a small village, where someone would be willing to put them up for the night while they figured out what to do next.

They walked side-by-side, climbing through the wet sand and skirting the remains of their voyage. Tristan found himself hoping Manuell, the captain, and the other men had washed up alive on another part of the shore. He owed them an incredible debt. It would be poor repayment if they had died because of his choice to delay their voyage home.

They didn't speak. Was she angry with him? He already felt a complete fool, she didn't have to punish him with silence as well, but every time he considered how he could start a conversation, his words caught in his throat. He looked at her sideways, noting her beauty even as she frowned.

As they walked, he thought he caught a glimpse of what she meant about the potion being a curse. Nothing could be the same between them; their easy conversation, their chance to discover their true feelings for each other, none of it would come naturally again.

Isolde didn't even trust that what he felt or did could be real. Resolve settled in Tristan's heart. He would do anything to give Isolde the confidence she needed to know his feelings were real. Only then could he convince her to find a way for them to be together.

CHAPTER SIXTEEN

Of all such woes as winter: what am I,
Love, that have strength but to desire and die,
That have but grace to love and do thee wrong,
What am I that my name should live so long,
Save as the star that crossed thy star-struck lot,
With hers whose light was life to Launcelot?
Life gave she him, and strength, and fame to be
Forever: I, what gift can I give thee?
Peril and sleepless watches, fearful breath
Of dread more bitter for my sake than death
When death came nigh to call me by my name.
"The Joyous Gard," from "Tristram of Lyonesse"
by Algernon Charles Swinburne

Rain streamed down Morgan's face, plastering her hair to her skin. Her cloak, though damp, kept the rain off her mostly-dry clothing. Tristan had it worse. Morgan wished she could do something. She knew his code of chivalry wouldn't allow him to take her cloak. They could only keep walking and hope they found a place to stay.

The first village met them with closed, merciless doors. The residents were, perhaps, too suspicious of travelers. It was too small a village, merely a cluster of homesteads, to have an inn. So, Morgan and her knight carried on, and the rain grew steadily worse.

"We have to find shelter," Morgan yelled above the wind and rain. She adjusted the strap of the makeshift carrier on her shoulder,

the bulk of the amber bottle thumping against the top of her thigh. Tristan questioned her need to carry it, but she knew if there was any chance of finding a cure, they would need a sample of the potion they had consumed.

"Do you see any?" Tristan shouted back.

Morgan's heart skipped a beat at the sound of his voice. She shook her head. She couldn't see even a single tree. They followed the muddy road, sticking to the grassy track beside it to avoid sinking into the mud. Tristan trailed behind her. She thought she could hear his labored breathing behind her. They were tired, and her stomach pinched with hunger.

Her parched throat and cotton-mouth made her turn her head to the sky, ignoring her instinct to hide her face from the rain, and open her mouth to let droplets of water trickle in. Her head ached where she'd been struck by wave-tossed debris before reaching shore earlier that day.

She stumbled, whether from fatigue or the severity of her head injury, she wasn't sure. And through it all, the pulsing, burning in her veins, urging her to turn and embrace Tristan, kiss him, to...

Morgan's feet slipped out from beneath her as she crested a low hill, and she fell, hitting her bottom hard and sliding in the rain-soaked grass and mud. A rock struck her hip, sending her end over end, tumbling down the steep hillside. Her arms flailed, fingers grasping.

She landed hard on her back in a stew-like puddle of mud and rocks at the bottom, scraped up and banged up, her chest tight like she couldn't breathe. She sucked air in and got mud instead, sputtering as she tried to get to her feet.

Panic set in. She was too far from Tristan. Her heart palpated within the cage of her ribs, frantic as a trapped butterfly. She heard a yell and turned as Tristan barreled into her. They slammed to the ground together, Tristan's bulk on top of her knocked the wind from her lungs.

She started to shove him off, but the potion's magic got to her before she could act. The proximity of his face and the blueness of his eyes captivated her. He leaned closer, his breath mingling with hers. Morgan's own breath caught in her throat.

"Look there, two pigs mating in the mud." A smooth, masculine voice broke through the spell, and Morgan turned her head.

Six or seven men surrounded them. She wasn't sure she could see them all from the ground where she lay. Tristan rolled off her and dragged her to her feet. Mud caked her so thoroughly that she saw no point in trying to wipe her face. The falling rain made it run, a muddy river making its way back to the earth.

"What do you want?" Tristan snarled, his arm barred across

Morgan protectively. Morgan noticed the men wore no armor, but held weapons, two with bow and arrow, several with knives and swords.

The man who had spoken before smiled disarmingly at him, one hand on the dagger in his belt. He reminded her of Lord Melwas, the horrible man who had captured her and made her his whore. Morgan shuddered, trying to stifle the warning bells screaming in her mind.

The men surrounded them, and being bonded to Tristan, she could not run even if she wanted to. The man eyed Tristan, then looked to Morgan, eyes lingering far longer. She grabbed the edge of her cloak, blocking the view of her clothes clinging to her lithe body from the man's dirty, conspiring gaze.

"Bring the woman; I have use for her. Kill the man." He turned, as if to walk away, hand gesturing dismissively.

Morgan looked in alarm at the advancing men, then glanced at Tristan. Rage made his face into a snarling, unrecognizable version of itself, unkempt beard and mud making him look more beast than man.

"Tristan?" Morgan said, watching his expression.

It flickered with recognition, but he never took his eyes off the advancing men. Fear clutched at Morgan's heart. One man against six made for terrible odds, not to mention his injuries, exhaustion, lack of food...

Tristan struck, quick as a viper, sword sinking into the stomach of a man to his right. He yanked it free and feinted forward, skidding on the mud, then whirled left as a man on that side dove in to catch him off guard, his blade meeting Tristan's instead of flesh. Tristan twisted the man's arm around, blades locked, until Morgan heard a popping sound and the man's shoulder dislocated. He screamed and dropped out of the fight.

An arrow darted past Tristan, embedding in the mud beyond, too close for Morgan's comfort. Fire lit in her soul and silver light sparked to life in the palm of her hand. She didn't have time to think.

The archers lifted arrows to their strings and pulled back.

Morgan whispered a quick incantation and sent energy towards the men, a flash of light arcing through the air, entering their bodies and dropping them in an instant.

Morgan's head throbbed, and her limbs felt suddenly sapped of their strength. She collapsed back into the mud, arms and legs too heavy to move. From the ground, her eyes followed Tristan's flowing form as he moved between the remaining two men, trying to keep them in his sights, but his strength waned.

The taller of the two edged around Tristan as the other launched a series of attacks, forcing Tristan into a defensive stance.

Morgan struggled to sit up, to do something, but her hand slipped, and her head splashed back down into the mud, ears ringing.

The man raised his sword, bringing it down hilt-first on the back of Tristan's skull.

Morgan felt a twinge in her own head, an echo of his pain. Weak as a newborn lamb, Morgan struggled in the mud as the men approached, eyes and teeth gleaming in the dark grey light of the stormy evening.

Her movements became frantic, panic overtook her. No. Not again. I will not be a slave to any man. She held up her hand, palm facing to the men, and coughed out a single word. A trickle of power came forth, bursting in a dim flash of nothing. The men laughed and leaned down towards her.

Delayed, a burst of strength flooded into her from her attempted spell. It wasn't much, but it had to be enough. She gritted her teeth and pushed off the ground, lunging at them with her final burst of energy, screaming with fury. Her hands clawed at their eyes, her fingernails scraped and scratched. One of them gripped her around the waist and pried her off, throwing her to the ground. She slapped into the mud. Her head struck, jarring her.

She tried to shake it off, but the men ran too fast. The taller one picked her up and slung her over his shoulder. She wrapped her forearm around his face, grabbed that hand with her opposite one, yanking the man's head around until his neck twisted so painfully he grunted and released her.

Morgan splashed down, keeping her footing, breath heaving. A roar came from behind and ducked, rolling to one side as Tristan charged up from behind her. He cracked the two stunned men's heads together, dropping them to the ground, then turned and stared blankly at Morgan.

Morgan walked to him, carefully eyeing the men that he felled, watching for any movement. She saw none. She took Tristan's right arm and pulled it over her shoulder. She turned and saw a light flicker to life in a distance, lit by some homesteader waiting for her husband to return. Without a word, he leaned on her.

A whispered spell and the remains of adrenaline helped her lift Tristan's bulk. Fortunately, he remained conscious and could help her, limping along with one arm draped over her shoulder. She kept her eyes trained on that flickering golden light.

Morgan half-carried Tristan for ages until he went limp, passing out and giving all of his weight to her. Morgan collapsed. Her real body was larger, stronger. Isolde's body was weak. She'd been poisoned for months, shipwrecked, and spent the day without food. She lay in the mud, pressing her cold, tired body against Tristan's bulk, listening to him breathe and praying to any deity that might be listening to let him live.

Bootsteps squelched through the mud. Through a haze of exhaustion, Morgan tried lifting her head.

"Yer codding me," a gruff voice rumbled. Lightning shot through the sky, illuminating a tall, thin man with a beard obscuring half his face.

Morgan couldn't speak. She tried, but only a low moan came out with a couple of slurred, nonsensical sounds.

The man stomped away, shouting. "Ida, come out 'ere, we got a couple o' live ones."

The door opened, spilling golden light out into the rainy darkness. Morgan could have wept with relief. She couldn't believe how close she had come, no more than thirty feet away.

It took the couple two trips, but they carried both Tristan and Isolde inside. They laid Tristan on a blanket on the floor and made certain he was angled in front of the fire with blankets piled on top.

Ida exclaimed at their mud-caked state, but when Morgan mentioned they hadn't eaten, the woman set to scrambling about the kitchen, pulling together bits and pieces of anything she had available.

Morgan told them about the shipwreck and the bandits in between bites of soft, delicious bread and hard cheese, dipping into the stew the woman, Ida, had made for her husband's supper.

"But what were ye doin' out on the ocean this time o' year?" The man, Ronan, said with a dubious expression on his face.

Morgan stuttered a moment, unsure what to tell them. The wife came to her rescue.

"Hush now, there dear. You are tired, I see. No need to spill the tale now." She cast a firm gaze on her husband, who opened and closed his mouth like a fish, but then smiled warmly at her and conceded, letting Morgan finish her stew in silence.

The couple explained they ran their home like a way stop, giving strangers a room and food for a little payment or trade, and they would be delighted to care for her and her knight until they felt well enough to leave again.

Morgan felt better than before but swayed with exhaustion, and when she started shivering, Ida revealed a freshly-poured bath. The water steamed, and Morgan sank into the small tub without hesitating. A plaid blanket hung in the rafters giving her privacy, as the small bedroom didn't have a proper door.

Beyond, she could hear Ida and Ronan whispering. She caught snippets of their conversation about the strangeness of their presence. They spent a good long time speculating, and then were cut off when Tristan groaned, regaining consciousness.

Ida looked in on Morgan, bringing her a simple, homespun dress and shift for her to change into. "Your companion is awake. I've given him something to eat. And I rinsed your wet things," the woman said, helping Morgan into the dress.

Morgan missed the Irish-style belt, she found, but she had to wait for her things to dry before putting them on again. She found them hanging from the rafters in the other room, dripping onto the floor in front of the fire where Tristan had lain.

The knight sat at the table, eating stew like a ravenous animal. A smile filled Morgan's face at the sight of him. He looked up at her and relief melted his strained gaze.

"I am...glad to see you looking so well." He glanced at Ida and Ronan, who sat smiling politely at the two of them. The company made things feel stilted and awkward.

Morgan sat down beside Tristan, close, but not too close. She longed to press herself against him, but they hadn't agreed on a story yet.

Ida stood, smoothing her apron. "I will heat more water for Sir Tristan's bath."

"Thank you, good woman," Tristan said.

Ida nodded, pursing her lips at the two of them, then bustled into the other room.

Tristan scraped the wooden bowl and put it aside before settling into some bread with cheese. The sound of his chewing filled the room.

"I haven't told them," Morgan whispered.

Tristan stared at her. "They don't know..."

"My name, Isolde, nothing more," Morgan replied.

"Why?" he asked.

Morgan bit her lip. Her fingers trailed across the table, making invisible swirls and circles.

"I wanted..." she began, then fell silent. She glanced up, meeting Tristan's eyes, seeing past the dark circles to the curiosity there. "Does it matter what I want?" she muttered.

His hand reached across the table. "Of course. This is your life, Isolde. You can have anything you want."

"But that isn't true. I can't have you."

"Why not?" He sighed. "Look, I am sorry that I did this to you. I meant to free you and I've enslaved us both, but perhaps the potion is a blessing, not a curse. We still have a choice. We can run away, live our lives together."

Ida bustled into the room, glancing at them. They remained silent, staring at each other until the woman left the room.

"Could you live with what that means?" Morgan replied, struggling to keep her voice down. She wanted to shout but suppressed the urge.

Tristan shrugged. "I could. You do not know me as well as you might think. I have not been a knight for long, and the love I claim for Cornwall and my uncle is tenuous, at best. He does not deserve you, Isolde."

"That seems rather selfish of you to say."

"It is," Tristan said, and he seemed unashamed

She hadn't expected Tristan to give in so easily when tempted. Did that disappoint her? She felt too tired to care at the moment.

"We have but the one room," Ronan said. "If it is too improper, we could find another arrangement..."

"No," Morgan said abruptly.

Tristan stared at her.

Ronan and Ida waited for her to continue.

Goddess give her strength. "That won't be necessary. We, ah, have just been wed." She rushed through the last part, glancing at Tristan for his reaction.

His eyes gleamed, his mouth splitting into a grin.

She gave him a relieved smile.

"Oh!" Ida exclaimed. "Why didn't you say so, dear? Blessings on you both." She still eyed them with suspicion, no doubt because they hadn't yet explained what they were doing at sea. Fabricating a story to satisfy the generous couple could wait until morning.

Ronan came over and slapped Tristan on the back. "A lucky lad, you are. In that case, your room is prepared." He gestured over Tristan's head, back toward the small room that Morgan had bathed in earlier.

Stomach full and body warmed through, Morgan didn't have to fake the yawn that overtook her body. She stretched her arms up, then stood and asked her leave of the couple that had taken them in.

“If you need anything, jus’ holler, we’re in the room on the other end of the house,” Ida said. Ronan stood next to her, his arm around

her shoulders, nodding in agreement. “And I will have breakfast for you in the mornin’.”

“Thank you, for all of your kindness,” Morgan said.

Tristan sat at the table, looking between the couple and Morgan. He seemed at a bit of a loss.

“Are you coming, love?” Morgan said, smiling innocently at him.

He gave a slow nod and stood, following her to the entrance.

Morgan moved farther into the room, and Tristan drew the blanket over the doorway behind them, eyes never leaving hers.

They stood in the flickering candlelight, staring at one another.

Morgan’s breath caught in her throat.

“I wasn’t expecting that,” Tristan said.

“No?” she laughed, releasing some of her nerves. “Maybe you don’t know me as well as you think, either. I have never been one to follow others’ expectations.”

Tristan chuckled. “I knew that much.” His expression sobered. “But what of the impending war? Can you live with knowing we caused it?”

Morgan swallowed past the lump of guilt rising in her throat and shrugged. “They would have found an excuse for war sooner or later. I choose to see this as initiating the inevitable, rather than fruitlessly attempting to prevent it.”

Tristan stepped closer.

Morgan's heart thudded in her chest.

"So, about finding a cure..."

"Forget it," she replied, watching him, longing for him.

He smiled, then closed the distance and took her in his arms, their lips meeting in a burning kiss, sweeping Morgan's guilt and fear away, heart soaring up to meet the stars.

As Morgan stirred awake the next morning, Tristan's bare shoulders rising with his breath beside her, she found she was grateful for the potion. It had taken away her fear of intimacy with its magically-induced desire burning through her veins, purging her of every past memory and filling her with love for Tristan.

She kissed Tristan's skin, lips lingering, satisfaction making her heart glow with warmth. She could have this. She could never again feel the pain of past mistakes, never again wonder about what might have been... except for the guilt.

In the morning's light, it showed stark, like the mud that had covered her white dress the night past. Her heart pounded, and her breath grew shallow. It wasn't so much about the war as it was about Isolde. If she knew where the woman had taken her body, what was happening for certain, perhaps she could rest easier.

Morgan got up from the bed, bringing a blanket with her. She peered into the main room, but Ida and Ronan were nowhere in sight, despite the breakfast that sat ready on the table.

Morgan went to a bucket in the corner, filled with clean water, a cup and a ladle beside. She dipped the ladle, bringing it up dripping until it filled the cup, then slipped back into the room she shared with Tristan. He stirred, and she froze, breathing out when he settled back down to sleep.

Water splashed over the rim of the cup as she set it down, wetting her hand. She sat on the bed next to the little table with the candle. She listened to Tristan breathing behind her. Soon, he would wake. She had to be finished by the time he did so.

The surface of the water stilled. Morgan glanced at it from the corner of her eyes and thought of Isolde. The image wavered, responding poorly to her exhaustion. She felt at the barrier that had broken her connection last time she scried Isolde and found it weaker than she expected.

Niviane might be too far from Isolde, or perhaps she neglected to renew the barrier at the proper time. Either way, Morgan found she could get through, though she felt as if she were straining for each moment, and she knew the connection wouldn't hold for long.

When had she last seen that expression of happiness on her own face? Isolde-as-Morgan beamed, her eyes gleaming with love and light. She looked at someone Morgan couldn't see, her bare shoulders an indication she was undressed, her posture indicating she laid in bed. Morgan's stomach clenched. She could not see who Isolde was with, but she could rule it out by scrying someone else.

She blinked, waving away the image of Isolde as herself, and the first face that leapt to her mind was Mordred's. She hadn't thought of him in ages. Her first love, her first mistake, her betrayal of Elaina. His handsome face filled the cup. Armor glinted above the edge of the image and he spoke earnestly with someone, sweeping black curls from his eyes with a swift movement of one hand.

Morgan didn't have time to consider who he might be talking with; it could be anyone. All that mattered was that Isolde wasn't with him. She sighed with relief and dropped the connection. Her body slumped, energy draining with the effort it took to scry.

Already, she had overextended herself, but she had to find out who Isolde was sleeping with, in her body, or rather, make sure there was another person she wasn't sleeping with. Morgan brought Arthur to mind. His eager blue eyes and sincere smile, his sandy hair and no beard, the way she preferred him. Her heart ached when his face appeared in the water. Clean shaven, beaming at her.

Chest and shoulders bare, looking down at someone she couldn't see.

Morgan's heart stopped.

It could be a coincidence. He could have found someone else, someone not Isolde.

Morgan glanced back at the cup, peering into the plain wood grain at the bottom through the clear liquid. Her mind and heart reeled. Even though it was Morgan's own body he made love to, she couldn't help feeling a hollow pit open up in her heart. It felt like he had moved on. How could he still love her, when the part that was her wasn't there?

Morgan's hands shook, making the water tremble in the cup.

Through the haze of her personal confusion, her mind worked on a larger problem. Would Camelot still fall? Or would Niviane fail to put all the pieces into play? Why should Morgan care?

A tiny voice whispered about Elaina, but Morgan shook it off. Elaina had freed herself without Morgan's help last time; surely, she could do the same now.

According to the priestesses, she couldn't prevent Arthur's downfall if she went to Camelot. Did they mean her as herself, in her own body? Would Isolde cause the same terrible fate by being there? It seemed more likely that Morgan herself caused all the trouble; bodies wouldn't make a difference. Whether she married Tristan or King Mark didn't matter in the grand scheme of things. Tristan at least loved her, even if it was only a byproduct of that tainted wine. After all this time, she could claim that much for herself.

A hand curled over her shoulder and Morgan jumped, knocking over the cup of water. Tristan chuckled, then sat up and scooted closer, pressing into her from behind.

"Did I startle you, my love?"

Morgan forced a nervous laugh. "Yes, you did. I was thirsty."

"Mm," Tristan replied, moving her hair aside and kissing the spot where her neck met her shoulder. "I think I am thirsty, too. But not for drink."

Morgan smiled. She pulled away from her thoughts of Isolde and Arthur, the potion like fire in her veins, allowing her to forget, even for only a moment. She had one last thought as he kissed her, his passion like that of a man dying of thirst; if she were to do this, to turn her back on Camelot, on Isolde, she had to find a way to forget.

Forget Arthur. Forget Avalon. Forget Elaina. Forget forever.

CHAPTER SEVENTEEN

"Dost thou repent thee of the sin we sinned?
Dost thou repent thee of the days and nights
That kindled and that quenched for us their lights,
The months that feasted us with all their hours,
The ways that breathed of us in all their flowers,
The dells that sang of us with all their doves?
Dost thou repent thee of the wildwood loves?"
"Tristram of Lyonesse"
by Algernon Charles Swinburne

One year later.

Morgan woke to her own screams. A heavy weight compressed her chest, suffocating her, and when she finally drew in a breath, the air tasted sweet. She gasped like a fish out of water, trying to restore the normal rhythm of her breath.

A full moon's face peered at her from the slat-like window formed in the stone and clay walls of their home.

Beside her, Tristan sat up, rubbing his eyes. He touched her shoulder, rubbing it.

"Again, Isolde?"

Morgan nodded, too stunned to speak. Memories rushed into her mind, swelling like a river during spring thaw. Her mind flashed with a thousand overwhelming details she had forgotten because of the last spell she cast, making her forget. Making her become Isolde.

"It isn't real, dearest. Try to rest."

Why had the spell ruptured? She recalled the nightmare, the same every night, except tonight, the face in the flames was hers. Not the face she wore, not Isolde's, but her own. Morgan's face. It had triggered the landslide of memories, the ones she had hidden behind a thin web of spells and herbs.

Tristan's hand left her back, and his comforting words trailed off into heavy breathing as he returned to sleep. Morgan could not do the same. She pushed the covers off and stumbled from their bed of straw on the floor. She poured herself a glass of water from the pitcher at the table and gulped the cool liquid, then stared into the bottom of the cup.

Flames flickered in the water. She dropped it, spilling the water. Flames danced toward her from the droplets on the ground.

Morgan gripped the chair before her, focusing on its hardness, its realness, to keep from screaming. She had seen only a vision, after all. No real flames licked the floor around her. Stillness and cool night air stifled her fears but did nothing for the restlessness that rose inside of her.

She wanted to forget the vision, to go back to sleep and let life return to its previous simplicity, but she couldn't. Memories demanded to have their place within her.

She went to the wooden chest, kneeling on the floor and reaching behind it for the sheaf of papers there. She lit the candle on the table, casting its flickering shadows over the pages. Morgan leafed through them, reading.

Queen Eithne, King Angeus. Elaina and Lancelot, King Arthur. She hadn't known the names when she wrote down the memories as they burst through hairline cracks in the spell over the past few months, but the descriptions were all there.

Guilt flooded into her chest. She recalled her most recent memory; a trip to the village for supplies. Merchants and farmers had asked for far more than their items' worth. She and Tristan returned from their last trip frustrated. They'd only been able to afford a fraction of the items they'd planned to purchase. Cornwall was at war, but with whom?

Morgan rubbed her head and slumped in the chair. Isolde's face, her face, flashed, the fiery scene making her rub at her arms, though the scars weren't there anymore. Was it happening now? Had it already happened? Or was it a vision of the future? She pushed to her feet.

Silver light gleamed in the small mirror on the wall across the room. She leaned back, trying to catch the silver surface in the glass, but the window wasn't angled right to reflect the moon in the mirror from where she stood.

Her own chest shone with silver light, winking from the top of her nightdress. Morgan pulled her neckline down and stared. The phoenix with the gold-tipped wings stared back, its feet now golden, too. The Rite of the Heart was not complete.

Morgan glanced behind her, at the bed on the floor where Tristan's form slept.

What had she done? What had they done? She had full awareness of the past year. As Guinevere she had lost time, but this was different. She remembered everything. Every night Tristan made love to her, every morning she woke curled up in his arms. All of it, selfishly stolen as they hid from duty, from responsibility, from preventing a war.

Morgan backed away from that peaceful sight, from the empty space in the bed that called for her to return to sleep and forget.

She could forget. Brew another potion. It would be much weaker this time, if she even managed it, and she would remember sooner. Maybe a few months and then she'd be right back where she started, and Isolde, the true Isolde, would be dead. Burned at the stake, a fate meant for Morgan.

And Elaina...had she escaped the tower? Would she rescue Isolde as she had once rescued Morgan? Or had the time-stream altered this new reality, one in which she would be caught weaving tapestries for eternity? Morgan couldn't let that happen. But she must. The priestesses had warned her what could happen if she returned to Camelot. Camelot would be ruined forever.

The taste of blood filled Morgan's mouth. Chewing on her lip with her worry had split it. She ignored the bleeding and began grabbing things. A potato sack, made of sturdy fibers, into which went a half loaf of slightly stale bread, two pears, and a wedge of cheese from the cupboard. A waterskin hung beside the door.

A floorboard creaked as Morgan crossed the floor to retrieve it, and Tristan mumbled, turning over and reaching for her in bed. Morgan froze, and he settled, hand resting on the empty bed beside him.

Her heart pounded, and her gut heaved. She couldn't leave. Their hearts were bound together. Neither could go anywhere without the other. If she wanted to save Elaina and Isolde, she had to tell him her true identity. Her heart plummeted.

A breeze blew into the room, carrying with it the whispering of the moor grass. It seemed so peaceful out there on the moonlit landscape, peace she could never partake of again.

Tristan deserved more. He deserved a wife who could love him without guilt reminding her every day of the mistakes she had made, of the lives that were lost because of her selfish decision to run away. He deserved a woman who wasn't plagued with memories of men she had loved long past, of children she couldn't bear, of madness and brokenness and everything Morgan had experienced.

Between telling him the truth and asking for his help and fighting to break the spell that bound their hearts as one, Morgan preferred the latter. She pulled the bag's drawstring tight, then quickly changed her clothes, shivering in the chilly morning air.

The sky lightened to a pale orange. If she made it to the village before the sun rose, she knew of a man who kept horses. She could take one, get away faster, maybe break the curse on her heart with sheer speed. At the very least, she could die trying.

There was only one thing that made her hesitate. Her eyes fell on him as she turned. She saw his face, relaxed in deep sleep. Tristan wouldn't understand her need to save Isolde, to save Elaina, and it would take too much time to tell him the truth and explain everything about her past, time she didn't have.

Morgan tiptoed to his side and kissed him softly on the forehead, apologizing in her heart at the pain she was about to put him through. He made an appreciative sound but fell back to sleep without waking further. She smiled, taking in his sleep-tossed hair and handsome face one last time, then walked out the door of the home they had built together.

She didn't make it past the rift. Tristan found her there, crumpled in heap, dry-heaving from pain and gazing out over the village below. He cried out, rushing to her side, pulling her close to him.

"Isolde, what were you thinking? You know we cannot be apart."

"I never should have given in, Tristan. There is a war, because of us."

She saw pain in his eyes, pain that she hadn't noticed before because of that horrid memory spell she had cast on herself.

He glanced away, holding her in his lap on the ground, then looked back. "We were happy, Isolde. Weren't we happy? Why ruin it now?"

Morgan shook her head. "This isn't who I am." Her blood no longer seethed and boiled. She would never make it to Camelot without him beside her.

"You said you wouldn't regret this. That you could live with the consequences."

He sounded angry, now. He had every right to be. She had promised him something she couldn't give.

Morgan closed her eyes, swallowing the pain that rose from her heart. Fatigue and pain squeezed at her heart. She was tired. So tired of running, of wrestling love from fate so she could be happy. Perhaps she wasn't meant to have happiness as others did.

"We have to fix our mistakes, Tristan. People are suffering because of us."

"What were you going to do? Go to Tintagel and marry King Mark?"

"Talk to him, at least."

Tristan's grip on her tightened. "He will never listen."

"He might. When he sees us, perhaps he'll take pity on our plight."

"You mean to tell him about the potion? He won't believe it."

Morgan reached up a hand to his cheek. "Have faith, my love. Perhaps God will have mercy on us." *And if not Him, perhaps the Goddess*, Morgan thought to herself. Tristan didn't know of her oaths to Avalon and the Goddess, another part of herself she had withheld from him.

"What if we're separated? Imprisoned? Or one of us is killed? We won't survive out in the world, Isolde. The bond on our hearts is too strong."

"Then we must find a cure." Morgan sat up, pulling herself out of his arms.

His face contorted with pain, and Morgan realized what she had said. "I still love you, Tristan. I do not intend to leave you."

"Isn't that what you were trying to do? What am I supposed to think?"

"We will be safer if we do not have this curse binding us together," she replied. "That is all I am thinking of. I want you at my side. I want to return to our home here and live out our days until we're old and grey." She smiled, but he did not return it, his blue eyes pained and serious.

"Once we reach Tintagel, Mark will never let us leave. We have betrayed him and his country. He will have us hung."

Morgan climbed to her feet, dusting off her hands. "I thought I could live with the guilt, Tristan, but I cannot. My life will be miserable if I do not at least try." She licked her lips, touching the throbbing wound where she had bitten her bottom one. "You can come with me, or... or I will die."

"Is that a threat?" Tristan leapt up, voice a deep-throated growl. He gripped her arm so tightly it hurt, but she didn't cry out. "You would rather take your own life than live your days with me?"

"That isn't what I said," Morgan replied, locking her eyes on his, fingers prying him from her arm. He let her, releasing his grip. "I love you, but I cannot enjoy my days with you if they are tainted with guilt reminding me that all of this is my fault." She gestured towards the village, where people stirred to start the day.

"I have seen the prices rising in the market. Soon, they will start recruiting men to feed the war. Families will be torn apart. I don't know how bad the fighting is, or if it has even begun, but I cannot stand by and watch knowing I took part in causing it. I am not noble or heroic, Tristan. I have done so many wrong things in my life. But this is one thing I cannot do."

Tristan glanced down at his feet, then to the village, then back to her. The wind blew his shoulder-length hair into his face, and he tucked it back behind one ear. His boots crunched on the rocky ground as he stepped toward her. His fingers rubbed the back of her arms up to her shoulders.

Morgan crossed her arms before her as he pulled her in, pinning her against his chest. She felt his lips on her hair.

"I am glad we had this time, at least."

"Me too," she replied, voice muffled. They stood like that for a moment, sun beaming down on them as it cracked the horizon with its light.

"I will come with you," he said at last.

Morgan smiled at him.

"Where do we go first?" He did not look at her.

Morgan focused on the horizon. "We head toward Tintagel. I have heard rumors of someone who might help with this potion. They call her the Rose Witch."

CHAPTER EIGHTEEN

As the dawn loves the sunlight I love thee;
As men that shall be swallowed of the sea
Love the sea's lovely beauty; as the night
That wanes before it loves the young sweet light,
And dies of loving; as the worn-out noon
Loves twilight, and as twilight loves the moon
That on its grave a silver seal shall set—
We have loved and slain each other, and love yet.
Slain; for we live not surely, being in twain:
In her I lived, and in me she is slain,
Who loved me that I brought her to her doom,
Who loved her that her love might be my tomb.
"Tristram at Brittany," from "Tristram of Lyonesse"
by Algernon Charles Swinburne

Tristan's hands ached to be doing something, anything, other than swinging at his sides as he walked. His sword bumped against his leg, an unfamiliar weight after his year of retirement from knighthood.

He'd left his harp, confident he would find Isolde and bring her back to their home. Tristan had never expected her change of heart, and she refused to return for anything, possibly afraid he wouldn't come with her once they were within the walls they had shared the past year. He should have insisted.

Tristan felt lopsided without the instrument, and the sword's weight made it worse. He itched to throw it into the bushes, but knew he'd want it when he faced his uncle. His fingers brushed the hilt, feeling the hard, smooth surface of the cut stones embedded there. A rich gift from a king he'd hoped he would never see again.

Mark would be furious, if he wasn't dead, though Tristan assumed that was more than he could hope. Tristan had broken the oaths of his knighthood and betrayed the king and his country. A war may have begun because of his actions with the Irish princess.

Isolde. Tristan glanced at her from the corner of his eyes. Her face held a look of determination that made him simultaneously proud of her and infuriated. What could have possibly changed her mind?

He had a vague suspicion that she'd done something with her herbs. At times she asked him things that made it seem as if she'd forgotten everything leading up to them choosing to be together. He worried about her, especially when she had started to wake up screaming about burning.

"Tristan?"

Tristan stumbled. His thoughts consumed him so thoroughly he didn't hear Isolde talking to him.

"You're distracted," Isolde said, her green eyes watching him with concern.

Fool woman, gallivanting off trying to break the potion's hold on their hearts. He grunted, not having any words to say.

She frowned. "I know you're angry with me, but you don't have to ignore me when I talk to you."

"What did you expect?" he snapped, harsher than he intended. His thumb rubbed the top of his sword again. Would he have to use it on Mark? Fight their way from Tintagel's keep? God help them if things went that poorly.

He sighed. "I have a lot on my mind."

Isolde nodded. "Me too." She eyed him sideways, a look he caught in his periphery, as if she were weighing him, judging him. He straightened, self-conscious of her scrutiny.

"Tristan?"

"Hm?"

"What if...what if we find the Rose Witch? And she removes the bond, and..." Isolde trailed off.

Tristan felt his throat tighten. He didn't want to consider that. He shrugged without speaking. Let her think he was angry. Damn it all, he was angry. Had she thought about how he might feel about this? Didn't she take one moment to consider the impact of her actions?

Even now, he wanted to drag her back to their hut on the rocks and keep her there, his forever. It burned furiously inside of him. He forced it down, reminding himself that wasn't a logical thing to do. Did he feel the potion's influence or his pride? How much of what he felt for her was because of that sickly, bitter drink they consumed together after washing up on the shore of Cornwall?

"Where are we headed, Isolde? Do you have any sort of direction? A landmark?" *Give me something to do*. He couldn't continue with the birds trilling and the leaves in the breeze and her damned silence condemning him.

She hesitated a long moment. "The witch lives in the shadow of the Castle Pleure, last heard." Then, after a moment, "I didn't think you would be interested."

He grunted, then caught her glare. She hated when he didn't give a thoughtful response. But what if he had nothing to say? "Sorry. I want this to be done."

She nodded, as if she understood. But how could she?

Tristan stopped on the path and took Isolde's arm, turning her to face him. "Are you sure this is what you want? There won't be any going back, after."

Unexpectedly, her face split into a grin. "Nonsense. I've got a small bottle of that potion left. We can always take a swig if we want this lust spell back."

"Who wouldn't?" he asked, tone joking, but his heart ached.

He swallowed and let her tug her arm free, and they continued on the path. He had told her the truth; he felt eager for this part to be done. After all, once they took care of this potion, she would see their feelings for one another were true. He believed their feelings began when they left Mumhan before the shipwreck.

The potion...hurried things along. Skipped the propriety, mainly. They only needed each other, as the past year had proved. But he couldn't get rid of the voice muttering in the back of his mind. *What if she never loved you at all? What if our feelings for one another are false?*

Tristan shivered, rubbing his arms against the frigid wind that picked up. White-grey clouds covered the sun. Over the tops of distant trees, the turrets of a tower could be seen. Castle Pleure, he assumed.

Tristan couldn't quite place where he had heard that name before. He peered into the forest on either side. Somewhere in those trees lived the witch that could help them.

He looked up at Isolde. She walked beside him, looking straight ahead, her face unreadable. He opened his mouth to speak several times, opening and closing it like a particularly slow fish. Was she angry? Should he apologize? Nothing came to his mind. Longing to hear her voice made his heart pound in his chest, and his palms sweated. They broke through the trees and the tower loomed before them. Isolde exclaimed, halting in the middle of the dirt road.

"It is impressive," Isolde said, looking up and down the height of the tower.

The familiarity of the castle's name came crashing down on Tristan. He gaped, gazing up the castle's height to the turrets, where a black flag flew. He couldn't make out the symbol on it at first; the flag folded in on itself, whipping in the breeze, then straightened to reveal a red rose on the black field.

"I have heard tales about this place," Tristan said, mouth gone dry. He licked his lips.

Isolde looked at him. "Do you know the lord or lady here? I hoped you might. We could inquire about the Rose Witch."

"We should not seek help here. I cannot tell you what we will find inside those walls, but none of the stories even hint at anything friendly."

"People fear what they cannot understand," Isolde said, gathering up her skirts and placing a foot on the first step. She glanced at him. "Are you coming?"

She was infuriating. And beautiful. Those eyes, those lips...that blasted castle.

Tristan put a hand to the pommel of his sword and gritted his teeth. "Do I have a choice?"

In answer, Isolde began climbing. The hair on Tristan's neck pricked with each step they climbed. The overcast sky seemed darker here than at the bottom of the steps.

A female gargoyle carved over the door frame, breasts bared, teeth gnashing towards the sky, caused tremors to move up his spine. He shook them off and climbed, legs burning.

Isolde stood before the door, seemingly frozen at the top.

"Are we going in?" Tristan asked, gesturing forward. When had they started arguing?

"We should at least knock. We don't want to be rude." Her dainty hand looked miniscule against the wide, blackened wooden door. She raised the massive bronze knocker and let it fall against the door, a thud echoing on the other side.

A chill wind picked up, whipping Tristan's hair into his face. He spit it out, shaking his head. The door creaked open, revealing darkness beyond. No one stood in attendance, and Tristan's heart clenched.

Unbelievably, Isolde stepped in as if she was mistress here, pushing the door open further. Tristan blew out a frustrated breath, hand rubbing the pommel of his sword, and followed her, the door closing off the relative light of day as it shut behind them.

His eyes adjusted to the flickering torchlight and dancing shadows on the walls. They darted around, searching for potential attackers, and found recesses dotted along the corridor. Anything, or anyone, could be hidden within, crouched, waiting for them to pass and ambush them.

Something brushed his arm, and Tristan half-drew the sword at his hip. Isolde's hand. He relaxed slightly, dropping the sword back into its sheath.

"What is this place?" she whispered, moving forward.

"It is called the Castle Pleure, as you know. The Weeping Castle," Tristan replied, keeping his voice low.

"What exactly have you heard about it that makes you so afraid?"

Tristan grimaced, following after her. "Knights and ladies alike entering, never to be seen again."

Isolde snorted. "You fear children's tales?"

Tristan ignored the jibe. Some things became legend for a reason.

Isolde headed towards a door at the end of the corridor. "Someone must live here. The torches wouldn't be lit otherwise."

"Unless it's enchanted," Tristan whispered, keeping his tone light. "Maybe ghosts light the torches?"

"Neither. Hush." She lifted a hand and appeared to be listening. "Do you hear voices?"

"No," Tristan said, listening. "Good to know you do. You might have told me sooner." She turned and glared at him.

The amount of venom in her stare surprised Tristan. And he saw a flash of something else...guilt? He didn't ask her about it then, only held his hands up in front of himself in defense of his jest.

She turned away without a word and took another step.

The hairs on Tristan's arms and the back of his neck rose. He opened his mouth to speak when the shadows seemed to bend. Knights in black armor melted from the walls, spear tips gleaming in the torchlight.

They stepped in otherworldly unison, but Tristan could see the humanness of their eyes through slits of their helms, even in the dim torchlight. It did little to slow Tristan's pounding heart. He swallowed, raising his arms up.

"You care to take these on?" Isolde muttered.

"I do not have a death wish," he snapped.

One of the knights stepped forward.

"Please, we have no ill intent. We only came seeking information," Isolde said, head held high, looking regal even in the dim light.

The knight held out his spear, visor obscuring any expression that might be on his face. He gestured down the corridor. A spear tip pressed into Tristan's back, forcing him forward. He swallowed hard and moved forward, praying Isolde would do the same. No words would save them, and he could not take on the dozen knights on his own.

The silent knights ushered them through the door and to the left. Another doorway at the end took them down a winding staircase. Here, the wall held no torches. The knight leading the way had taken one from the bracket before the stairs, its jittery light illuminating dripping, algae-covered walls.

The smell of moisture and earthy rot filled Tristan's nose, making it tickle. He sniffed several times, then reached a hand up and rubbed at it.

The spearman behind him pressed his point into Tristan, and he hurried ahead, keeping Isolde in his sights. If anyone occupied the neighboring cells, they didn't make themselves known. Tristan and Isolde were ushered inside, the barred door clanging shut behind them, the key making a final clanking sound as it turned in the lock.

Tristan approached the bars, facing the knight who had led them here. He didn't want to use his connection to his uncle so soon. It would be better if they held the advantage of surprise, but the situation appeared desperate.

"My name is Sir Tristan de Liones, knight of Cornwall. It is imperative we be released and allowed to continue on our way. I am certain if you tell your lord who I am, he..."

"Your fate has been decided," the knight said, voice raspy, as if it hadn't been used in a long time. "A meal will be brought. There are blankets in the corner, and a pail." He did not explain further. He put the torch in a nearby bracket, a small mercy, and walked from the dungeon.

Frustration made Tristan smack his hand, palm-first, on the bars. The sound reverberated through the dungeon, and his hand smarted. A foolish move. He leaned on the bars, their cool, curved surfaces pressing into his forehead.

"Now what?" he muttered. He turned his head sideways to look at Isolde.

She looked around the dungeon with interested eyes, scanning every corner she could see in the near-darkness. When they connected with his, they seemed haunted.

Tristan shook his head. Certainly, the Irish princess had never experienced conditions as hard as these, and yet she shed no tears, made no complaints. Tristan had an underlying sense that, despite their year together, he didn't know her as well as he wanted to believe.

"If you are going to joke about how I got us here, don't," she said.

Her voice quavered. Perhaps she wasn't as calm as she appeared.

Tristan took a step towards her, arms open, and she fell into them. Her body relaxed, and she let out a long, relieved breath. Having her here, head pressed up against his galloping heart, was like being fed a warm meal after a long journey. He let his lips brush the top of her head, a familiar fire igniting in his chest. He felt the urge to keep going; to hold her, and kiss her, to let his hands roam her body until...

Isolde sighed and moved, pushing lightly against his chest until he released her. It left emptiness inside of him. Would he ever hold her like that again? He pushed the thought away. He couldn't think like that. There must be some mercy in Mark, a sentimental side that Tristan had never seen.

Isolde crouched down and rummaged through her pack. "It is odd that they didn't take anything from us. You still have your sword."

Tristan grasped his sheath, looking down at the hilt that stuck obtrusively from the opening. That he did. "That means we have food."

"We ate already," Isolde said, staring at him.

"I didn't say I was hungry, just stating facts," he replied, crouching down beside her.

Isolde rummaged through, rearranging, counting, a crease appearing in her brow. "It isn't much. I wasn't expecting company."

It stung, but he let it go. "The guard said a meal would be brought," Tristan replied.

"Have you ever eaten dungeon food?" Isolde asked.

"No, but it's starting to sound as if you have." He gazed at her until her eyes dropped from his, and she went back to organizing the pack, biting her lip as if to keep from speaking. Tristan reached out his hand, touching the back of hers.

"Whatever it is, you can tell me," he said, keeping his voice and his eyes soft, suppressing his urge to know.

She looked at him, then nodded slightly, turning back to the pack without speaking.

Tristan took an opportunity to glance around the cell. No rotting corpses or skeletons hung from the walls. More an expectation of his overactive imagination, he realized. Clean straw lay piled in the corner, and two blankets that appeared well-mended and in good condition, nothing threadbare or filthy. Two buckets sat on opposite sides of the room.

Tristan stood and walked over to the first one, noticing a ladle handle that curved over the edge. He took it and raised it, dripping, to his nose, sniffing, and found the scent fresh. Then his tongue flicked out and he tasted it.

"It's clean," he exclaimed.

Isolde looked up from the pack and glanced around the dungeon. "Either they treat visitors well here, or they were expecting us somehow."

"Anyone watching from the height of the tower would have seen us coming from miles away," Tristan replied, walking over and noting another bucket meant as a latrine.

They waited. Isolde dozed, head bobbing on her chest. Somewhere, water dripped.

Tristan opened his mouth to break the maddening silence, but before he could speak, footsteps sounded on the staircase. He rose to his feet, legs complaining as they unwound from their cramped position.

A twitchy little man in a plain tunic walked up to the prison bars. "You have arrived at Castle Pleure, holding of Lord Bruenor and Lady Arian."

"Why are we being held? We have done nothing wrong," Tristan said, gripping the bars in his hands. The cold of the metal seeped into his skin. Isolde came up behind him, radiating warmth in contrast to the chill prison air.

The messenger eyed them both, then cleared his throat and continued, clearly having repeated his message numerous times.

"It is tradition in this castle that any lord and lady who are found therein must participate in a challenge. The people shall thereby be gathered together and brought into the castle proper, where a contest shall be held between the lady of the castle and the other lady, and the lord of the castle and the other lord. The ladies shall be judged of their comparative beauty, and the one decreed fairer than the other shall keep her head. The opposing lord shall strike off the head of the less fortunate lady.

"Then the lords shall take up their swords and enter a duel forthwith for possession of the successful lady, and the victor shall rule, the fairest lady by his side. Thus, the fairest and the strongest shall rule in Castle Pleure." The messenger stopped and sniffed, then wiped his beaked nose with spindly fingers.

"That is barbaric," Isolde spoke at last, stepping up through the bars. Her hand darted out, too fast for Tristan to react, and gripped the neckline of the messenger's tunic. "We refuse to participate. Release us, now," she growled.

Tristan stared from her to the panicked messenger. The messenger grasped her hands and yanked them from his tunic, stepping away quickly.

"I have no power here. Your freedom must come of yourselves."

"At least the men have a fair contest of skill and strength! Who is to judge my looks and compare them with this mysterious lady's?" Isolde asked, voice laced with bitterness.

"The people of the village, men and women alike. They will agree amongst themselves, then choose a spokesperson." The messenger hesitated, then leaned in a little closer. "It is not mine to tell, but I would give you some hope: the people are discontented with the current lady. She practices wicked magic and preys on the people. They wish for her to be removed. Flaunt your kindness, have you any, and you will be rewarded."

Tristan found himself smiling in the flickering dimness of the prison. It would be easy for Isolde to show herself as kind. Until now, he hadn't seen much that would mar that reputation.

"Will I at least have the decency of a bath and a change of clothing? The contest will hardly be fair, otherwise," Isolde said, arms crossed over her chest.

"Both of you shall receive all that you need from within the castle." The messenger bowed crisply at the waist and left with haste, leaving the couple alone in their cell.

Tristan found Isolde's eyes in the darkness.

"You must hate me," she said, glancing away.

"I was going to do it if you hadn't," Tristan replied, feeling a bit perplexed.

Isolde's forehead creased. "What?"

He shook his head, snorting. "Not what I meant, love. I thought you were talking about the man and how you... never mind." He cleared his throat, looking at her. How could it feel so difficult to communicate after an entire year of bliss together? He thought he knew her, but she seemed like a new person, a stranger. Would it be this way once the potion's influence left them?

"I don't hate you. I could never hate you."

Her expression didn't change. She didn't believe him.

"Tell me what I can say to convince you. I'm here, aren't I? And I think there are better things we could be doing right now. Like making love for the last time in dirty hay in a prison cell on the eve of our deaths."

"Not even funny, Sir Tristan," Isolde said. She folded her arms and her eyes grew red, her expression tense. Another woman would cry, but Isolde never had in the entire year he had been with her. Odd, that.

Tristan brought her close into his chest once more, wishing it could last forever. "A jest in bad taste, I'm afraid."

"You are good at those."

"Forgive me?" he asked.

"Always," she replied.

He smiled at the familiar exchange. "We should try to escape," he said at last, letting her pull away from him.

"Do you think we would succeed?" Isolde asked. She sounded distant, as if her mind wasn't there in the cell with him, but somewhere else. Did she think they were going to die?

"Perhaps," he said, shrugging. He waited for her to reply, but she rummaged in the bag again.

She pulled out a pear, considering it before biting into the bruised yellow flesh.

"You are the loveliest woman I have ever laid eyes on," he said, voice hoarse. "Do I tell you enough?"

Isolde paused in her chewing, gazing at him. "You have told me a thousand times, and a thousand more." She swallowed, the hand holding the fruit dropping into her lap. "I never considered myself pretty. My younger sister..." she stopped as the words left her lips, and her eyes darted up to him, then back to her hands. She cleared her throat.

"You have a sister? Why did I not meet her in my time at the castle of Mumhan? Or ever hear of her?"

"I...she..." Why wouldn't she meet his gaze? Tristan wondered, watching her. "I do not like to consider her fate," she mumbled.

"Did your mother...?" Tristan asked. Her mother had tried to kill her, so it wasn't an absurd assumption to make. Isolde didn't reply at first.

"What happened was my fault," she said at last. She held up a hand, cutting off his protest. "And before you object and claim it was surely not my fault, I would say that you know nothing of what I speak, and I will not go into details now, so you cannot consider yourself any authority on the subject."

She took a trembling breath. "Suffice it to say, she was far prettier than I, and always has been. Eyes like a summer sky, petite in form and fair in face. Oh, how I envied her." She laughed, a choked, broken laugh, then took another swift bite of pear, looking away as she chewed.

Tristan could not take his eyes from her face. Seeing expressions on it he never had before made him wish he could capture this moment forever, no matter the sorrow found in it.

"Her person was even lovelier than her body. Nothing I could ever hope to match."

"You are the kindest, most generous...why, in our time together, you healed half of Ireland and several villages besides with little compensation for your own time or supplies," Tristan sputtered, shock overwhelming him at her degradation of herself.

She smiled at him, a smile that didn't reach the sadness of her eyes. "I have been compensating, for my sister's sake, trying to be everything she was, and everything I have never been. You do not know the real me, Tristan."

He didn't know how to feel about that revelation. She had a sister, likely dead, whom she had never spoken of to him in their year together. She claimed to not be the person he knew. She knew about potions and had mentioned magic on more than one occasion. Had she been the one behind the love potion?

She looked as benign as any other person, not like the sort who could cast spells or bewitch a man. But then, he hadn't known any sorceresses. He had only heard them described as ancient women who tucked themselves away in secluded huts and handed out remedies that worked far better than they should, sometimes asking for nothing in return, other times... other times taking what they wanted when their payment came due.

The more he thought about it, the more he realized how much that sounded like Isolde, except for the ancient part. Could she possibly be a hag who enchanted herself to look young and beautiful, trying to win her way to the heart of Cornwall through Tristan?

“Are you thinking about tomorrow?” Isolde asked, breaking through his thoughts. As soon as he laid eyes on her, his ridiculous assumptions fled his mind. Sincerity shone through her gaze and her body, in the way she leaned towards him. How could he ever assume the worst of her?

“Tristan?” she asked again.

Tristan blinked. “I am sorry, my thoughts are... confusing. I don’t wish to trouble you.”

“It is no trouble,” she said. “Though, I have been anything but forthcoming. I understand if you do not feel you can trust me after all this.”

“I trust you, Isolde.” She flinched at the harsh way he said her name, and he tried to calm himself. “I don’t understand how, after all we have been through, you can be so distrusting of me. And then to accuse me of the same. I trust you with my life, and more importantly, my heart.” She looked away at that. “I wish I could convince you it is sincere.”

“I have had my share of...insincere love from men,” Isolde said, her hesitant voice reverberating off the cell walls. “You are anything but that, Tristan. Anything but. Though at times I wonder how much the potion...” she bit off her words.

Tristan went to her, crouching on the floor at her side, lifting her chin with his fingers so she looked into his eyes. He wanted her to see him, not just hear his words.

“The potion does not make me someone I am not,” he said. “I love you, Isolde. Almost from the moment I woke in that bed in your infirmary, I felt something different for you than I have ever felt before.”

Her eyes glittered, but no tears fell. “We ought to rest,” she said at last.

He did not reply but took the blanket she offered to him and placed it, folded, under his head, adjusting until his head did not feel the stone floor beneath. He wished he could say the same for his back. Isolde dragged hay over and settled next to him, body pressed against his, the heat of her overwhelming.

Tristan rubbed his hand down the length of her, a motion he had made a hundred times, but never before had he felt her stiffen beneath his touch the way she did now. He leaned over and kissed her temple, then draped his arm over her. Looking at her, the curve of her body visible in the dim light, his ribs constricted. He wanted... well, he would not say what he wanted.

She seemed to sense something in his silence. She shifted, rolling slightly, until her hand found his in the dark, grasping it in her chilled fingers, and her head snuggled into his chest.

He breathed in the scent of her hair in the darkness of the prison, rubbing her slender fingers until warmth came back to them. By that time, her breathing evened out. Sleep came for Tristan a long time after.

They came at dawn, a group of soldiers with unmoving expressions. They held the cell door open. Tristan walked through, but they stopped Isolde when she tried to follow. Tristan protested, refusing to leave her side.

"Another will come for her. She will receive different treatment." The cell door clanged shut, trapping her back inside.

He kept his eyes on her as long as he could, until they rounded the corner and he could crane his neck no farther. His fingers itched, flexing on the hilt of his sword, considering taking it to hand and fighting his way back to her and out of the castle, but he restrained himself.

They would succeed. They had to. He would not let them slay Isolde, no matter the beauty of their mistress. He would not let it happen. Whatever the vile traditions of this place, he would break them without hesitation if anyone dared lay a hand on his precious Isolde. His heart pounded in his chest, threatening to burst as it filled with hot, dark, fearsome anger at the prospect of losing her, of her head being removed by this foul and villainous man, Lord Bruenor, and his Lady Arian.

They led him to the armory and outfitted him with the finest in mail and plate. A faint shred of pain tugged at his heart as they helped him, his distance from Isolde enough to cause discomfort, but not harm.

The assortment of armor astounded him; all different shapes, sizes, styles, and levels of finery. Some dented and terrible, some even beginning to rust and wear from age and use, others gleaming and new, engraved with delicate designs. No two pieces seemed exactly the same, unusual for a castle armory.

He had never worn anything like the polished black plate armor they found for him. It allowed for better movement at his joints and it was so quiet. He followed the silent soldiers to a wall that held a thousand glittering weapons, again such an assortment as to be unfathomable. Sword and shield, mace and axe, crossbows, knives, even some weapons that Tristan wasn't sure he recognized.

"I will use my own sword," he said, resting his hand on the hilt attached to his side. They offered a new sheath, and he took it, a beautiful leather casing with metalwork on the ends.

Then, he turned his attention to the wall of shields, an overwhelming assortment of colors and symbols. He had a choice between square, rectangular, circular, and pointed shields, wood and metal, leather-covered, metal- studded or plain, all bearing a different coat of arms.

Now, he realized where the assortment of weaponry and armor had come from; other men who had fought the lord of the Castle Pleure and lost.

Tristan's throat tightened. He chose a circular metal shield with a black eagle emblazoned on a field of red. It provided the perfect balance to his sword. He walked around for a while with the entire ensemble, sword out, falling into various stances, getting used to the odd, easy way the armor moved. He had practiced the past year by fighting straw dummies and dead trees.

He wasn't at peak fighting form any longer but felt heartened by how readily the stances came to him. He turned to the man at his side, a taller man with a bushy, light brown mustache and wide eyes.

"I need to care for my sword. It is in desperate need of cleaning, sharpening, and polish."

The man nodded to one of the five other soldiers with him, who split off from the group and returned moments later with the materials Tristan needed. Tristan sat on a bench, feeling awkward at first. He usually cleaned his weapon in private; being watched made his movements hesitant. He set everything out before him, breathing slow and deep to calm his nerves, then picked up the heavy metal file. He laid the sword parallel to himself on a large block of wood, then filed down the edge.

Eventually, all other persons seemed to disappear from the room. A bottle of oil came next, poured onto the whetstone before him. Back and forth strokes, uniform in pressure and speed, polished the rough edge on the blade with the file. When he had finished one side, he moved to the other.

He had done this hundreds of times with his swords throughout the years. Going to a blacksmith was convenient, but he found that doing it himself, especially before or right after a battle, soothed his nerves. He let thoughts come and go, not giving them any particular attention, as he moved on to the large felted cloth. He held it carefully in one hand and rubbed it across the flat of his blade, using the oil left from the whetstone to clean off the remaining residue.

"That is a fine weapon." A female voice, slick like oil, glided into the room and reached his ears.

Tristan turned and faced a tall, lanky woman dressed in vibrant red, her silk gown clinging to her thin form. A metal belt rested on her bony hips.

She raised a thin arm towards him, offering her hand. Tristan leaned forward and brushed the papery skin with his lips. He suppressed a shudder as he pulled away and resisted the urge to scrub the feel of her from his lips. He looked into the woman's dark eyes, observing her high, pointed cheekbones and straight, narrow face.

"May I assume you are the Lady Arian?" he asked, turning back to his sword and giving it several extra rubs with the cloth as an excuse to avoid staring at the purported sorceress.

Lady Arian smiled, stretching her face into an unnaturally wide grin, showing all of her straight, white teeth that, in the semi-darkness, almost seemed pointed. Tristan shook his head, trying to erase that demonic image.

"Do you hope that I am, Sir Knight?" Lady Arian's hand rested at the base of his scalp, her fingertips digging in, massaging. Tristan moved his head away from the scratch of her nails, standing, bare sword held before him. "I see all of your instincts are intact."

She tilted her head back and laughed, her black hair cascading down past her waist. "Good. I like a man who is fully present. You're going to win this duel; the fight is in you." Her eyes flashed. "Just as I am going to win the contest, for none of my subjects will dare vote for that wench you brought." She laughed again. His skin crawled at her presence as she circled around him again. She stopped at the group of guards standing at attention, twirling the mustache of the man with the wide- set eyes.

"Because I like you, I'll give you a little advantage," Lady Arian said, passing her arm over his head.

Tristan thought he felt a tingle move through his entire body. It made him itch.

Before he could ask what she meant, what she had done, the Lady Arian vanished. Whatever she did to him, he could do nothing about it. He only had to hope it was truly an advantage, as she said, and not something that would cripple or inhibit his fighting.

As much as it left a bad taste in his mouth to use magic in an honest duel, part of him was a bit relieved, in a way that made him feel guilty. His thoughts went to Isolde, wondering what her preparations included. He hoped it would be enough.

CHAPTER NINETEEN

And know not if they know if dead these be?
Oh love, are thy days my days, and to thee
Are all nights like as my nights? does the sun
Grieve thee? art thou soul-sick till day be done,
And weary till day rises? is thine heart
Full of dead things as mine is? Nay, thou art
Man, with man's strength and praise and pride of life,
No bondwoman, no queen, no loveless wife
That would be shamed albeit she had not sinned.
"Iseult at Tintagel," from "Tristram of Lyonesse"
by Algernon Charles Swinburne

Morgan watched Tristan leave, heart pounding as he moved out of sight. She stopped herself from reaching out and pleading for them to take her with them. She hated it. She had no control, like the times when her personality split half a dozen ways, trapping her in her own body, unable to move or think.

She had no choice in loving Tristan now. No opportunity to discover whether her love for him was true or not, lasting or fleeting. The potion coated her nerves and organs, attached to her brain, sending false signals shooting to her core, which, in turn, made her move and act without conscious choice.

An ache started in her chest as Tristan drew further away. The pain pulsed, distracting but not crippling. She stood at the bars of the cell, feeling that ache in her chest when the group of women came for her.

A short, large-bosomed woman with a strawberry-shaped face and a huge gap in her upper lip that almost connected to her nose smiled at Morgan, the gap in her lip making it more of a sneer.

She unlocked the cell and beckoned Morgan out. Her three companions, beautiful in comparison, remained stone-faced and silent.

"Where are you taking me? Where's Sir Tristan?" Morgan asked as they surrounded her and ushered her towards the stairs.

"He be gettin' ready, milady," the gap-lipped woman said in a muffled sort of way. Her voice dropped to a mutter. "...today is a good day...today I get my pretty face..."

Morgan assumed the woman must be addled in the mind, as well as disfigured. She tried to memorize their path, to glimpse the hallway where they'd first entered, but they never seemed to cross it. Each door they passed remained shut, and they met no other people.

The ever-present tug of pain in Morgan's chest loosened, then tightened, fluctuating as they must have drawn near to the room that held Tristan.

A door opened before Morgan, and she stepped into a comfortably warm room. A steaming meal rested on a table next to a large decanter of wine. Two fires burned in identical grates on opposite sides of the room. A huge tub sat in the middle of a red-brick floor.

Morgan gaped in spite of herself. She had never seen the like. The women each took up a station. The first indicated she should undress, and they allowed her the small privacy of removing her own clothing, then helped her into the tub.

Soreness melted from her body. Her muscles relaxed as she rested her head against the back of the tub. She relished the cocoon of warmth that wrapped her body, so much so that she barely registered when several pairs of hands started gently cleaning her body. Their hands moved in rhythm, dipping beneath the water, sponging away the traumas of the past few days.

Morgan let them do their work, focusing on breathing and letting go. It felt good to be taken care of. They poured water over her head, wetting her hair, and rubbed a lilac- scented soap into it.

As they washed her, Morgan wondered about the castle, about this foolish, barbaric tradition. She watched the faces of the women tending her. Would they answer her questions?

"What do you hope happens today?"

All four faces glanced to one another, then to her. Two of the women draped clothing on a bed across the room while the others, a ruddy, round-faced woman and a taller, broad-shouldered woman rinsed Morgan's hair.

"We should not speak of it, milady," the taller woman said, brushing her dark hair from her face as she held out an arm to aid Morgan as she stepped over the steep sides of the tub. "Our lives are in jeopardy as it is, serving you."

"Were you forced? Or did you choose?"

"We were assigned. We are her ladyship's servants."

"Has no one tried to stop his horrid tradition?" Morgan asked, the relaxation from her bath fleeing in the face of the morbid conversation. She glanced between the three ladies in front of her. The fourth stood somewhere behind, supplying a warm towel to be draped around Morgan's shivering form.

"There are rumors that Lady Arian has ruled here from the beginning, occasionally taking the faces of her competition to maintain an illusion of fairness. No one can prove her deceit. The servants are replaced after each new arrival." The taller woman led her to the wardrobe area, where she helped Morgan into a delicate, white shift.

"Replaced?" Morgan asked. "You mean killed," she answered herself.

They invited her to sit in a chair near the fire, while one of the women, timid-faced and petite, brushed scented oils through her hair, then tied it in rags to encourage curls when it dried.

"Princess Isolde, let us dress you so you can eat," the tallest woman said.

She took Morgan's arm and encouraged her to stand. A dazzling array of dresses glittered like gemstones in the firelight. Amethyst and diamonds, emeralds, sapphires, and garnets.

Morgan took them in with wide eyes. She should choose wisely; the choice could mean the difference between keeping her head and not.

She eventually selected a deep violet dress with flowing sleeves down to the floor that hugged her hips, accentuating what little curve Isolde's body had. At her elbows and waist, gold-wrapped thread made intricate Celtic knots, and a necklace of amethyst gemstones glittered in little clusters along her neckline, set in delicate gold. Morgan touched the cold stones.

In Ireland, Isolde had kept plain things. The last time someone treated Morgan like, well, a queen, was in Camelot. She swallowed hard to get past the lump in her throat and clenched her fists to keep from ripping the jewels free and flinging them away.

The smiling, large-bosomed woman led her to a chair at the table where still-steaming food waited for her. Juicy meats and delicate fruits blossomed with flavor on her tongue. She started in on the food as if she hadn't eaten in days, but halfway through the meal, surrounded by the smiling women, she realized that this could be her last meal.

She swallowed a piece of chicken without tasting it, and every bite she took after tasted like ash. She forced herself to finish a few more bites, then pushed her plate away and took a final sip of wine.

The women untied the strips of fabric and her hair cascaded in tumbling curls down past her shoulders, silky against her skin. Morgan kept her eyes closed and relished the feeling of security that enveloped her. Against all reason, she felt safe with these women. No matter that she could lose her head all over a perceived beauty that wasn't even her own.

The door to the room creaked open. Morgan turned to see a man in a black doublet step gracefully in. She gazed at him, eyes lingering on his wide, handsome face and the onyx rings decorating his broad fingers.

"Who are you?" she croaked, then cleared her throat.

The man smiled and bent at the waist. "I am Lord Bruenor. And you must be the Princess Isolde."

"How do you know who I am?" Morgan asked, throat dry. A chill seemed to sweep through the room. Her body went rigid, as if a predator had entered.

"We have our ways," Lord Bruenor said.

Morgan's eyes narrowed. Did they know that Morgan wasn't the Princess Isolde? Is that how Tristan would find out, revealed as they took off her head? She forced the thoughts down. She had to focus, to find out what he wanted.

"Stand up," he commanded. His voice held a compelling power and Morgan found her muscles and limbs responding involuntarily. She jerked out of her seat, leaning on the table for support. "Come over here," he said from the center of the room. She complied.

He walked around her, muttering, hand reaching out to touch her elbow, her waist, her neck, fingers trailing. Morgan's face grew hot, though he never touched her where he ought not. The intimacy of it made her skin crawl, her blood boil. She found her fingers fidgeting, and her stomach grew taut, almost nauseated at the thought of his hands on her, as if he owned her.

"Sir, remove your hands," she said evenly.

Lord Bruenor chuckled, thankfully taking his hands away. The crawling sensation remained on the surface of her arms and neck. "You are right, Princess. You are not mine to play with. Yet."

Nor will I ever be, Morgan thought. She moistened her lips. "Where is Sir Tristan? You have treated him well?" Her voice trembled, though she tried to hide it by adjusting her gown, brushing off invisible dirt.

"It is tradition to be sure our guests are well-rested and cared for before their trial," Lord Bruenor said, turning to face the fire.

Morgan gasped. A large, twisted scar ran from behind his ear, down the length of his neck and disappeared inside his doublet. Lord Bruenor noticed her stare. "I have been lord of this castle longer than any before me. I received this several years ago from a rather skilled knight. He nearly had me." He bared his teeth, and a hand reached up, stroking one of Morgan's blonde curls.

"Sorry, I could not resist." He turned suddenly, facing the line of serving women that stood to Morgan's left. "Tabitha, fetch the special pots for this one. I appreciate her beauty; it deserves unique attention."

Tabitha, the tallest of the four women, inclined her head and walked to a tall cupboard on the far side of the room.

Lord Bruenor smiled at Morgan again, making her spine crawl with discomfort. His blue eyes sparkled with mischief. "You will like this gift, I think." He leaned forward, closing the gap between their faces, nose touching her ear, breath tickling her neck. "I want you to win, Isolde. This will help against her enchantments."

He moved away, abruptly turning on his heel and heading for the door. "I will leave you ladies to it," he said, then shut the door with force, its closure seeming to reverberate as a sound of finality through Morgan.

One of the nameless women, her brown hair coiffed on top of her head with an admirable delicacy, took Morgan's hand and led her back to the chair by the fire.

Tabitha placed a tray of little pots down on a small table within arms' reach and took the lids off one by one. The contents shimmered.

Morgan stared at them, then looked into the eyes of the woman kneeling before her.

"What is this?"

"Maquillage magique, milady," she said, a perfect French accent rolling naturally off her tongue. She picked up a pot and a wide brush, dipping it into the glittering white powder. She continued talking as she brushed with wide, confident strokes across Morgan's brow. "It is a secret recipe, passed down through the generations of my family. It will enhance your beauty in a way no other rouge or perfume could."

"Magic," Morgan murmured. Her skin went colder with each stroke of the brush. "What is your name?" she asked.

"Annora," the woman said, setting down the pot and brush and picking up a smaller set. "Close your eyes."

Morgan did so, feeling pressure as Annora stroked across her eyelids with a smaller gesture, painting around Morgan's eyes. Her cheeks received rouge and her lips a thick red paste.

"Miroir, si'l vous plait."

The large-bosomed woman held out a small handled mirror.

Morgan stared at the reflection. An angel gazed back. The dark circles under her eyes were gone. A bright gold and amber streak smudged each eyelid. Her lips looked darker than the deep-red of poppies. Her once-wan cheeks now appeared flawless and rosy, and soft sparkles shimmered when she moved her head. Her hair fell in flowing waves, curling past her shoulders. The violet dress accentuated her pale hair and skin. She looked perfect, like a statue, but with warmth and softness.

Her hand drifted towards her face, but Annora slapped it away.

"No, you mustn't touch, mon cher," Annora exclaimed, pressing Morgan's hand into her lap and patting it.

"What happens now?" Morgan asked, tearing her gaze away from the mirror. The pride and satisfaction she felt in how she looked in this body that wasn't hers disoriented her.

"Soon, they will come for you. The Hall of Decision has the best lighting. There you will be judged by the villagers," the large-bosomed woman said.

"Should I be concerned about Lady Arian? Is her magic strong? Will she try to harm me?"

"No, she is bound by tradition. Even her magic cannot interfere."

"That isn't true, Herriette," Annora broke in, facing the well- endowed woman. "How else has she maintained her position so long? She has found a way."

"And our lord tires of her, which is why he petitioned you for your magic pots and skill with the brush," Herriette replied, fists on her wide hips. "The princess need not be concerned."

Morgan licked her lips, and a cherry flavoring coated her tongue with sickly sweetness. Must be something in the paste on her lips. She considered what she could do if she felt an enchantment laid on her, but her mind seemed blank. In fact, she had trouble keeping her eyes open at all. She leaned, hands reaching for a surface to lay on.

"Just need a rest," she slurred.

Several sets of hands braced her upright. "Annora, your lip paste!"

Annora gasped.

Morgan's vision blurred, then sharpened, then went sideways as her head flopped.

"She must have found my pots! What could she have used?" The voices blended, becoming faint and indiscernible.

The heavy enchantment reminded her of the magic pills Merlin had once given her, only much stronger.

Fingers thrust under her nose, fumbling. She jerked upright.

"Sniff," the distorted voice commanded, holding the back of her skull, forcing her head down.

Morgan sniffed, and fire lanced through her nostrils to the top of her head. Her limbs started jerking uncontrollably. Strong hands held her down. Someone shouted. Another set of hands forced her mouth open, placing a hard, bitter object on her tongue, then braced her chin shut.

Morgan struggled against her captors, the bitterness dissolving on her tongue, numbing her jaw, spreading fast through her limbs, down to fingers and toes. She relaxed. Frantic hands rubbed at her lips, taking off the poisonous lip paste. Gradually, her mind cleared.

Four faces peered at her, watching with concern.

"So sorry, princess..." the words trailed off.

Morgan squinted at the woman's blurred face. Annora, she thought.

Tingling started in the very tips of her fingers, like what she felt after resting in one position too long. It spread like fire, licking up her legs, arms, and torso. Morgan gritted her teeth and stamped her legs, trying to shake it off faster. Her jaw worked. She gulped air.

"Lady Arian won't try anything? Isn't that what you said?" she asked at last, raising her eyebrows at Herriette.

Herriette's eyes widened.

"This incident implicates Annora, but we both know she didn't do it. You four, besides Lord Bruenor, are the only ones who know of these pots. Unless Lord Bruenor was bewitched by Lady Arian or ordered me murdered himself, both of which I doubt," Morgan said.

Herriette stuttered. "N-no, milady. 'Tweren't me, honest."

"I heard you, in the hall, muttering about getting your pretty face today. Is that what she promised you in exchange for killing me?"

Herriette whimpered, hunching her shoulders.

The other women gasped together. Morgan sat back in the chair, feeling spent. She clasped her hands together to keep from rubbing her face and ruining it further.

"Beauty," Herriette said with a sob. "No man will have me like...like this. I've seen thirty-five years. She's been promising for five of them that if I helped get rid of the ladies who threatened her position, she would give me an elixir for youth and beauty."

She buried her red, blotchy face in her hands and wailed. "And now, she'll kill me because ye are still alive."

Morgan grimaced, then slapped her thighs and stood up. "Well, so long as I am chosen in this ridiculous beauty competition, Lady Arian will lose her head and you have no fears."

Herriette shook her head. "She wears an emerald necklace that makes her skin stronger than steel. She cannot be killed."

"Of course. Her failsafe," Morgan muttered, pacing. She found herself running her tongue along her lips, as if searching for any traces of that cherry taste. She stopped and looked up. "Do any of you have access to the lady's chambers?"

The others shook their heads. Herriette tried to make herself smaller.

"It has to be you, then," Morgan said. "You can make this right, Herriette. And you must. Steal the necklace. Bring it to me."

Herriette's wide eyes gazed at Morgan without blinking. "W-what?" she stammered.

Morgan locked eyes with her. "Steal the necklace. Get it from the Lady Arian. The others will spread word of my arrival, convince the villagers to select me. When I am chosen, her head will be removed, and you will be free."

Herriette put her head down.

"Listen, Herriette, no one can promise the kind of beauty you seek. It comes with a heavy price and is not without pain. A sacrifice must be made, one I can tell you are not ready to make, nor should anyone expect it of you. You can be happy without youth and beauty."

"That is easy for you to say," she mumbled, voice thick with emotion. "You are a beautiful princess. Wars are fought over you. I am nobody. No one notices me, except to ridicule."

Morgan breathed through her nose. She had to convince Herriette. "You are right about one thing; a war will be fought if I do not leave this place, if it hasn't started already. I was like you once, Herriette; I believed I could live with the consequences of my actions. But when I learned that others would die because of what I had done, I chose to make it right. If I don't meet with King Mark of Cornwall, hundreds of good people may die, innocent ones. Children. Are you prepared to share responsibility for that, Herriette?"

Tears flooded the shorter woman's eyes. She sniffled. "I jus' am afraid," she replied. "She'll kill me."

"I understand. But life is not without risks. And you very nearly killed me. A debt is owed," Morgan replied.

Herriette nodded, tears spilling down her cheeks. "Aye, milady, that there is. Me mam taught me better." She nodded resolutely. "I'll do it."

"Thank you," Morgan said. She felt no relief. She wouldn't until she held the necklace in her hand. Morgan turned to Annora, Tabitha, and the third woman, who hadn't given her name yet. "Tabitha, take your friend..."

"That's Perinne, my sister," Annora cut in. "I will go with her."

Morgan nodded. "Very well. Annora and Perinne, go to the villagers and tell them to select me. Whomever you can reach. Assure them all will be well, and their families will be safe." Morgan turned to the taller woman. "Tabitha, can you create a distraction for Lady Arian, and get her to leave her rooms? Herriette will need help getting out of there before she returns. You can be lookout."

Tabitha hesitated, then nodded. Herriette gave her a relieved look.

"It will take all of us to make this work. How much time do we have?" Fatigue overwhelmed Morgan, but she forced herself to remain alert and standing.

"A few hours. They will make the announcement soon and select a group of villagers to represent the entire village. I will try to get to them as soon as they are chosen," Annora said.

"Don't tell them about the necklace. We can't have Lady Arian hearing of it, and sorceresses have ways of hearing the wind's whispers."

The four women nodded.

"What will you do, milady?" Tabitha asked.

"You look about to drop," Herriette said, looking guilty. "Let me bring you some blankets. There's a lounge chair in the back of the room, there."

"Yes, thank you," Morgan said.

They moved at the same time, heading to complete their tasks. Morgan moved towards the fur-strewn lounge Herriette had indicated. Being imprisoned, awake most of the night, and almost murdered brought a bone-deep weariness upon her.

She sank into the furs, drawing a thick, wool blanket over her as she laid down, adjusting her hair so she didn't lay on it and ruin the curls. The crackling fire made the room warm. It was her first time without Tristan within calling distance since they first drank the potion.

She wished she had magic for scrying, to find out if what she had seen in her night visions was a premonition or a reality. Perhaps Niviane sent it as a warning. On the other hand, it could be a trap.

That made her think of Elaina, trapped in the tower at Niviane's hand. Morgan put a hand to her head, groaning. Her thoughts scattered, trying to predict Niviane's next move, trying to decide how she felt about Tristan, about Arthur.

Her last thought before falling asleep was of the priestesses. They had sent her back in time to save Camelot, to prevent its fall and preserve the Knights of the Round Table. And by all accounts, it seemed she had failed.

Morgan woke to someone shaking her shoulder. Her eyes blinked open to a glittering green and gold object swaying before her face. She sat up and reached out, touching the smooth, glassy surface of the emerald necklace.

"How did you manage, Herriette?"

"I told her it needed to be cleaned and polished. She is ever so vain." Herriette looked over her shoulder, her hair even frizzier than before, tufts sticking out like a lion's mane around her beet-red face. She panted as if she had run from Lady Arian's room back here. "Please, Princess Isolde, what should I do? When I don't return, she will search for me and punish me. She'll want to wear it to the contest."

"Take the magic pots and find Annora. She can give you a disguise, I am certain of it. Then lose yourself in the village or surrounding forest. Is there someone who would hide you? She won't have time to search for you at this point if you leave the castle quickly. If this goes wrong and I am killed, take to the road and find a new home. Better to lose your job than your life." Morgan placed her hand on Herriette's shoulder. "Thank you for doing the right thing, Herriette. I am certain that, with time, you will find happiness."

Herriette's eyes watered. "Thank you, milady, for your kindness. I'm sorry I tried to kill you."

"There is enough happiness to go around without harming others to get it," Morgan said, brushing several strands of golden curls away from her face. "A lesson I have learned the difficult way."

Herriette clasped her hand for a moment, then rushed away, disappearing through the doors.

Morgan stared at the emerald necklace beside her. She could wear it herself, a move certain to incur the wrath of Lady Arian and perhaps cause her to kill Morgan before the villagers even had a say. She wrapped the fine chain around her fingers, then tucked the coiled metal into her bodice. It would be close, but undetected, she hoped. She stood, stretching.

A knock sounded at the door, and Tabitha slipped in looking around for Morgan. She smiled when she saw her.

"Is it done?"

"It is," Morgan replied.

"Where is it?" Tabitha asked, peering curiously at Morgan, then around the room.

"Hidden well. There is no need for concern; I will take care of it."

Tabitha nodded. "That is well. Are you ready? The villagers have been gathered. They await your presence in the Hall of Decision."

"The Hall of Decision?" Morgan echoed, walking across the room.

Tabitha produced a pair of black slippers with silver thread woven throughout. She indicated Morgan should sit in a chair across from her.

"It is where the contests of beauty and strength have always been held," she explained, bending over and pulling the slippers onto Morgan's feet. "Ever since I was a little girl, and before."

"How long has this been tradition?"

"As long as this castle has been here." Tabitha stood and held out a hand for Morgan who took it, rising from her seat. Tabitha made a few quick adjustments to her hair, untangling some unruly curls, then led her silently from the room.

The hall was dark and quiet. A low murmur came from somewhere below them; perhaps the villagers gathering in the Hall of Decision. Morgan clasped her dress with clammy fingers. She felt calm but could feel the tension in the air. Tabitha radiated with it, every movement stiff.

"Tabitha, what do you hope happens today?"

"I have been taught not to hope," she said quietly. "When I was chosen as maid to Lady Arian, my mother and father wept for weeks. They begged me to run away, knowing that once someone like you and your knight arrived, they would never see me again." Her voice broke.

Morgan's gut twisted. Her death would mean Tabitha's death as well. The emotion created a new sense within her, something of a responsibility for another person's well-being.

Tabitha continued. "I suppose...it would be nice if both you and your man won the day. You seem kind. But if only one of you should win..." Her words stopped as she did.

Two tall, wooden doors stood before them, shut tight. Beyond, Morgan could hear nothing but silence.

Tabitha's hand on her arm made her look up. "I fear Lord Bruenor and Lady Arian have the capacity to corrupt either one of you. You must succeed."

She squeezed Morgan's arm lightly, and Morgan gave her a small smile, feeling a sudden rush of insecurity. Tabitha rapped on the doors and they swung wide, pushed by two armored guards bearing spears.

Morgan stepped inside, and the silence grew heavy, thick as fog on a moor. She walked through the hall towards the regal couple sitting in thrones at the far end of the room. Peasants lined the edges of the carpet she tread, watching her with wide eyes and pinched faces. They huddled beside each other and whispered at her back.

Morgan dared to glance at Lady Arian; her dark eyes thunderous, her expression livid. She sat in a plum-colored dress, shades darker than the violet dress Morgan wore. Her long fingers trailed at her neckline, as if used to stroking a certain emerald necklace. Morgan straightened her head and deliberately looked away from the sorceress's furious glare.

Lord Bruenor stood, arms open, smiling charismatically as he descended the steps to greet her. He walked like a predator, pacing before the people who shied away from him like animals lined up for slaughter. He towered at over six feet tall, which, combined with his rippling muscles, made for an intimidating stature. Lord Bruenor took Morgan by the hand, raising it between them, and escorted her to the top of the dais, standing above the peasants.

"I present to you, la belle Isolde, the Irish princess!" The breath knocked out of her in the midst of the false-sounding cheers the peasants gave. Morgan glanced at him, and he smiled at her.

"You'll start a war," Lady Arian hissed.

Lord Bruenor's eyes glittered. "It is tradition," he said, as if that were explanation enough, then he looked away, dropping her arm and sitting back into his throne, leaving her standing, alone at the top of the steps.

The doors opened again, and in strode Tristan. Morgan's breath caught in her throat at the sight of him in gleaming black armor, his broadsword naked in his hand. It seemed he had bathed as well, and she hoped he had eaten. His eyes were hard, until, halfway down the carpet, he noticed her. His steps faltered a moment, and she saw him working to maintain a fierce, intimidating air. He stopped at the bottom of the stairs to the dais, looking up with a face of anger at Lord Bruenor.

"Do we fight here or in the outer yard?" he asked, practically growling. The timber of his voice went up through Morgan's spine, making her shiver.

Lord Bruenor laughed. "The ladies make their battle first, Sir Knight." He looked over to Lady Arian. "Are you going to announce your champion?" he asked, gesturing towards Tristan.

Lady Arian huffed, then slapped her hands on the arms of her throne and stood. She forced a smile, more like a grimace, as she gestured towards Tristan.

"Sir Tristan de Liones," she said. She pulled her hand towards her, urging Tristan to climb the steps and stand beside Morgan. The crowd cheered again, sounding deflated.

Morgan could only imagine what they expected to see now.

"First, the presentation of the ladies." Bruenor's voice boomed, filling the silence that followed the cheers. "Choose wisely; your next lady of the castle awaits your judgment. The unlucky one," he paused, "will lose her head at the hand of the other lady's champion." His face split with a feral grin.

Morgan felt sick. The man actually enjoyed this. She watched below as two men rolled the red carpet away, all the way back to the doors, and Morgan's stomach roiled. A hideous, dark brown stain spread from the foot of the throne to the edge of the crowd. She swallowed hard and covered her mouth with her hand. How many men and women had lost their lives there on that floor?

Tristan's hand brushed hers, and warmth moved through her at his touch.

She glanced at him, found him staring at her with open admiration.

Beautiful, he mouthed, then grasped her fingers in his and squeezed.

"Ladies, present yourselves before the court," Lord Bruenor said.

Lady Arian stepped down onto the first stair, and Morgan mirrored her, keeping her chin raised, her heart pounding so hard she thought everyone could hear it. They moved down the five steps together, halted at the bottom, then gave a turn. Lady Arian placed her hand on her hip, smirking. Even without the emerald necklace, she held the advantage of having struck fear into the hearts of the people.

Morgan rubbed her clammy fingers against each other, trying not to clutch at her dress. *Smile, Morgan.* She felt wooden; her face didn't seem to respond. *Look friendly. Look genuine. Look strong.*

How had she gotten herself into this mess? Her arms trembled. She looked out over the small crowd staring at her and Lady Arian.

Lord Bruenor cleared his throat. "Who is your spokesperson?"

A woman stepped forward, hands clutching at her grey and blue homespun dress. "I am, my lord," she replied. She glanced upward at the nobles, then back to the ground.

"Count the selections. You may ascend the stairs and tell me of the final choice when you are finished."

The spokeswoman nodded, then turned and wove her way among the dozen or so village people. It did not take long. Each person whispered in her ear, and she made a small mark on a slip of white parchment with a charcoal nub.

Morgan craned her neck and strained her ears but could hear nothing. She glanced to Lady Arian, who stood stone-faced.

The woman chosen as spokesperson ascended the steps, eyes carefully averted from Lady Arian's burning glare and Morgan's curious stare. She handed the folded parchment to Lord Bruenor then hurried back down to where her fellow villagers waited.

Lord Bruenor unfolded the parchment, and a smile split his face as he read.

"Princess Isolde has won the affection of the people with her beauty!" he shouted.

Morgan heard as if from far away. She couldn't believe it; she had actually won the contest!

Beside her, Lady Arian crumpled into a heap of silk and jewels. Morgan stared at her. She almost reached out to touch her, to tell her it would be all right, but Lord Bruenor rushed in from behind and clasped an iron collar with a long chain around Lady Arian's neck.

"No, no!" Lady Arian gave an agonized scream. Her fingernails scrabbled against the bar, chipping their long, carefully crafted points on the hard metal.

Lord Bruenor fixed the chain to a bolt on the floor, holding Lady Arian trapped like a beast prepared for slaughter. She collapsed, crying out hysterically, grasping the bar as if she could tear it off. Lord Bruenor looked on in disgust. He turned toward Tristan, who stood frozen at the top of the steps, sword half-raised. Morgan's heart skipped. Would he...?

"Well, finish her off, then," Lord Bruenor said, gesturing to the frantic woman, sobbing on the blood-stained floor.

Tristan's gaze hardened. He dropped his sword point towards the ground. "I will not participate in your barbaric traditions."

Morgan's heart soared. She swallowed the lump in her throat and started up the stairs towards him, to stand by him.

The ring of a sword made her wheel around, barely keeping her balance on the narrow steps. Lord Bruenor's sword whistled through the air and silenced the unfortunate sorceress.

Morgan collapsed, stomach heaving, retching.

She heard Tristan's boots on the stone staircase and he bent down, placing a gauntleted hand on her back.

Morgan reached her hand up to his arm and pulled herself to sitting. She could not look toward Lord Bruenor, not without seeing that horrific pool of blood, and a headless body in a plum-colored dress.

"You are a monster," Tristan growled.

Morgan felt the rumble of his anger vibrate against her body. She clutched his arm. The emerald and gold necklace caught her eye, poking out from the top of her bodice. She pulled it out, quickly winding it around Tristan's wrist and clasping it. Tristan didn't take notice. All of his focus on the cruel man in black standing at the bottom of the stairs with blood on his sword. Morgan tugged at the crude knot, securing it.

Tristan stood, bringing her with him. She faced the empty thrones atop the dais, listening to the silence behind her, marked by the occasional retching from someone within the group of villagers. Could such a thin chain really save his life?

"It is your turn, Sir Tristan. I am ready for you."

Feet shuffled. Morgan glanced from the corner of her eye and saw the villagers scattering backward, making room away from the newly deceased body for the men to fight their battle.

Tristan moved her hand from his arm. "Wait here," he snarled, gaze fixed on Lord Bruenor.

"Tristan…" Morgan started, but he was already gone, sword raised, racing down the steps towards the man who had murdered his own wife.

Morgan forced herself to watch. She sat on the steps, legs trembling too much to hold her upright, hands clenching the smooth fabric of her dress that draped over her knees.

She knew little about fighting. Back and forth, the men danced. Lord Bruenor had a strange grace about his fighting, like a stork, balance and strike, sword darting out to catch Tristan unawares. But Tristan was a lion, fierce and powerful despite everything that had happened the past few days. He struck out relentlessly, hammering his sword down again and again, always on the offense, face clenched in an expression of righteous anger.

Lord Bruenor deftly stepped aside from an attack. Tristan stumbled, falling to the floor.

Morgan gasped and stood. The villagers looked on in horror, some hiding their faces, as Lord Bruenor's gleaming sword flashed down and rebounded with a flash of green light. Some of the villagers shouted in shock.

A shriek erupted from Morgan's throat, calling out for Tristan.

Tristan rose to his feet, glancing at the chain on his wrist before wheeling around, sword clashing with Lord Bruenor's next attempt on his life. He roared, a sound unlike any Morgan had heard before, and pursued Lord Bruenor until the lord of the castle fell to his knees, pleading for his life.

Morgan saw Tristan hesitate. She thought she could see the wheels of his mind turning. In the end, Tristan was a man who valued honor above all things, and that honor included avenging the woman and countless others whom Lord Bruenor had slain in the name of this horrifying tradition.

Morgan closed her eyes, not opening them until the cheers of the people erupted in the dreadful silence of the Hall of Decision.

Lord Bruenor was dead.

Tears pricked at the corners of her eyes. A soft hand on her arm made her look up into Tristan's face. He had removed his helm, and he gazed at her with a tender concern that made her want to embrace him. Somehow, he knew she wouldn't appreciate the embrace, even though her limbs trembled, and her body cried out for her to reach out and claim him. She breathed in deeply, then let it all out in a rush. They had won.

She looked up. The twenty or so gathered villagers stared at her and Tristan. Their faces held a hopeful expectation, some mixed with understandable wariness, that brought a lump to Morgan's throat.

She opened her mouth to speak to the people, to tell them she could not do as they desired, but Tristan's hand tightened on her arm, stopping her words before they flowed out. He had something to say.

CHAPTER TWENTY

So far was my love born beneath his love.
I loved him as the sea-wind loves the sea,
To rend and ruin it only and waste: but he,
As the sea loves a sea-bird loved he me,
To foster and uphold my tired life's wing,
And bounteously beneath me spread forth spring,
A springtide space whereon to float or fly,
A world of happy water, whence the sky
Glowed goodlier, lightening from so glad a glass,
Than with its own light only. Now, alas!
"Iseult at Tintagel," from "Tristram of Lyonesse"
by Algernon Charles Swinburne

"We cannot stay, Tristan," Isolde whispered.

Her breath tickled his ear, making a thrill of pleasure travel up and down his spine. He shivered slightly. Anger surged inside him, mixing with the passion in a strange whirlpool in his gut.

Why not? He wanted to ask. She expected him to go to a witch who could break this so-called curse on them and present themselves to King Mark like hawked rabbits on a kill line, and in doing so destroy everything they built together. He thought he knew why, but he wanted to hear it from her. He would ask, as soon as these people were satisfied.

Tristan looked out on the gathered people, their rags and wan, pinched faces making his heart plummet in his chest. If it weren't for the matter at hand, he would rule fairly for these people, with Isolde at his side until the end of his days. But King Mark would find them before long if they remained on his lands. It seemed whatever direction Tristan looked, happiness could not last.

He raised his arms, calling their attention. "I know your traditions dictate that the victors of this gruesome contest are to be your lord and lady. Those traditions died with the tyrants who have ruled your lives for these many generations. All curses are broken with their deaths, and you are free to choose your way."

"Who will lead us?" A tall bearded man in the front of the group came forward, concern on his broad face.

"The people shall choose."

"How?"

"The same way they always have, except the lord and lady shall be chosen for their fairness, nobility, regard, and honor, traits that will better serve the people. And no deaths."

Heads nodded and smiles broke through the solemnity on their faces.

Tristan raised his arms again. Isolde glanced at him, brow creasing. "We give you this one gift, before we depart; Castle Pleure shall, from this day, be known as Castle Bel Content. Let this castle and its vassals no longer weep, but rejoice."

The gathered people cheered.

"That was well said," Isolde said.

Her praise warmed him. He expected her to suggest they leave, but instead she straightened her shoulders and faced the group of villagers.

"We seek a witch, or wise woman, in the area. The Rose Witch. Do you know of whom we speak?"

Silence covered the group like a blanket, stilling their happy chatter until the murmurs began again. Tristan caught their whispers in his ears. Rose Mère. Rose Mother.

A woman stepped forward, age beginning to grace her with crow's feet at the corners of her eyes and streaks of grey through her dark brown hair.

"You seek the Rose Mother, good lord and lady. Some may call her witch, but she is a kind, gentle, wise woman who has served our people endlessly, and often at little cost but the items she needs to survive. She has a house in the marshland north of here, about half a day's walk."

"Thank you," Tristan said, nodding. "We will prey on your hospitality a little longer. We require a days' worth of rations and some other items."

Many of the villagers gradually left to return to their families and neighbors and tell of the events that had happened at the now-named

Castle Bel Content. Those that remained helped Tristan and Isolde find the castle's steward, an aging man who was slightly deaf. He recruited guards to remove the bodies and their heads from the Hall of Decision and found servants to scour the blood from the floor, as well as provided the provisions Tristan and Isolde required for the rest of their journey.

They took two bulging bags from the servants, one of whom Isolde knew. She threw her arms around the petite woman the moment she saw her, receiving comforting words in French that Tristan could barely hear. The French gave him an urge to stay that he had to shake free again. It wasn't for him to rule here, even though the people would clearly have him.

The steward bowed to him, and Tristan sighed, opening his mouth to explain that they weren't the lord and lady of the castle, but Isolde interrupted.

"Annora says the people have already chosen a day to vote, in a few weeks' time. You can come back and check on them, after..." she choked on her words, looking up at him.

"Why couldn't we come back?" He gritted his teeth, fists clenching before him. "It's high time you told me your plan, Isolde. I can't keep following blindly like this. Tell me now, or I'll..."

"What? Leave?" Isolde folded her arms. "I do not know everything yet, Tristan. I only know that I need to try to set things right. I thought you might feel the same way. What we did was wrong. Why are you fighting doing the honorable thing?"

"Because I'm not an honorable man!" Tristan shouted.

The maid beside Isolde took a step back, hand to her mouth in shock. Isolde set her jaw.

They had never fought like this. They had never needed to. "I am not a knight, Isolde. I was made one because my uncle wanted me to fight that foolish battle with Sir Marhaus. I have never desired the title. I never found myself worthy of it."

"You are wrong in that regard. Where I come from, you were among the noblest of men that ever served King Arthur." She bit her lip and glanced away from him, as if she said too much.

Tristan stared at her, stunned.

She turned away. "Come on. Let us find the Rose Witch."

"What did you say?" Tristan asked.

Isolde ignored him, waving to the French woman and marching down the hall.

He cursed and jogged after her, toward the double doors at the end of the hallway they had walked down when they first entered the Castle Pleure.

Castle Bel Content shrank behind them. As the forest disappeared and the land opened up into rolling hills, Isolde slipped her hand into his. It felt like an apology, and though Tristan took it, confusion and anger simmered below the surface.

He smelled the marsh before he saw it. Cresting a steep hill, hand-in-hand with Isolde, he looked out over the marsh spread before them, water glistening, hidden among tall green and brown rushes and grass.

Birds called, flitting from one perch to another. The water rippled. Probably a mink or beaver, Tristan guessed. He could see the animal's glistening, dark head as it made its way through the shallow water. The ocean glittered in the noon-day sun, just beyond the marsh.

Even farther, Tintagel clung to a tiny outcropping of wave-lashed land. Tristan gripped Isolde's hand tighter, then scanned the marsh.

"Do you see..." he began, just as Isolde pointed.

"Over there," she said, her lilting, Irish accent overlapping with his rounded British one.

He followed the line of her delicate wrist and fingers to where she pointed. A tiny grey-brown hut with crooked wooden slats and patchy, rotting thatch slumped against the marshy backdrop.

Tristan raised his hand, blocking the sun's glare. "Are you certain that's it? I wouldn't think anyone lived there."

"I can see her herb garden. Us healer-types often get caught up in our work and neglect our surroundings, but her herb garden is neat enough. I'd be willing to trust any witch that keeps up her garden; it indicates a sound mind. Come on, perhaps she can tell us something about this potion."

"Not so fast." Tristan held her hand, their arms stretched out between them as she tried to pull away.

He reeled her into him, wrapping her tightly in his arms, her back against his chest. He nuzzled his face against her cheek, making her squirm as the beard on his face tickled her skin.

"Let me go," she said after a moment. "We need to keep moving."

"Not until you tell me what is so urgent. What's gotten into you, Isolde? One moment we're happy, living our lives peacefully, comfortably. The next, you're running from me, as if you'd do anything to get away. You say it's to right this wrong you think we committed, but I still don't understand what wrong that is." He released her, turning her to face him, holding her hands in his. "We love each other. That love started on Mumhan. At least, for me it did. I thank God every day we drank that potion and have never felt guilty. You were never supposed to marry King Mark."

"Who do we have to thank for that, then?" Isolde asked, eyebrow raising.

Tristan licked his lips, shifting his feet.

She took a breath in, keeping her eyes locked on his. "I had it under control, a plan to escape. And then you offered my hand in marriage to someone else." Isolde closed her eyes, turning her face away from him. "I didn't see the potion as a bad thing either, not once I decided to be with you."

"Tristan, to make that decision, I had to erase my own memories. There are potions strong enough to do so, if they're made right, and in those first few months I made a draught and took it. That's why I didn't remember all the things about how we met."

She reached up a hand and touched his face, her green eyes searching his for a reaction.

Tristan kept his face impassive, but his mind spun. He hadn't given her patchy memory much thought before, thinking it a side-effect of the love potion.

"Then your memories returned," he guessed.

Isolde nodded. "It was enough to make me feel guilty. I couldn't live with myself knowing we started a war."

"Possibly," he corrected. "We don't know for sure yet."

"And we won't until we talk with King Mark."

Tristan ran a hand through his hair, then rested a fist on his hip, looking out across the moor at that tiny shack.

"Why find the witch, then? Why break the curse? We could tell Mark there is no cure."

She smiled at him, a look she gave him when she had already thought of something and knew why it wouldn't work.

"What happens when he banishes you and keeps me in the castle? Or kills one of us? The other would go mad, Tristan."

"I'd rather go mad then see you marry him."

"No one is marrying anyone. We already did that," she said, twining her fingers in his and coming closer.

"Not officially."

"In the eyes of the church, we are heathens, perhaps. But in the eyes of my people, consummation is the same as any words a priest could say."

"There you go again, saying things that only make sense if you aren't Irish," Tristan said. He watched her face and saw guilt flicker in her gaze. He brought his forehead to meet hers, listening to her breathing. "Whatever it is, you can tell me, Isolde."

She laughed breathlessly. "I don't want it to change what we have."

"It won't."

"You don't know that."

"I'll try," he replied. She smiled, and it made him smile, even though his heart beat with a kind of fear he had never known. What could she possibly say that would change his mind?

"Tristan, I..."

"Oy, lovebirds! Get off that patch of murkweed!" a woman's graveled voice shouted at them, making them jump and look up together. A tiny old woman, mostly skin and bones, stood in the doorway of the hovel. A furious expression twisted her ancient face.

Tristan looked down. His feet stood on a rather flattened patch of some brown plant that oozed slime; it glistened against the bottom of his boots. He stepped back, and Isolde did the same, the movement separating them.

"Sorry," Isolde called out, waving to the woman. "Hold on, we're here to see you!"

The woman's lip jutted out and she crossed her arms.

"She looks like you when you're being stubborn," Tristan said to Isolde, nudging her with his elbow. Isolde gave him a withering glare. Tristan sobered. "I haven't forgotten what we were discussing, you know."

"I know. I will tell you, in the right moment."

As they made their way across the moor, trying to keep on the driest path, Tristan wondered if the right moment would ever come.

"So, you got yourselves hitched at the heart, I see?" the old woman asked, chuckling gleefully to herself. "I've made a few of those potions for local sods who want nothing more than to be bound to their sweetheart forever. Or to urge an unwilling mate to take the bait. What makes you two want to be apart so much?"

Tristan's eyes watered as a wave of putridity assaulted his nose. He pinched it shut and looked to Isolde. She looked as if she'd swallowed horse dung but was trying to be polite; or at least more polite than Tristan. The hovel stank something fierce.

"We didn't take it willingly. And it is imperative we are separated. We might...well, we don't want to risk going mad."

The Rose Witch nodded. "That's a side-effect you could expect if one of you was killed, captured, or made love to by anyone besides your bond mate."

She muttered the last part, then made a loud clucking sound. Tristan jumped and dropped his grip on his nose. He groaned at the smell that assaulted him.

"I guess I can't blame you. You'll need an antidote. It takes months to make. Distilling in the light of two full moons, adding ingredients on days three, fifteen, and fifty-three. And the final ingredient can't be added until right before it is to be used."

Tristan's heart rose in his chest. His shoulders dropped, and he let out a long breath. Two moons?

Surely, Isolde couldn't expect them to sit here and wait for it to be finished. Hopefully, by the end of two moons' time he would convince her to let go of this foolish sense of honor.

"Lucky for you folks, I have some on hand," the Rose Witch replied, winking at them.

Isolde sighed with relief. Did she have to look so damn happy about it? Tristan folded his arms over his chest as the woman tumbled from her stool holding a tiny, rose-colored glass bottle with a cork stopper.

"Oh, thank you," Isolde breathed. "How much?"

The Rose Witch considered Isolde's face, pursing her lips. "How about payment for now is you fetch that last ingredient?"

Tristan couldn't help noticing the way she slipped that in there—payment for now. What did that mean?

"What is it?" Isolde asked, eyes narrowing.

The witch tapped her chin with the bottle. "Oh, let me see, now. Was it fritillary? No, nothing so fancy as that. Ah ha!"

Tristan jumped at her exclamation. She held out a single finger, the nail on it long and yellowing, quivering below Tristan's chin. The witch's green eyes held his gaze. He couldn't help but stare at the extra-long hair trembling from the mole on her forehead.

"Thyme broomrape," she said at last, glancing at Isolde.

"Thyme broomrape?" Isolde asked, wrinkling her nose. "It's a weed, isn't it?"

"It's not too common anymore, I'm afraid. I can make some extract if you find some. It likes to grow around the rocks and is always near thyme. Can you identify thyme?" The witch asked, raising an eyebrow at Isolde and holding out a small basket made with dried rushes and clay.

"I know what thyme looks like," Isolde snapped, snatching the basket away and looping the handle over her arm. She stormed past Tristan, who stared after her, bewildered.

"Do not try to understand the tempest, Sir Knight, it will pass." The Rose Witch chuckled to herself. "Make sure you bring me some thyme, while you're at it. A small bunch will do," she called after him as he left, the creaking, crooked door banging shut behind him.

Tristan caught up to Isolde muttering to herself as she squatted and ducked, scanning the ground for any hint of the plant they sought. "What does..." he couldn't remember the name the witch had used for it. "What does it look like?" he called, skirting a marshy area that housed a deep-looking miniature pool. The wind caught his voice and carried it back behind him.

Isolde didn't seem to hear for a moment, then straightened and turned back to him.

"Red flowers on a thick, red stalk, lower than knee-height. Grows near a spiky, kind of bushy plant with tiny purple flowers, though they aren't out this time of year."

She ripped a strip off the brown shawl she wore and tied her hair back, keeping the wind from blowing it back into her face. She looked more beautiful than Tristan had ever seen her. In his haste to catch up with her, he sloshed through several muddy pits, getting a boot full of mossy brown water. It chilled his toes, squelching with each new step he took.

A bird startled up from a nest at his feet, squawking as it took flight, feathers flapping in Tristan's face. He scrambled back, arms up for protection, and slipped, falling rear-end first into marsh-land. He sputtered and coughed, spitting marsh-water from his mouth and attempting to wipe mud from his face with a sopping wet sleeve.

Isolde, laughter making her hysterical, reached down and grasped his hand. Their grip slipped, and the momentum sent her backward, making a spectacular splash of her own. Tristan roared with laughter, slapping his damp breeches and rocking back and forth.

Isolde sputtered for a moment, flicking her hands as if that would do anything to dry her off, then joined him, her joyful laughter bubbling up over the marshland. She climbed to her feet and Tristan followed suit, noting the way her wet dress clung to her curves, and the slick strands of hair, darker when wet, trailing down her neck towards her breast.

She caught him staring, and in a rush of heat Tristan wondered if they would fall down together and make love, marsh, mud and all. Isolde's breath made her chest heave, the swell of her breasts making Tristan's blood rush downward. He stepped toward her, but she looked away, breaking the brief spell between them.

Tristan swallowed, licking his lips to get the moisture back. Would they ever make love like that again? Filled with abandon and burning passion for each other? Or would all of that be lost when they took this antidote?

Isolde tossed aside the bent and broken basket. It had suffered in her fall into the marsh and wasn't worth saving. She scoured the brush less delicately this time, tromping through the shallow, wet places without fear of getting muddy.

Tristan followed the same path several feet away, looking for anything red. Some of the reeds were a rusty brownish color, making the search difficult.

The wind picked up again and a bank of clouds moved across the sky like an army on the march. The sun disappeared behind them, consumed in a blanket of grey. Tristan shivered in his damp clothes, mud gritty between his toes. He had mud in places he didn't even want to think about at the moment.

A shriek from Isolde made him jump, nearly sending him into the bog again. He reeled around to see her crouched down, grasping a bunch of a red plant in her hand.

"Here it is, Tristan!"

His heart regulated its rhythm once more when he saw no danger, though it felt as though a rock weighed in his stomach, and pressure built up in his chest. Now the Rose Witch would finish her potion.

Tristan contemplated "accidentally" tripping into Isolde and sending them both into the bog again, in the hopes that the red plant would be lost. But Isolde would find more and the childish attempt to thwart her would cause additional frustration.

No, he couldn't prevent it. But he could talk to Mark. Perhaps he could convince him to relinquish his right to Isolde as his bride. After all, Tristan and Isolde had consummated their marriage to each other. Surely, Mark wouldn't accept her after knowing that.

It was Tristan's only hope; a weak flame that a single doubt could douse.

Isolde's hand dropped to her side, and she gazed at him, her expression pained. He looked away from her, unwilling to let her see the vulnerability shining through his eyes or the tears that dripped down his nose and across his cheeks.

Her boots squelched as she pulled them free of the bog's grip and came closer to him. Her hand touched his face, drawing it up to look into hers. He reached his hand up and cupped hers. Heat spread from the point of contact, moving through his veins.

"If there were any other way..." her eyes searched his. "Why does this hurt you so much? It isn't as if there will be no chance of us being together. It will be more real, even, without the potion muddling up our feelings."

He took her hand away from his cheek, holding her cold fingers. His other hand moved automatically, brushing a wet strand of hair from her face, tucking it behind her ear.

"We don't know that." His voice came out hoarse. He cleared it, then tried again. "Everything could change after this."

"You can speak with the king. You know him, don't you? Talk with him. Tell him what happened."

Tristan shook his head and barked a laugh. He hadn't been talking about Mark. "You don't know Mark, how he can be. He has been alone a long time; that is, if he didn't meet anyone this past year. And he wouldn't have gotten married if he thought your father was withholding you from him. Every king wants a woman to bear him sons. Once he meets you..."

"You think he will be that enamored? On sight?"

"I was," Tristan replied, feeling a strange sense of satisfaction at the flash of guilt he saw in Isolde's eyes. He continued. "Mark looks for the most convenient way to get what he wants. Having your hand offered to him, you being beautiful and intelligent by reputation, plus being able to avoid future war with your father's kingdom, it was too great an opportunity to pass up. He will be furious that I took you, his pride wounded. I may be run through by his guards or hanged on sight, with no hope for trial."

Isolde gripped his arm with her other hand, stepping closer to him. "He won't want me after I've been with you." She didn't sound too sure of herself, and Tristan noticed a distance in her eyes. But her words...he clung to them as if they were a rope thrown to the man dangling over a cliff.

"That is my hope, as well."

She released him and found a dry path out of the bog. Their clothes were ruined, and since the hag clearly did not have suitable accommodations, they'd have to find a place to get clean before confronting Mark.

Isolde ducked under the doorway's low beam. The witch's door pounded shut behind her. Tristan put his hand on the door, taking a slow breath. His heart pounded, though he wasn't sure why. Did Isolde not feel this way, or was she better at hiding it? Curse her.

Tristan shook his head, then opened the door to find the women glaring at one another. Isolde clenched the red flowers, thyme broomrape, in fists that trembled with anger.

"I must insist on paying you in some way," Isolde said through gritted teeth, staring the Rose Witch down.

"I do not accept regular payment in exchange for my service. You understand the old ways. You know why I do this," the witch said. The wrinkles around her eyes tightened as they narrowed, and Tristan could see a storm raging in those pale blue eyes.

Isolde's fist tightened, threatening to decapitate the blossoms. "What is going on, Isolde?" Tristan asked.

"Dealing with a witch who doesn't accept payment is dangerous. You never know when the payment will come, or what it will be. It might be something small. A hair, a fingernail, a drop of blood, which can later be used in enchantments binding you to the witch's will, or to the highest bidder. Or perhaps she'll require your first or last-born child, or the love of your life, or your sight." She spat to the side. "It is often accomplished with dark magic, and it is rarely convenient."

"Then why come here in the first place?" Tristan snapped, throwing his hands into the air, disturbing a bunch of dried leaves with a crunch and making a small shower of them fall to the dirt floor. The witch made a strained sound but didn't say anything. "You knew it might be like this, didn't you?"

"Yes," Isolde replied. She glanced down at the wilting red flowers. Her grip loosened. "But I hoped..." she swallowed. Her free hand came up and rubbed unconsciously at her chest.

"You aren't the only one this will affect, and I am not willing to risk giving up a future child to this witch simply because you think it's the worst fate in the world to be forced to love me!" Tristan shouted, the anger inside surging out of him.

The witch and Isolde both stared at him. Dust floated down from the rafters above his head.

"I promise payment will not be a child," the witch offered, her tone far too confident for Tristan's liking. He turned his gaze to her.

"Is that so? Well then, perhaps you can tell us what it might be?" He kept his face firm, staring the Rose Witch down until she broke her gaze.

"I do not always know the price of my items, Sir Knight. It isn't so simple as that," she muttered, moving towards her shelves. "I move at the whim of the Goddess, as your pretty Irish pet should understand, with her experience." Her voice grew muffled as she went to the back of the hut. The sound of clinking bottles echoed as she rummaged through the clutter. She dropped something and yelped a curse that made Tristan's ears want to curl in.

He took a few steps closer to Isolde, who seemed intent on avoiding his gaze. "What did she mean, just now?"

"You know witches, always twisting the truth to avoid being scrutinized," she replied off-hand. She avoided looking at him.

He would get the truth from her sooner or later. For now, he straightened as the witch came out from behind the shelves, the same rose-tinted glass bottle from earlier clutched in her hand.

She faced their accusing stares with a grimace. "I couldn't risk you two circling back and taking this from me, now could I? I hid it. Now, here it is." She held it out towards them.

"Finish it," Isolde said, her voice hard. She held out the bruised flowers.

The Rose Witch looked at them and sniffed, then snatched them from Isolde's hand. She grumbled as she set the bottle down, then dropped the flowers into a small mortar and began working them with a pestle that seemed, rather oddly, to be the bone of a small creature. She added a tiny drop of oil to the petals and mashed it into a lumpy ball of paste. She used a shell fragment to scrape the mortar clean, pressed the blackish paste into the narrow neck of the rose-tinted bottle, reapplied the stopper and shook vigorously.

The contents turned a murky red color, difficult to see in the fading light of day that filtered through the hut's tiny windows and wood slats. She held the bottle up to the light, flicking the glass a few times and muttering to herself. Then she smacked her lips and held it out toward Isolde and Tristan between her thumb and forefinger.

"There you have it. The cure for a bonding potion." Isolde reached for it, but the Rose Witch snatched it away, eyes narrowing again.

"Now, my eyesight isn't too good these days, and Goddess knows I am terrible with people, but it seems to me you two aren't in agreement about what's to be done with your current situation." Isolde opened her mouth, but the witch cut her off. "Now, it's none of my affair what you two do with your lives. But love potions, and their cures, are finicky. Sometimes cures won't stick if they don't want to. Are you certain you want to do this?"

Isolde nodded, firmly, then glanced up at Tristan.

He gave a short nod. Whatever it took to get them away from this place.

The Rose Witch cradled the potion close to her chest. Her nose stuck into the air, and she huffed loudly. "You must consume it within two days, or it will not be effective. Do not eat or drink within two hours of taking. Do not have intercourse with the person you are bonded to within two hours of taking it. You have been well warned. I will not be held accountable for your foolishness if it doesn't work. The price, as mentioned, is unknown, and you may discover you do not like it. Don't bother looking for me to exact any sort of revenge, you will not find me again." Her eyes flashed, and Tristan shuddered, not doubting she had otherworldly guardians to hide her from unsatisfied customers.

"Yes, of course, thank you." Isolde said impatiently, holding out her hand. The Rose Witch slapped the bottle into her palm and turned on her heel, disappearing into the recesses of her hut. Isolde turned without a word and headed outside, Tristan on her heels. The rickety door to the witch's hut thudded shut behind him.

"Isolde, I don't think..."

He wasn't two steps away from the threshold before Isolde wheeled around and confronted him.

"You understand, don't you Tristan? We have to do this. Love potions can kill. I didn't want to risk losing you that way."

He stood there, blinking against the golden splendor of the sunset that shone at her back. Her words shouldn't hurt as much as they did. Love, or anger, or the potion; it burned inside of him hot and furious, making his emotion rise to the surface so fast he thought he might burst.

"You know, Isolde, I get the feeling this isn't about me. It's about you. You are too afraid to spend the rest of your life loving me and wondering if you wasted it; as if a life spent loving someone else could ever be a waste." He breathed in, the fresh, cool air invigorating him.

"You think I can convince King Mark to let you go? To be with me? He would never. He is a selfish man, like so many men. And I am no better. I would kill him if it would prevent you from being forced to marry. Don't ask me to do this," he commanded.

Isolde gaped at him. Tristan looked away from her, at the golden landscape. He thought he could smell the sea. Tintagel lay over the next rise. They could be there before dawn.

"Maybe there never was any hope. But I wonder... would you..." he broke off, gaping at Isolde as she sniffed the bottle and made a face, then tipped her head back. Tristan grabbed her hand before the bottle made it to her lips.

"Isolde, wait."

She froze, lowering her hand.

"I'm sorry. I'm selfish, you know I am. But I can't let you do this, not without..." he paused, licking his lips as he watched her, frozen there, silhouette backed by a purple sky and the setting sun.

"Without saying goodbye?" Isolde whispered. "I can see it in your eyes. You're afraid we won't love one another after taking it."

"It would pain me more than I could bear if that happened. I want to hold you in my arms one last time, hoping without hope that it won't be the last time."

"Tristan, I have loved you most in all my life. That won't change; I won't let it." She smiled the beaming smile that could light up the darkest of places, even within his heart. "I can give you that much," she said.

Tristan's shoulders sagged with relief. He wished it didn't feel so much like one of them was dying, but he wanted this. He wanted her.

Tristan reached out and took her hand. Touching her felt like fire and ice at the same time; fire in his chest, ice on her skin. He rubbed her frigid hand between both of his, bringing warmth back into it. She stared at their hands, avoiding his gaze. A breeze swept past, sweeping her matted, filthy curls across her face. She still looked beautiful.

She pulled her hand from his and moved forward, tucking herself against his chest. It took Tristan a moment to wrap his arms around her, but when he did, his heart threatened to gallop away. Her hair smelled like peat, not entirely pleasant, but the warmth of her was enough to make him ignore it. He nuzzled in deeper, finding her own scent.

"Is that a yes?" he murmured.

Isolde moved her head, adjusting where her face lay below his collarbone. Her chin tilted up and she pulled away to look at him.

"One more night. I promised...I promised I would tell you the whole truth."

Tristan nodded once. "Fair enough. But not until after." He found himself grinning, and he tickled Isolde at her rib cage, making her laugh.

"I will enjoy getting to know you better."

"Even if it isn't pleasant?"

"Especially then. You're far too perfect, you know. Irish princess, healer to the masses, love of my life. It will be good to have proof of your humanity."

She rolled her eyes. "What does Irish have anything to do with it?"

Tristan laughed. "I don't know. It sounded better in my head." She smiled, then found her place again, head resting on his chest. Tristan cleared his throat. "I know a place we can get cleaned up, though there may be little hope for our clothing."

"I have an extra dress. It will be crumpled, but I kept that violet one from the castle. I didn't want to approach King Mark in rags."

"I suppose there's clothing for me in one of these bags. I have something to wear after all. A shame," he said, a boyish feeling of mischief turning up the corners of his mouth.

Her hand slapped his chest, and she pushed away from him. “Tristan!” Her eyes glittered, her indigence clearly false. “Where are we headed?” she asked, adjusting the small pack on her shoulder.

“Food or bath first?”

“Ooh.” She clutched at her stomach. “Food, as long as I don’t have to be presentable.”

Tristan raised two fingers to his lips and gave a sharp whistle, letting it sound three times. It was a long shot that Astor was still alive and near Tintagel, but it didn’t hurt to try. Silence followed his call. Isolde watched him as he waited. After a time, he tried again; three sharp whistles.

A hawk’s piercing cry cut through the evening air. There was enough light for Astor to get a decent hunt in. Tristan grinned and turned to Isolde. “How does fresh meat sound?”

Her eyes widened, making him laugh. Tristan’s stomach grumbled thinking about it. He wiped his mouth before the saliva could escape, then held out his hand.

Isolde took it, her laughter at his wilderness chivalry floating into the air, and they began walking. Astor’s shadowy form caught up and followed them, the golden light of late afternoon gleaming off his wings.

CHAPTER TWENTY-ONE

Iseult, Iseult, what grace hath life to give
More than we twain have had of life, and live?
Iseult, Iseult, what grace may death not keep
As sweet for us to win of death, and sleep?
Come therefore, let us twain pass hence and try
If it be better not to live but die,
With love for lamp to light us out of life."
"The Last Pilgrimage," from "Tristram of Lyonesse"
by Algernon Charles Swinburne

Watching the red-tailed hawk hunt fascinated Morgan. Its flight was somehow elegant, even as it plummeted towards the earth and ended the life of the hare that became their dinner. A few clicks of his tongue and Tristan could get it to release the prey and send it off into the purple dusk to find its roost at Tintagel castle.

"That was amazing," she told Tristan, crouching beside him as he skinned the rabbit.

It was a stomach-churning sight, but Tristan's sideways grin and the way his brown curls fell forward along his jaw as he leaned over the kill helped alleviate the nausea. Her heart beat faster as she listened to Tristan's happy chatter about his hawk, Astor.

"You know how to start a fire, right? Here."

He reached into the satchel nearby and pulled out a flint. A bunch of finely shredded bark and dry grass came from his pocket. His fingers fumbled against her hand as he deposited the items, and she stared at them stupidly for a second. He smiled at her, cocking his head. His stare made her cheeks flush, and his knowing grin caused her hands to tremble.

Morgan shook her head and set up the fire, drawing a few smaller sticks from the pile and stacking them in an alternating square pattern around the kindling. Then she took the flint and struck it, making sparks that smoldered against the delicate branches and brought them flaming to life. She blew gently, trying to ignore Tristan's eyes on her.

As it began to eat its way through the meager meal of kindling and twigs, she stacked several larger sticks and a small log delicately against the blaze so the fingers of the small fire could lick at them without being smothered. She dusted off her hands and sat back, glancing at Tristan.

The stars began to show through the streaks of clouds above them. A gentle breeze blew through the grass of the plain around them. Hills rose and fell, blocking the horizon. Somewhere beyond lay the ocean, and Tintagel was built on the rocky shore of Cornwall.

Morgan guessed they were north of Tintagel now, but barely. Close enough that Tristan knew the lay of the land, close enough for him to call his hawk. Close enough that their time was limited. Close enough to make her heart pound in her chest. She had to tell him, tonight.

Tristan trimmed some limbs with a knife he had found in the pack, carving out the y-shapes before digging into the dirt beside the fire. He used another sturdy stick, which he had scraped the bark off of and sharpened, to skewer the rabbit's skinned corpse. Placing it on top of the two y-shaped sticks, he cleverly arranged a spit. He twisted it occasionally, and soon, juicy bits of fat began dripping into the flames.

"Well, there's that. It will take a while to cook. What did you want to tell me?" he asked, sitting cross-legged and looking at her, the fire's flickering orange light making shadows on his face.

Morgan glanced at the sky. *Goddess, help me.* She looked at the piece of grass she twisted between her fingers.

"Perhaps it should wait until after dinner," she muttered, not wanting to look up. She did anyway, glancing towards him to see his expression. His face remained straight, neutral.

"Could I ask you a question?" She nodded.

"Why are you so afraid to tell me, whatever it is?" he asked.

Morgan stared into the fire. "It will change how you see me."

"It won't alter how I feel," he insisted. "I cannot imagine not...well, not feeling the way I do." He swallowed. He hadn't said it. Love. They exchanged that word back and forth as easily as breathing the past year. Now, everything had changed. His hand brushed her cheek, and she looked up. His face was so open, his concerned smile so sincere.

"Take your time," he said.

"I wish we had more time," she said softly, meeting his gaze. Her heart beat faster. "Can we forget for right now? I promise I will tell you, but I can't, not yet. I want..." She couldn't finish that sentence. *I want you to always see me as you do right now. I don't want your feelings for me to change, not yet.*

"You mean, pretend? Like the rest of the world doesn't exist?" She nodded, words caught in the web of emotion at her throat. "I would like that, very much," he said, voice dropping, cracking at the end. He cleared his throat.

He watched her and waited for her to come to him, as if she were a wild horse being tamed.

Morgan scooted across the dirt towards him, then rested her head against his shoulder.

His hand came up behind and stroked her hair. His lips pressed against the top of her head, and a wave of pleasure washed through her body. They sat like that for a long while, the cool night air not seeming to touch them, the sounds of night filling in.

Morgan pushed her thoughts away, forcing them down, trying to enjoy the sensation of being near Tristan.

It didn't last long. The thoughts pressed on her until the dam she had built in her mind broke and they rushed forward, choking the pleasure she felt at Tristan's touch. She sighed, opened her mouth, then closed it as Tristan nudged her.

She moved, chill air closing in on the space left by her absence. He leaned forward and turned the rabbit on the spit, dropping bits of juicy fat into the fire, letting off a delightful aroma. He settled back, pulling her into him. "This will take quite a while," Tristan said, gesturing towards their meal. “Perhaps you would like to bathe while it cooks? There’s a place I know nearby.”

She nodded. That would give her time to think. She gathered her clothes from their pack.

Tristan stood, wrapping an oil-soaked rag from their pack around a long, sturdy branch. He lit it with their fire, making a torch, and held his hand out to Morgan. She stared at him a moment before taking it, feeling the roughness of his palm as his larger hand encased hers.

As she followed him onto a forested path, climbing up over rocks, crossing a large, rushing river, she realized she wanted nothing more than to love him the rest of her days, and the depth of it made her heart climb into her throat. Would he still want her when he knew who she was? And would they survive what lay before them?

He led her down a well-worn path through a narrow gorge. Ahead, she could hear the crashing of a waterfall. Her skin itched and the brand on her chest heated up. She rounded a final bend.

The moonlight gleamed in the clearing. Water cascaded into a deep pool through a perfect circular rock formation. Tree branches bent down, laden with rags and ribbons, coins, metal beads, and gems; tokens for the fair folk.

Morgan breathed out, reaching her hand toward a nearby log, running her fingers over the hundreds of coins embedded in its surface.

“What is this place called?” she asked. It would look spectacular in daylight. Clearly a sacred place, a place of healing. Already she could feel the peace of it seeping into her skin, melting away the tension in her shoulders.

“It is a clootie well,” he replied, lifting his torch and making the metal bits gleam. “People come and wash, then leave a coin or ribbon to take away pain, or for luck. You should be safe enough here. It's not a place vagabonds dare frequent. Protective spirits and the like. Do you want me to leave the torch?"

I want you to stay. She turned her face up and pressed her lips into his, her hands on either side of his face, breathing in his scent as they kissed.

She broke away, breathless, and bit her lip. "I want this, Tristan. I want you. But...I want to bathe first."

Tristan's concerned expression broke as he chuckled. He rubbed her hands between his fingers. "I thought you were going to say something far more serious. Very well. I can understand wanting to be clean. Get a head start. I'll leave the torch here and return in a moment. I saw a blanket in one of the packs. I don't fancy making love on the rocks."

"No?" Morgan asked, teasing. He kissed her again.

"Take the torch," she said, "the moon is bright enough for me."

"I'll be just a moment," Tristan said, his grip loosening. "Oh!" He reached into one pocket, then pressed a smooth, round object into her hand; lavender-scented soap. He pecked her lips and left the way they had come.

She watched him go, the smile slipping from her face. Somehow, she had to prevent two wars, and she feared she wouldn't be able to do so without breaking two hearts.

She undressed, letting her mind wander. She had to convince Tristan to speak with King Mark. Failing that, she would marry the king and then disappear, feign being captured or killed without implicating anyone important, especially Tristan.

Morgan dipped her toes into the water. Goosebumps rippled over her bare skin. She took a breath and waded in until the cool water lapped at her thighs. She shivered, then put her hands before her and pushed off in a shallow dive.

Her head broke the water, gasping. A quick swim back to shore exposed her to the air, now freezing, so she could grab the soap, and then she headed back into the deep water, where it felt relatively warm.

Isolde would need her in Camelot. And Elaina might as well. Should she visit the tower first? Perhaps she would get up the courage to tell Tristan, and if he wasn't furious at learning that she had withheld who she was, he might help her plan her escape from Cornwall. Or he would go berserk and storm the castle, kill the king, and take her away, and she would fail on all counts.

Thinking through her options, she realized she knew little of the knight who escorted her, despite the year they spent together. He'd started as an invalid who played the harp like an angel and became an enchanted, love-sick warrior who would do anything to keep her safe.

The lavender scent of the soap reminded her of magic pills. Of Arthur. *Don't make the same mistakes. Better to leave him while he's still safe.* She ducked under to rinse her hair and came up, wiping water from her eyes.

The metal offerings hanging low from the surrounding branches clinked together like a warning. Morgan's neck prickled, and goosebumps rose on her skin. She could practically hear whispered voices, urging her to dress, to flee.

Where is Tristan? she thought, moving as quickly as she could, first swimming, then pressing against the water as her feet touched the rocky bottom. She splashed to the shore, trembling in the cool, not- quite spring air. She had no towel, nothing to dry off with, so, dripping and shivering, Morgan pulled on her dry clothes. They clung to her skin, but at least she felt warmer. Her hair hung past her face.

She felt an urgency to find Tristan and leave this place, though the night was silent, except for the chiming of the charms in the trees. She wanted to get back to the fire, to sit beside Tristan and let the fire's heat dry her hair and warm her bones. She combed through her hair with her fingers and turned back towards the water.

What she saw made her freeze, eyes locked on a reflection in the water. Flickering flames. She glanced behind, expecting Tristan with the torch and blanket. The entrance to the shallow gorge stood empty, and the only light came from the full moon glaring down at her like an empty, baleful eye. She looked back at the water.

An image rippled in the place the moon's reflection should have shone; a young woman's face, Morgan's true face, the face Isolde wore, black hair falling forward, white shift vivid, flames licking upward. She was open-mouthed, screaming. The vision from before.

"No," Morgan whispered. It had happened, or was about to happen. She could not fail, not after all this...

Footsteps crunched across the stones behind her and she whirled around to find Tristan, holding a darkened torch, and no blanket. He looked her up and down, and his shoulders sagged with relief.

"I thought I heard you screaming for help. It's spooky out on that plain alone in the dark." He gestured with the stick in his hand. "It's gone out. That gust of wind took it out just now, as I was running. Fire's still good, though.

Think we can find our way in the dark?" he asked, grinning.

Morgan stood, unable to respond. The charms in the trees hung dead-still. Her skin crawled, and though she rubbed at her arms, the sensation remained.

"Something is coming," she whispered.

Confusion crossed Tristan's shadowed face. "I didn't see anyone, Isolde. Come now, you're safe with me." His hand reached out towards her.

She shied away from his touch, a sudden fear striking her heart. Her chest burned. The phoenix reared up in her mind's eye, burning red, its feathers like flames.

Tristan closed the distance between them, hands clasping her face, bringing it towards his, his lips melding with hers and warmth stirred inside, sparking a fire that burned through her chest, her face, down her stomach, into the deepest parts of her. She pushed him away, gasping, but he held her tight against him, crushing his lips against hers. Her body responded, wrapping her arms around him, pressing into his curves, longing to be closer, to let him lift her against the rocks and take her at last. She bit his lip, making him release her.

"Tristan, no! We cannot do this."

"Why not?" He breathed, wiping his lip and looking at the blood that glistened darkly in the moonlight against his skin.

"I'm not who you think I am, Tristan." she exclaimed, breath heaving. Her chest and throat burned. Her heart ached.

Tristan halted, staring at her. "Then who are you, Isolde? Tell me." He moved closer as if she were a skittish animal that might be frightened off.

She let him come, both wanting him and praying he would be hurt or offended and leave her so she wouldn't have to. She swallowed, moistening her throat. She couldn't stand the confusion in his gaze.

She could feel the truth clenching at her heart like a clawed beast, making it hard to think, to reason her way out. She had to tell him, now, with the moon shining down and no one listening but the wind and the trees and the rocks around them.

She licked her lips. "My true name is Morgan le Fay, and I come from another time." She glanced around. She couldn't be certain the vision she received wasn't happening now.

She rubbed at her arms. This body didn't remember the flames licking her skin, but her mind did.

"I..." Morgan stopped. Her ears picked up the sound of boots stamping towards them, and torchlight flickered against the rock wall opposite.

Tristan heard it too, frowning as he turned and looked toward the mouth of the narrow gorge, just as eight men emerged.

"There they are," one man said, gesturing with his sword. Several came forward, faces obscured by helms, brandishing spears.

Tristan put himself before Morgan, sword appearing in his hand almost like magic. Morgan hadn't even noticed he carried it.

"Who sent you?" Tristan asked as the men advanced. "How did you find us?"

"You are wanted for treason, Sir Tristan, by King Mark of Cornwall."

"Treason?" Tristan said.

"Kidnapping a princess and defecting in the line of duty." At the man's signal, the guards swooped in and took them. Tristan's sword dropped to his side without a fight.

Morgan let two of the guards flank her. They brought her to the center of the group, Tristan being held behind her, his sword in the hand of one of the guards. She stumbled a little on the rocky path, shallow cliff walls rising on either side of her, giant, warped shadows dancing across their surface in the torches the guards carried.

They left the gorge behind them, and Morgan glanced to the side, noticing the extinguished fire, the rabbit and spit laying in the dirt. She looked among the men and spotted their bags, slung over the shoulders of a short guard with an impassive face.

The lateness of the hour took its toll on her. She hadn't slept in what felt like days. Between the events at Castle Bel Content that morning and hiking all over the moors searching for the flower that would break the bond between them, she was bone-weary. Possibilities for escape flickered through her mind.

She glanced behind. Tristan walked on his own now, but his head and shoulders slumped over his tied hands. He looked like a prisoner being lead to his execution, which, she supposed, he might be. She didn't know the laws of Cornwall. Would his uncle have him killed for this accusation of treason?

The darkness started to lift as they crested a final craggy mountain. Morgan smelled the salty tang of the ocean and took in the grey waves, dull in the early dawn light. Tintagel lay below, built on a narrow outcropping that linked Tintagel Island, a peninsula reaching into the ocean. The long, thin castle keep maintained a highly defensible position, but lived in danger of being washed away by the gradual erosion of ocean water on the rock that supported it.

They started down towards it, descending on a steep, well-worn path. No sound but the clink of weapons and armor, and Morgan's own breath loud in her ears. She focused on planting each step surely, afraid to slip and tumble down the mountain. White-tipped waves crashed against the cliffs that held Tintagel.

Morgan followed the guards down the path, crossing beneath a high stone arch. They would reach the castle as the sun crested the horizon.

Fear brought her heart to her throat, but she steeled herself, straightening. She had survived being burned at the stake. Surely, she could handle appealing to a king to save the life of the man she loved.

CHAPTER TWENTY-TWO

What tears are like the wondering tears
Of that entranced embrace,
When out of desolate and divided years
Face meets belovèd face?
What cry most exquisite of grief or bliss
The too full heart shall tell,
When the new-recovered kiss
Is the kiss of last farewell?
"Tristram's End" by Robert Laurence Binyon

Tristan's head ached abominably where the head guard, a man he thought he recognized, but wasn't certain, had struck him with the hilt of his sword. The pain made his vision blur, and whenever he slowed the men on either side would shove him forward, making him stumble.

Isolde, of course, walked in front of him, her clothes dried off, her hair laying tangled down her back as it had dried. He supposed he shouldn't think of her as Isolde. Hadn't she said another name, Morgan, and that she came from another time? Whatever the hell that meant.

He cursed internally. If Mark's men had found them moments later, she could have answered his questions. A pit opened in his stomach, thoughts of the worst possible explanations spinning in his mind, and a longing to go back to before all this happened, back when things were simpler, and he was certain he loved her.

He didn't know how to think of her now. She remained Isolde to him. The fact that she had another name, supposedly, didn't change how he saw her. And it still made his heart ache and his blood boil to think of King Mark having her. Damn that man.

They passed the knights standing at attention at the drawbridge. It lowered with a loud creaking and a final thud. Sixteen pairs of boots stomped across it, and one pair of mud-stained slippers.

Daylight streamed into the courtyard, and Tristan was pressed forward into a corridor that lead into the inner part of the castle, Isolde ahead of him. They passed the heavy double doors that led to King Mark's receiving hall. They weren't on trial; not yet.

Tristan didn't get a chance to be relieved, however, when the guards led them down towards the lower holdings. The guards' mail clinked as their boots clomped down the steps.

Scattered torchlight lit the lower holdings, and it smelled of unwashed bodies and musty water. A few figures stirred, watching the guards lead Tristan and Isolde past their cells until they stopped before an open door and ushered them in. They clapped heavy iron manacles on Tristan's arms and linked it to a chain on the wall.

"How did you know where to find us?" Tristan demanded.

"We were tipped off," one of the guards said. They turned as one and moved out of the dungeon, leaving one posted near the stairs.

"My bet is on the witch," Tristan said.

Isolde remained silent, staring at their surroundings. She shivered in her damp hair and wet clothes. The cell had no blankets. Nothing but a little moldy hay and two buckets.

"This dungeon is worse than the last one," Tristan joked bitterly, kicking at the rusted bucket filled with stagnant water. "I thought my uncle would maintain his better."

"I don't have the money, Sir Tristan," a familiar voice drawled.

A silk and velvet-robed figure approached the bars, hands clasped behind his back.

Isolde lifted her chin, looking proud and stubborn.

Tristan stepped up, lifting his manacled hands and gripping the iron bars before him.

"What did you spend it on? Clothes, no doubt," Tristan said, looking the portly man up and down. "Food is my second wager. You're still fat."

"I spent it trying to appease an Irish king hell-bent on invading Cornwall to find his stolen daughter!" King Mark bellowed, ruddy face flushing an even deeper color. "By God, man, have you no shame? Don't you see what you've done?"

"I fell in love," Tristan said. "You've ruined countless lives!"

Isolde stepped up. "It was my fault, King Mark. I made the decision to run away with him."

"Silence, you whore." The king's spittle flecked Isolde's cheek. She didn't move. "I am glad you ran off before we wedded, rather than after. I would rather make an example of you than be made a fool."

“What do you mean?” Tristan said, lip curling. Only the bars prevented him from ripping out the man’s throat for insulting Isolde.

King Mark smirked. “I plan to marry this wench, Sir Tristan, if for no other reason than to show you that I am your king, that I have the power to crush you, to destroy you, and maybe for once you’ll show me the deference I deserve.” He closed in on the cell, his face separated from Tristan’s by the bars. “And when I am done with her, I will hang her by her neck while you watch, then banish you so you can live out the rest of your days with the knowledge that it was you who killed her.”

Tristan’s entire body went rigid, his throat dry. For once, he couldn’t think of a comeback and had to watch as King Mark walked away. He was going to kill Isolde. Marry her, then kill her.

Something scuffled in another cell, filling the silence before it stilled. Isolde regained her tongue and spoke.

“I thought he might at least listen to us first,” she said.

Foolish woman, you wanted it too much to see anything else, Tristan thought.

“I could’ve told you he isn’t one to bargain when he could lose what he wants. Oh wait, I did,” Tristan muttered darkly. The chains on his wrists rattled as he shifted away from her.

“You have every right to be angry.”

“Damned right, I do. You stole my wife from me.”

She sucked in a sharp breath, looking as if he had struck her. “Tristan, I am your wife.”

“You aren’t acting like it. And you won’t be after that brute has his way with you, then hangs you, or didn’t you hear?”

"He isn't going to get that chance, I promise you."

Tristan shook his head. "How can you be so calm about this?"

"This isn't the first time a king has married me and tried to kill me."

He stared at her, blinking. "It isn't?" The knowledge that he never truly knew her built inside his chest, making it hard to breathe.

Isolde glanced away from him. "I should have told you sooner. It was selfish not to. You have always been honest with me. I...I have always been other than I led you to assume. I am not the Princess Isolde, daughter of the Irish king."

Her chest moved with her next inhalation. "I am Morgan le Fay, daughter of Avalon. A priestess in training. But I have been many other things. I have been Morgause, a frightened, abused little girl. I have been Morgaine, a bitter and resentful young woman, wounded and angry. I have been Morgan, an overprotective sister, and a thief. And I have been Guinevere, queen of Camelot, wife of King Arthur Pendragon, lost and turned mad by my past. I have lived so many lives, and I would be dead if it weren't for the sacrifice of many, my sister first among them."

Shock rang through Tristan's body, stiffening him until he felt paralyzed and unable to move. His breath came shallow. He waited, letting her say her piece.

"I was sent back in time by the priestesses on Avalon. They believed if I returned to my life as Guinevere and avoided Camelot, King Arthur would be saved. Something went wrong with the spell, and my body was switched with another.

"The real Isolde is in Camelot, and according to a vision I received, she is in danger of suffering the same fate I suffered. Nothing has changed; Camelot is still in jeopardy. And consequences be damned, I am responsible and must do my part to change fate. At least Isolde's fate. I stole her life from her. She deserves to have her body back, if it isn't too late. And someone must save Elaina. I owe her as well," she finished, chest heaving.

Tristan could see the fear in her eyes, waiting for his reaction. A swirl of emotions filled him. The confusion fled, and curiosity won out over anger at her deceit.

"What do I call you?" he asked.

"Morgan," she replied, without hesitation. "You must be..."

Tristan held up a hand, the motion limited by the shackle bar he wore around his wrists. "Do not pretend to know how I feel. I have been betrayed by the one I loved, I have been misled as to her identity. I do not even know who you are."

She glanced down, hand going to a pocket in her dress.

Tristan's chains clinked as he moved his feet. "Why didn't you tell me sooner? You could have told me in Mumhan, in the infirmary."

"I didn't know you well enough, then. I tried to play the part, to avoid suspicion. Would you have believed me? Would you have thought me mad? And..." she trailed off, looking back to him. "I wanted to hope that I hadn't missed out on my last chance at love, but I was afraid to tell you who I was; a woman healing from countless abuses, so broken that even magic couldn't save me."

"You lied."

"I was always myself, as much as I could be. I just pretended...I pretended I was whole, is all. In a way, you saw my best self."

"I wanted to see all of you. Even the broken parts."

Her eyes glistened, but no tears fell.

Tristan glanced out through the bars in front of their cell. She wasn't the woman he fell in love with. And yet, was she really different now that he knew the truth? He had heard of Avalon and knew of sorcerers. He never thought he would meet one of them

Could she truly have come from another time? Queen of Camelot, wife of the great Arthur Pendragon?

Tristan sat across from her, from the woman who called herself Morgan. He didn't have the words to say, to make it right, to explain. A thousand questions poured through his mind.

At some point, he fell asleep, head bobbing on his chest, mind swimming with dark dreams, body shivering in the damp, cold air of the lower holding cell of Tintagel castle.

When he woke, stretching his stiff neck, the place where Morgan had fallen asleep was vacant. She was gone.

CHAPTER TWENTY-THREE

None, unless the saints above,
Knew the secret of their love;
For with calm and stately grace
Isolde held her queenly place,
Tho' the courtiers' hundred eyes
Sought the lovers to surprise,
Or to read the mysteries
Of a love - so rumour said -
By a magic philtre fed,
Which for ever in their veins
Burn'd with love's consuming pains.
"Tristan and Isolde; The Love Sin"
by Jane Fraqncesca Wilde

Mark barely looked at Morgan as he assigned her maids to lead her to her chambers. Her chest heaved with nausea at the thought of being with this horrendous man in any intimate way, but she let herself be led to the upper floors.

Once in her appointed chambers, Morgan excused the curtseying chambermaids, two young, wide-eyed girls who left with a plethora of "Yes, milady," and "By your leave, milady," as they went

Morgan collapsed to the floor, sliding down the wooden surface of her bedroom door, face in her hands. She trembled, trying to catch her breath.

Gradually, her efforts seemed to work; she could breathe easily again, and her hands came away from her face to rest on her raised knees before her.

What have I done?

She went into that room so poised, filled with assurance that this was the best course of action to save Tristan's life and prevent war with Ireland. Now, the throbbing in her chest filled her, confusing her, reminding her of the day she lost her mother.

She'd been seven years old, almost eight, when her mother died of a wasting sickness. She had looked forward to her birthday, when her step-father returned home, and they would be together as a family. As a family.

Morgan didn't know anything about a real family. Her relationship with Elaina was the closest she'd ever gotten. She thought she had found it with Arthur, but all she learned in that experience was to never trust a king; they were more married to their land than to their wives.

Tristan seemed to fill her with the same sense of fierce protection she'd had for Elaina, a willingness to sacrifice anything for his happiness, even to the point of self-destruction. Did he love her since finding out her true identity? Would he love her when she switched places with Isolde and became, once more, Morgan le Fay?

A headache pounded at her temples. She rubbed the muscles there, moving her fingers in small, circular motions down to her neck, the muscles tight as a rope holding a ship on the mooring during a storm.

She looked at the fire blazing in the grate. Its heat made her sweat profusely. Or perhaps it was her headache, or this horrid, stifling dress.

Morgan stood and stripped off her dress. She stood in her shift and stockings, staring into the mirror at herself.

The makeup from Castle Bel Content had washed off in her bath in the well, and deep shadows under her eyes the color of deathly belladonna flowers indicated the lack of quality rest, caused by her constant worrying over what to do about Camelot, the real Isolde, and this whole mess she had gotten herself into.

She frowned and stepped closer, tilting the mirror so it showed the phoenix on her chest in full light. The entirety of its wings shimmered a new color...gold. It startled her so much she stumbled back several steps, glancing around the room, hand rubbing across that painted image. The Rite of the Heart somehow, inexplicably, continued to heal her.

She had lost sight of her purpose in the year she spent with Tristan. Getting to know him, his love of life and of music, was one of the purest joys she had known. Argante, the head priestess of Avalon, said clearly that Morgan shouldn't go to Camelot. But she hadn't gone, Isolde had, as her, and won Arthur's affection just the same. Is this what the Goddess had intended?

A solid lump formed in Morgan's throat. She felt like she would choke on the emotion welling up inside of her. If the true Isolde had perished and Morgan's body with her, Morgan would be forced to live out her days with the face and responsibilities of the princess.

Morgan's mind danced and reeled, thoughts cycling through her mind like a spinning wheel. She felt a tap on her shoulder and whirled around, a strand of blonde hair coming free and sticking to her mouth. She sputtered, dragging it out with her finger, and stared with wild eyes at the empty room behind her. A plate of food and a goblet sat untouched on a table. The fire crackled and a log snapped, sending up a shower of sparks.

Another tap, more distinct this time. Morgan spun again and caught a glimpse of a shadow that darted away before rushing straight at her. Before she could move out of the way, it shot like a black arrow into her chest and disappeared. She gasped, her vision turned black, and she heard them in her mind again; voices.

There is nothing you can do. Why put yourself through this any longer?

And another voice. *There is no point, Morgan.*

Who is this? Morgan shouted in her own mind. The conversation continued with her words ignored.

She has every choice. She could choose love.

Recognition flashed through Morgan. That voice was Guinevere, or rather, her sense of self that divided all those years before. All Guinevere ever wanted was a relationship filled with respect and mutual admiration. She almost got killed instead.

I think she should go find him. A younger voice. Morgause? That meant the first voice...

She doesn't deserve love. She deserves to die. We all do. What have any of us given to the world but sorrow? What need does anyone have for us? Living would only be the source of more torment. You are selfish fools if you think otherwise.

Morgaine. Bitter, resentful Morgaine.

Morgan used to be afraid of her and expected to feel the same rush of emotion rise within her. When it didn't, she sat for a moment, stunned as the three voices argued over her, and their, fates.

She would have agreed with Morgaine, once. What had changed?

Why are you here? she spoke above the cacophony in her mind.

She sensed several presences turn their full attention on her.

Silence.

You haven't decided, Guinevere's voice replied.

Decided what? Morgan asked.

Whether your life has meaning. Whether what you do makes a difference.

Does it? Morgan asked.

You ruin the life of everyone you meet, Morgaine broke in. *Look at Elaina and Arthur. Look at Tristan. Banished, dead, isolated, betrayed. Why keep trying?*

Morgan felt herself shrink away from the truth of those words. Nothing good had come of her betrayal of Elaina, her relationship with Arthur, or her time with Tristan.

Here I find you, full circle again, a fourth voice echoed.

Who are you? Morgan asked.

The pressure of another presence filled her mind, accompanied by a strong sense of warmth and brightness. *Do you not recognize me?*

Blue, green, and violet light flooded her vision, as if lit from behind by the sun. A flawless female face, filled with compassion, her arms outstretched toward Morgan, her brown hair rippling. Her favorite rendition of the Goddess from the temple on Avalon, come to life.

Morgan gasped. The Goddess was here, in her mind, speaking to her.

Mother, Morgan said reverently. She would fall prostrate, if she had any awareness of a physical form to do it with. *I have failed you.*

Failed? No, *my dear, you have, in fact, succeeded rather splendidly. You were told only to stay away from Arthur, Niviane, and Mordred, a task you have completed to the fullest.*

But Isolde; our bodies were switched, and my scrying has revealed her with Arthur.

Yes, Isolde. Not you.

But my body—

Is not you. The calm voice of the Goddess permeated Morgan's being, and despite the thousand questions that rose, especially an overwhelming desire to contradict the Goddess about her success.

Morgan relaxed, as if she stepped into a warm bath in the safest place imaginable.

You have done well, daughter. But I have a new task for you, now.

Anything, Morgan replied.

Marry the King of Cornwall, then follow through with your plan to escape. Go to the tower of Shalott.

Morgan's heart leapt to her throat. *Is she there? Is she in danger?*

You will find all you seek there, came the Goddess's cryptic reply.

Why couldn't she just tell her? Morgan forced a rush of anger down, trying to keep her heart penitent before this almighty, all-powerful being that she revered.

What would you have me do?

You will know.

She had said that before, and Morgan thought she had known, and then all of this had happened. She bowed her inner self before the Goddess, swallowing every furious, insecure word that tried to burst forth from her.

Yes, Great Mother.

The word came with a sense of finality. Morgan felt breath return to her body and opened her eyes one at a time, the blurry room coming into focus.

Two chambermaids, concern on their youthful faces, leaned over her with a bottle of smelling salts and a fan, attempting to bring her to.

"Oh, thanks be to God!" the brunette one said, fanning her own face for a moment. "I thought you were...well, I am so glad you aren't..."

"Dead?" Morgan asked, grunting as they helped her stand. She waved off their attempts to support her across the room.

Neither commented on her state of undress, nor on the phoenix with golden wings emblazoned across her chest. Morgan had long ago learned that no one but her could see it. The outline of it burned into her skin, making it itch. She resisted the urge to rub at it, and instead, asked the girls for a cup of water.

Morgan drank it down, then clapped her hands and requested help dressing. Time to plan her wedding.

Morgan slid her hands down the gold fabric stretched taut across her waist and hips. Heavy trimming and red embroidery lined the entire thing. Several tailors worked through the night to make sure the dress fit her. Morgan pursed her lips, then tugged at the edge of her bodice. It was far more revealing than she preferred, but she couldn't do anything about that now.

"Even your sulking is lovely. Pout again, dearest." King Mark chuckled, coming up behind her. Morgan saw his perpetually red face in the mirror and turned before he could grab her backside, smacking his hand away.

"You are feisty," King Mark replied, pouting.

Morgan backed up, bumping into the mirror and gripping its frame to keep herself from falling into it. That look on King Mark's face was so like Lord Melwas's, Morgan's mind spun into despair and fear...and then it cleared. She felt the warm, sweaty surface of the rose-colored bottle tucked between her breasts, and with one hand drew it out, pulling the stopper and bringing it to her lips.

King Mark cried out, stepping towards her. Morgan held out a hand to stop him. "What is that? What are you doing?"

"Killing myself. If I drink this poison, you will have a corpse instead of a bride."

King Mark brought both hands up before him, sweat breaking out on his wide, bald brow. "Dearest," he said, laughing nervously. "Come now, don't ruin our big day. You will be queen. Queen of Cornwall. I won't hang you; I planned to hang a serving maid in your place, to make Tristan believe you were dead. See, an easy remedy."

Morgan dropped the bottle slightly. "Titles don't interest me. My own life means little. I want Tristan's. Let him go and promise you won't pursue him. And no killing the maid, either." She swallowed past the dryness in her mouth, watching the king.

His eyes narrowed. "Release him? He'll come after you. No, if I free him, you have to promise you will stay with me all your days, even should he approach you with an option of escape. You must stay at Tintagel."

"Yes. For his life, yes," Morgan said, without hesitation. She put the stopper back in the bottle, and King Mark reached out his hand for it, but she slipped it back in her bodice.

"I need to be certain you'll keep your side of the bargain," Morgan said.

"Of course," King Mark replied, curling his hand back, only smiling with half of his mouth. He dropped a hand into his pocket and pulled out a key. "My guards will take you to the lower holding. This key will unlock Tristan's cell. I don't wish to sully myself with his presence today. If you try anything, my guards have orders to kill Tristan on the spot, and you will be hung."

Morgan grasped the key, and Mark turned, hands clasped behind his back. He spoke to a small contingency of guards outside the door, five that Morgan could see.

The rose-colored bottle came out of her bodice easily. She eyed it for a moment, then pulled the cork and brought it swiftly to her lips. It tasted sour and lingered on her tongue, coating her entire mouth with a taste so strong her face puckered. She stopped it up again, and returned it to its nest between her breasts, hands shaking.

Her heart stopped. Life spilled from her in one great rush, and her lungs froze. She couldn't draw air, couldn't move, couldn't cry out for help.

Her heart beat again. Her lungs released, and she took a painful breath in, filling her lungs with sweet air, gasping slightly. Would Tristan feel the release too? Would he know she had broken their bond?

Morgan held her head up as she walked out the doors between two lines of guards. She counted seven now, each looking stoically at her. She walked through the midst of them and they followed on both sides and behind, preventing escape. Not that she would try without making sure Tristan was freed first, and he would need both the key and the little rose bottle to survive leaving her.

She still had to convince him to go.

CHAPTER TWENTY-FOUR

O Tristram!"--How her low voice strangely rings!--
There comes a ship, ah, rise not, turn not pale.
I know not what this means, it is a sail
Black, black as night!" She shot her word, and fled.
But Tristram cried
With a great cry, and rose upon his side.
It cannot be, it cannot, shall not be!
I will not die until mine own eyes see."
"Tristram's End" by Robert Laurence Binyon

The cell door behind Tristan swung open with a screech that jerked him out of his thoughts.

Two guards escorted Isolde inside. She gazed at him, her hair brushed and braided. It shone like the sun where it lay across her back. She wore a white-gold dress after British fashion, with wide, flowing sleeves, hemmed with lace and gold stitches, a band of gold embroidery at her narrow waist. She stood with her fists clenched at her sides, a stubborn set in her jaw that Tristan recognized.

The pain in his chest immediately eased; pain he had forgotten was there until its absence brought sweet relief. He wanted to reach out, to touch her, to see her eyes soften as they looked on him, but the time for that had passed.

"You never wore a wedding dress when we..." His voice broke.

He licked his lips.

"I never needed one," she replied softly. The distance between them seemed impossible to cross. "I have bargained with the king. He has allowed me to free you."

"In return for what?" Tristan snapped.

"My marriage to him, and the promise that I will remain." She turned her head to one side, to the guards she had bribed. "Leave us."

"We will return in a moment, milady," one guard said firmly.

She nodded, then looked back at Tristan as they left. He couldn't read her expression. She seemed cold, as if his presence did nothing for her, not like hers did to him, making his heart race, his body heat. Did she still feel the same?

"The guards will escort you from the castle, a hundred paces out. Your title has been revoked, and you are banished from Cornwall. Found herein, you will be killed. There is a bounty placed on your head."

"Why are you doing this, Morgan? Have I not loved you well?" Tristan asked.

She blinked, then continued in a rush. "As long as you don't remain, you will live. You could return to France."

"I don't want to go back there. I want to stay with you. Surely, there is another way."

"If I knew another way out of this, Tristan, I would..." She swallowed, pain flashing in her gaze.

It gave him a small thrill, knowing this was difficult for her, as well. But nothing she said could make it right.

Tristan moved closer, manacles clinking.

"You could at least be grateful," she said. Tristan stopped just short of reaching her.

"For what? You saving my life?" He laughed thickly, blinking at the moisture in his eyes. "If you think you've saved it, you are wrong."

"Would you rather rot here?" Morgan snapped. She reached into her bodice and pulled something out, then came close to him, grabbing his collar and kissing him. Their lips moved together as one.

Tristan cursed as she pulled away, feeling her hand slip from his pocket.

"I still love you, Isolde. Morgan. Whoever you are."

"You are the greatest love of my life," Morgan whispered back. "The potion may have started it, but I know the truth; I will never love another more than I have loved you."

"Then do not do this. Free me, we will run away together, as before. It isn't too late."

Morgan shook her head, her heart tearing in her chest. "I can't, Tristan. This is the best way."

"Wait for me. I'll come with you."

"You have to leave now, before the wedding." Morgan said, emotion choking her. She backed away from him.

The guards appeared in the doorway. Only three. Tristan could take them all and be away with Morgan before anyone had a chance to raise the alarm, if only he could get his hands free.

Morgan handed a key to one of the guards. "Free him."

"There's another way. There has to be."

Morgan turned and walked away, torchlight glinting off her gold hair.

Tristan rubbed his wrists and stepped after her. “Morgan, wait!”

She continued walking.

His hand dropped to his pocket as he broke into a jog to catch up to her. What had she put there? His fingers grasped the narrow top of a glass bottle and pulled it out. He glanced at the rose-tinted glass, gaping.

She rounded the corner ahead, the tip of her braid disappearing as she ran.

“Have you drunk any of this? Isolde...Morgan!” he cried.

Some of it seemed to be missing, but he couldn’t remember; had it been full when the witch gave it to them? Morgan was smart enough not to leave him without drinking her portion. Unless that was her plan all along, to set him free while she died as their bond severed.

He moved to follow, but a hand clapped on his shoulder, and several guards surrounded him. They marched him up the stairs, and met four more guards at the top.

They led him down the corridor, past the open door of the throne room. She knelt on the floor before King Mark, surrounded by a golden sun-lit halo, head bowing towards the floor.

“Morgan!” He shouted, but she did not look towards him, and the guards grabbed him by the arms, half-carrying, half-dragging Tristan through the outer doors.

She sacrificed her freedom, and possibly her life, to give him his. In that moment, he realized it didn’t matter whose body she wore. He couldn’t live without her.

This reality hit him as they stepped from the keep into the open courtyard. From castle darkness to sunlight. He turned. He would go back. He wouldn't let her do this.

The men halted after exactly a hundred paces, facing him with their swords and shields.

"You heard our king," one man said, gesturing with his sword. "Get out of Cornwall, or you're a dead man."

Tristan walked backward a few paces, saluting the men, then pivoted. His heart grew sorer by the moment.

Literally sore. Should it be hurting this much? He rubbed his sternum, where a burning sensation pulsed with each heartbeat. He had to keep moving while the guards watched.

The glass bottle burned in his hand, still warm from where it had sat against her skin. Tristan gripped it so tightly, he thought it might break, but the glass held.

She gave it to him so he would drink and be free from their bond. But had she drunk from it? Would she die of madness if he went too far? Was that her plan to escape marriage to King Mark?

Tristan would not drink it, not until he knew if she had. If she went mad, so would he. After all, he had promised her once that he'd rather go mad than see her wed to his uncle Mark.

He pressed forward, gritting his teeth at the pain pulsing through him. He broke into a jog.

Morgan's face wouldn't leave his mind. He could try to forget her, but between the tightness in his chest and the intermittent stabbing pain beginning at heart-level, he knew it would be impossible.

Tristan broke into a full run. He headed north, towards Camelot. He had always wanted to see what those famed Knights of the Round Table were like. Perhaps there would be room for him among them. First, he needed to get away from here and focus on surviving with nothing. He had done it before, only now he didn't have her. The loss of a woman often destroyed good men. Would it destroy him?

He couldn't tell yet, and that terrified him. So, he ran. From the fear, from the feeling of losing her. From the memory of her that replayed in his mind. Tree shadows speckled the path, then covered it. This forest stretched for miles.

It would be two days until he was out of Cornwall. He had to avoid bounty hunters until then, but unless King Mark sent horses out with missives to the farthest reaches of Cornwall, no one would yet be aware of it when Tristan passed.

Besides, the king would be busy with his wedding.

Tristan's chest twinged with pain. His breath sounded loud in his ears, growing harsh. He ran too hard, too fast. Memories burst to life in his mind's eye, blinding him so he barely registered his surroundings. The way her delicate fingers would tuck that stray strand of hair behind her ear, only for it to slip out again moments later.

Her sideways smile. The softness of her lips when he kissed them. And beyond that, the sound of her laugh. The softening of her eyes when he undressed her. The way she listened raptly as he played his harp. His harp. Left behind in King Mark's castle. He would mourn its loss later.

He tucked his chin and let out an extra burst of speed. He flew through the forest, trees blurring past, sunlight flickering through the tree branches.

He burst through the trees onto a cliff top, feet scrambling to a halt. Sweat dripped down his brow, and he wiped it away on his sleeve before it could reach his eyes.

He stood, chest heaving, lungs burning from his run in the cool spring air. Below, waves crashed at the base of the cliff. His heart threatened to burst with the intensity of feeling for her.

Tristan clenched his fists and drew in a breath, then bellowed.

"Morgan!" Her true name erupted from the depths inside of him and startled a pair of birds flying past, scattering them away from each other. He yelled again, tears pricking at his eyes, then forcing their way out and trailing down his cheeks, cold in the wind that blew past.

Tristan rubbed them away with his fists and sniffed; the cold air was making his nose start to run. Wiping it on his shirt sleeve, he turned away from the cliff. He tried to stop himself, to glance past without pausing, but he couldn't help it. He looked toward Tintagel, that castle perched precariously by the sea.

Somewhere inside, Morgan prepared for the wedding. Somewhere inside, she stood alone, possibly afraid, possibly in pain from their severing bond, although he wouldn't put it past her to hide it from the world.

In her life as Morgan, she had seen and done things he didn't even know of. As all the other names and lives she claimed to lead. How could one woman have been through so much?

My name is Morgan le Fay, and I come from another time.

Another time. Another name. What did she mean by that? He rubbed at his chest. The burning from overexertion should've stopped, in fact, his lungs felt clear, and he breathed easily, but he still felt the pain of the potion that bound him to Isolde...no, Morgan.

Tristan walked now, kicking at the damp green and brown grass beneath his boots. He took it easy at first, then broke out into a run again as he re-entered the forest and struck out northward once more. This time, Tristan didn't think of her. At least, he tried not to.

Fearful pain pulsed with each beat of his heart. His muscles split with each breath. At first, the sensation centered in his chest, but the farther he ran, the more it spread.

His shoulders and abdomen grew heavy, then burned with flashes of pain as if it were moving through his veins, like fire in his blood. He pumped his legs and arms, pushing it.

He had spent so many days afraid of parting from her, and he couldn't let that fear control him. He could drink the potion. It wouldn't kill him to be apart from her.

Tristan pushed harder. He couldn't keep running like this. His throat tightened, parched, and his empty stomach complained, but he pressed forward, as if he could outrun the pain and leave it on the path somewhere behind him.

Tristan's vision narrowed, black spots forming. He thought about slowing, but his arms and legs didn't want to obey. They maintained an impossible pace. He startled birds as he passed, woodland critters darted out of his way, some crossing his path. A deer watched from a distance, watched the madman run through the forest.

A knife lanced through Tristan's chest, and his foot struck a protruding rock in the path. He skidded face-first to the ground, spitting leaves and dirt, hand pinned beneath him. The musty, earthen smell of rotting leaves filled his nostrils.

Grimacing at the pain pulsing through his body, each breath came out as a wheeze. He rested his forehead on his arm, remaining sprawled on the ground.

A squirrel chittered somewhere above him. Birds called back and forth. Leaves rustled. Silence filled the spaces between.

Tristan grunted and dragged himself upright, looking back the way he had come. He couldn't return. He had to keep going, or he was a dead man. But he wouldn't make it through this agony that moved through his blood. He reached into his pocket for the bottle, cursing his weak soul.

It gleamed innocently in the sun.

Tristan popped the cork, hesitating. He didn't want to let go of her; this curse was all he had left.

He turned the bottle upside down and watched the potion run out, dribbling into the ground. He tossed the bottle to the side, scuffed dirt over the potion, and got to his feet, not bothering to brush off his clothes. His legs wobbled like a newborn colt's.

Tristan stumbled forward, leaning on a tree for support, pressed his forehead into the rough bark just for a moment, then pushed off and moved forward down the path.

Agony lanced through his body, a sharp tugging sensation that pulled him backward even as he moved forward. He strained against it, fists tightening, arms clenching, as if someone held his arms and kept him back. He pulled, neck tightening.

He couldn't move.

For a moment, he stood like that, suspended, panting, then in a sudden burst of speed and force he pulled against that barrier until it broke.

His heart and mind broke with it.

Tristan's arms wind-milled as he fell forward and his knees struck the ground. Spittle flew from his mouth, dripping onto a broken, brown leaf between his hands.

The pain reverberated through his head and chest in brief waves. Breath shuddered through his body. Thoughts reeled around in his mind, none sticking. He had lost the one thing that mattered to him most in all of life.

A strange sound came from inside him; a keening that carried through the forest. He rocked on his hands, body shifting back and forth rhythmically. His arms trembled. He wanted to simultaneously curl up in a ball and start sprinting again.

Instead, he rocked, voice rising and falling, until he lost all track of time or meaning. After a time, the sound ended, halting as suddenly as it had begun.

The forest fell quiet. Nothing stirred for a single, eternal moment, and then Tristan began to scream.

CHAPTER TWENTY-FIVE

Yea, shame's own fire that burned upon his brow
To bear the brand there of a broken vow
Was frozen again for very fear thereof
That wrung his heart with keener pangs than love.
And all things rose upon him, all things past
Ere last they parted, cloven in twain at last,
Iseult from Tristram, Tristram from the queen;
And how men found them in the wild woods green
Sleeping, but sundered by the sword between,
Dividing breast from amorous breast a span,
But scarce in heart the woman from the man.
"The Maiden Marriage," from "Tristram of Lyonesse"
by Algernon Charles Swinburne

Morgan leaned against the windowsill, staring out over the ocean as white-crested waves crashed against the cliffs below the castle. She could just throw herself from the window, end it all now, never worry again...

She shook her head and stepped back from the window, rubbing the silk elbows of her impossibly tight dress.

Her wedding dress. For the second time, she found herself wedded in the eyes of the laws of the land and the Christian Lord. Only sheepherders and a few minor lords attended the brief ceremony. Important sheepherders, King Mark assured her, as if she cared.

As soon as the words were spoken by the droning voice of the priest, servants ushered Morgan off to the king's chambers to await his claim on her virtue. Whatever was left of it.

Great, fat droplets of sweat ran down from her hairline and soaked her armpits. Her hands and thighs felt clammy.

It is all right. I have a plan. Morgan reminded herself. She glanced furtively at the narrow-necked bottle she placed on the bedside table earlier that morning. A strong sleeping draught, one found in the apothecary.

Morgan had asked the healer for a simple headache remedy, lavender, to be precise, and tricked a page into calling him away at just the right moment, so she could sort through his shelves and take what she needed.

She wasn't sure how effective it would be, but it looked similar to some of the recipes she had seen in Isolde's books. It wouldn't kill him, but it could be too mild as well, a thought that didn't banish the images of the King of Cornwall advancing on her, hands on her, undressing her...

Morgan shuddered and paced, wringing her hands. At least she convinced the attending women to let her prepare herself, against tradition. She didn't intend on undressing or getting into that bed at all, if she could help it.

The chamber door opened. Morgan jumped. Her eyes darted around the room, looking for a place to hide, before she got a grip on her sanity and forced the panic down, turning to face the door, hands clasped before her.

King Mark stepped in, shutting the door behind him and latching it. He smiled at her. Was that meant to be reassuring? He started unbuttoning his doublet.

"My king." Morgan swallowed. "My husband. I had this wine prepared for us. Please, allow me to pour."

He hesitated, his hairy chest peeking out from the opening in his coat, then his smile widened, and he nodded.

Morgan tried not to let her relief show too much. She walked around the bed and picked up the wine bottle, then poured some into both silver goblets on the table. She brought the first to the king, hoping he wouldn't notice her quivering hands.

He took a long swallow, smacking his lips, swishing the liquid around.

Morgan pulled her stare from him. She took a sip, pretending to take as long a drink as he had done, and faked swallowing. She figured a man Mark's size would have to drink a full cup of the brew.

Mark took another swig and sighed with pleasure, then set the goblet down.

"Now then, my dear, shall we..."

"No!" Morgan blurted, sloshing the liquid from her goblet. A splash landed on the floor, just shy of her toe. "I mean, my king, if you please, I had hoped to drink a little more. It...it will help me relax."

King Mark chuckled. "Feeling nervous? There's no need."

There is every need, Morgan thought. Her knuckles turned white as she gripped her goblet. She smiled disarmingly at the king.

He moved towards her, and she hastily tipped up the cup, taking another tiny sip. He hesitated, then picked up his goblet and took several long drinks, eyes wandering all the while. She could feel them stripping her frame without a shred of discretion, and it made her insides writhe. She felt like she needed to bathe, and he hadn't even touched her.

King Mark's goblet clanked on the table, and Morgan jumped again, sloshing the liquid brimming in her cup.

"I am not a patient man," the king said, unbuttoning the rest of his doublet and pulling it off as he walked towards her.

Morgan's blood ran cold. She craned, trying to see into his goblet. She had to know if he had taken enough of the draught for it to be effective. Any moment, it would take effect, and the giant of a man would collapse to the floor. She backed up, feigning another sip at her goblet, trying to smile.

"The bed, Isolde, now." His voice had a tone of command; the command of a king to his subject, of a controlling man to his submissive wife. He expected her to obey, and his eyes flashed at her slight hesitation.

She reached back behind her as if to undo her gown, but he growled, stopping her.

"I'll do that."

She collapsed onto the covers.

It wasn't going to work. He came at her, his doublet removed, that enormous stomach protruding over the belt that his fingers worked to remove. Her gut clenched, her throat open and ready to scream. This wasn't happening; not again, not with him.

She leaned back as he bent down towards her, his presence cutting off her air, making her breath come shallow and fast, her heartbeat escalating to a dangerous point, until his breath suffocated her, and his weight pressed her into the bed.

He paused, shaking his head, then turned his head back towards her, lips readied to press a kiss on his new bride. He paused again, frowning. “That wine...it tasted strange. What was...”

And then he fell.

Morgan’s breath squeezed from her lungs as his bulk collapsed on top of her. Grimacing and wheezing, she placed her hands against his bare, hairy chest and heaved.

He might have guessed at the end that she had done something.

Morgan didn’t have time to consider the implications. She dragged the blanket off the bed and tucked it around the deeply snoring king, propped a pillow under his head, then slapped him soundly. He didn’t respond. She felt only a tiny smidge of guilt at the bright white-red imprint of her hand on his face. He was a complete ass of a man, and she considered for a long moment whether she ought to kill him after all.

She had already had a letter sent to King Angeus of Muhman in Ireland. Isolde, urging him to stop the war. She described having been waylaid and lost after the ship crashed, but finally made it to Tintagel and wed King Mark.

By the time Mark woke, the letter would be long gone. Would he pursue the war? If he did, he was a fool beyond imagining.

Morgan struggled for far longer than she was comfortable before stepping from the dress with relief. The cool air raised goosebumps on her skin. She scrambled to dress in a plain, homespun gown and retrieved the pack hidden beneath the bed.

Morgan used the pins in her hair to pile the locks on top of her head, then wrapped a large, stained kerchief around it all, tying it the way she had seen women do when they tended the wash. She rubbed her fingers inside a pot filled with black powder; walnut, ash, dirt, a bit of everything.

She rubbed it into her hairline, darkening it, smudging with her fingers until she hoped it looked natural, then went to work on her face. She found no mirrors in the king's rooms, so she did her best to even out the filth, avoiding making any sharp lines and putting just enough on her face and hands so she could distract from her distinct features.

Morgan took her pack containing a massive sum of money for the peasant she pretended to be, as well as a few other things, and slung it over her shoulder, then adopted her practiced hunched-over posture.

King Mark had ordered the guards away from his doors, perhaps preferring to make love to his new bride in private. The servants and wedding attendees enjoyed the feast downstairs, leaving the corridors empty.

Morgan hugged the wall, making it out of the castle without being confronted, then turned right and made her way towards the stables. As she ducked under a stone archway in the cool blue twilight, a hawk's cry pierced the air. So distinct from the harsher cry of a seabird, it made Morgan glance up, and her chest twinged unexpectedly.

She had taken the potion, and her bond with Tristan was severed, but she still felt for him, still wished to be near him. True feelings developed after all, beneath the influence of the potion's enchantment. Would she ever see him again?

Morgan set her jaw, breathing deeply to keep a handle on her emotion. Should the Goddess keep her alive, she would find him after she made it to Camelot.

With the old stable master drunk from Morgan's earlier gift of wine, Morgan led a bay mare named Mira from the stable, saddled and bridled. The waning moon showed her the path that led from Tintagel.

Mira nudged Morgan's back, hands, and sides, as if searching for an expected treat.

Morgan threw her bag over the saddle. It didn't contain much in the way of provisions, but she had plenty of wealth to bargain with. She just had to avoid calling too much attention to herself, lest she attract thieves on the road.

She mounted Mira, grateful for her extra wide skirts that let her ride normally without showing an unseemly amount of leg, and with a click of her tongue, the horse moved forward. Adrenaline from her escape and the brisk night air kept her wide awake, and she gazed about like a child at the night-darkened landscape, half-lit by the waning moon.

A gentle breeze rustled through the long grasses, and patches of bright stars peeked out from behind banks of storm clouds. A large, dark form lumbered beside her for a time, before veering off into the grass; a badger, if her eyes told her correctly.

Mira snorted, and Morgan patted her neck, murmuring encouraging words. It felt good to be atop a horse again. She hadn't done as much riding in her life as Isolde. She took a deep breath of the fresh, late-spring air.

Ahead, a forest awaited her, treetops stretching over the road she rode like giant lovers reaching for each other.

For the first time in weeks, Morgan felt as if she could truly breathe.

CHAPTER TWENTY-SIX

Not now, Isoult, not now!
I am thine while I have breath.
Words part us not, nor vow--
No, nor King Mark, but death.
I hold thee to my breast.
Our sins, our woes are past;
Thy lips were the first I prest,
Thou art mine, thou art mine at the last!
"Tristram's End" by Robert Laurence Binyon

"It seems like 'e might be enchanted or sommat," one man said.

"Yeah? What's it to us?" his companion sneered, looking Tristan's filthy form up and down with contempt.

Spittle dribbled from Tristan's mouth. He didn't move to wipe it away.

"Well it isn't 'is fault, now is it?"

The person's companion grunted. "Poor bloke. We better 'elp 'im."

"What do you mean?" the other man asked.

The first man gripped Tristan's arm and pulled him gently forward. Tristan yanked his arm away, thrashing and yelling as the man came closer.

"Now, see 'ere bloke, we be trying to help ya."

Tristan strained against his grip, scrabbling to get away. His mind filled with panic and a red fog that grew darker every moment they detained him.

"Oy, be useful! Grab that rope there."

The man caught a thick brown rope in his hands and deftly wrapped it around Tristan's hands, then wound it up his arms.

Tristan jerked against the confines of the binding but settled after it wouldn't budge.

"Where do you think to take him?" The second man asked. "I ain't holing him up at my place. My lady would have a fit."

The first man nudged Tristan forward. He took a few halting steps. "The Rose Witch will know whot to do with 'im," he announced.

That name triggered a thought in Tristan's mind. Everything was so muddled, hidden beneath a fog and a layer of pain that he shuddered to think about breaking through. It was safer here, beneath it all, not thinking or feeling.

He walked with the men, them on their horses, him following behind, head bowed, feet dragging on the ground. He kept just enough slack in the rope to avoid getting dragged.

They stopped midday and tried to feed Tristan some bread, but he sputtered and spit it out, staring dejectedly out to the distance. He allowed them to trickle water in his mouth, only enough for a swallow. Just enough to stay alive. For now.

The men shook their heads and pitied him. They didn't even know what he had lost.

They retraced Tristan's steps from the days prior. They saw no one, except an errant farmer tending the fields. The part of him that hung stubbornly onto lucidity shouted, trying to bring the rest of his mind to its senses, to no avail. He stared, the echo of pain in his heart as he passed Tintagel enough to make him shudder.

He would not think of her. Would not think of her betrayal, of his broken heart, of the man she now married. His common sense screamed at him to wake, to take charge of his life, to go back towards Camelot. But he was far beyond that, now.

The voice yelled and tried to shake him free of his thoughts. *Think, man! Even broken-hearted, you shouldn't be this incompetent.* Tristan couldn't block out his own inner voice, but he could ignore it. He pushed away the guilt, the fear, the intelligence, in favor of numbness, an intellectual and emotional death.

The long, green-brown grass on the moors bent at his feet in the breeze that ruffled his matted hair. It wafted the stench of his own unwashed body into his nostrils, and he sniffed, stifling an urge to sneeze and failing to prevent the involuntary convulsion.

The men guiding him wrinkled their noses and turned their heads away as the wind blew his stench towards them. Up on those horses, speaking in low tones and glancing at him. Did they think he didn't see?

Tristan stumbled along behind, trying to keep his mind as free of lucid thoughts as possible. When they came upon the broken-down shack in the middle of the moor, with its crooked, thatched roof and greying wooden sides with boards a kilter, he didn't recognize it. Not immediately, anyway.

No, it took actually seeing the bent, frizz-haired woman with the cheeks that blushed a deep, unnatural rose color, to rustle up the memory of a few days prior. She was the reason he had lost the bond with the woman he loved.

He ripped his hands free of the loosened ropes around his wrists, snarling as he lunged. Spittle flew from his mouth and his hands closed around paper-thin skin to grip the old woman's neck.

He growled and squeezed, while she calmly looked into his eyes with her clear blue ones, then gripped his massive arm in her dainty hand and squeezed. The nerve she struck sent fire lancing up Tristan's arm, and he howled.

The two men stammered excuses and fled, the lopsided door banging behind them as they ran.

Tristan's fingers released their hold. Quicker than he could ever anticipate, the Rose Witch grabbed a length of rope and tied it expertly about his wrists, bringing them so tight together it made the rope dig into his skin and burn as he struggled.

"There," she said, only a mite out of breath. "I think that might hold you. I expected something like this, you know. The package you came in was a bit different than I thought, but I expected it all the same. You would have found your way here eventually, begging me to reverse whatever potion I gave you." She eyed him up and down.

When Tristan didn't reply, the Rose Witch cackled and turned away, rummaging in the baskets at the bottom of one of her shelves. She came up with another rope, a triumphant look on her wizened face, and rolled up the sleeves of her tattered green dress before tying the rope about Tristan's shoulders, and using another length to tie a lead coming off of him, like an unruly stallion she intended on breaking. She tied the other end of the lead to the side of a shelf.

He jerked at it, hoping to topple the shelf on both of them and end the old woman and perhaps himself at the same time, but it held firm. It must have been the firmest structure in this ruined house; it didn't even wobble.

A gag came next, a dirty cloth stuffed into his mouth that tasted of dust and mold and made him gag, followed by a longer strip of fabric tied about his head, keeping the wad of cloth in place.

He watched the Rose Witch, hatred filling his core.

"These love potions are devastating, aren't they? And so often couples actually ask for them, thinking it seals their fate together. It does, but not in the way they imagine. It's worse when someone is given a potion alone, and there's no one bonded to him. Those ones go mad, begging to be released or killed."

She eyed him, bushy grey eyebrows raising. "I wager you side with the latter, Sir Knight? Your missus drank and you didn't." She tsked, then smacked her lips and rubbed her hands together. "All right, then, enough chatter. We have somewhere to be."

Tristan grunted, the first sound he'd made since attacking her. He tried to make it sound insistent, or questioning.

She seemed to get what he meant. "There's that much sense left in you, eh? That won't last long. Soon the sorrow will set in, then fatigue, then…" She shrugged, then cocked her head, staring at him. "I suppose I'll need a horse," she mused, then turned back to him. "What do I want with you?"

He nodded, despite his desire to ignore the mad old woman and let her do what she wished with him, consequences be damned.

"It is your lady's doing, really. You have her to thank for so much. After all, she's the reason you're here, isn't she?" The Rose Witch didn't wait for his reply but lifted her skirt up past her knee and stepped on a lower shelf to reach higher. "She isn't who you think she is, my pretty boy. Did you know she lied to you? And she has had another intention this entire time, using you to get to Camelot and her precious Arthur." The woman muttered to herself.

Tristan shook his head, wishing for the first time that he had all of his wits about him and could process what she said. Something about Arthur. King Arthur? Morgan had said something about Arthur, too.

The witch came down with a grunt, a squat, brown jar clutched in her hand. She unscrewed the lid and sniffed, making a face, then grinning. She set it next to a growing pile of items on a low counter behind Tristan.

"There is so much to tell that you won't know a thing about, so I'll enter the story where you might understand. I learned that Morgan, that's your Isolde's true name, Sir Knight, posed as the reclusive healer-princess in Ireland. Well, I needed her to come to me. A debt gone unpaid between us, you see, and she must be held accountable for that. I impersonated someone close to her, planted that love potion you so obligingly gave her. I thought I was done when that storm cast me from the ship, but I survived."

Tristan gaped, half-aware that drool dribbled down from his open mouth and made a wet spot on the dusty floor. The Rose Witch stopped moving about and stood before him, smiling, a beam of dim light cast on her from a fair-sized hole in the roof. As he stared, mind sluggishly trying to catch up with what the witch had told him, her face changed.

The homey, unremarkable face of the Irish queen's maid, Aideen, flashed before him, a wicked edge to her grin. Her face morphed a second time, taking on the flawless visage of a stunning, silvery blonde- haired woman. He gaped, stuttering, unable to bring up the words to ask, but the sorceress before him anticipated his question.

"You want to know how? When I caught Morgan scrying, trying to fix some foolish mistake she thought she made. It didn't take me long to figure out what had happened, but you don't need to be confused with those details." The sorceress grasped Tristan's chin and shook his head back and forth, making a pursed-lip, simpering kind of face before releasing him. "I did some magic of my own. My plans were being cast awry, and I had to work fast to preserve them.

"I planted the love potion, intending to give it to Morgan the eve of her wedding with King Mark, leading her to a miserable end trapped in love with that foolish brute and keeping her out of my way, but then it got better."

The witch's voice brightened. "Because you drank the potion, and gave it to Morgan, I knew you would seek an antidote, so I holed up here and awaited your arrival. When you came, I gave Morgan the antidote. Either you would both drink it, and she would run off to Camelot, miserable without you, or one of you wouldn't take it. It wasn't a foolproof plan, but I would win either way."

She laughed, the musical sound not matching the horror that filled Tristan at his center, the part of him that could still think and feel, at least for now. "So you, my good knight, are going mad. You will eventually accept your fate and die, but not for an agonizingly long while. And I hope not before Morgan gets to see what she has done to you. It is the perfect punishment for her attempt to evade the debt she owes me, you see. The love of her life, destroyed by the very feelings he has for her, and she gets to watch."

The woman snatched a large satchel from a nail and piled her things into it, then slung it over her shoulder. She untied the rope from the shelf and clicked her tongue, tugging at the rope until Tristan stood, keeping his head down to avoid hitting the roof, and followed the sorceress out. He cleared his throat and forced a single word past the fog in his mind.

"Where?" he rasped.

The deceitfully beautiful face turned back toward him and laughed again, tapping his nose with a single sharp fingernail.

"You'll see."

CHAPTER TWENTY-SEVEN

And ere her ear might hear her heart had heard,
Nor sought she sign for witness of the word;
But came and stood above him newly dead,
And felt his death upon her: and her head
Bowed, as to reach the spring that slakes all drouth;
And their four lips became one silent mouth.
So came their hour on them that were in life
Tristram and Iseult: so from love and strife
The stroke of love's own hand felt last and best
Gave them deliverance to perpetual rest.
"The Sailing of the Swan," from "Tristram of Lyonesse"
by Algernon Charles Swinburne

Morgan thought she would pick up rumors of the goings on of Camelot along the way, but the tavern gossip was strangely silent. She would sit in a common room of an inn or tavern until the last travelers turned in, and then turn in herself.

She heard some talk of the queen, an apparently beautiful, quiet, generous woman who kept to the castle. Morgan assumed they spoke of Isolde.

On the third day of travel, the road broadened before her and became heavier with foot traffic, merchants and traders, knights and farmers, women laden with goods to sell in the marketplace, children running and yelling. It seemed far busier than she remembered it being, except at festival times. With a start, Morgan realized it had to be near Beltane time.

"Young lad," Morgan called out to a passing boy of ten or twelve. He stopped dragging his stick through the dirt and looked back at her.

"Aye, milady?"

The horse gave her away, or perhaps the way she held herself. You couldn't always hide a lifetime of nobility with clothes and dirt.

"When is the Beltane celebration?"

He looked at her, cocking his head sideways. "You a recluse, or sommat? It be tomorrow night, milady, everyone be gettin' ready."

"Thank you."

She tossed him a coin, which he caught deftly between his two palms, grinning up at her, showing the gaps in his teeth, before running to catch up with the others he played with.

Hours later, Morgan tugged on Mira's reins, bringing her to a stop. She patted the horse's neck. She deserved oats and rest, only one of which Morgan could provide. The tower rose before her, casting its late-afternoon shadow over the bank and road where Mira stood.

The horse lowered her head to pull at some fresh, green grass; grass made greener by the wide river that surrounded the tower. Morgan shaded her eyes from the bright sun. Her heart thumped out an anxious rhythm in her chest, and her breathing came shallow, as if her throat constricted and she couldn't draw in enough air.

The tower looked the same as she remembered, and somehow different.

"They say there's a fairie woman in there," a woman piped up from the ground beside her, a basket of neatly folded linen gowns balanced on her head with one hand, the other holding the hand of a dirty-faced little girl, who looked up at Morgan with wide, serious brown eyes.

"Aye, I have heard that. What is the quickest way to the other side of the river, pray tell?"

The woman blinked, a little startled by her question, then nodded her head forward slightly, so as not to disturb the basket or its contents.

"Ahead a bit, you'll find a bridge to cross."

Morgan thanked the woman, smiled at the child, then urged Mira forward. She crossed the wide bridge and entered the forest on the other side, relishing the cool, dappled light in the heat of the day.

She didn't have to go far. Morgan dismounted off the path, beneath the shelter of the trees where plenty of new grass made a perfect feast for the horse. She tied the reins loosely around a low- hanging branch. She didn't know what faced her in that tower, but if she didn't return, Mira would be able to free herself if she tugged hard enough.

Morgan gave the mare a final, friendly pat, then stepped onto the bank of the river. She remembered a narrow bridge of land nearby. Her heart sank when she saw the inches of water rushing over it.

The winter snow melt made the river high this time of year. Crossing would be slick and not without risk of falling into the frigid water.

Morgan gritted her teeth, removed her boots and stockings, then stepped into the water, holding them in one hand. She gasped at the shocking temperature and moved quickly, keeping her skirts high, mud squishing beneath her feet as she ran.

On the far side, she propped her boots against the mossy base of the tower. She didn't want to put them on with her feet so wet. Green grass tickled her feet as she walked around to find the wooden door she remembered.

Everything looked the same; the mossy sides of the tower reached up towards the blue spring sky and vines covered the aging wooden door. She had no doubt that when she saw her sister, she wouldn't have aged a single day, either.

Morgan's ribs felt constricted and her head swam as she reached for the door, brushing aside vines to get to the handle. The warm, rusted metal moved hesitantly beneath her hand, then clicked open, and Morgan stepped into the darkness.

Musty air tickled her nose and made her feel like sneezing. Morgan suppressed it, tensing her neck and constricting her own breathing until the urge passed, even though the irritating sensation remained for a moment, burning the inside of her nose.

To her right, a staircase wound down. How far it went, she did not know. Last time she had ignored it. Should she take a look? She peered into the darkness, ears and eyes straining. It seemed abandoned. The stairs looked as if all they'd carried in decades was a thick layer of dust and cobwebs in every corner. She looked to her left.

Another staircase, lit by several tiny window slits, wound upward to the top of the tower. She couldn't hear anything coming from there, either; she must not be close enough. Tapestries hung on the walls, all woven by Elaina and the enchantment on her.

Morgan walked up the staircase on her left, leading up. She ran her hand along the tapestries briefly, feeling the texture of the thousands of rows of thread that made up the image. She stopped before the door. It hung open a crack.

She pushed against it, the rusted hinges stiff and creaking.

Her foot brushed something sharp. It clinked as it slid across the floor. Broken glass, reflecting the wooden timbers of the tower roof. Morgan looked across the room to the mirror.

A few large, jagged pieces clung to the sides of the ornate frame. The rest carpeted the floor in a thousand glittering shards. Morgan swallowed, then edged to her left towards the bed, avoiding most of the glass. She sat down on the mussed covers and found her breath again.

The room was empty except for the shattered mirror, the unmoving loom with a half-finished tapestry, and a few pieces of simple furniture.

Elaina had escaped, as before. Had she rescued Isolde from the flames? Would she return to the tower, as she did when she rescued Morgan?

"Hello?" she called out on a whim, the stiffness of the room's silence making her feel uneasy. She cleared her throat and clasped her hands in her lap. What did the Goddess expect her to do here? Why not send her to Camelot, to stop Arthur from going to war, or save Isolde herself? Why...

You ask many questions. The male voice startled her into standing.

A piece of glass crunched, and Morgan winced, sitting back down and brushing the piece from her skin.

"Who's there?" she asked aloud. Her eyes scanned every nook and cranny. They hesitated on a chest against the far wall, the ornate carvings etched deep into the dark cherry wood.

Alas, my fate seems to be the same in this alternate timeline.

This timeline? "Merlin?"

Indeed.

"How are you still here? I thought..."

You thought more would be changed.

"I thought you could see the future!"

Ah. That, I cannot. My Sight is clouded on the best days. I can tell you, when I counseled the Avalon priestesses, my impression of the outcome of this timeline was positive.

"Positive for whom? Not you, clearly."

No? You are here.

"Where is Elaina?" Morgan asked, glancing around the room again. "Will she return?"

I assume she will. She saw a vision of her sister burning at the stake and broke the curse.

"What of Arthur?"

He may be dead already. His fate was unclear to me, though I saw him killed at Mordred's hand all the same.

Her heart seemed to skip a beat. He was dead. Shouldn't she feel more than simple sorrow? Morgan reached up and rubbed at her chest, suddenly feeling a powerful itch.

As she scratched, her ears picked up the muttering of a female voice in the stairwell and the sound of heavy panting with the clank of armor. Morgan bolted from the bed, skipping over the glass, and threw open the door.

She ran down the stairs, getting halfway before she met Elaina, dressed in full armor, a half-unconscious woman draped over her shoulder. A ragged line of black hair hung down, covering the woman's face, but Morgan knew it would be like looking in a mirror at her own face; her true face.

Elaina froze, one booted foot on the next step up, her hair tied back from her ash-smudged cheeks.

"Who are you?" she asked, in the same moment Morgan blurted, "Are you all right?"

Elaina's expression shifted to bewilderment. Isolde groaned and shifted, then cried out.

"Oh goodness, never mind introductions. Can you help me?" Elaina asked, voice straining as she awkwardly held onto Isolde.

Morgan nodded and came down the steps, managing to get Isolde's other arm up over her shoulder. It was a tight squeeze in the narrow stairwell, but they made it up the steps and into the room.

A small piece of glass pinched the underside of her foot, but she limped to the bed and lay Isolde down with Elaina.

The burns exposed raw, weeping flesh on the woman's legs and feet. The brown dress she wore lay draped across her legs in blackened tatters.

"What happened?" Morgan asked, staring into her own face, unable to look away.

It wasn't as bad as what happened to her, so perhaps Elaina got there sooner this time. Morgan saw no marks on Elaina, though she wheezed, probably from the smoke she had inhaled.

Elaina eyed Morgan, as if weighing whether she should find out more about her before answering.

"This is Queen Guinevere," she said, hesitating to judge Morgan's reaction.

Morgan raised her eyebrows. She knew this already but figured she should try to act at least a little surprised.

Elaina sighed and rubbed her face. "Condemned to burn at the stake for adultery that I don't think she committed."

"And the king?"

"Dead." Elaina choked out the word, seeming oddly emotional until Morgan remembered that Arthur was her son.

"I am sorry," Morgan whispered. There it was again; the infuriating itch. She rubbed at it again. She felt an ache too. She had loved him once, after all, but the ache was old, like a war wound in an aged knight, a stiffness rather than a sharpness. The sharpness she felt came from her failure. She had failed. Camelot had fallen.

Elaina nodded, then gave her a strange look. "What do you have to be sorry for?"

So much, Morgan thought. She opened her mouth to explain, but the sound of someone dashing up the stairs made her start.

She and Elaina both looked to the door as a man burst in, breathless, chest heaving, pushing brown hair out of his face. Hands on his hips, he looked back and forth from Elaina to Morgan, then saw the woman on the bed. His hands went to his face.

"She looks terrible, Elaina. We need a healer, an apothecary, a..." he stopped and looked at Morgan. "Is that you? Brilliant, Elaina."

"No, that isn't..." Elaina began.

"I am, actually," Morgan said, sitting up straighter. "I mean, I have some training, a little skill. I could make her stable. Could someone fetch clean water from the river below?"

"In the corner, Gereck. There is a pitcher behind the bed. There may be water in it." Elaina said.

Morgan's hand went to the satchel at her side. It had a few things in it; herbs to make Isolde sleep, to make the pain diminish. It would stop her moaning at least. Morgan flipped mentally through the books she had read, remembering anything she could about treating bad burns.

Calendula. Comfrey. Lavender. Dry, treat, dress, keep the victim hydrated.

Morgan's hands hovered over Isolde's legs, damp cloth in one hand, pot of salve in the other. Elaina sat near Isolde's head, touching her face, murmuring.

Morgan licked her dry lips. She stared into her own unconscious face, about to attempt to heal her own damaged body. She took a breath and moved to press the cloth against the worst of the burns.

"Do not touch her." A harsh, deep female voice commanded.

Morgan froze, then looked up. Standing in the doorway, her beautiful face rigid, expression one of cold anger, was Niviane in the youthful guise she had worn as Nimue.

Elaina stood. "You!" she said.

"Niviane," Morgan whispered.

Elaina glanced at her. "You know this sorceress?" Elaina spat. "Who are you?"

Niviane laughed, crossing her arms over her chest and leaning on the door frame. "You haven't told her yet, my dear? Oh, this is better than I thought. Go ahead, I can wait."

Morgan's gaze shifted from Niviane's cold smile to Elaina's confused and angry expression. She stood, her fists clenching, eyes darting. She had gone through so much; Morgan didn't want to increase her burden, but she had little choice now.

"It may be difficult to believe, but I am your sister, Morgan le Fay." Morgan nodded to Isolde, who lay on the bed, the shallow rise and fall of her chest the only discernible sign of life. "I was enchanted, and my body was switched with another's. The woman you see wearing my face is the Irish princess, Isolde. King Angeus's daughter."

Morgan glanced down into her lap, then forced her eyes upward.

She wouldn't hide from this.

Hurt creased Elaina's brow. "It wasn't you that I saved from the flames?"

Morgan shook her head. "Yes, and no. She wears my body, which is part of me."

Emotion warred in Elaina's pale blue eyes. It seemed she couldn't decide what to feel; did she know of Morgan's part in her years spent in the tower?

"The truth is out, now we can proceed," Niviane declared.

"Proceed?" Morgan echoed.

"Yes, my dear. With your trial." Niviane gestured with her hand and walked into the room, her elegant green dress brushing the glass-covered floor, making the broken shards clink as they swept together behind her. And, floating through the air, arms and legs limp, face pale and sweaty, was Tristan.

He drifted forward a few more feet, then the magic released him and he fell to the floor, moaning.

Morgan gasped, dropping the cloth and salve and putting her hands to her mouth. "What did you do to him?"

"It's rather what you did, dearest. You took the potion, your knight did not. A future I predicted and worked for." She grinned, and in a flash, her face changed from the young and achingly-lovely Nimue to the creased, bent-nosed visage of the Rose Witch.

"It was you all along? But how..."

"Yes, I am sure you are wondering how I knew to be there when I did. When I intercepted your message to Isolde, I performed some magic of my own. I intended for you to take the potion with your, or rather Isolde's, intended, the King of Cornwall, and put you out of my way for good, but it was just as well that Sir Tristan was bound to you instead. When I discovered the mistake, I made my way to Cornwall. It wasn't difficult to guess you would make your way to Camelot to try to stop the fall of King Arthur, and rescue Elaina. The Rose Witch is an identity I have cultivated for decades."

Niviane waved her hand, lowering Tristan to the ground on the floor beside the bed.

"There is much for you to answer for, Morgan le Fay. You have neglected your agreement with me, a contract you are bound to with no simple promise, but an Oath, witnessed by a druid council with authority from Avalon. You have harmed Elaina, stolen her life from her in a misguided attempt to protect her. You are responsible for stealing the identity of the Irish princess, Isolde, condemning her to die the death meant for you, and now the noble knight Sir Tristan suffers, even unto death, with the potion-inflicted bond of love still tied to you."

Anger flashed inside of Morgan, and she looked to Niviane. "Do you deny the part you have had in all of this? It was your magic that bound Elaina to the mirror and the loom. All I asked was for you to protect her! I take full responsibility for what has happened to Isolde, I admit it was my ignorance that forced her here, away from her own life. You do what suits your own intentions, your own plans for power and gain, and yet you claim to follow the will of the Goddess."

Morgan's voice sounded clear and strong, power thrummed through her words, her chest vibrated. "You know nothing of the Goddess, her power to nurture and love. You know only greed and selfishness! You can prevent this, and yet you choose to withhold your hand." Morgan clenched her fists and stepped toward Niviane.

"So would you, if you hadn't run from everything," Niviane replied coldly. "You ran from Avalon, you ran from your agreement with me, you ran from your past and rejected yourself." She paused, running a hand along the wood of the loom. "I admit I have done wrong. Placing Elaina in the tower fit our agreement but was also self-serving. This is nothing in the face of the debt you still owe me."

"You got what you wanted, Niviane. Arthur is dead; Camelot is ruined."

"A priestess of Avalon was supposed to retain the throne, Morgan," Niviane said, eyes flashing. "A vessel of the Goddess, whether it be you or myself. In this, you have failed, and so your debt comes due. In the face of all that has happened, I will show you mercy, but justice must also be served."

Morgan's heart thudded in her chest.

Niviane gestured to Tristan and Isolde, both unconscious, both laboring to breathe, reaching for life, and failing. "I claim one life for my debt. Thus, I will save the other. Choose the love of your life, your last chance at true love, or Princess Isolde, who wears your body. Choose the first, you get your happy ending. Choose the second, you redeem yourself, regain your body, stop a war."

Sacrifice my integrity or sacrifice my happiness.

Morgan stepped toward Tristan and fell to the floor. She lifted his head and pulled it into her lap, stroking his brow.

"Tristan, please wake up." She wanted to talk to him, wanted to hear his voice before...before she made her choice.

His breathing hitched, and then his eyes flickered open. He smiled.

Morgan ran her fingers through his thick, brown hair, twirling the length of it around and between them as she had done a thousand times before.

"I thought my heart would mend when I saw you, when we were near again, but we..." He grunted, and pain creased his brow, echoed in his eyes. She recognized the look from when she healed him of his wounds before, in Mumhan.

Her hand soothed his brow. "We aren't bonded anymore," she whispered. "Oh, Tristan, why didn't you take the potion? You had it in your hand."

"I couldn't...I didn't know for certain if you had drunk it. You never said, and I couldn't...I couldn't risk this being your fate."

Guilt flooded Morgan. "Of course, I drank it, Tristan! I never could have left you if I hadn't. I thought you would listen to me, that you would drink it. I didn't think..."

"That I would be so foolish. I always intended to follow you. Why didn't you wait for me?"

"I thought I could save you the pain of seeing me...of seeing the real me."

Tristan reached a hand up to stroke her face. "Oh, Morgan. Isolde's body is beautiful, but she isn't you. She could never be you."

Silence filled the space.

Neither Elaina or Gereck tried to speak, to fix with their words what could not be fixed, to persuade her to make one decision or another.

Tristan reached a hand up to her face. His fingers brushed her cheek, and Morgan leaned into the touch, closing her eyes as his warm palm cupped the side of her face, her hand reaching up and holding his.

"What I've wanted, more than anything, is to be able to show you who I am," she said, "but I was foolish, and now there isn't time. You will never know me."

Tristan shook his head, a subtle movement she felt more than saw as his weight shifted against her thigh.

"Does anyone ever know another completely?" His eyes gazed past her, and for one, terrifying moment she thought that he would never look at her again, but his eyes focused back on hers and her body relaxed. "When I first met you, I didn't think I needed anything, or anyone. I was just living, and I thought I was happy."

Morgan shifted. It was the potion, of course. That horrible, nasty potion, filling his heart with lies and a need for her that would kill him. "I discovered a need I didn't know I had. I need you. The time we had together...was the greatest I've known. Is it selfish to want more? I want to grow old with you, to have children with you and live our lives in peace and safety and comfort. We deserve that, don't we Morgan?" His use of her true name sent chills down her spine. She reached out and stroked his brow.

"You deserve that, Tristan." And as she said it, she knew. She could never live with herself if, after all that had happened, she chose to be selfish again. "Can you ever forgive me?" she whispered.

He nodded once, though the pain in his eyes spoke for him. They closed. His hand gripped hers, trembling as he squeezed it.

A tear trickled down the side of her nose and fell from her face. Morgan touched it, staring at the glistening liquid on her fingertip.

She was crying.

A surge of fire filled her chest and rushed down her arms, towards her legs, into her head. It burned through her, pulsing with each beat of her heart.

Who knew love burned? She felt pain from the heat, and also cleansed, as if the fire purged everything, leaving behind a fertile ground for new growth to spring up. She looked to Elaina, who stood by the bed, her own eyes wet with tears. Staring into her sister's eyes, Morgan spoke the words she knew she must.

"Save Isolde, Niviane."

CHAPTER TWENTY-EIGHT

Tristram, 'twas I that healed thy hurt,
That old, fierce wound of Morolt's poisoned sword.
Stricken to death, pale, pale as now thou wert:
Yet was thy strength restored.
Have I forgot my skill?
This wound shall yet be healed.
Love shall be master still,
And Death again shall yield!
"Tristram's End" by Robert Laurence Binyon

Morgan felt Tristan's last breath shudder through him, and then his weight sank into her arms, his body having let go of this life at last.

He was dead.

"It is done," Niviane replied.

And then the sorceress began chanting.

Morgan pushed Tristan's head from her lap, bolting to her feet, hand reaching out toward the sorceress. "No!" she yelled.

Wind whipped up around her, picking Elaina and Gereck up into the air behind her, grasping at their throats as if someone invisible strangled them.

“What are you doing?” Morgan screamed. Tendrils of wind wrapped themselves around her arms, pinning them to her sides.

“Did you think I would be satisfied with such a pitiful payment in exchange for what you promised me? One life? Leaving you to find another chance at happiness? No, nothing but your life, filled with suffering, will serve to fill your debt,” Niviane snarled. Her beautiful face contorted, darkness casting over her eyes, her red lips grinning. “You are my slave, Morgan le Fay.”

“Let them live, at least!” Morgan begged. “They have nothing to do with this.”

“I don’t want these hero-types getting some idea in their pretty heads about rescuing you.”

Morgan looked over her shoulder, tears pouring down her face now, sobs shaking her shoulders, the whipping wind making it hard to draw in breath. Elaina was already unconscious. Gereck struggled, his efforts faltering.

No. She would not let this happen. She would rather die than see them killed. Morgan strained against the wind that held her arms. She felt heat boil up inside her chest, coursing through her veins, burning through to her skin until golden light shone out from every pore on her body.

A field of light blossomed around Morgan, then grew to surround Elaina and Gereck. They collapsed to the floor with two simultaneous thuds. The shield around them shimmered like a giant, transparent pearl. The wind could not reach them here.

Wind whipped around Niviane, her silvery hair reaching towards the sky, her feet lifted from the ground as she shrieked.

It sounded so muted from inside the bubble of light. Morgan reached out in amazement, touching the inside surface of what she'd created. She noticed a thin strand of light connecting the shield to her chest. Beneath her dress, a golden light pulsed; the phoenix tattoo, painted pure gold and shining.

The Rite of the Heart had completed.

Morgan, Merlin said. *Morgan, free me.*

How? Morgan cried out in her mind, unable to speak for the emotion that coursed through her.

Touch the chest that contains me. It requires but a little magic.

If I move, Niviane will kill them and turn on me.

All it takes is your touch. You have enough of Avalon in you to break the enchantment. Trust me.

Niviane chanted a new phrase now, and lightning crackled in her hands. It darted towards the shield around Morgan, crackling across the surface.

Morgan ducked, and the shield faltered, large patches beginning to lose the pearlescent shine, fading, losing strength.

Now, Morgan!

Morgan ran. The shield burst behind her in a shower of gold dust. Morgan ignored the glass shards pinching her feet. Her hip struck the loom when she got too close. She cried out in pain and stumbled, but kept her feet and lunged for the wooden chest.

Niviane shouted. Lightning arced toward her, illuminating the tower room.

Her fingers brushed the carved wood, and Merlin burst free. He flew out chanting, aged hand reaching for Niviane. His voice groaned and scraped like the earth itself moved.

Niviane shrieked, her words unintelligible as her body contorted and stretched, arms reaching upward. Texture, like bark, mottled her once-fair skin. Branches broke through the roof of the tower, sending thatch and clay down on Morgan's head. Then the leaves sprouted, and a tree stood in the midst of that tower room, roots reaching down through the floor.

Morgan stepped forward, hand up as if to touch it.

"Do not touch her, Morgan. You have enough magic remaining to unset the spell I cast," Merlin said, blue eyes iridescent. They dimmed, and she looked into his usual, brilliant blue gaze, a storm still visible in his irises.

"Is she...dead?"

"No. Merely contained, as I was in that chest. Do not fear, I will watch this place to ensure she is never released."

Gereck and Elaina stared at Morgan from the floor. "What happened?" Gereck asked.

No one answered him.

Isolde sat up in bed, a bewildered expression on her face. After examining all the people in the tower, her eyes landed on Morgan. They widened. She pushed the covers off and stood up.

Gereck and Elaina moved apart so Isolde could pass them, her bare feet crossing the glass floor, her tattered, charred dress swaying at her knees. She reached Morgan and they stared at each other, each one seeing her own face.

Morgan's hand moved at the same time as Isolde's, palms pressing against the other woman's cheek. Isolde's palm felt soft on Morgan's skin. She closed her eyes and breathed in, sharp and deep, then out, long and slow.

When Morgan opened her eyes again, she stared at a blonde-haired woman, shorter than herself, a smile on her heart-shaped face, pale green eyes glistening with tears.

"It feels good to be in my own body again," Isolde said, her lilting accent so familiar to Morgan's ears.

Morgan glanced down at her hands, flawless and healed.

"It does," she murmured.

She glanced over Isolde's shoulder, to where Elaina stood holding Gereck's hand and speaking to him. She noticed Morgan's stare and stopped talking. They had won, hadn't they? Morgan's body felt tight and hard, her throat constricted. They had stopped Niviane, for now, and saved Isolde. She had her own body, her own life back. And yet, she felt too much sadness to celebrate.

Morgan's eyes dropped, finding Tristan's body on the floor, then walked to it, kneeling down beside him. She looked into his face, her hair falling past her shoulders and brushing his cheek. She swept it behind one ear and looked up again, mind racing.

There has to be a spell, something Niviane taught me, something I read somewhere. You're not dead; not really.

But the magic from the Rite of the Heart had diminished to a dim, flickering flame. What little magic she could do now would never be powerful enough to bring him back to life.

The priestesses were too far away; they wouldn't get there in time. Even if they could, raising the dead was not done lightly. Often, the person raised was altered in mind or body; they became resentful, even to the point of suicide or murder. It wouldn't be worth it to have Tristan back, only to have him want nothing to do with her for tearing him away from whatever paradise lay beyond.

"You can still save him," Merlin said, stepping up beside her. He reached into his robe and pulled out a bottle, handing it down towards Morgan. "He is not dead, only near. Break the bond, and he will live."

Morgan stared at the smooth, rose-colored bottle, her distorted reflection stared back. A tiny residue remained inside; would it be enough?

"How?" she asked, glancing up at Merlin.

He smiled, deepening the crow's feet around his eyes. "I will tell you, some day."

She tugged the cork out with her fingers. Her hand trembled as she tipped it against Tristan's lips, waiting for several agonizing moments before the remaining drops slid from the bottle's mouth into Tristan's.

Tristan stirred in her arms, and she cried out. Blue eyes blinked open, as if he'd been sleeping.

He stared at her changed face. Morgan held her breath.

"Is that you, Morgan?"

She nodded, biting her lip, then burst into tears. Tristan sat up, holding her against him, rocking as she cried.

"You're here, with me. You're alive," she managed, heart bubbling with warmth. This was what true love felt like. No threats, no betrayals, no power struggle, no manipulation or guilt, and no potion. True love.

She took his face in her hands, gazing into his eyes with surety pulsing through her heart, confirming what she knew for certain to be true with each rapid beat.

"I love you, Tristan," she said.

His face split into a beaming grin. His hand slid across the back of her head, bringing her close, pressing her lips to his. She brought her arms up underneath his shoulders, holding him close to her, feeling his heartbeat, the warmth of his mouth, and his breath on her face. He was alive, and he loved her.

Merlin clapped his hands, drawing their attention. "I am needed elsewhere."

"Wait," Morgan said, hand reaching towards Merlin. "Please, I have a question."

Merlin inclined his grey head toward her, beckoning for her to go on.

"What was the purpose of sending me back, if Camelot fell and Arthur died all the same? I have failed in almost every regard."

"I would not say failed," Merlin said, a small smile appearing on his lips. "You have found love, you have regained your form while returning Isolde's to her, and you have aided in the capture of the sorceress Niviane, so that justice might be sought for her actions." He peered down at her, hands clasped before him. "That, my dear, would appear to be quite a lot to call success."

"Is it what the Goddess intended?" Morgan asked.

Merlin glanced up toward the ceiling and sighed before returning his gaze to her.

"Traveling through time is an unknown, even to me. You never can quite tell how it will turn out, but some things are certain; these things are branches in the tree of time, rather than changeable leaves. The Avalon priestesses assumed the Goddess intended for Camelot's outcome to be altered, but, as evidenced by the way events unfolded, that was not the case. King Arthur was killed at the hand of Mordred, who has also died.

Camelot is at war with the Saxons and will be for some time as various kings and lords vie for their place on the vacant throne."

Merlin nodded toward where Elaina held Gereck's hand. They sat together on the stone window ledge, speaking to one another.

"I happen to know that for Elaina matters turned out quite similarly. Because Niviane intercepted your message to Isolde, she sent the shield to Mordred sooner rather than later, and Gereck lost it. In losing it, he was fated to climb this tower and meet Elaina. Her happiness, therefore, and her freedom, were little affected by your movement back in time." His smile widened, reaching his dancing blue eyes. "Much ill has come of your mistakes, Morgan, but I believe if you think on it a while, you will find that so has much good. Trust in your higher purpose, seek learning and growth all of your days, and you will find you have lived a life worth living, no matter the choices or mistakes you have made in the past or will make going forward."

"Then it does matter? Or it doesn't? I am confused," Tristan said from beside her.

"I do not think he meant to answer the question for us," Morgan murmured. "It is not his way."

Merlin's eyes twinkled. Morgan blinked, and dust swirled in a sunbeam on the wood floor where the wizard had stood. The tree branches above them rustled in a strange wind.

Morgan shivered. It would've been peaceful if she hadn't watched the tree grow from the body of a person. She stood, and Tristan moved with her.

The others looked at them.

"All right then, now what?" Tristan asked, clapping his hands together. Morgan realized that he didn't know Elaina or Gereck. She opened her mouth to introduce them, but Elaina spoke first.

"Gereck and I were just discussing that," Elaina said, "and we agree that our first step is to leave this place."

No one disagreed. The five of them filed down the winding staircase, past the dusty, enormous tapestries, through the small wooden door, and splashed out across the bridge of grass and dirt to the other side of the river to sit in the shade and decide their fate.

Mira stamped her hoof and snorted a welcome to Morgan.

A long moment passed before anyone spoke.

"If we leave, a war will start," Morgan said. Elaina looked up in surprise.

"A war has already begun, Morgan. Haven't you heard of the Saxon hoards?"

"No, I mean that we will cause a war. Another one. Between Cornwall and Ireland."

"What did you do?" Isolde asked. Morgan let Tristan explain. She picked at the grass while they talked, feeling the full weight of her selfish decisions.

"It is easily solved," Isolde said.

Morgan glanced up, releasing a tortured blade of grass from her grip. "How?"

Isolde shrugged. "I will write to my father, tell him of my decision not to marry the King of Cornwall. He will not deny me my freedom, not after working so hard to keep me safe from my mother. I think he will be rather relieved to be done with the whole thing. He isn't a war monger, nor is he a tyrant. Tristan already won the agreed-on duel to resolve the unpaid tribute, so King

Angeus will have no quarrel with King Mark, once he knows I am safe."

It was so simple that Morgan couldn't believe she hadn't thought of it herself. But then, she couldn't have understood the full context of Isolde's relationship with her father. It would all work out. They continued their conversation, discussing possible locations, even telling snippets of their recent stories.

Morgan leaned against Tristan, taking in the security she felt with his warmth against her side. Gradually, the conversation turned to Camelot, and inevitably, King Arthur.

"Did you love him?" Morgan asked, looking at Isolde, surprising herself with her own boldness.

Tristan gripped her hand in his own, their hips and shoulders touching. He kissed her hair.

"Arthur?" Isolde asked. Morgan noticed a familiar look in Isolde's eyes; she had seen it in herself when she looked in the mirror at times. "I suppose I did, though I am certain I was enchanted, the way you were with Tristan. Compelled to love him as part of Niviane's plan. Echoes of our love linger in my heart."

That will fade, Morgan thought. She understood more now how the heart healed. With time. With new life lived, new connections made.

Isolde furrowed her brow. "I don't understand why Sir Lancelot tried to engage me in romantic activities. How did you know him?"

Morgan glanced at Elaina, who avoided looking at her, staring at the river instead.

"He was my sister's lover," Morgan said quietly. "At the time, I was impulsive and bitter. I took advantage of Beltane's call and drew his attention away from my sister. I told myself I was protecting her." Morgan swallowed, looking at the back of Elaina's head. She turned to meet her sister's gaze. Her eyes watered, tears threatening to spill over. "I was a fool, and a coward. I am sorry."

Elaina didn't speak. Morgan didn't expect forgiveness; not after what she had done.

"He was Arthur's father," Elaina said.

"I know," Morgan said. She did know. Elaina had told her, once, in another time. The four of them stood, silence filtering between them like the afternoon sunlight.

"Ah. Perhaps it is well that everything happened as it did," Isolde said at last.

In the end, no one had any desire to remain in Camelot; but where else could they go? Morgan's face could be recognized as Queen Guinevere.

Elaina and the man she had met and fallen in love with, Sir Gereck, wished to leave and start anew.

Isolde had no desire to return to her homeland, convinced that she would be recognized by one of her mother's mercenaries and hunted. She mentioned going to Northumberland, where she could continue her healing practice and perhaps have hope for a normal life.

Morgan turned in Tristan's arms, craning her neck to look up at him. "And you, Sir Tristan? Where would you like to go?" she asked. She thought he might say France. He spoke of it often, and fondly.

Tristan rubbed his beard on her cheek, a scruffy, tickling feeling that made her inner body yawn with pleasure. "I will go anywhere with you," he said at last, "though I lean toward Northumberland. I happen to know it is beautiful there, a wide expanse of mountainous land and lakes."

"You've been to the north?" Morgan asked with surprise.

Tristan nodded. "I've been here and there. Not many places overseas, but everything that touches Britain, and then some. I think we could be happy there."

"Then we go north," Morgan said, snuggling into Tristan's chest. Some piece inside her fell into place, then, and it all had a feeling of rightness.

"We go north," Tristan replied.

Along the way, Morgan heard that Gereck's wife Winna had perished at the hand of Mordred, who Gereck knew as Sir Lancelot. They retrieved Gereck's two beautiful young children, Cai and Ada, from the care of his cousin. They brightened the entire journey, and everyone fell in love with them.

They set up in a beautiful, peaceful homestead, tucked away in the highlands of Northumberland.

Fields of heather waved whenever the winds blew, and hawks flew through the mountainous skies. Tristan made short work of capturing and taming one to start hawking game.

Under those skies, both couples married, with simple vows to each other and none but Isolde and the children to witness.

They built a home before the frigid winter set in, and as it thawed, Morgan fell ill. She woke each day and vomited so violently she could eat nothing.

Tristan held her hair and rubbed her back, coaxing her to drink and eat. It took Isolde to convince her of the reality she had never anticipated, never before wanted.

She was pregnant.

"I can't be pregnant," Morgan stammered. "The herbs, the miscarriages, my womb never..." she trailed off, hand touching the golden phoenix on her chest, then moving down towards her growing stomach.

She burst into tears and threw her arms around Tristan's neck.

"You can expect as much for the next few months," Isolde told him. He laughed, and Morgan felt dampness on his face as it pressed against hers. They had started their family together.

Morgan gave birth to a little black-haired girl at the close of summer, and soon after, Elaina and Gereck announced their pregnancy.

Morgan never knew she could have this kind of happiness. It was a better life than she had ever been able to dream of on her own.

Sometimes, she longed for the sanctuary of Avalon, the wild freedom of being a priestess, but she felt strongly that the Goddess wanted her on the path she trod. One day, perhaps, the path might reconnect with Avalon, but for now, she was content to remain with Tristan, with her family.

What she had with Tristan was still a bond. Not the kind of bond that forced them to stay together, but the kind that kept them from wanting to leave. Some days, she wanted anything but to be near him, and days where she longed for him in a deep and aching way; days where she hurt him with her words or emotions, days where he hurt her, too, and they would separate, only to come together again, sorry they had caused harm, stronger for their forgiveness of each other.

Morgan dreamed of a life where she wouldn't have nightmares of past abuse, of relationships that could have been something more but weren't; at times, her mistakes haunted her.

Despite her past, she found that she could be grateful for what she had. She was loved by someone who respected and cared for her. And it was enough, from that moment until the end of her days.

About the Author

Bree Moore lives in Utah with her amazing husband, six children, and two cats. When she's not busy homeschooling or folding laundry, she sneaks off to write more urban fantasy.

Bree has a passion for pregnancy and childbirth, which influences her female-led stories. She loves shopping for groceries like other women like shopping for shoes (no, seriously), movies that make her cry, and Celtic music. She likes both her chocolate and her novels dark.

Subscribe to her newsletter and get a FREE fantasy story! You can subscribe at www.authobreemoore.com

THANKS

Writing a book is an enormous endeavor, and while so much of the work is done by me, alone at my keyboard, there are players behind the scenes making sure everything comes together.

Huge thanks to my writing group, Writing Through Brambles, who, as always, cheered me on, read early drafts, and helped me get back on track when I was stuck.

Thanks to my editor, Amy Cissell with Cissell Ink, for doing a fantastic job.

I can't forget my tireless beta readers, Rachel, Amanda, Skye, and Kayla for making this book the best it could be.

I owe so much gratitude to everyone at Phase Publishing, LLC, for bringing the first edition of this book to fruition, and with it my dreams of being a published author.

A giant thank you to all my readers, especially those who have taken the time to write a review on Goodreads or Amazon. Reading about how much you enjoy my stories makes my day every time.

Finally, thanks to my eternal companion and best friend, Tyler. Without you watching our six crazy kids and picking up on the housework during NANOWRIMO 2017, this book would still be in first-draft stages and our house would be a perpetual disaster (well, more than it already is).

I can't count the number of ways in which you have supported me in becoming a published writer, and I can't thank you enough for the fact that you've never complained about my tendencies to get lost in my fantasy worlds or chatter endlessly about plots and characters. I couldn't have picked a better match.

Also by Bree Moore

www.ingramcontent.com/pod-product-compliance
Lightning Source LLC
Chambersburg PA
CBHW020601310726
48979CB00008B/1298/J

* 9 7 8 1 9 5 6 6 6 8 1 5 5 *